'Geoff Ryman's new novel is swift, smart and convincing. *Air* is a wonderful and frightening examination of old and new, and survival on the interface between'
Greg Bear

'This is a liminal book: its characters are on the threshold of something new; their village is on the brink of change; the world is launching into a new way to connect; humanity, at the end of the novel, is on the cusp of evolution . . . its plot is exciting and suspenseful, its characters gripping, its wisdom lightly and gracefully offered, its language clear and beautiful. Like *The Child Garden*, *Air* is both humane and wise. This novel is such a village. I cannot recommend it highly enough. It becomes finer as I think back on it, and I look forward to rereading it. I only wish Ryman's work were more widely available and more widely read, as it deserves'
Joan Gordon *New York Review of Science Fiction*

'Ryman renders the village and people of Kizuldah with such humane insight and sympathy that we experience the novel almost like the Air it describes: It's around us and in us, more real than real, and it leaves us changed as surely as Mae's contact with Air changes her. This amazing balance that Ryman maintains – mourning change while embracing it – renders *Air* not merely powerful, thought-provoking, and profoundly moving, but indispensable. It's a map of our world, written in the imaginary terrain of Karzistan. It's a guide for all of us, who will endure change, mourn our losses, and must find a way to love the new sea that swamps our houses, if we are not to grow bitter and small and afraid'
Robert Killheffer, *The Magazine of Fantasy and Science Fiction*

'The wondrous art wrought in Ryman's *Air* shows some of its meaning plainly, calling forth grins, astonishment and tears. More of its meaning is tucked away inside, like the seven hidden curled-up dimensions of spacetime, like the final pages of the third book of Dante, beyond words or imagining high and low. Treasure this book'
Damien Broderick, *Locus*

D1387071

Also by Geoff Ryman in Gollancz

The Child Garden
Was

AIR

(or Have Not Have)

GEOFF RYMAN

GOLLANCZ

LONDON

Copyright © Geoff Ryman 2004
All rights reserved

The right of Geoff Ryman to be identified as the
author of this work has been asserted by him in accordance
with the Copyright, Designs and Patents Act 1988.

First published in Great Britain in 2005 by
Gollancz
An imprint of the Orion Publishing Group
Orion House, 5 Upper St Martin's Lane,
London WC2H 9EA

This edition published in Great Britain in 2006 by
Gollancz

3 5 7 9 10 8 6 4

A CIP catalogue record for this book is
available from the British Library

ISBN-13 9 780 57507 811 6
ISBN-10 0 57507 811 1

Printed in Great Britain by
Clays Ltd, St Ives plc

The Orion Publishing Group's policy is to use papers
that are natural, renewable and recyclable products and
made from wood grown in sustainable forests. The logging
and manufacturing processes are expected to conform to the
environmental regulations of the country of origin.

www.orionbooks.co.uk

Dedicated to Doris McPherson
and what is left of (the original) Meadowvale, Ontario, Canada

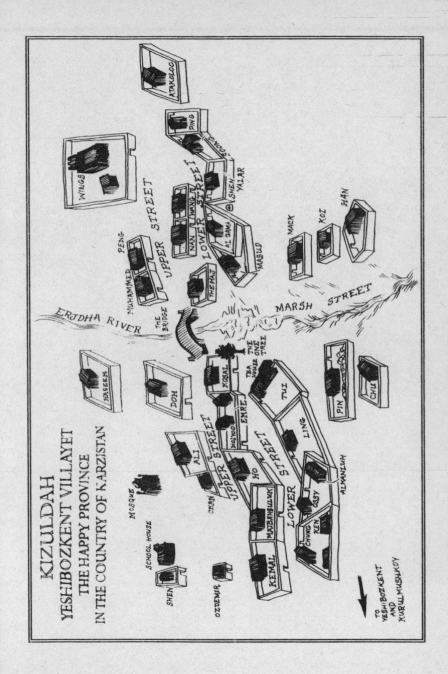

Mae lived in the last village in the world to go online.
After that, everyone else went on Air.

Mae was the village's fashion expert. She advised on makeup, sold cosmetics, and provided good dresses. Every farmer's wife needed at least one good dress.

Mae would sketch what was being worn in the capital. She would always add a special touch: a lime-green scarf with sequins; or a lacy ruffle with colourful embroidery. A good dress was for display. 'We are a happier people and we can wear these gay colours,' Mae would advise.

'Yes, that is true,' her customer might reply, entranced that fashion expressed their happy culture. 'In the photographs, the Japanese women all look so solemn.'

'So full of themselves,' said Mae, and lowered her head and scowled, and she and her customer would laugh, feeling as sophisticated as anyone in the world.

Mae got her ideas as well as her mascara and lipsticks from her trips to the town. It was a long way and she needed to be driven. When Sunni Haseem offered to drive her down in exchange for a fashion expedition, Mae had to agree. Apart from anything else, Mae had a wedding dress to collect.

Sunni herself was from an old village family, but her husband was a beefy brute from farther down the hill. He puffed on cigarettes and his tanned fingers were as thick and weathered as the necks of turtles. In the backseat with Mae, Sunni giggled and prodded and gleamed with the thought of visiting town with her friend and confidante who was going to unleash her beauty secrets.

Mae smiled and whispered, promising much. 'I hope my source will be present today,' she said. 'She brings me my special colours, you cannot get them anywhere else. I don't ask where she gets them.' Mae lowered her eyes and her voice. 'I think her husband . . .'

A dubious gesture, meaning that perhaps the goods were stolen,

stolen from – who knows? – supplies meant for foreign diplomats? The tips of Mae's fingers rattled once, in provocation, across her client's arm.

The town was called Yeshibozkent, which meant Green Valley City. It was now approached through corridors of raw apartment blocks set on beige desert soil. It had billboards, a new jail, discos with mirror balls, illuminated shop signs, and Toyota jeeps that belched out blue smoke.

The town centre was as Mae remembered it from childhood. Traditional wooden houses crowded crookedly together. Wooden shingles covered the roofs and gables. The shop signs were tiny, faded, and sometimes hand-lettered. The old market square was still full of peasants selling vegetables laid out on mats. Middle-aged men still played chess outside tiny cafes; youths still prowled in packs.

There was still the public-address system. The address system barked out news and music from the top of the electricity poles. Its sounds drifted over the city, announcing public events or new initiatives against drug dealers. It told of progress on the new highway, and boasted of the well known entertainers who were visiting the town.

Mr Haseem parked near the market, and the address system seemed to enter Mae's lungs, like cigarette smoke, perfume, or hairspray. She stepped out of the van and breathed it in. The excitement of being in the city trembled in her belly. The address system made Mae's spirits rise as much as the bellowing of shoppers, farmers, and donkeys; as much as the smell of raw petrol and cut greenery and drains. She and her middle-aged client looked at each other and gasped and giggled at themselves.

'Now,' Mae said, stroking Sunni's hair, her cheek. 'It is time for a complete makeover. Let's really do you up. I cannot do as good a workup in the hills.'

Mae took her client to Halat's, the same hairdresser as Sunni might have gone to anyway. But Mae was greeted by Halat with cries and smiles and kisses on the cheek. That implied a promise that Mae's client would get special treatment. There was a pretence of consultancy. Mae offered advice, comments, cautions. Careful! – she has such delicate skin! The hair could use more shaping there. And Halat hummed as if perceiving what had been hidden before and then agreed to give the client what she would otherwise have had. But Sunni's nails were soaking, and she sat back in the centre of attention, like a queen.

All of this allowed the hairdresser to charge more. Mae had never pressed her luck and asked for a cut. Something beady in Halat's eyes told Mae there would be no point. What Mae got out of it was standing, and that would lead to more work later.

With cucumbers over her eyes, Sunni was safely trapped. Mae announced, 'I just have a few errands to run. You relax and let all cares fall away.' She disappeared before Sunni could protest.

Mae ran to collect the dress. A disabled girl, a very good seamstress called Miss Soo, had opened up a tiny shop of her own.

Miss Soo was grateful for any business, poor thing, skinny as a rail and twisted. After the usual greetings, Miss Soo shifted around and hobbled and dragged her way to the back of the shop to fetch the dress. Her feet hissed sideways across the uneven concrete floor. Poor little thing, Mae thought. How can she sew?

Yet Miss Soo had a boyfriend in the fashion business – *genuinely* in the fashion business, far away in the capital city, Balshang. The girl often showed Mae his photograph. It was like a magazine photograph. The boy was very handsome, with a shiny shirt and coiffed-up hair. She kept saying she was saving up money to join him. It was a mystery to Mae what such a boy was doing with a cripple for a girlfriend. Why did he keep contact with her? Publicly Mae would say to friends of the girl: It is the miracle of love, what a good heart he must have. Otherwise she kept her own counsel which was this: You would be very wise not to visit him in Balshang.

The boyfriend sent Miss Soo the patterns of dresses, photographs, magazines, or even whole catalogues. There was one particularly treasured thing; a showcase publication. The cover was like the lid of a box, and it showed in full colour the best of the nation's fashion design.

Models so rich and thin they looked like ghosts. They looked half asleep, as if the only place they carried the weight of their wealth was on their eyelids. It was like looking at Western or Japanese women, and yet these were their own people, so long-legged, so modern, so ethereal, as if they were made of air.

Mae hated the clothes. They looked like washing-up towels. Oatmeal or grey in one colour, and without a trace of adornment.

Mae sighed with lament. 'Why do these rich women go about in their underwear?'

The girl shuffled back with the dress, past piles of unsold oatmeal cloth. Miss Soo had a skinny face full of teeth, and she always looked like she was staring ahead in fear. 'If you are rich you have no need to try to look rich.' Her voice was soft. She made Mae feel like a peasant without meaning to. She made Mae yearn to escape herself, to be someone else, for the child was effortlessly talented, somehow effortlessly in touch with the outside world.

'Ah, yes,' Mae sighed. 'But my clients, you know, they live in the hills.' She shared a conspiratorial smile with the girl. 'Their taste! Speaking of which, let's have a look at my wedding cake of a dress.'

The dress was actually meant to look like a cake, all pink and white sugar icing, except that it kept moving all by itself. White wires with styrofoam bobbles on the ends were surrounded with clouds of white netting.

'Does it need to be quite so busy?' the girl asked doubtfully, encouraged too much by Mae's smile.

'I know my clients,' replied Mae, coolly. This is, at least, she thought, a dress that makes some effort. She inspected the work. The needlework was delicious, as if the white cloth were cream that had flowed together. The poor creature could certainly sew, even when she hated the dress.

'That will be fine,' said Mae, and made a move towards her purse.

'You are so kind!' murmured Miss Soo, bowing slightly.

Like Mae, Miss Soo was of Chinese extraction. That was meant to make no difference, but somehow it did. Mae and Miss Soo knew what to expect of each other.

The dress was packed in brown paper and carefully tied so it would not crease. There were farewells, and Mae scurried back to the hairdressers. Sunni was only just finished, hairspray and scent rising off her like steam.

'This is the dress,' said Mae and peeled back part of the paper, to give Halat and Sunni a glimpse of the tulle and styrofoam.

'Oh!' the women said, as if all that white were clouds, in dreams.

And Halat was paid. There were smiles and nods and compliments and then they left.

Outside the shop, Mae breathed out as though she could now finally speak her mind. 'Oh! She is good, that little viper, but you have to watch her, you have to make her work. Did she give you proper attention?'

'Oh, yes, very special attention. I am lucky to have you for a friend,' said Sunni. 'Let me pay you something for your trouble.'

Mae hissed through her teeth. 'No, no, I did nothing, I will not hear of it.' It was a kind of ritual.

There was no dream in finding Sunni's surly husband. Mr Haseem was red-faced, half drunk in a club with unvarnished walls and a television.

'You spend my money,' he declared. His eyes were on Mae.

'My friend Mae makes no charges,' snapped Sunni.

'She takes something from what they charge you.' Mr Haseem glowered like a thunderstorm.

'She makes them charge me less, not more,' replied Sunni, her face going like stone.

The two women exchanged glances. Mae's eyes could say: How can you bear it, a woman of culture like you?

It is my tragedy, came the reply, aching out of the ashamed eyes.

So they sat while the husband sobered up and watched television. Mae contemplated the husband's hostility to her, and what might lie behind it.

On the screen, the local female newsreader talked: Talents, such people were called. She wore a red dress with a large gold brooch. Something had been done to her hair to make it stand up in a sweep before falling away. She was groomed as smooth as ice. She chattered in a high voice, perky through a battery of tiger's teeth.

'She goes to Halat's as well,' Mae whispered to Sunni. Weather, maps, shots of the honoured President and the full cabinet one by one, making big decisions.

The men in the club chose what movie they wanted. Since the satellites, they could do that. Satellites had ruined visits to the town. Before, it used to be that the men were made to sit through something the children or families might also like to watch, so you got everyone together for the watching of the television. The clubs had to be more polite. Now, women hardly saw TV at all and the clubs were full of drinking. The men chose another kung fu movie. Mae and Sunni endured it, sipping Coca-Cola. It became apparent that Mr Haseem would not buy them dinner.

Finally, late in the evening, Mr Haseem loaded himself into the van. Enduring, unstoppable, and quite dangerous, he drove them back up into the mountains, weaving across the middle of the road.

'You make a lot of money out of all this,' Mr Haseem said to Mae.

'I . . . I make a little something. I try to maintain the standards of the village. I do not want people to see us as peasants. Just because we live on the high road.'

Sunni's husband barked out a laugh. 'We are peasants!' Then he added, 'You do it for the money.'

Sunni sighed in embarrassment. And Mae smiled a hard smile to herself in the darkness. You give yourself away, Sunni's-man. You want my husband's land. You want him to be your dependant. And you don't like your wife's money coming to me to prevent it. You want to make both me and my husband your slaves.

It is a strange thing to spend four hours in the dark listening to an engine roar with a man who seeks to destroy you.

In late May, school ended.

There were no fewer than six girls graduating and each one of them needed a new dress. Miss Soo was making two of them; Mae would have to do the others, but she needed to buy the cloth. She had a mobile phone, a potent fashion symbol. But she needed another trip to Yeshibozkent.

Mr Wing was going to town to collect a new television set for the village. It was going to be connected to the Net. Mr Wing was something of a politician in his way. He had applied for a national grant to set up a company to provide information services to the village. Swallow Communications, he called himself, and the villagers said it would make him rich.

Kwan, Mr Wing's wife, was one of Mae's favourite women: She was intelligent and sensible; there was less dissembling with her. Mae enjoyed the drive.

Mr Wing parked the van in the market square. As Mae reached into the back for her hat, she heard the public-address system. The voice of the Talent was squawking.

'. . . *a tremendous advance for culture,*' the Talent said. '*Now the Green Valley is no farther from the centre of the world than Paris, Singapore, or Tokyo.*'

Mae sniffed, 'Hmm. Another choice on this fishing net of theirs.'

Wing stood outside the van, ramrod-straight in his brown-and-tan town shirt. 'I want to hear this,' he said, smiling slightly, taking nips of smoke from his cigarette.

Kwan fanned the air. 'Your modern wires say that smoking is dangerous. I wish you would follow all this news you hear.'

'Sssh!' he insisted.

The bright female voice still enthused: *'Previously all such advances left the Valley far behind because of wiring and machines. This advance will be in the air we breathe. This new thing will be like TV in your head. All you need is the wires in the human mind.'*

Kwan gathered up her things. 'Some nonsense or another,' she murmured.

'Next Sunday, there will be a Test. The Test will happen in Tokyo and Singapore but also here in the Valley at the same time. What Tokyo sees and hears, we will see and hear. Tell everyone you know: Next Sunday, there will be a Test. There is no need for fear, alarm, or panic.'

Mae listened then. There would certainly be a need for fear and panic if the address system said there was none.

'What test, what kind of test? What? What?' the women demanded of the husband.

Mr Wing played the relaxed, superior male. He chuckled. 'Ho-ho, now you are interested, yes?'

Another man looked up and grinned. 'You should watch more TV,' he called. He was selling radishes and shook them at the women.

Kwan demanded, 'What are they talking about?'

'They will be able to put TV in our heads,' said the husband, smiling. He looked down, thinking, perhaps wistfully, of his own new venture. 'There has been talk of nothing else on the TV for the last year. But I didn't think it would happen.'

All the old market was buzzing like flies on carrion, as if it were still news to them. Two youths in strange puffy clothes spun on their heels and slapped each other's palms, in a gesture that Mae had seen only once or twice before. An old granny waved it all away and kept on accusing a dealer of short measures.

Mae felt grave doubts. 'TV in our heads. I don't want TV in my head.' She thought of viper newsreaders and kung fu.

Wing said, 'It's not just TV. It is more than TV. It is the whole world.'

'What does that mean?'

'It will be the Net – only, in your head. The fools and drunks in these parts know nothing about it; it is a word they use to sound modern. But you go to the cafes, you see it. The Net is all things.' He began to falter.

'Explain! How can one thing be all things?'

There was a crowd of people gathering to listen.

'Everything is on it. You will see on our new TV. It will be a Net TV.' Kwan's husband did not really know, either.

The routine had been soured. Halat the hairdresser was in a very strange mood, giggly, chattery, her teeth clicking together as if it were cold.

'Oh, nonsense,' she said, when Mae went into her usual performance. 'Is this for a wedding? For a feast?'

'No,' said Mae. 'It is for my special friend.'

The little hussy put both hands either side of her mouth as if in awe. 'Oh! Uh!'

'Are you going to do a special job for her or not?' Mae demanded. Her eyes were able to say: I see no one else in your shop.

Oh, how the girl would have loved to say, I am very busy – if you need something special, come back tomorrow. But money spoke. Halat slightly amended her tone. 'Of course. For you.'

'I bring my friends to you regularly because you do such good work for them.'

'Of course,' the child said. 'It is all this news; it makes me forget myself.'

Mae drew herself up, and looked fierce, forbidding – in a word, older. Her entire body said: *Do not forget yourself again*. The way the child dug away at Kwan's hair with the long comb-handle said back: *Peasants*.

The rest of the day did not go well. Mae felt tired, distracted. She made a terrible mistake and, with nothing else to do, accidentally took Kwan to the place where she bought her lipsticks.

'Oh! It is a treasure trove!' exclaimed Kwan.

Idiot, thought Mae to herself. Kwan was good-natured and would not take advantage. But, if she talked . . . ! There would be clients who would not take such a good-natured attitude, not to have been shown this themselves.

'I do not take everyone here,' whispered Mae, 'hmm? This is for special friends only.'

Kwan was good-natured, but very far from stupid. Mae remembered, in school Kwan had always been best at letters, best at maths. Kwan was pasting on false eyelashes in a mirror and said, very simply and quickly, 'Don't worry, I won't tell anyone.'

And that was far too simple and direct. As if Kwan were saying:

Fashion expert, we all know you. She even looked around and smiled at Mae, and batted her now-huge eyes, as if mocking fashion itself.

'Not for you,' said Mae. 'The false eyelashes. You don't need them.'

The dealer wanted a sale. 'Why listen to her?' she asked Kwan.

Because, thought Mae, I buy fifty riels' worth of cosmetics from you a year.

'My friend is right,' said Kwan, to the dealer. The sad fact was that Kwan was almost magazine-beautiful anyway, except for her teeth and gums. 'Thank you for showing me this,' said Kwan, and touched Mae's arm. 'Thank you,' she said to the dealer, having bought one lowly lipstick.

Mae and the dealer glared at each other, briefly. I'll go somewhere else next time, Mae promised herself.

The worst came last. Kwan's ramrod husband was not a man for drinking. He was in the promised cafe at the promised time, sipping tea, having had a haircut and a professional shave.

A young man called Sloop, a tribesman, was with him. Sloop was a telephone engineer and thus a member of the aristocracy as far as Mae was concerned. He was going to wire up their new TV. Sloop said, with a woman's voice, 'It will work like your mobile phone, no cable. We can't lay cable in our mountains. But before MMN, there was not enough space on the line for the TV.' He might as well have been talking English, for all Mae understood him.

Mr Wing maintained his cheerfulness. 'Come,' he said to the ladies, 'I will show you what this is all about.'

He went up to the communal TV and turned it on with an expert's flourish. Up came not a movie or the local news, but a screenful of other buttons.

'You see? You can choose what you want. You can choose anything.' And he touched the screen.

Up came the local Talent, still baring her perfect teeth. She piped in a high, enthusiastic voice that was meant to appeal to men and Bright Young Things:

'Hello. Welcome to the Airnet Information Service. For too long the world has been divided into information haves and have-nots.' She held up one hand towards the heavens of information and the other out towards the citizens of the Green Valley, inviting them to consider themselves as have-nots.

'Those in the developed world can use their TVs to find any informa-tion they need at any time. They do this through the Net.'

Incomprehension followed. There were circles and squares linked by wires in diagrams. Then they jumped up into the sky, into the air – only the air was full of arcing lines. 'The field,' they called it, but it was nothing like a field. In Karzistani, it was called the Lightning-Flow, Compass-Point Yearning Field. 'Everywhere in the world.' Then the lightning flow was shown striking people's heads. 'There have been many medical tests to show this is safe.'

'Hitting people with lightning?' Kwan asked in crooked amuse-ment. 'That does sound so safe, doesn't it?'

'It's only the Formatting that uses the Yearning Field,' said Sloop. 'That happens only once. It makes a complete map of minds, and that's what exists in Air, and Air happens in other dimensions.'

'What?'

'There are eleven dimensions,' he began, and began to see the hopelessness of it. 'They were left over after the Big Bang.'

'I know what will interest you ladies,' said her husband. And with another flourish, he touched the screen. 'You'll be able to have this in your heads, whenever you want.'

Suddenly the screen was full of cream colour.

One of the capital's ladies spun on her high heel. She was wearing the best of the nation's fashion design. She was one of the ladies in Mae's secret treasure book.

'Oh!' Kwan breathed out. 'Oh, Mae, look, isn't she lovely!'

'This channel shows nothing but fashion,' said her husband.

'All the time?' Kwan exclaimed, and looked back at Mae in wonder. For a moment, she stared up at the screen, her own face reflected over those of the models. Then, thankfully, she became Kwan again. 'Doesn't that get boring?'

Her husband chuckled. 'You can choose something else. Anything else.'

It was happening very quickly and Mae's guts churned faster than her brain to certain knowledge: Kwan and her husband would be fine with all this.

'Look,' he said, 'This is what two-ways does. You can buy the dress.'

Kwan shook her head in amazement. Then a voice said the price and Kwan gasped again. 'Oh, yes, all I have to do is sell one of our four farms, and I can have a dress like that.'

'I saw all that two years ago,' said Mae. 'It is too plain for the likes of us. We want people to see everything.'

Kwan's face went sad. 'That is because we are poor, back in the hills.' It was the common yearning, the common forlorn knowledge.

Sometimes it had to cease, all the business-making, you had to draw a breath, because after all, you had known your people for as long as you had lived.

Mae said, 'None of them are as beautiful as you are, Kwan.' It was true, except for her teeth.

'Flattery-talk from a fashion expert,' Kwan said lightly. But she took Mae's hand. Her eyes yearned up at the screen, as secret after secret was spilled like blood.

'With all this in our heads,' Kwan said to her husband, 'we won't need your TV.'

It was a busy week.
It was not only the six dresses. For some reason, there was much extra business.

On Wednesday, Mae had a discreet morning call to make on Tsang Muhammed. Mae liked Tsang. She looked like a peach that was overripe, round and soft to the touch and very slightly wrinkled. Everything about her was off-kilter. She was Chinese with a religious Karz husband, who was ten years her senior. He was a Muslim who allowed – or perhaps could not prevent – his Chinese wife keeping a pig.

The family pig was in the front room being fattened: half the room was full of old shucks. The beast looked lordly and pleased with itself. Tsang's four-year-old son sat tamely beside it, feeding it the greener leaves, as if the animal could not find them for itself.

'Is it all right to talk?' Mae whispered, her eyes going sideways towards the boy.

'Who is it?' Mae mouthed.

Tsang simply waggled a finger.

So it was someone they knew. Mae suspected it was Kwan's oldest boy, Luk. Luk was sixteen, but he was kept in pressed white shirt and shorts like a baby. The shorts only showed he had hair on his football-player calves. His face was still round and soft and babylike but lately had been full of a new and different confusion.

'Tsang. Oh!' Mae gasped.

'Sssh,' giggled Tsang, who was red as a radish. As if either of them could be certain what the other one meant. 'I need a repair job!' So it was someone younger.

Almost certainly Kwan's handsome son.

'Well, they have to be taught by someone,' whispered Mae.

Tsang simply dissolved into giggles. She could hardly stop laughing.

'I can do nothing for you. You certainly don't need redder cheeks,' said Mae.

Tsang uttered a squawk of laughter.

'There is nothing like it for a woman's complexion.' Mae pretended to put away the tools of her trade. 'No, I can effect no improvement. Certainly I cannot compete with the effects of a certain young man.'

'Nothing . . . Nothing . . .' gasped Tsang. 'Nothing like a good prick!'

Mae howled in mock outrage and Tsang squealed, and both squealed and pressed down their cheeks, and shushed each other. Mae noted exactly which part of the cheeks were blushing so she would know where the colour should go later.

As Mae painted, Tsang explained how she escaped her husband's view. 'I tell him that I have to get fresh garbage for the pig,' whispered Tsang. 'So I go out with the empty bucket . . .'

'And come back with a full bucket,' Mae said airily.

'Oh!' Tsang pretended to hit her. 'You are as bad as me!'

'What do you think I get up to in the City?' asked Mae, who arched an eyebrow, lying.

Love, she realized later, walking back down the track and clutching her cloth bag of secrets, love is not mine. She thought of the boy's naked calves.

On Thursday, Kwan wanted her teeth to be flossed. This was new. Kwan had never been vain before. This touched Mae, because it meant her friend was getting older. Or was it because she had seen the TV models with their impossible teeth? How were real people supposed to have teeth like that?

Kwan's handsome son ducked as he entered, wearing his shorts, showing smooth, full thighs, and a secret swelling about his groin. He ducked as he went out again. Guilty, Mae thought. For certain it is him.

She laid Kwan's head back over a pillow with a towel under her.

Should she not warn her friend to keep watch on her son? Which friend should she betray? To herself, she shook her head; there was no possibility of choosing between them. She could only keep silent. 'Just say if I hit a nerve,' Mae said.

Kwan had teeth like an old horse, worn, brown, black. Her gums were scarred from a childhood disease, and her teeth felt loose as Mae rubbed the floss between them. She had a neat little bag into which she flipped each strand after it was used.

It was Mae's job to talk: Kwan could not. Mae said she did not know how she would finish the dresses in time. The girls' mothers were never satisfied, each wanted her daughter to have the best. Well, the richest would have the best in the end because they bought the best cloth. Oh! Some of them had asked to pay for the fabric later! As if Mae could afford to buy cloth for six dresses without being paid!

'They all think their fashion expert is a woman of wealth.' Mae sometimes found the whole pretence funny. Kwan's eyes crinkled into a smile; but they were almost moist from pain. It was hurting.

'You should have told me your teeth were sore,' said Mae, and inspected the gums. In the back, they were raw.

If you were rich, Kwan, you would have good teeth; rich people keep their teeth, and somehow keep them white, not brown. Mae pulled stray hair out of Kwan's face.

'I will have to pull some of them,' Mae said quietly. 'Not today, but soon.'

Kwan closed her mouth and swallowed. 'I will be an old lady,' she said, and managed a smile.

'A granny with a thumping stick.'

'Who always hides her mouth when she laughs.'

Both of them chuckled. 'And thick glasses that make your eyes look like a fish.'

Kwan rested her hand on her friend's arm. 'Do you remember, years ago? We would all get together and make little boats, out of paper or shells. And we would put candles in them, and send them out on the ditches.'

'Yes!' Mae sat forward. 'We don't do that anymore.'

'We don't wear pillows and a cummerbund anymore, either.'

There had once been a festival of wishes every year, and the canals would be full of little glowing candles, that floated for a while and then sank with a hiss. 'We would always wish for love,' said Mae, remembering.

Next morning, Mae mentioned the wish boats to her neighbour, Old Mrs Tung. Mae visited her nearly every day. Mrs Tung had been her teacher during the flurry of what had passed for Mae's schooling. She was ninety years old, and spent her days turned towards the tiny loft window that looked out over the valley. She was blind, her eyes pale and unfocused. She could see nothing through the window. Perhaps she breathed in the smell of the fields.

When Mae reminded her about the boats of wishes, Mrs Tung said, 'And we would roast pumpkin seeds. And the ones we didn't eat, we would turn into jewelry. Do you remember that?'

Mrs Tung was still beautiful, at least in Mae's eyes. Mrs Tung's face had grown even more delicate in extreme old age, like the skeleton of a cat, small and fine. She gave an impression of great merriment, by continually laughing at not very much. She repeated herself.

'I remember the day you first came to me,' she said. Before Shen's village school, Mrs Tung had kept a nursery, there in their courtyard. 'I thought: "Is that the girl whose father has been killed? She is so pretty." I remember you looking at all my dresses hanging on the line.'

'And you asked me which one I liked best.'

Mrs Tung giggled. 'Oh yes, and you said the butterflies.' Blindness meant that she could only see the past. 'We had tennis courts, you know. Here in Kizuldah.'

'Did we?' Mae pretended she had not heard that before.

'Oh yes, oh yes. When the Chinese were here, just before the Communists came. Part of the Chinese army was here, and they built them. We all played tennis, in our school uniforms.'

The Chinese officers had supplied the tennis rackets. The traces of the courts were broken and grassy, where Mr Pin now ran his car-repair business.

'Oh! They were all so handsome, all the village girls were so in love.' Mrs Tung chuckled. 'I remember, I couldn't have been more than ten years old, and one of them adopted me, because he said I looked like his daughter. He sent me a teddy bear after the war.' She chuckled and shook her head. 'I was too old for teddy bears by then. But I told everyone it meant we were getting married. Oh!' Mrs Tung shook her head at her foolishness. 'I wish I had married him,' she confided, feeling naughty. She always said that.

Mrs Tung, even now, had the power to make Mae feel calm and protected. Mrs Tung had come from a family of educated people and once had had a house full of books. The books had all been lost in a flood many years ago, but Mrs Tung could still recite to Mae the poems of the Turks, the Karz, or the Chinese. She had sat the child Mae on her lap and rocked her. She could recite now, the same poems.

'*Listen to the reed flute,*' she began now, '*How it tells a tale!*' Her old blind face, swayed with the words, the beginning of *The Mathnawi.* ' *"This noise of the reed is fire, it is not the wind."* '

Mae yearned. 'Oh, I wish I remembered all those poems!' When she saw Mrs Tung, she could visit the best of her childhood.

Mae then visited the Ozdemirs for a fitting.

The mother was called Hatijah, and her daughter was Sezen. Hatijah was a shy, slow little thing, terrified of being overcharged by Mae, and of being underserved. Hatijah's low, old stone house was tangy with the smells of burning charcoal, sweat, dung, and the constantly stewing tea. From behind the house came a continual, agonized bleating from the family goat. It needed milking. The poor animal's voice was going raw and harsh. Hatijah seemed not to hear it. Hatijah had four children, and a skinny shiftless husband who probably had worms. Half of the main room was heaped up with corncobs. The youngest of her babes wore only shirts and sat with their dirty naked bottoms on the corn.

Oh, this was a filthy house. Perhaps Hatijah was a bit simple. She offered Mae roasted corn. Not with your child's wet shit on it, thought Mae, but managed to be polite.

The daughter, Sezen, stomped in barefoot for her fitting, wearing the dress. It was a shade of lemon yellow that seared the eyes. Sezen was a tough, raunchy brute of a girl and kept rolling her eyes at everything: at her nervous mother, at Mae's efforts to make the yellow dress hang properly, at anything either one of the adults said.

'Does . . . will . . . tomorrow . . .' Sezen's mother tried to begin.

Yes, thought Mae with some bitterness, tomorrow Sezen will finally have to wash. Sezen's bare feet were slashed with infected cuts.

'What my mother means is,' Sezen said, 'will you make up my face?' Sezen blinked, her unkempt hair making her eyes itch.

'Yes, of course,' said Mae, curtly to a younger person who was so forward.

'What, with all those other girls on the same day? For someone as lowly as us?'

The girl's eyes were angry. Mae pulled in a breath.

'No one can make you feel inferior without you agreeing with them first,' said Mae. It was something Old Mrs Tung had once told Mae when she herself was poor and famished for magic.

'Take off the dress,' Mae said. 'I'll have to take it back for finishing.'

Sezen stepped out of it, right there, naked on the dirt floor. Hatijah did not chastise her, but offered Mae tea. Because she had refused the corn, Mae had to accept the tea. At least that would be boiled.

Hatijah scuttled off to the black kettle and her daughter leaned back in full insolence, her supposedly virgin pubes plucked as bare as the baby's bottom.

Mae fussed with the dress, folding it, so she would have somewhere else to look. The daughter just stared. Mae could take no more. 'Do you want people to see you? Go put something on!'

'I don't have anything else,' said Sezen.

Her other sisters had gone shopping in the town for graduation gifts. They would have taken all the family's good dresses.

'You mean you have nothing else you will deign to put on.' Mae glanced at Hatijah: she really should not be having to do this woman's work for her. 'You have other clothes, old clothes – put them on.'

The girl stared at her with even greater insolence.

Mae lost her temper. 'I do not work for pigs. You have paid nothing so far for this dress. If you stand there like that, I will leave, now, and the dress will not be yours. Wear what you like to the graduation. Come to it naked like a whore, for all I care.'

Sezen turned and slowly walked towards the side room.

Hatijah, the mother, still squatted over the kettle, boiling more water to dilute the stew of leaves. She lived on tea and burnt corn that was more usually fed to cattle. Her cow's-eyes were averted. Untended, the family goat still made noises like a howling baby.

Mae sat and blew out air from stress. This week! She looked at Hatijah's dress. It was a patchwork assembly of her husband's old shirts, beautifully stitched. Hatijah could sew. Mae could not. With all these changes, Mae was going to have to find something else to do besides sketch photographs of dresses. She had a sudden thought.

'Would you be interested in working for me?' Mae asked. Hatijah looked fearful and pleased and said she would have to ask her husband. In the end she agreed to do the finishing on three of the dresses.

Everything is going to have to change, thought Mae, as if to convince herself.

That night Mae worked nearly to dawn on the other three dresses.
Her noisy old sewing machine sat silent in the corner. It was fine for rough work, but not for finishing, not for graduation dresses.

The bare electric light glared down at her like a headache, as Mae's husband Joe snored. Above them in the loft, Joe's brother Siao and his father snored, too, as they had done for twenty years. In the morning they would scamper out to the water butt to wash, holding towels over their Y-fronts.

Mae looked into Joe's open mouth like a mystery. When he was sixteen, Joe had been handsome – in the context of the village – wild and clever. They'd been married a year when she first went to Yeshibozkent with him, where he worked between harvests building a house. She saw the clever city man, an acupuncturist who had money. She saw her husband bullied, made to look foolish, asked questions for which he had no answer. The acupuncturist made Joe do the work again. In Yeshibozkent, her handsome husband was a dolt.

Here they were, both of them now middle-aged. Their son Lung was a major in the army. They had sent him to Balshang. He mailed Mae parcels of orange skins for potpourri; he sent cards and matches in picture boxes. He had met some city girl. Lung would not be back. Their daughter Ying had been pulled into Lung's orbit. She had gone to stay with him, met trainee officers, and eventually married one. She lived in an army housing compound, in a bungalow with a toilet.

At this hour of the morning, Mae could hear their little river, rushing down the steep slope to the valley. Then a door slammed in the North End. Mae knew who it would be: their Muerain, Mr Shenyalar. He would be walking across the village to the mosque. A dog started to bark at him; Mrs Doh's, by the bridge.

Mae knew that Kwan would be cradled in her husband's arms, and that Kwan was beautiful because she was an Eloi tribeswoman. All the Eloi had fine features. Her husband Wing did not mind and no one now mentioned it. But Mae could see Kwan shiver now in her sleep. Kwan had dreams, visions, she had tribal blood, and it made her shift at night as if she had another, tribal life.

Mae knew that Kwan's clean and noble athlete son would be breathing like a moist baby in his bed, cradling his younger brother.

Without seeing them, Mae could imagine the moon and clouds over their village. The moon would be reflected shimmering on the water of the irrigation canals which had once borne their paper boats of wishes. There would be old candles, deep in the mud.

Then, the slow, sad voice of their Muerain began to sing. Even amplified, his voice was deep and soft, like pillows that allowed the unfaithful to sleep. In the byres, the lonely cows would be stirring. The beasts would walk themselves to the village square, for a lick of salt, and then wait to be herded down to valley pastures. In the evening, they would walk themselves home. Mae heard the first clanking of a cowbell.

At that moment something came into the room, something she did not want to see, something dark and whole like a black dog with froth around its mouth that sat in her corner and would not go away, nameless yet.

Mae started sewing faster.

The dresses were finished on time, all six, each a different colour. Mae ran barefoot in her shift to deliver them. The mothers bowed sleepily in greeting. The daughters were hopping with anxiety like water on a skillet.

It all went well. Under banners the children stood together, including Kwan's son Luk, Sezen, all ten children of the village, all smiles, all for a moment looking like an official poster of the future, brave, red-cheeked, with perfect teeth.

Teacher Shen read out each of their achievements. Sezen had none, except in animal husbandry, but she still collected her certificate to applause. And then Mae's friend Shen did something special.

He began to talk about a friend to all of the village, who had spent more time on this ceremony than anyone else, whose only aim was to bring a breath of beauty into this tiny village – the seamstress who worked only to adorn other people . . .

He was talking about her.

. . . One who was devoted to the daughters and mothers of rich and poor alike and who spread kindness and goodwill.

The whole village was applauding her, under the white clouds, the blue sky. All were smiling at her. Someone, Kwan perhaps, gave her a push from behind and she stumbled forward.

And her friend Shen was holding out a certificate for her.

'In our day, Mrs Chung-ma'am,' he said, 'there were no schools for the likes of us, not after early childhood. So. This is a graduation certificate for you. From all your friends. It is in "Fashion Studies."'

There was applause. Mae tried to speak, and found that only fluttering sounds came out, and she saw the faces all in smiles, ranged around her, friends and enemies, cousins and non-kin alike.

'This is unexpected,' she finally said, and they all chuckled. She looked at the high school certificate, surprised by the power it had, surprised that she still cared about her lack of education. She couldn't read it. 'I do not do fashion as a student, you know.'

They knew well enough that she did it for money and how precariously she balanced things.

Something stirred, like the wind in the clouds.

'After tomorrow, you may not need a fashion expert. After tomorrow, everything changes. They will give us TV in our heads, all the knowledge we want. We can talk to the President. We can pretend to order cars from Tokyo. We'll all be experts.' She looked at her certificate, hand-lettered, so small.

Mae found she was angry, and her voice seemed to come from her belly, an octave lower.

'I'm sure that it is a good thing. I am sure the people who do this think they do a good thing. They worry about us, like we were children.' Her eyes were like two hearts, pumping furiously. 'We don't have time for TV or computers. We face sun, rain, wind, sickness, and each other. It is good that they want to help us.' She wanted to shake her certificate; she wished it was one of them, who had upended everything. 'But how dare they? How dare they call us have-nots?'

2

The next morning was the day of the test.

Mrs Tung came calling, on the arm of her grandson Mr Ken Kuei.

'Granny Tung!' exclaimed Mae, delighted and alert. She was doing her laundry, and the cauldron was huge and unsteady on the kitchen brazier. Mr Ken gracefully passed his grandmother across to Mae.

Mrs Tung was still in her robe and slippers, hooting to herself like an owl. 'I thought I would just pop in, dear,' said Old Mrs Tung. It was a great adventure for her to go visiting. She laughed at her daring, as Mae eased her onto a chair.

Mr Ken was a handsome, orderly man. 'I told my grandmother about your certificate, and she wanted to see it.'

'Oh! It is nothing, but please sit down, Mr Ken.' Mae wanted Mr Ken to sit. She liked his calming influence. 'I meant to visit you this morning with some graduation cakes. Please have some.'

Mr Ken smiled and bowed slightly. 'It would be delightful, but my wife is doing the laundry, and I said I would help her.'

'Oh, perhaps you could come and help me!' Mae joked. Mae got no help.

Mr Ken bowed and left.

Mrs Tung ran her hands over the certificate with its frame and glass.

'It shows how we all love you,' said Old Mrs Tung. 'Read it for me, dear.'

Mae could not read. This was embarrassing. She recited what she remembered it said:

TO *Chung Mae Wang*

CERTIFICATE OF APPRECIATION FROM THE GRADUATING CLASS OF 2020

FOR FASHION STUDIES

Mae had to stop. Something was swimming in her eyes. There was an area out of focus. 'I think I need glasses,' said Mae.

The blur shifted, changing size and shape like a slug. Mae's fingers began to buzz.

Mrs Tung's head was cocked to one side. 'Do you hear something, dear?'

There was a flash as if someone had taken a photograph. 'Oh!' Mae said, and was thrown back onto a chair. Everything tingled – her feet, her hands, even her eyes. Worst of all, her brain tingled; she could feel it dance. The room went dim.

'Chocolate. I smell chocolate,' cooed Old Mrs Tung.

Mae smelled wine, perfume, sweat, onions, rain on cobbles, scorched rice, old shoe leather. Colours danced in her eyes; green-yellow red-blue, as if colour had become toffee to be stretched and mixed. And there was music – all kinds of music – as if hundreds of radios were being played at once, and a rearing-up of screeching, tinkling sounds like thousands of birds.

'I don't feel well,' said Old Mrs Tung. She raised her hand to her forehead, and for Mae it seemed to open up in stages like a fan.

'It must be this Test of theirs,' said Mae.

'Mae, dear,' Mrs Tung said, 'I need to get home.'

And then Mae had a sense of déjà vu, so strong that the words seemed to echo. It was not as if she had been here once before. It was as if she had always been here, and would go on being here, for ever. It was as if an image of herself had been copied in layers, off into eternity.

Mae stood up, but the room seemed to be stuffed full of sponges. She had to fight her way forward, giddy with sensation.

Colours, lights, stars, sounds, smells . . . Mae's hand touched a skillet, or so she thought, and she yelped and jumped back. She felt silk on her cheek. A baby kissed her toes. Her fingers were plunged into paddy mud.

Mrs Tung rose shuddering to her feet. 'Flies,' she said, and began to wave her stick.

Pork, cheese, tomatoes, oak bark, ginger – all skittered about Mae's tongue.

'All these flies!' Old Mrs Tung's blind eyes looked wild.

'I'm here, Granny!' said Mae, trying to sound calm. She waded her way through sight and sound. The world chattered, screeched, stank, glittered, rippled, stroked, soured, sweetened, burned. The air seemed set solid against her. Mae had to push herself from one second into the next. Time was gluing shut.

Mrs Tung spun around. 'Ugh. Flies!' She stumbled, and tottered sideways into the brazier.

Granny Tung!

Everything was slow. The cauldron rolled like a world making up its mind to fall. A wash of boiling water poured over Mrs Tung's thighs and legs, and the cauldron toppled against her, ringing like a slow gong and knocking her off her feet. Mrs Tung fell forward onto the ground and a steaming white sheet poured out with the chalky water and enveloped her, clinging.

Suddenly, stillness.

Mae panted for a moment. She had the sensation of having been fired from a gun, shot a great distance to somewhere else—

Here.

She jumped forward, and jostled the scalding sheet away from Mrs Tung. The boiling water had settled into her earthen floor, turning it into steaming mud. Hopping barefoot, Mae grabbed hold of Mrs Tung's arms and pulled. The old woman howled. The skin of Mrs Tung's hands was rucked-up and red like old tomatoes.

'I will get your grandson,' Mae said. It seemed as if hundreds of versions of Mae were speaking all at once, and would be stuck saying the same thing for ever.

Mae ran out into the courtyard.

A vortex of hens was running round and round in a perfect circle. All the village dogs were barking, their voices echoing from the amphitheatre of the surrounding hills. In the far corner, was a lump of what Mae at first thought was Mrs Ken's laundry in a heap.

Mae ran towards Mr Ken's kitchen.

Something tickled the inside of her ear. A mosquito. Go away! Mae tossed her head.

The buzzing returned, more insistent and louder. Mae remembered that once, a louse had got trapped inside her ear. I don't need this now!

The noise mounted to a roar. Mae had to stop, and she dug a finger in her ear, to prise it loose.

The sound motorboated forward inside her head as if changing gears, whining and roaring at the same time.

Nothing for it but to push on. The roar deafened Mae. It numbed her hands as she fumbled with the latch on Mr Ken's door.

The Ken family – Mr Ken, his mother, his two little girls – all sat around the table as if at a séance. They all held hands, and it seemed to Mae, because she could hear nothing, that they were all chanting in unison.

Mr Ken rose up at the table and mouthed at her. She began to make out what he was saying.

'. . . *no need for fear and alarm.*'

'Mr Ken,' Mae began, and the noise in her head rose to an all-consuming lion's roar . . .

The two girls and Old Mrs Ken waved her forward, nodding. *Join in!* they seemed to say. They all stood up and worked their mouths like fish at her.

'*Just listen to the words. Try talking along with them. You will find that will help.*'

Mae listened, and the roaring seemed to narrow into something like a line of surf breaking along a beach. She focused and there seemed to be voices, like mermaids in the waves.

Mae started to repeat them and they suddenly came clear.

'*Imagine that your mind is a courtyard. Assign these words like livestock to a pen. They are instructions. They will be in that pen whenever you need them.*'

The roaring stopped. Mae sighed, 'Oh!' with relief. Mae nodded to indicate to Ken that she got it.

'*Try to see the courtyard. You will find that you have a very clear picture of it in your head.*'

Echoing after each word, a great sigh rolled all around their house, rising and falling with Mae's own voice. Everyone in the village was saying the same thing at once.

Mae grabbed hold of Mr Ken's forearm and started to pull.

'*Can you see it? There are four pens in the courtyard, and they have signs over them. Can you see the signs? Can you read them?*'

'Mr Ken,' cried Mae. 'Your grandmother!'

The words rocked the room like a ship at sea and Mae was nearly thrown from her feet. The unfocused motorboat sound roared again.

Mae winced. She rejoined the chanting of the choir.

'*The signs say: "Help." "Information." "Airmail." And "That's Enter-tainment!"*'

Mr Ken looked quizzical. Mae signalled desperately towards her house. She saw him remember: *Granny!* He waved wildly to his mother and his daughter, and then turned and ran with Mae.

Outside, all the voices of the village tolled around them like a thousand calls to prayer.

'We call the pens and things inside them the Format.'

The laundry in the corner of the courtyard had sat up. Mrs Ken Tui sat with her elbows pressed tightly over her ears. Mr Ken moved towards her. Mae pulled him and signalled, *No, no – in here, in here!*

'Go to "Help" when you need help using Air. "Info" will tell you about everything from weather reports to what's available in the shops . . .'

Mae dragged Mr Ken into her kitchen. On the floor Granny Tung lay with her back arched, her hands claws of pain. Mr Ken ran forward and slipped on the steaming mud floor.

' "Airmail" is where you go to send messages to other people. Anyone, anywhere!'

Old Mrs Tung felt her grandson's hands. She looked up, her blind eyes staring, her face smeared with trails of tears. She quailed, in a thin voice, *' "That's Entertainment" is full of Air versions of your favourite films . . .'*

Mr Ken tried to pull her out of the steaming water. He touched her and she howled with pain. He winced and looked up at Mae in horror.

'Let's rest for just a moment. Take some time to think about the Format . . . and in a few moments, you'll see what Air really can do.'

Like the sound of a rockfall dying away, everything went still. There was the sound of wind moving in the courtyard. Was that it? Was it finished?

'I'm so sorry, Mr Ken, she stood up and knocked the brazier—'

'Anything to make a bandage?' Mr Ken asked.

'All the sheets were boiling. Everything will still be hot.'

He nodded. 'I must see to my wife. I'll get a sheet.' He stood and left them.

Mae knelt. 'Do you hear that, Mrs Tung? Your grandson Ken Kuei is bringing bandages.'

Mrs Tung seized Mae's hand. Mae winced at the ruined flesh. 'I can see,' Mrs Tung whispered. Her blind eyes moved back and forth in unison.

Blind Mrs Tung said she could see, and something moved behind the curtain of the world.

The world had always been a curtain, it seemed – one drawn shut inside Mae's head. Now it parted.

'Oh, God . . . oh, please,' said Mae. *'Inshallah!'*

The village dogs began to howl again.

The world pulled back and suddenly Mae stood in a blue courtyard. Everything was blue, even her own glowing hands. Neon signs glowed over the livestock pens. They were green, red, yellow, and mauve, and the flowing scripts were in the three languages of Karzistan and Mae knew, as if in a dream, what the words meant. In Air, Mae could read: Help, Info, Airmail.

The voice of Air said, *'Perhaps you see the Format more clearly now. This is how Air will look from now on. This is an Aircast, an image we can send out to you. It will be there whenever you need it. Let's see what an Aircast looks like. Go into the area called "That's Entertainment." '*

Mae! Mae! said a voice, far too closely, far too intimate, as if someone were whispering in her ear. *Mae, Mae – help!*

'Today, we have an Aircast from National Opera!'

'Granny Tung!' Mae heard her own voice. But she had not spoken.

The voice of Air said, *'We will see part of the opera* Turandot. *The opera is a favourite with audiences in the capital.'*

The whisper came again. It was Granny Tung. *Mae. Where is the world?*

'I'm trying to find you, Granny!'

Air said, *'Perhaps we like to think that the opera's hero, Kalaf, is Karzistani.'*

Mae raged. 'I don't want to go to an opera! I need to talk to Granny Tung!'

Immediately, the sound of the opera dimmed. A new, calmer voice spoke. *'To send messages, go to the area called Airmail.'*

Mae shot forward. She went through a blue wall, and into it. Mae crashed into metaphor. Information swallowed her. Information was blue and she was lost in it.

Mae! Mae!

'Do not attempt to send or receive Airmail until you have configured your personal airmail address. This is like putting your house name on your letterbox.'

If Mae had had a voice, she would have shouted. 'I've got no time, this is an emergency!'

'For an emergency configuration, simply repeat your own name several times.'

Mae said her own name over and over.

Mae! Mrs Tung seemed to cry out.

'Mae, Mae, Mae . . .'

Mae!

Something seemed to go click. It felt like a small electric shock. Something was connected.

Immediately, Mae was seized, hugged, held in terror as if she were a strong tree in a flood.

Can you feel it? It's pulling us back, Mae!

The voice of Air slowed to a crawl. *'Your . . . mailbox . . . is configured . . .'* Time was stopping.

Old Mrs Tung said one small, forlorn, unexpected word, full of dread.

Water.

Time reversed. Everything, the Format, the voices, the whitewashed stone walls, the people in them were sucked back in, down. It all collapsed, and everything was gone.

The past is so very different, we know it at once.

Mae knew she was in the past because of the smells. The wood beams stank of creosote; the house had a stewed odour of bodies and tea and fermenting beanshoots.

She was in a house at night, with no lights on; the walls were in unexpected places. A stairwell opened up underneath her feet. A woman stumbled, rolled down the steps and landed up to her knees in water.

My books, someone thought, *all my beautiful books!*

The woman stumbled to her feet, tried to find a candle. A candle, fool, in this?! She waded across the floor of her main room, water lapping around her shins. How much water is there? Where can it come from? She reached out and touched a leather binding on the shelf and in that moment knew the books were lost.

She heard a laugh behind her and turned. A woman's voice said, 'What is it worth now, all the money you married?' The voice was rough and silky at the same time; an old woman's voice.

'Is it still coming in?' Mrs Tung screamed, twisting around. Mrs Tung was young, supple, and strong.

'It is roaring down every slope.' Hearing that voice, Mrs Tung's heart sank with a sense of oppression, overruling, and contempt.

Mrs Tung waded her way through the flood. 'Are the children upstairs?' she demanded.

'Oh,' said the dark voice, 'so now you remember you have children?' The voice was bitter, triumphant, and full of hatred.

Mrs Tung pushed past her, feeling her old, quilted overcoat. The old woman laughed again, a familiar hooting, a slightly hollow laugh.

Then, from outside the house, from the slopes above, there came a spreading hiss and clatter like applause, as if all the stones of the valley were rising in tribute.

'Lily! Ahmet!' Mrs Tung called, in the dark, to her children. A thousand rolling pebbles clattered against the house like rain. There was a *boom!* and the house shuddered.

'Mrs Tung,' Mae tried to say. The words went somewhere else.

'Lily!' Mrs Tung shouted again, her voice breaking. The house groaned, and something made a snapping sound.

Mrs Tung bashed her head on a doorway, heard a wailing in a corner. She scooped up a child in thick pyjamas. Mae could feel the button-up suit made of flannel, smelling of damp dust.

'Where is your brother?'

The child could only wail.

'Lily! Where is Ahmet?'

The child buried her head and screamed.

Mae thought: Lily? Ahmet? Mrs Tung had another family? Another family before the Kens? Who?

Mrs Tung turned and begged the quilted coat, 'Mrs Yuksel, please! Have you seen Ahmet? Has he gone down the stairs?'

'Yes,' said the calm dark voice. 'He went out the front door.'

And the certain, terrible knowledge: Ahmet's grandmother did not want a half-Chinese grandson.

'You let him out!'

The laugh.

'You let him out to die!'

Carrying Lily, Mrs Tung thrust herself past her mother-in-law.

'Ahmet! Ahmet!' Mrs Tung wailed a whole broken heart. She plunged down into her front room and into mud up to her waist. The front room was choked with it. The child in her arms kicked and screamed.

It was all Mrs Tung could do to shrug herself around, turn, and wrestle her way back towards the stairs. As her foot struck the lowest step, still under mud, she felt a scurrying sensation round her knees. Water was flowing in over the top of the mud. The water was still coming for them, inexhaustible. Bearing Lily, she hauled herself up.

'Mrs Tung! Mrs Tung!' A voice was pleading.

Her own voice. If this voice was her voice then who was she?

'Mrs Tung, this is just a memory. Mrs Tung . . .'

What? What?

'This is all Air, Mrs Tung!'

'Water!' she shouted back, and rose out of the mud. Hatred swelled out of her heart. She felt the wall of the staircase. On the wall was a family sword.

'So you will not inherit my beautiful room,' said the laugh.

Mrs Tung swung the sword. The laugh was cut off. Mrs Tung turned and ran into the upstairs corridor. The wooden timbers creaked, like a ship. The entire house shuddered, heaved, and moved forward from its foundations. It twisted and began to break apart; she ran towards its end room, the one with the beautiful window, the one that looked back towards home, to Kizuldah.

She heard a great collapsing behind her, felt timbers separate, fall, rumble like barrels. Somehow she kicked glass from the window. Lily screamed. Reflected in the roaring water was fire, leaping along roof-tops. Mrs Tung jumped, falling many feet, out over the downside of the slope, awash in a wake of water. She fell through warm air down into a snow-cold, icy torrent.

Everything pulled. Lily was pulled from her. She slipped away like a scarf into the current.

'Mrs Tung!'

The water was blue.

'Mrs Tung, this is just a memory, this is not really happening!'

Then why is the air warm? Why is the water cold? Can you feel water in memory?

Mae held and pulled, resisted the Flood and the backwards pull.

Somewhere dimly there was singing. *Turandot* was being performed. Three old men sung about their lost homes. *'Kiu . . . Tsiang . . . Honan.'*

'There, Mrs Tung! We need to get back there!'

From somewhere, Old Mrs Tung said: *It was real. It was as real as now and as important. My Lily was real.*

Mae said, 'We need to get home!'

That was home! That is real! It all gets washed away. I can die, that means nothing, but a whole universe dies every day, slowly, slowly, it deserves remembrance, here, see it was beautiful, beautiful!

'Dear Mrs Tung. Sssh. See? See?'

Life like a mountain, huge, cold, fearsome, ice with water wreathed in cloud and air and sunset, too big, too strange.

Suddenly they were standing in a courtyard, a courtyard at night.

Mae said, 'Mrs Tung, that is the Format.'

Why are there neon signs? Help? Entertainment? I have done with all that, I am too old. In the corner there is a TV set. When did we get a TV?

It is showing an opera. I have never seen an opera. It is the opera in Balshang, and I have always, always wanted to see that, oh, the red and the gold! And look at the jewels as they sing! I have heard this on radio, and dreamed, there she is, there she is, the Princess, singing of a beautiful woman who died centuries ago.

In the opera, a woman sang, *'Principessa Loo Ling, my ancestress, sweet and serene . . .'*

'Mrs Tung? Mrs Tung? I'm afraid, Mrs Tung. I have to go.'

Then go, child.

'I have to get back.'

You go on. I will stay here.

Mae pulled herself away, and felt herself stretching, held by someone else's thoughts.

She goes. I always thought Lily would be here to meet me. Instead it is Mae, faithful little Mae, who helps me across.

Our flesh is earth and fire our desires, and the fire burns through the flesh, the water washes it all away. And what is left is air. And air rises towards heaven.

There was a sense of parting, like a sprain.

Mae was separated from Mrs Tung, and standing in the Format, demanding in terror, 'How do I get back?'

Air answered.

'Leaving Airmail in the event of an emergency: every message area has its own entry protocol which should prevent access to the full mind.'

Mae cried, 'I've got access to the full mind!'

It was cold inside Mrs Tung, and the cold seemed to clasp and hold and freeze.

'Protocols can break down in the event of illness or extremes of emotion. If you find your mind in contact with more than the Airmail area of the person you are contacting, first find your own Airmail address. Concentrate on that area as if in meditation. Repeat your address like a mantra . . .'

Her address? Mae remembered. 'Mae, Mae, Mae, Mae . . .'

Something brushed past her. *Darling child*, it seemed to say.

'Mae, Mae, Mae, Mae, Mae . . .'

That was what Mae was saying, over and over when she woke up, lying on the floor, holding Mrs Tung.

Mae knew then why the old woman had laughed through the last sixty years of her life. It was not to keep up her spirits. Mrs Tung had hooted all her life from heartbreak.

And the dear old creature was dead.

3

Mae was finding everything funny.
She lay in bed, pushing herself into the corner of the alcove, her face stretched into a grin she could not explain. Her family and friends were crowded around. They knew Mae had been inside Mrs Tung when she died.

Mae's mother sat beside the bed in state and that was funny. 'Allah!' her mother said, calling on the God of the Prophet with hands raised. Mae's mother was a Buddhist.

'A terrible thing,' said Mae's brother Ju-mei, shaking his head. He had put on his best city suit and long city coat for the occasion. He sweated, steaming for his respectability.

Kwan passed Mae tea, and that was funny. Someone dies and so you make a cup of tea?

Kwan intoned, 'Many people say that they did not find death so terrible.'

Mae laughed. It was the soft, hooting sound of heartbreak that was part of her now. 'How can they say anything if they're dead?'

Kwan said, calmly, 'Sometimes the doctors bring them back.'

'Isn't science wonderful?' Mae chuckled. 'Did they ask the people if they wanted to come back?'

Mae's mother cursed the devil. 'It is Shytan, the work of Shytan!'

'We will take care of you now,' promised Mae's brother, heavy-faced.

That made Mae laugh, too. More like you want me to go on taking care of you, she thought.

Mae remembered Mr Ken's wife, lying in the courtyard. 'How is Mrs Ken Tui?' Mae asked.

Everything went silent. Joe, sitting at the kitchen table, lifted up his baseball cap and scratched his head.

Kwan answered. 'Tui is dead, too.' Mae's brother leaned forward and took her hand. Kwan hesitated, then spoke. 'She ran out of the yard. She was crying that she was going mad. She threw herself down into the well.'

Mae squawked with laughter. It was terrible, but she did. 'You all went to see an opera and meanwhile the rest of us lived one.' She was still chuckling when she asked the next question. 'Do they count the Test as a success?'

Mr Wing looked grim. 'No,' he said.

Mae found that funny, too, and chuckled again and waved her hand. 'It would seem not,' she replied.

Mr Wing said, 'They said that the process was proved physically safe but there were still many instances of panic and injury.'

'And no one can drink from their wells, they are so stuffed with the bodies of neighbours.' Mae laughed again, and alarmed herself. She was laughing too much.

Mr Wing kept doggedly informing her, to calm her, which only made things funnier. 'They will not begin Aircasting for another year.'

'So, we have a year to live,' Mae said.

'There is to be an international program of education.'

Mae imitated the voices, out of pure, hilarious rage. You all now have a pigpen inside your head and we do not know how to clean it up. 'The Pig' is called 'Terror.' You also have another area marked 'Death.' Please do not choose 'Death.' You can choose 'Terror' and 'Panic' whenever you like.

'There is also,' Kwan said calmly, 'a world of the spirit. And you have travelled that.'

Mae stopped laughing, abruptly.

The next morning, Mae tried to go back to work.
She tried once more to boil the clothes. It took all morning. She kept dropping things, distracted. She was aware that as a fashion expert she should look her best. She put on a best dress, but it wouldn't hang right, as though it were on backwards. She started to apply makeup in the mirror and burst into tears.

The face was alive but alone.

The brazier was moved outside the kitchen. Mae found herself standing outside in the courtyard, with the long wooden laundry spoon still in her hand, remembering.

She was remembering all the children who had run in that yard, the girls in dirty flowered trousers, the littlest boys in shorts, the biggest lads in sweatshirts, sports gear. She saw them in waves, coming and going. She found herself remembering children like Woo, who had died, caught in a thresher.

Before Mae was born.

Mae was remembering what Old Mrs Tung had seen.

She remembered a farming village owned by a landlord who the Communists later killed. She remembered his car, all polished cream metal, too large and fast for local roads. It was pulled by oxen and the landlord waved from its back seat. He was fat, childish. He gave little Miss Hu a bonbon. Hu Ai-Ling had been Mrs Tung's name once.

Mae remembered weaving pots from reed. She remembered women whose faces were almost familiar, whose names she could almost recall, and she heard them agree that it was best to be a middle wife. First wives were supposed to lead, and lived in fear of being usurped. The youngest wife would always be the lowest in the house. 'So how can you be a middle wife without being the youngest first?' someone asked.

Mae remembered how to make cucumber pickles that would survive crisp and free from vinegar taste for three years. She remembered bean harvests, sitting in groups sorting good from bad, shelling, grilling, drying, pickling. The women had worn quilted jackets, no makeup, and they all smoked chervil in their soapstone pipes. They tried to get rid of teeth; teeth just caused trouble and pain.

Mae remembered the poems.

'Tis the fire of Love that is in the reed, it is the fervour of Love that is in the wine

'Mrs Chung?' It was Mr Ken, standing in front of her.

The reed is the comrade of everyone who has been parted from a friend

His neatly trimmed hair, his round face, all seemed newly widowed and alone. She saw his face as a boy, as a grandmother would see it, the face of the future. Now grown up, now bereft, now without her. The chasm of the future into which we all fall, and decline, and disappear. The hollow that is left in the world by our own missing shape.

'Oh,' she said, and hugged him.

She wept into his shoulder.

'Mrs Chung,' he said again, and gingerly patted her back.

'I . . . have . . . your grandmother's memories!' Mae blurted it out all in a rush, fearful, terrified, and she covered her mouth.

'You had a blue plastic truck, I remember that, and you drove the family crazy making truck noises. You wanted to be a truck driver.' Her face was stained with tears. She was shaken with the mystery and sadness of life. 'Why did you never become a truck driver?'

Ken Kuei's round and handsome face was slack, unmanned by the sudden intimacy. The question was a good one. His grandmother had never asked it.

'The farm,' he murmured. The shrug said there was much more to be said. He glanced about the courtyard. Mae was still in her morning robe.

'Come inside, Mrs Chung,' he said, and began to lead her. 'Do you want me to get Joe?'

'I don't know.' She wanted Mr Ken. She wanted to talk to him about his childhood. She had a terribly strong sense of who he was. She had held him as a baby. She had known that even as a baby he was a reserve of quiet, calm strength. He never wept or wailed. He could fight, but only when he needed to. He had been so good at football.

Like Ahmet had been.

All of this made her weep for what had gone, as if Kuei's childhood was the distant shore of some beautiful retreating land. For Mrs Tung, taking care of the family's long-awaited grandson had been the last time she was useful.

'I was a skeleton for years,' said Mae, confused.

Mr Ken's face was seriously worried for her.

'Your grandmother loved **you**,' said Mae. 'She was so sad when you went away.'

He had managed to get her back into her own house. 'I did not go away.'

'You grew up,' she accused him, and started to weep. 'We should come out of shells,' she said. 'The shells should be the babies, and the babies should be left behind, alive. For the mothers. For the mothers to cradle.'

'Stay here,' said Mr Ken. And he ran.

And Mae was left alone, and she wept; she wept for the village that had already died, the old Kizuldah.

You should be able to turn a corner and find home again, with its undrained marshes in the valley floor. The valley was left unploughed for the waterfowl, the foxes, the stars, and young lovers.

Oh, Mrs Tung, I was a friend of yours, and still I did not know you. I never came close. After you had sat me on your knee and showed me pages of clothes and beautiful women. Even though I saw you every day, still I did not know you. I never asked you about Japanese airplanes. Was it true that the landlord put poachers' heads on spikes?

An answer came from somewhere. *Yes.*

You see? No one believes that now. People think it was just Communist fairy tales. We lose, we lose so much.

The voice came back. *Only everything.*

It was as though Old Mrs Tung had come in and sat down.

Once there was a cold snap and I dropped a shirt from the laundry line and it broke.

And Mae saw that world: of rising with the dawn, of bending all day jamming rice plants into mud.

In the morning, you would hear all the men going off, singing songs.

Sing them for me, said Mae in her mind. And stood up to work.

Both of them sang old work songs that only Mrs Tung remembered – simple songs about someone whose work trousers would not stay up, or about the love of the porcupine for the wood louse. She remembered jokes that the villagers had told, jokes about moths. Who was so innocent now to joke about moths, sole leather, or candles?

Mae hung up her laundry, singing to herself in a loud, rough, peasant voice.

'Mrs Chung?' asked a young voice.

Mae turned and had to blink. The round young face could have been from any era: the 1940s, the 1980s, or the 2000s. The low rope collar of the dress told her what year it was.

This was one of Saturday's graduates, Han An. 'I came to thank you for my graduation dress.'

'You are welcome,' said Mae, and bowed. An was the daughter of a woman who had been Mae's best friend when they were children. They hardly saw each other now.

'We heard that you were not well after the Test.'

Mae shook her head. No, she was not well at all.

The young woman looked shaken. 'We all thought that, as fashion expert, you would be most at home with the new things . . .'

Mae started to say what had happened, and found she could not. It was too complicated and too simple at the same time. She could phrase it, I am haunted by a ghost. She could say: I stole part of Mrs Tung's soul. She could say, I was in Airmail when she died. She could say: I think Airmail is a place.

All of it would be true and all of it false. Language, like Mrs Tung herself, was an old, fragile footbridge, breaking through.

Mae stood with the wet sheets folded over her arm. Everything foxed her. An saw this. 'Let me help you,' said An.

An had bought cakes of gratitude. She passed these to Mae to hold out of reach of Mr Ken's dog, and began to nip clothes pegs onto the sheets.

If I was still concerned about being fashion expert, Mae thought, I would be alarmed. I would be alarmed at this loss of status. But I cannot be alarmed. I cannot help it.

An led her back into her own kitchen. She made Mae tea. Mae unwrapped the cakes, and she began to weep. She wept copiously, like a natural spring welling up out of the depths of the earth.

They were old-fashioned cakes, cakes such as the villagers had baked for each other for hundreds of years; beautiful little cakes made mostly from air, old rice, spare sugar, preserved sweet things in tiny precious slices. A story of hundreds of years of poverty and gratitude was told in those cakes. It seemed to her that Old Mrs Tung, all her friends and her mother's friends, all of the village women from the hard centuries, had clustered around to receive that thank-you.

Joe came home early, with Dr Bauschu, the county doctor.

'You cannot work, wife,' said Joe, heartsick, as if she were a favourite machine that had broken.

She paused and contemplated what must be true. 'My heart is too full,' she replied.

And suddenly, she remembered him, she saw him. Tiny, mischievous, in shorts – the child Joe. She saw him as Mrs Tung saw him. Oh, what an angel! A beautiful, merry little fellow in shorts, running amongst the others, chuckling and buffing them on the head, still laughing when they cuffed him back. He grew quickly and was too soon developed. Joe had ceased to learn.

There was little enough mischief in Joe now, or laughter.

'Oh, husband! What we have all lost, what we will all go on losing through all of history, it cannot be weighed. It cannot be measured!'

Her handsome, comic husband stood helpless, scratching his head.

Whoever had heard of a wife who could not work because she perceived the weight of history?

Dr Bauschu asked her to sit down and roll up her sleeve. He was a hard, thin man who circulated among half a dozen villages with a battered old black briefcase. He had always been highly critical of the fashion expert – she did too much massaging with oils, too much dental flossing, services on the borderline where beauty crossed into health.

He seemed quite pleased that she was ill. 'So, you see, when illness really comes, even you call for the doctor.'

How unpleasant could he be? I am in mourning, fool, for a whole way of life.

Dr Bauschu insisted on taking her temperature, her pulse. He prodded her for lumps and peered down her throat. 'It is a nervous condition triggered by the trauma of that Test. Otherwise, there is nothing wrong. I suggest a drawing-off of humours.'

Even Mae knew that he had ceased to be scientific. He heated her good glasses, and set them on her lower back, to suck and draw.

'The doctor used to come every six months,' said Mae, sleepily, 'in a white van with a red crescent. We would all line up for treatment, even if there were nothing wrong. There always was something to cure: a tooth or a cut or head lice.'

The doctor's glasses gleamed as he snapped shut his bag. She was talking nonsense. The fashion expert had fallen.

That night most of the village crowded into Mae's single room. Mae's sister-in-law, Mrs Wang, barracked around Mae's kitchen, trying to brew tea by looking in all the wrong places, scattering arrangements. Joe's brother Siao quietly followed her, replacing things. Ten of the Soongs, who were connected to Mae by various marriages crowded into her house. She couldn't even think of some of their names.

Mae's mother exclaimed to Old Mrs Soong. 'It is God's will. We have sinned and gone on sinning, so God punishes us.'

'Nonsense, Mother,' said Mae. 'God doesn't punish. He doesn't reward. He lets us get on with it.'

'Her father was murdered,' said her desolate mother, handkerchief gesturing towards Mae, as if that explained everything. 'She lost her sister and her daughter . . .'

All the family legends came out. Mae was too tired and harassed for them now. Wasted love was wearisome. Her handsome older sister Missy, who died . . . Mae's elder daughter, who also died . . . Why remind her of that now? Being with people, feeling so ill, reminded Mae of the worst of her past. She wanted everything gone. She wanted sleep, but they had all come to make her feel better.

Teacher Shen came, looking solemn. He brought his beautiful wife Suloi, in case anyone misunderstood his friendship with Mae.

'Teacher Shen,' Mae said, pleased to see him. Suloi had Kwan's face, the face of their minority, the Eloi. Mrs Shen was just as beautiful as Kwan. Even now, here, she was merry.

Mrs Shen asked, 'How is our fashion expert?'

'Very confused,' Mae replied. 'I am more a history expert now.'

She looked up at Teacher Shen's face and, lo, remembered him as a skinny, put-upon little boy. Old Mrs Tung had worried so about him. She had wished she had more books to give this solemn child.

'You should have gone for that exam,' Mae said sleepily, 'to be a civil servant.'

Teacher Shen blinked, his face darted up towards Kwan, who nodded once downwards.

'I could not afford the time or the books,' he said quietly. 'So I took the teaching course.'

'Remember the tiny white book? About the rabbits?' Mae murmured. Old Mrs Tung had found it for him, a book of his very own.

His face was a wan smile, his eyes unblinking. He produced from his pack. 'This one,' he said.

It was a tiny battered book, stained by childhood, and it said in the language of their people *The Tale of Peter Rabbit*.

The Teacher turned to others in the room about him, and his staring eyes were filling. 'It's true,' he whispered to the room. 'It's true.'

Shen's Eloi wife edged closer to Mae, on her knees, smiling. She took Mae's other hand.

'You have become a prophet,' she said, in a very quiet voice.

'Of the past,' said Mae. What would it be like, just once, to have a moment to herself?

Standing among her friends were Sunni and her husband Mr Haseem. He wanted this house.

The next day was Mrs Tung's funeral.

Mae watched impassively as the cardboard coffin was lowered into the rocky ground. The mosque looked small, high on the hill, its white-wash peeling. The whole hillside looked peeling.

It was somewhat strange to see your own body buried, to see people you did not really know daub their faces. To know that you had lived so long that there was no one left to mourn you. Mrs Tung's grand-sons were grown men, sad, yes, discomfited in suits. One was a mechanic in Yeshibozkent, another drove buses. They would be back to business by the afternoon.

Mae was not in mourning; for her, Mrs Tung was not dead. A body was only earth. Mrs Tung was with her in Air.

Sunni Haseem came to her and took Mae's hand. 'I am so sorry,' said Sunni, conventionally.

'Why?' Mae asked.

'She led a full life,' Sunni agreed.

And Mae remembered Mrs Tung making love in the middle of battle, in the marsh.

She remembered the tops of the reeds being cut down by bullets as Mrs Tung embraced. Mrs Tung's young man leaned back and smiled, and Mae remembered that smile. It was careless, as if to say, *Life is not worth having if it's not worth losing*. And Mae knew: The boy was killed.

'She died at an honourable age,' said Sunni.

Oh, fashion wife with your little kitchen and lack of love, what do you know about it? What have you ever given for anything?

'Honourable?' Mae repeated. As if all Mrs Tung had done was darn tea towels. 'She was a guerrilla; she hid soldiers in the school.'

Kwan and Joe came forward, and took her arm. 'Let's get you back home,' Kwan said.

Mae stood her ground. 'Why do people treat the past as if it had lost a battle that the present won?' she demanded, fists clenched. 'Why do they treat it as if it faded because it was weak?'

Joe looked baffled and distressed.

'I don't know,' said Kwan.

'The past is real,' said Mae. 'It's still here.'

'Then maybe so is the future,' said Kwan.

Through those weeks, into June, Mae slept late and long.
She grew plump through inactivity, dreaming of ninety years' worth of human voices: children, adults, the barking of favourite dogs long since dead, the sloshing of water on burnt-out canoes long since rotted away.

Gradually she found she could make meals again, do some tidying-up, or sweep. She managed to banish her sister-in-law from her kitchen. Her husband Joe began to look relieved. His work clothes were ready again for him in the mornings, and his breakfast of steamed noodles.

But Mae would stand near her tiny kitchen window, to catch a glimpse of Mr Ken. Her heart would go out to him, with two young daughters late in life, leaving for his fields in the earliest dawn, long before her Joe. Her heart would go out to him, for the infant and small boy he had been, and for his plump face, thin waist, and the quick, nimble way he did things.

She kept thinking of Old Mrs Tung in the reeds. How the dress had come up, the trousers down, and how Mrs Tung had opened up to her lover, fully, completely, loose and abandoned like a sail in the wind, wanting him to fill her with babies, nothing held back.

Old Mrs Tung had known that, prim and delicate as she may have looked.

The fashion expert had not, for all her talk of beauty.

The lipsticks, the oil in the hair, the flower hairgrips – they were all signals; signals that said, *Love me, I have not been loved*. That was why they had power over her, why she was drawn to them, why she needed them. She had wanted to festoon herself with flags, saying, *Come to me, I cannot come to you*.

Now she simply wanted Mr Ken.

4

It was night and Mae was half asleep in bed when she heard Joe come home.

Back from the Teahouse, Joe hissed and giggled at his brother Siao. Someone else was with them. 'So where is the wife?' a man asked. Mae recognized the voice: Sunni's husband had come back with them.

Joe murmured something polite and indistinct.

'Back at work? In the fashion business?'

Joe chuckled something; Sunni's husband chuckled back.

'Good to be the man of the house again, ah? Ha-ha!'

Joe told his brother Siao to fetch the whisky. Siao grumbled, fed up with Joe playing the older brother.

'Oh! No – the good stuff for Mr Haseem!' Joe exclaimed in frustration. A clink of glasses. Joe would be pink-faced in the evening and red-eyed in the morning. Joe was worst when drunk; he simply became a sheepish goon. Why couldn't Sunni's husband just come bearing good wishes and go?

Because, thought Mae, Sunni's husband does not bear good wishes. Mae lay still and focused with her ears.

'I can help,' said Sunni's husband. Mae could almost hear the wallet unflap, unfold. She kicked her way free from the sheets, and threw on a robe. Then she thought: No. That is not enough. She needed to look like a fashion expert.

Everything worked against her: the dark and the slovenly disorder the alcove had become. She tried to move quietly; she wanted to appear suddenly, in order, pristine, to say, *We do not need your help Sunni's-man, sir.*

'*How* much?' Joe exclaimed in wonder.

Mae fumbled for her best dress in the dark. Her hand struck a hanger, and she felt the dress. The curtain-folds of the collar seemed to be right. She hauled it on over her head and ran her fingers through the bird's-nest tangle of her hair. She patted the windowsill and found a hairgrip. Hands shaking with urgency, she pulled her hair back as tightly as she could bear it and slipped on the grip.

Everything felt lopsided – her face, the grip, the dress hanging off one shoulder but straining around her belly. Shoes. Where were her shoes?

Mr Haseem's voice drawled as if over a woman. 'Enough to clean up the old barn, set up a byre, buy a few goats. Ah? Ha-ha.'

Don't, Joe, fool, that's how he does it, he loans too much money and then takes the farm in payment. Sandals. Inappropriate with a best dress, but anything, now. I feel like a haystack, thought Mae. And pulled back her curtain with gracious slowness.

Around her table, Sunni's husband was leaning back, at home, feet on a chair, rice-whisky bottle opened and half empty.

'Wife!' called Joe, as if overjoyed to see her. Siao looked up in drunken dolefulness.

Faysal Haseem appraised her with narrow eyes, and a grin.

'We are honoured,' said Sunni's husband, pushing a whisky glass to her in her own kitchen. 'You wear your best dress for us.'

'She couldn't find another!' Joe thought this was very funny and laughed, opening his mouth like a duck's bill.

Mae said, 'You are very kind to offer us help.'

'Aren't I?' said Sunni's-man, and lifted up the glass.

'He has already loaned us one hundred riels!' said Joe.

'Oh,' said Mae. 'Then you must give them back.'

'Naw,' growled Sunni's husband, and sloshed the whisky around in his mouth.

'One hundred riels, wife! A new barn! Goats! We will be rich.'

'Mr Haseem is far too kind.' Mae sat down, trying to get her business brain to work. She was not up to cunning. 'But how will you pay him back, husband?'

'Oh, we can come to some kind of arrangement,' said Joe, besotted, foolish.

'No problem about payments!' said Sunni's husband, not so drunk that his eyes did not fix on Mae and twinkle with mischief. 'If it comes to it, you can pay out of your fashion business.'

'Ah,' said Joe in scorn. 'We will not need that.'

'You do not have it,' said Mae, with a sick and weary chuckle. Could not Joe see that? Mae had been ill through the spring fashion season.

'We will have an ox, two oxen,' said Joe, with a bit of swagger.

'Two oxen cannot pay back one hundred riels.' Mae clasped her head to keep her brains together. All she could do was play the game as if everything were above board.

So she asked straight out: 'Please, Mr Haseem, there is no way for us to pay the money back. This is a very bad business proposition for you.'

'I think it is a good one,' he said, red-faced, knowing exactly what he was doing.

'You will lose the money!' Oh, she had been a fool to try to dress! Why did she dress? To show him they still had an extra source of money? All the village knew now that was unlikely. All her dressing-up had done was delay her until it was too late. So much for fashion.

'I won't lose the money,' said Sunni's husband. 'Will I, Joe?'

'Certainly not,' said Joe, dazzled. He unfolded the actual money in a fan.

'Joe, you are drunk,' Mae said in desperation. She looked at Siao, who took light little puffs of his cigarette and gazed at his shoes. He didn't like this, either.

'Siao,' she pleaded. 'Tell him. This is your father's house! Tell him that we won't be able to pay back the money!'

Siao glanced up at her and rubbed his whole face, once, with his hand. He had managed to grow a wispy beard, and around his mouth were strings of muscle. He flicked ash. 'Mr Haseem has been very kind, but we've all hit the bottle. Perhaps we should say thank you, Mr Haseem, and give our answer in the morning.'

'Answer in the morning?' Joe said. 'A friend generously offers money and you insult him by saying we have to consider?'

'I am saying that perhaps Mr Haseem and ourselves will feel different in the morning,' Siao said.

Joe glanced sideways at Mr Haseem. He needed to look like the boss of the house. 'Sometimes it is necessary to take a risk. You never have done that, Siao. You have never left home.'

'Neither have you,' said Siao, quietly. 'But I think perhaps soon you may have to.'

Mae spoke. 'Joe, your brother is right.'

'Wife. This is between men.'

Mae turned. 'Mr Haseem, please, my husband does not know what he is doing, please take the money back, there is no way we can pay you. Except to give you the farm.'

She was being honest. She was much reduced; she had no weapons.

'I think that is for your husband to say,' said Mr Haseem.

Mae leaned forward. 'Mr Haseem, please don't take the farm, please don't do this, I am a friend of your wife's, think of the friendship and please don't swallow us. Please, I beg of you!'

Terror and confusion from the Test, hatred of what was happening, overwhelmed her. Mae got down on her knees. In the dust in her best white dress with the heart-shaped patterns, she abased herself.

'Please don't take our farm!'

'I think it is your wife who is drunk,' chuckled Sunni's husband.

'Wife!' barked Joe. 'You are making a scene. You are ill. Ill in the head.' He jabbed a finger at his own.

'Take the money back!' sobbed Mae, seizing it from Joe and pushing it at Mr Haseem. 'Please.' It fell on the ground. She cradled it up, poison money, and tried to push it at him again. He took it, rolled it neatly, leaned across the table, and put it into Joe's pocket, patted it, grunted, and leaned back. He looked content, exactly as though he had eaten well.

So, Mae thought. You have your loan and you even had me begging on my knees. You know that I know, and that I am helpless. I should have denied you that, at least. I give nothing else away to you.

Mae stood up and wiped her cheeks. She had a blinding headache, suddenly, and the entire room seemed filthy, dull, and wearisome.

'One hundred riels is not a bad price to pay for a farm,' she said. 'It is good business, Mr Haseem. For you.'

Joe looked befuddled.

'Here, husband.' She poured him another whisky. 'It is best that you be merry now. It is best that you forget.' She stroked his crisp, slicked-back hair, then lightly batted it.

He took the glass with a hazy swagger. *The wife pours her man a drink, that is right and proper behaviour.* Mae slipped her hand into his pocket, and took the money. She counted it.

'One hundred riels,' she said, in acknowledgement to Sunni's husband. 'It is all there.'

'Of course,' said Mr Haseem, leaning back. 'I am an honest man.'

'An honest man!' insisted Joe, and held up the glass.

'The wife always keeps the money,' Mae said, folding the money into the collar of her best dress. She thought, I would not put it beyond you to steal it back from my husband while he drops off.

Sunni's husband tipped his glass towards her in mock salute.

Mae could not bear to see any more. She left and pulled the curtain shut behind her, but did not lie down. She stood riveted to the spot by panic. He has us, he has us, just like he got the others, the loans, the further loans, the money that could not be paid, the seizing of the house, the lands. This whole house is only worth three hundred riels! Our fields only bring in about a hundred. We have to find a year's extra income, with interest.

Mae thought of Sunni. Men's business, is it? Well it can be women's business as well.

Now she could turn on the light. The bare bulb glowed over sewing machine, toiletries, and heaps of cloth. It showed her crumpled face, bags and lines around the eyes, a puffy mouth as if her husband beat her. There was her comb. She pulled it through her hair. There was her lipstick. She precisely placed it, outlining the lips she wished she had. She pinched her cheeks and found the right shoes, and threw on a sweater. She strode back out into the kitchen.

'I'm going for a walk,' she announced, and stalked out into the courtyard. Sunni's husband roared with laughter, and saluted her. 'Walk well, fashion expert!'

Mae walked across Upper Street then up the steep slope to Mr Haseem's riverside house. She knew that Sunni would be awake, bitter, watchful.

Mae pushed open the courtyard gate, walked to the kitchen door, ducked down, and entered. The kitchen light was on, but Sunni was not there. Best not to surprise her if she was not looking her best. 'Friend Sunni!' she called. 'It is just Mae. Can I come to talk?'

In fact Sunni was ready for her. Mae knew that from the way the curtain snapped back on its rings, the way Sunni's hair and makeup were perfect, but most of all from the way she stood straight and tall with her plump face set.

'This is late for a social call,' Sunni informed her.

'Indeed. But I need your help.'

'Indeed. You have not been yourself lately,' said Sunni. 'Standards have been allowed to slip.'

Mae knew then in her gut that this was pointless, she knew in her gut what the situation was. But at least later she would be able to say that she had asked.

'Are you going to ask me to sit down?' Mae asked. 'I do not intend to stay long. As you say, I have not been well lately.'

Sunni motioned for her to sit, at the kitchen table, not to enter her main rooms. Sunni chose to stand.

Mae announced: 'I will, of course stay in the fashion business.'

Sunni's head inclined. 'That is the first time I have heard you admit that it is a business. It has always been couched before in terms of friendly advice.'

'And indeed much advice was given for free. Out of friendship,' said Mae. Her voice was sad, she felt sad. 'And one can tell, of course, who one's friends are in adversity.' *Sunni, Sunni, I know what you are, but you are better than this.* Sunni said nothing.

Mae continued: 'Your husband, of course, is in the farm-buying business.'

Sunni was still unmoved. All of this, so far, she would have been expecting; she would have known that the loan would be offered. Sunni may even have tried to dissuade her husband, but right now, as far as she was concerned, the decision had been taken.

Sunni took her time to respond. 'It is more clever than being a farmer. It is the way to prosperity. It is, of course, prosperity that pays for fashion.'

'Your husband has got Joe drunk, and fired him up with wild imaginings and loaned him one hundred riels.'

'Tuh. More like your Joe has got my husband drunk, to loan you that much.'

'We can't pay, Sunni, and you know as well as I do that that is how your husband gets rich. And I am asking you as a friend to use your good offices to get your husband to take back the money now. Or, indeed' – Mae reached down into her dress – 'to take the money back from me now yourself. And plead our case with him, and ask him to spare us.'

Mae held out the money, printed so elaborately with the portrait of President Kubla Khan. Sunni seemed to falter in her resolve.

'Please, Sunni,' said Mae, and felt the weakness of the illness return, as her voice shook, near tears again. 'Otherwise we will lose everything.'

'This loan nonsense,' said Sunni, faltering. 'It is men's business, my husband's business, I cannot interfere.'

'Sunni. He will destroy us!'

'I cannot help you.' She turned to go.

'Sunni, if you were ever my friend . . .' Mae stood to follow her, unbidden, into the rich man's house.

There were embroidered curtains, embroidered cushions, gold on green, everything overstuffed, the very room overstuffed, a small farm room full of glass decanters, snowstorm domes, and a set of billiard balls without a table.

'This is none of my business!' said Sunni, more fiercely now. Her arm was across her tummy, as if she had cramps. She suddenly spun. 'And as for being friends, you were a servant, do you understand? I bought your services, your, your, advice, your, your fawning over me, I purchased it, and you know that.'

Sunni, Sunni, you hate this, you are made clumsy.

'Of course it was business, we both knew that.' Mae was growing annoyed. 'But you cannot have a business without a relationship, and ours was straightforward and good, with no misunderstandings. That can continue. But only if this nonsense – as you so rightly call it – this nonsense over the loan is put to bed!'

Sunni looked cornered, her head was shaking slightly, *No, no, no.*

Mae understood. 'You are frightened of him.'

'What nonsense, how dare you!'

'Of course you are frightened of him; I am frightened of him. He is a brute, Sunni.'

The two women stared at each other. The money was between them. Mae looked at it, considering its power.

'But,' Mae sighed, 'he makes you rich. That is why you married him. And therefore you cannot question the way he makes his money. As you say: It pays for fashion.'

She put it back into her dress.

Sunni's face had crumpled, her mouth working. She wanted revenge now – revenge for being so coldly, clearly described.

'Fashion expert. Who will need you, ah? Who will want your advice, servant, when your friend Wing's TV gives us all advice, and better advice than you ever gave. Peasant. Farmer's wife!'

'Whore,' said Mae, coldly. I will regret that, she thought. But I do not need to take insults now. 'At least I am not a whore, Sunni.'

Sunni had no response to that at all. Mae turned and quickly walked away.

Sunni started to bellow: 'I was going to say something, something to him to help you.' Sunni followed Mae into the kitchen. 'I was, but I will not now! How dare you call me names? "Friend?" You? You do anything for money, and you call me whore?'

Mae stood at the kitchen door. 'Save it, Sunni, save it. Everything you have said about me is true. And I am sorry you sold your life for this house. I might have done the same.'

And out into the night, out under the stars and clouds, that were eternal. A moon that was nearly full.

What now! she wondered. Dear God, what now?

Mae got back to find both her husband and Sunni's-man asleep at the table. Siao had climbed upstairs.

'Out,' Mae said, and shook Mr Haseem. 'Drunken man, get out, up, out.'

Blearily, Mr Haseem gazed up at her and grinned.

I know you, she thought. You are the strong man who rules by force. You will have heads on spikes if we let you.

'Out of my house,' she said again, and hit him.

'Hey!' he bellowed, and looked for assistance at Joe. Her useless husband was dead to the world, too deadened even to help his enemy.

'Out, out, out,' was all she could think of saying, raining blows about his head. He began to chuckle; he seemed to think it funny.

'She-wolf,' he chuckled. Oh yes, that was it, the image of the angry wife, chastising her husband's drunken friends. It enraged her still further to find herself cast in such an ancient role.

'I am not throwing you out because you are drunk! I am throwing you out because you are an enemy to us. Because you want to steal everything from us. Get out before I slice open your eyes!'

Mae grabbed her big kitchen knife. He stopped laughing and jumped back, away from the table. She saw his eyes flicker and she seized the cleaver before he did. 'I will kill you and then we do not have to pay you back the money. I will kill you and spare the village a strongman.'

She meant it. She swiped the cleaver at him and he yelped and jumped back, shouting, 'Hey! Madwoman! The air has entered your head and – hey!'

'I . . . will . . .' she promised and came at him, knife and cleaver flashing '. . . kill you!' Her voice became a screech.

He ran for the door and seized his coat, his thick tobacco-yellow fingers trembling, face crossed in surprise, fear, confusion. The world was suddenly upside down for him to be chased by a madwoman with knives. One last gasp of surprise and he ducked out of the house.

Mae chased him across the courtyard, howling insults. 'Run, dog! Run, donkey! Go, go, go!'

There was light on courtyard walls, lights springing on throughout the village. Mr Ken's dog, awakened, began to bark. She heard the sound of Mr Haseem's feet outside the gates, the flapping of his loose shoeheel. Other dogs began to bark; all the village was awake, all the village would know by morning what had happened.

'Mrs Chung?'

There, in his underpants only, was Mr Ken.

She began to sob. She dropped the knives, they clattered to the stone. She hid her eyes in shame, in fear. How had things gone so far so quickly?

'What is happening?' Mr Ken said. He stood still, looking at her, aghast. She didn't want him to think her mad. She gathered herself in and explained.

'Mr Haseem has loaned Joe one hundred riels. He got Joe drunk, and Joe took the money.'

Mr Ken knew what that meant. 'Ah,' he said.

'We will never pay it back. He will get our farm!'

'Won't he take the money back?' Mr Ken shifted, aware now of his nakedness.

She yearned to hold him. That would comfort her, that would stop the world spinning, make everything stop.

'No, he doesn't want the money, he wants us, and our land. He wants to make us slaves. He wants to do the same to you, too.'

A pause, a beat. The lights were still on. 'You'd best go inside,' he said.

She felt frozen in place, still shaking, still helpless. He knelt down to pick up her knives; she saw how the top of his back swelled outwards to broad shoulders. She saw the crease down the middle of his strong back where the spine was buried deep.

Then he put an arm around her and in silence turned her not towards her house, but his own.

'Sssh,' he said.

He guided her into his own kitchen. He did not turn on the light. Very carefully, her knives were placed on the table, almost without a sound.

What are we doing here in the darkness, each of us? Are we doing what I think we are doing?

'My mother will be awake,' he said, in a voice as quiet as water on reeds. She smelled his breath: sleepy, garlicky, but somehow not unpleasant.

It was Old Mrs Tung who moved her, Old Mrs Tung who knew how to get what she wanted.

Somehow her hands were on his shoulders, then down his smooth broad back. Then his hands were on her breasts, and her heart was thumping, she could hardly breathe. This was dangerous, madness, but she found she did not care. One should not do this, one should make men stand off and away, but she had been doing that all her life and all she had to show for it was Joe.

She must have tugged at him, for suddenly his smooth upholstered chest seemed to surround her. His thick bowed legs and his underpants, loose but also now full with a small hard penis, were pressed against her. She was wearing no underpants. Such a tiny penis, it would be inside her so quickly, it could be done so quickly so simply, as simply and as sweetly as a kiss.

She found herself pulling up her good white dress. He kissed her, she slipped down the last of his clothing, and finally, finally, finally, for the first time in her life, she had it. This was foolish, he would despise her later.

But she had just tried to kill someone with knives and she no longer cared. It was softly done, it was quiet. She felt his spasm, felt something shoot against an inner wall. Then his forehead leaned against hers.

He had not left her body yet. Suddenly, as if clubbed, she was overwhelmed; something clenched shook and moistened inside her. She couldn't stop herself saying, oh, oh, oh.

'Sssh,' he said, and slipped out of her.

Her dress fell down, covering her. He stepped out of his underwear, and walked with her, to the courtyard. The village lights were off now; the moon was still out. He was blue and naked and she had never seen anything as beautiful.

They looked at each other. *What now?* both their faces seemed to say. Then they both smiled, overwhelmed by the speed of what had happened. Let tomorrow take care of itself. He nodded once, meaning, *Swift now, hide now.*

She turned and walked back into her house, turned and looked at his dark and empty doorway.

She got back in, and Joe was still asleep. You are not a bad man, she thought, you are just a bit of a fool and I do not want you the way I want Mr Ken. She left him sleeping at the table. She fell onto their disordered bed.

5

In the morning, Joe had a hangover.
He would not stop moaning and holding his head. Mae was abrupt with him. She took back his plate of cold uneaten breakfast.

'You'll have a headache longer than that; you'll have a headache all your life when you find yourself the slave of Mr Haseem.'

Joe's eyes were fearful as well as pained. 'We will have to make money. We might as well buy goats and make cheese.'

Mae said, 'We should spend none of it. Then all we have to do is earn back the interest.'

'The interest!' Joe groaned, and held his head. 'We agreed no interest.'

'Then we will say that, and give him back just the hundred.'

Joe looked fearful. 'He will say it was fifty per cent. He always says that.'

'Then you had best get to work,' she told him.

Joe left, looking guilty. He left Mae alone with all the terrors of adultery.

If Joe looked guilty, what was she? The village did not forgive women who strayed. They would say Mr Ken was a widower, he had his needs. But what had Mae been thinking of? You can't be a fallen woman and a fashion expert; the husbands won't let you in the house. The best she could hope for was that they would blame Air. So who buys fashion from a crazy woman with Air in her head who chases men with knives? What was she going to do?

Well, Mae, apart from anything else, you have to make money. All your life you have done that by staying ahead of the village. You better get to that TV and find out what everyone has been watching on it.

With no more precise thought than that, she stood up and walked out into the courtyard.

And in the courtyard, Mr Ken was staggering with a wheelbarrow of mucked straw.

Oh, wonderful.

'Good morning, Mr Ken-sir!' Mae called brightly, for the village to hear. She walked more quickly to escape. To her horror, Mr Ken lowered the barrow and began to walk towards her with an expression of perplexed sincerity, even solemnity. At least this time he was fully dressed.

Mae started to walk more quickly. She wanted to avoid any chat in public places such as her house. He began to smile slightly. He walked faster.

He stood in the gateway, of all the silly places! There was still a hint of a smile in the creases of his mature face, but he said the most direct thing: 'Do you regret last night?'

'No,' she said, before realizing that she had spoken. She wanted to escape.

'Do you want to go on?'

Mae felt something akin to panic; she wanted him to stand out of the gate, to keep his voice down. He looked like both her husband and her son at once.

'Yes,' she said, quickly.

So, this was love. Ken Kuei stood before her and she could scarcely bear to look at him. She felt old and misshapen in comparison. He was her boy, her baby, she saw in him the beauty and sadness of passing generations. It was as though Mr Ken were a corridor into which she could shout and hear echoes resonate like sad voices. Into a lost past, into lost chances.

No wonder she had never had love. Mae knew now that she had avoided it. Love hurt. She had known inside that love would make her guts twist, her eyes weep. She wanted to be with Ken Kuei; it hurt that she found no light and easy words with him, it hurt that their situation was dreadful, that they would have to slip and slide, hide, do it in corners like something dirty. It hurt worse than childbirth, worse than anything.

Mr Ken said, 'I will see you when I can.' His jaw worked with something unsaid. 'I do not want to cause you trouble.'

Mae cupped her forehead between her hands. Oh, that is nice. Trouble, what trouble could there be, fucking another man than your husband? All disaster loomed there.

'I am a widower, there will be no blame on me,' he said, looking at the ground.

'We have been talking long enough, and too solemnly,' she murmured, and mimed the pleased and neighbourly smile that kept distance.

Mae raised her voice for the sake of the walls. 'It is so sad about your wife, I still feel for you,' she said. 'If there is anything you need, please ask my husband.'

Mr Ken was still smiling. 'There's no one to hear you.'

She felt silly, frightened, but she couldn't help it. She remembered the listening lights of the night before.

'It will be no trouble. Just talk to Joe.' She felt like weeping in panic.

'When. How?' he demanded.

'I will leave my house tonight,' she whispered. 'We can go out into the fields, into the reeds. Three A.M.?'

That firm, old light was in his eyes again. He kept shifting in her vision between man and boy. Now he seemed older. He nodded once: Good.

'This will end well,' he promised her.

She shook her head with misgiving, and left him.

And so she was reduced to being a young girl, addled by love instead of money. Love catches up with you if you ignore it, she thought. She wanted to be with him, now. She wanted to suckle on his nipples as though they were breasts. All these things shocked her, overturned her. She was upended like a boat.

'I am bereft,' Mae said. She said it to Old Mrs Tung.

She answered. *When I was in trouble, I started a school.*

Mae walked on, towards the television set.

And there were the men of the village, at this hour of the morning, watching kung fu.

There was Joe.

'I knew!' she exclaimed. 'I knew I would find you here! Shiftless, feckless man!'

Joe shifted his feet staring at them, wincing with hangover and embarrassment.

'You *comic* character,' she told him, more in frustration, sadness, and affection than anything else. Young Mr Doh, Old Mr Doh, Mr Ali – they all chuckled, too.

'Your wife is well again, I see, Joe,' said Young Mr Doh.

'And a good hand with knives I hear, too,' said Old Mr Doh. And they all laughed. Which meant that yes, they all knew she had chased Mr Haseem out of her house. Did Joe? He kept grinning, looking baffled.

Mae needed the men to be away. She needed the television. 'What are we to do with you small boys?' Mae said, shaking her head. 'Ah? You have families, you have fields, you have duties, what are you doing here?'

'Watching the movie?' shrugged Joe. More laughter.

'Joe, you dolt,' she said, simply, quickly. That made the men laugh again.

'Wifely humours,' Young Mr Doh said. It was a way of saying a woman was right. He leaned forward and pushed some buttons. 'Okay, I've saved the movie. What time?'

The men frowned and wobbled their heads. They murmured times, but Old Mr Doh was something of a leader. 'Eight o'clock,' he said.

With a flourish, his son moved the hands of the clock to eight.

Mae felt a stab of something icy in her chest. They can do that? Go back to a movie? The movie folded up like a picture and was dropped into a pink piggy bank. Mae thought, Mr Doh knows how to do that? And I don't? The men stood up with a murmuring and an exchange of cigarettes. They nodded goodbye to Mae.

She was left standing alone in the courtyard.

The screen showed nothing but a door.

Mae sat in front of the screen. She touched the door. It creaked, it opened.

There were pictures with words underneath. Mae couldn't read. On the screen was a picture of an hourglass with running sand, like her life draining away, and there were rows of pictures: books and magnifying glasses and things that had no meaning for Mae at all. Mae saw a drawing of a newsreader. News would be good. She touched the newsreader and up came a screen of words.

Too many words, too complicated. It assumed so much, this machine – that you understood what the signs meant, that you could read, that you could guess what lay behind each door or each word. Her heart was sinking.

Then she saw a picture of an ear.

'Touch the ear,' said a woman's voice: Kwan, behind her.

Kwan was wearing a folded headdress, the peasant dress of her ethnic minority. She had never done that before. She stood over Mae.

'Go on,' she said.

Mae did.

The TV replied, *'You have chosen the talking option.'* Mae felt both relief and shame. Kwan knew the fashion expert found it difficult to read.

'It is good you are learning,' said Kwan, suddenly relaxing. 'It is good you are not afraid of it.'

Afraid? Well, yes, this was new stuff.

The TV kept talking. *'The list of available topics is very long. It is probably easier if you tell me what you want to know.'* It was as if the television were inhabited by a ghost. Like Old Mrs Tung.

'Fashion,' said Mae.

And for some reason, as if on impulse or from affection, Kwan had taken hold of the muscles between Mae's neck and shoulder and given them a squeeze.

'So you are going to fight,' said Kwan.

Mae paused. 'You know,' she sighed.

'In this village? There is nothing to do but talk.'

Mae was ashamed, fearful, and angry. 'There is everything to do!'

Mae amazed herself again with the passion, almost the frenzy, that welled up inside her. 'The village is like a goose without a head when the legs keep twitching. The whole world has died, and we have a year to learn how to live all over again!'

She spun around to look at Kwan. Kwan was blinking in surprise.

The television said in a honeyed voice, *'You have a choice of looking at the Paris spring collections, the Beijing Festival of Culture, or the Vogue channel.'*

'I do not need to be beholden to that dog of a man now! I need to be doing this!'

'Pause,' Kwan said once, to the machine. It whirred in place. 'Mae, we could loan you the money to pay him back. What is the interest?'

'Joe was so drunk, he did not even ask!' Mae swayed under the weight of it all.

'We would not charge interest,' murmured Kwan.

Mae felt many things, all at once – gratitude, relief, and wariness. She feared that they would end up replacing one loan with another. You and Wing make yourselves rich the same way Haseem does, she thought, only, you are more polite. Though she loved Kwan, Mae did not entirely trust her.

'We would stand in an echoing corridor of loans,' Mae said quietly.

'That is true,' said Kwan, calmly. 'But the offer will stay open, if you need it.'

'Thank you, Wing's-wife, ma'am.'

'Don't be silly,' said Kwan, for Mae had addressed her as an employer.

Mae sighed. 'Until we have money, I am everyone's servant,' she said. 'The offer is kind and will be remembered. Paris,' she told the television. 'Show me Paris.'

'I will leave you to it, then,' said Kwan. She turned and walked away.

She has changed, too, thought Mae. We will all change.

So Mae looked at the ghosts of Paris, and they were no help. These were clothes that no human being could wear, let alone farming women in the Happy Province. The television talked and talked. It explained why it was such a revolution that long flaps of cloth hung uselessly down to the knees from the shoulders, or that someone called Giannini had gone for splashes of colour.

Mae already knew. It is just a special way of talking. It sounds grand, but it offers nothing to actually do.

What . . . she asked herself, what actually am I trying to do?

I am trying to find something that will make me money. I think if I spend more time at this machine, then I can stay ahead of my clients, find something to sell them. But they are ahead of me . . .

Paris fashion kept parading, as if to say, look, peasant, look what you cannot afford to even look at. Look at what your world could never have in it. Learn the lesson of your poverty and your distance and your unimportance.

She looked around. Two little village girls stood in Kwan's court-yard, twisting in place with coy naughtiness.

'Who told you you could come to Mrs Wing's house? Go on, go away.'

'We want to watch the television,' one of them said – determined to stay, hopeful of being allowed to.

'You should be in school,' Mae said.

They said nothing, but their eyes and smiles grew brighter. A little boy ran up to them and stopped, dead, to see an adult by the tele-vision. The girls burst into fits of naughty giggles.

Then An, Kai-hui's daughter, sauntered in. Her eyes widened, she bowed briefly towards Mae. 'Children,' said An, newly graduated. 'You should be in school.'

More giggles.

Mae reached up, to find some way to turn it off, to hoard the fashion information. How had Young Mr Doh done it? Mae touched something and another screenful of words appeared. *'Main menu,'* said the screen. Were they in a restaurant?

An said, 'No, no, don't change it for my sake.' Then she used a new word. 'Undo,' she said, and they went back to the fashion show.

The sun kept rising, the courtyard kept filling. An's friend Ling-so walked in as well. Ling-so said that she had preferred the Singapore fashion show last week. But then she said, 'Eastern couture suits our tastes better.'

Mae felt like she had swallowed an ice cube whole. While she had been ill and wasting time, all the village had been watching television. Mae felt a kind of hungry panic. She had fallen so far behind!

In desperation she turned around. 'What do the children want?' she asked.

She knew the answer: kung fu. She knew also that the children would run forward and push the button for themselves.

The children sat openmouthed as the kung fu hero met a man whom they all knew was a dragon in disguise. The secret dragon breathed out fire. For some reason he could fly, with a sound like a sliding whistle. Even An and Ling appeared to be content. This confirmed Mae's suspicion that people would watch anything so long as it was on TV.

Mae didn't watch. She sat thinking over and over, What do I do? What can I do?

At high noon, Mr Shen arrived from the school.

He was shaking with rage. 'All of you, back into class. All of you, what are you doing, when you should be at your lessons!' He cuffed the boys about the head. They ran off giggling.

Mr Shen glared at Mae. 'You have let this sickness take you over!'

Mae was shocked to have Teacher Shen, of all people, be angry with her.

'I was trying to use it for information . . .' she began. Her voice sounded weak, even to her.

'Oh, yes, it looks like it! Hong Kong indulgence. This whole country is sinking into it.' He spun on his heel and marched to the television set. He pulled out its plug. In a fury, he pulled at the plug until, by adrenaline strength, he succeeded in hauling the wires free from their screws.

'There,' he said, shaking the naked wires at Mae. Then he walked away, taking the plug with him. He stopped at the foot of the stone staircase leading up to the Wing house.

'Mrs Wing-ma'am!' Shen shouted. 'I have taken the liberty of turning off your machine. Perhaps I can advise you to keep it inside your house and away from my students.'

The children were gone, still giggling, like laughing leaves blown in the wind. Shen marched off, through the dust, without a further word to Mae. She looked up and saw Kwan already descending the stairs to the courtyard. She had a screwdriver and a replacement plug.

The village was a boat that had come free from its anchor. Mae shook her head.

An was elegantly scornful. 'He's scared because he is Teacher and he knows nothing about all this.'

'*Tuh.* My parents pretend nothing has happened,' said Ling-so, even more beautifully turning away. Her lipstick was perfect.

Kwan knelt beside the TV, quietly replacing the plug.

'Why don't you take it inside?' Mae asked.

'Because we want the village to have it,' said Kwan, still kneeling.

'At least now we can look at fashion in peace,' said An.

On came Paris again. Kwan walked back up the stairs to her laundry or her sweeping. The Paris show ended, and the two girls changed to the Vogue Channel. More ghosts, in silver fabric, and Mae found that she had nothing to say that was any different from what the two girls said. Finally, when a shadow had crept across the wall and touched the screen, it was like a sorrowful spell. Quietly she bid the girls farewell. Young, poised, beautiful. They could read. They had no dinners to cook. This new world was theirs.

When Mae got home, Joe was waiting with Mr Haseem.
Joe did not look like a dolt now. He looked very upright and angry. 'You will apologize to Mr Haseem,' he demanded.

Mr Haseem's face seemed to be made of old porridge – heavy, dour, unmoving – and he looked without blinking at Mae. She looked back. She calculated quickly, knowing what had happened. Someone had told Joe about the attack, and honest Joe, moral Joe, was appalled. He had no understanding that sometimes morality was not enough. There was one quick way out.

'I'm very sorry, Mr Haseem,' Mae said coolly. 'I have not been myself lately.'

Joe nodded once, abruptly. *Quite right and proper*, the nod said. 'To chase a guest with knives from our house!' Joe murmured.

You have to cling to something, if all the world is changing. Joe clung to rules. He was stiff, formal, but dignified. Mae's heart wanted to break for him; he just did not understand.

'Mr Haseem-sir,' said Joe, 'please accept an invitation to dinner.'

Haseem was as slow as a frog on a lily-pad, with its sticky tongue curled up, waiting to lunge. 'I am afraid, Mr Chung-sir, that my wife would not consent. She is too upset by the events of last night.'

'Oh!' said Joe, in shock. He turned and glared at his wife.

'Things were said to her that cannot be easily forgiven.' Mr Haseem pressed his advantage. 'I accept the apology for your good sake, Mr Chung. I have to say that nothing in your wife's manner makes me think her apology is genuine.'

He was trying to enlist Joe, force more out of her. *No*, thought Mae. You will not humiliate me further. Mae said, 'It was genuine enough, Mr Haseem-sir, when I got down to you on my knees and begged you to take back the money. If you are so insulted, perhaps you will withdraw your generous loan.'

She held out the money again.

Sunni's-man leapt to his feet. 'Really, this is too much. You let your wife drive you, Joe. She has no place in interfering with our business! You and I are friends, but I want no dealings with her.'

That's because, thought Mae, I am a match for you.

'Any further business will be conducted in my house. She is not welcome there.' Mr Haseem stalked out.

Joe blinked at her in fury, speechless. He was not used to scenes of any sort, least of all in his own kitchen.

Mae felt detached. It was strange, the mix of feelings. She thought of Joe in a kindly, distanced way. It was part of the beauty of their way of life that he should be so small, so constrained, and so insistent on good behaviour. That way of life was dead.

'What is the interest rate?' Mae asked Joe, in a small, clear voice.

'What?' He clamped a hand on his forehead. His head shook in disbelief. 'Do you care only for money?'

She stayed in the same mode, still and cool. 'Is anything in writing?'

'Yes,' he said fiercely, proudly thinking: *See how businesslike I am?* Her heart sank for him.

'So. I ask again. What is the interest rate?'

'Two per cent,' he said, with a diagonal jerk of the head that seemed to say: *See how unfounded were your fears?*

'A month?' she asked.

He blinked at her. Poor Joe.

'That means that in a year's time, we not only have to pay him back the hundred, but also find a further twenty-four riels.' A quarter of a year's income. 'And that is only if he does not compound it monthly.'

She let the roll of notes fall like leaves onto the table. 'There is your money, Joe. I suggest that you do not spend one riel of it. It will be hard enough for us to find the extra twenty-four.'

She turned and began to cook supper: the blackened pot, the single electric ring. She looked at him, and he was looking at the money. 'Make no mistake, Joe. I will not work for Mr Haseem.' Her voice was cool with promise. She cooked. Joe drank.

Come, darkness; come, three A.M., she prayed.

In the courtyard of the Wings' great house, Kwan had an air of someone cleaning up after the party, collecting cigarette butts.

'Kung fu?' Mae asked ruefully.

'Oh!' sighed Kwan.

'You begin to regret your generosity?' said Mae.

'I begin to regret that people do not get bored!' said Kwan, and slumped on a chair.

'I know. I know,' said Mae, her eyes going hard like boiled eggs in agreement. 'I am bored.'

Kwan looked around, questioning.

'Is there anything on that thing other than fashion and kung fu? Junk for women, junk for men?'

'Ask it,' said Kwan.

'But ask it for what?'

'Ah,' said Kwan, 'that is the question. When you are an ignorant peasant, you do not even know what to ask.'

Mae's mind danced in the Format like a moth around an electric light.

'Search,' she told the television.

The TV replied. *'Please tell me which word or keywords.'*

'Eloi,' Mae said. The name of Kwan's national minority. Kwan sat up, with a sharp intake of breath.

'Ah. That does not bore you.' *Tonight*, thought Mae, I am as sharp as a knife.

The TV asked, *'What aspect of the Eloi interests you?'*

Kwan intervened. 'History. Politics.'

The TV whirred to itself.

The TV said, *'We have found sixteen listings whose main subject is the history or politics of the Eloi minority.'*

Kwan's face softened. 'I thought there would be nothing.'

'Fourteen of these listings are held in our professional or academic files. If you are a professional or academic subscriber, say "Yes." Say "No" if you are not a subscriber.'

To get the good listings you had to pay. To pay you had to have something called a Clever Card which established that you were Believable.

Kwan said that she was a director of Swallow Communications.

'We're sorry. Your account covers a range of popular entertainment and documentary options, but full text searches must be paid for by corporate subscription. Please say "Yes" if you want to subscribe, and have your Clever Card ready . . .'

Mae asked, 'What's a Clever Card?'

Kwan looked worn. 'You have to go to the bank. You have to have a passport. You have to have money. More than we have.'

'But you pay! The government pays.'

Kwan sighed. 'Not enough for that. We'll have the two free listings.'

The first offering was the official Karzistani government files. It gave a picture of a happy, modern people. A model spun around in traditional garb.

'Fashion!' exclaimed Mae, and began to laugh.

The model was a Balshang beauty, all Beijing-styled angular elegance, face composted with layers of paint and powder. Mae suddenly thought she had never seen anything as funny.

'Traditional . . . Eloi . . . woman!' Mae gasped for breath. 'Fresh from mucking out stable and making shitcakes for the fire.'

Kwan stood still and icy.

There was a government video of a modern-day Eloi, relocated to Balshang apartments. The woman was plainly of Eloi stock, but was drab in a loose white shirt, blue trousers, and an awkward headscarf to appease the city's Muslims. She proudly showed her new toilet, her new icebox.

Mae could not help but laugh again. The boldness of it! Not one mountain, not one pony, not one terraced field, not one dirty hungry child. Not one destroyed Buddhist temple. Oh, everything was modern about the Eloi.

'Hmm,' said Mae. 'They call it "information." That does not make it true.'

Kwan paused for a moment, then suddenly looked around. 'Do you have a lover?' she asked.

Mae's heart stopped. 'How do you mean?'

'When a woman gets bold and heedless, as if she had gone through a door, when she gets harder, cynical, and brighter . . . well . . .'

And Mae knew something, too: 'Do you have a lover, then?' Mae thought of the beautiful Kwan and her older husband.

'Long ago,' said Kwan, and tapped the screen to select the next article.

'Who?' asked Mae, edging forward.

Kwan looked back. 'Who is yours?' she asked.

'Yours was long ago and does not matter. The past is dead.'

The next free offering was in German, from a museum. It was about some show or exhibition in Berlin that was long since closed. Kwan scrolled down a menu, hoping to find something else. 'He was an Eloi shepherd, high in the hills,' she said.

Mae was fascinated. 'Oh! Was he beautiful?'

Eloi men could be beautiful, like their women. Some of them had tattoos like stockings on their bare smooth legs, and bracelets, and wild stallion-manes of hair.

'He was to me,' said Kwan. She looked old under the harsh yellow light; old, but in a good way – handsome, lined, smiling with endurance. 'He was blind in one eye.'

'What happened?'

'The usual things,' said Kwan, amused, with a bit of a swagger.

'No. I mean, the end.'

Kwan's endurance was even more rocklike. 'He said I was too Chinese.' She shrugged. 'He was right. I stayed with Wing.' She sighed with concern. 'Be careful, Mae.'

'Oh, I have been careful all my life! Do not tell me to be careful.'

'It's not Sunni's-man is it?'

'Ah!' squawked Mae, and pretended to spit.

'I had to ask, chasing a man with knives. It could mean . . .'

'It meant I really wanted to kill him! That bastard! He wants to take everything.'

'Everyone laughed,' said Kwan.

'Did they? It was not funny at the time, I tell you – old Sunni's-man knew I was mad, and he went running.'

Kwan started talking like a Talent. 'Our fashion expert, all delicate femininity, the sweetness of flowers, the wistfulness of morning mist, the gentleness of the butterfly.' Kwan shook her head. 'Chasing the headman with cleavers!'

Mae suddenly understood. It was funny. 'This year, all village fashion experts will wear an adornment of knives. We see Kizuldah beauty Mrs Chung in a necklace of real murder weapons used on friends of drunken husband. Note the subtle arrangement of cleavers about the shoulders.'

Kwan smirked in mild amusement and then said, 'So who is he?'

'Mine is not yet in the past,' said Mae.

'Mmm-hmm,' said Kwan. She thought she had guessed who it was.

Mae gave her a slap on the back of the arm. 'You be careful. You know nothing.'

'I am saying nothing,' replied Kwan.

The voice droned on in a language they could not speak. The advertisement showed rare photographs of the Eloi. They looked as if they had been taken one hundred years before. They were as alien to modern-day Eloi as the propaganda video had been. Alien faces stained with dirt, with tense lines of muscle around the chin and cheeks. They wore headdresses and boots that were wrappings of animal hides. These worn people stared accusingly out of the screen, from the past.

'Oh, Allah be praised,' said Mae shaking her head, feeling disappointment for Kwan's sake.

'There is nothing in between,' said Kwan, her head shaking quickly from side to side. 'We are either like angels descending at the end of an old pageant, all costume, or we are refrigerators for the Karz.'

Their choices came to an end. That was it. Kwan was hard-faced.

'Save,' she said. 'Print.'

The TV buzzed as if it were sewing something. A tongue of paper began to emerge. Mae saw letters stick out, and then the top of an Eloi head.

'It prints?' she said, almost in despair.

Kwan nodded. 'In the West, children make screens for this thing. They do all their business on it. You can even make movies for Aircasting on this thing. That knob on top is a camera. In America, children make Air music out of their own heads and then share it. They call it "Ko-lab Oh."'

'We are so far behind,' said Mae.

'We live in a different world,' said Kwan. 'Sometimes I think we can never catch up. Now, with Air, they will be ready, and we will not be. We will be like children wandering around, lost.'

Kwan pulled out her sheet of paper. It was all laid out with information about her people that she had not written. Suddenly, she snapped to. 'I'm going to bed,' she announced. 'You be good.'

Finally Mae was left alone with the screen.

'Money,' she asked it.

There were offerings of books she could buy or courses she could pay to take. There was a course in 'How to Have a Bank Account,' offered by the Balshang Older Citizen's Institute. Someone in a place called *Mi Wok Ee* was offering loans. The text came up and the TV read it for her, but much of it made no sense.

Suddenly there was an avalanche: loans, courses, 'HOW TO GET RICH QUICK!' Many windows all at once on the screen, all babbling. One window on top of another, cutting off the other voice before it had finished.

'Stop.' said Mae. Nothing happened.

Say yes if you want to ring this telephone number to have personal, on-TV counselling on making money. Please have your Clever Card or Believability Card ready. Calls cost two dollars a minute. Buy this book; join this bank. Just say yes.

'No, no, no, no,' Mae kept saying.

They crowded round like wasps on shit. One little window sliding on top of another one, a little babbling voice talking over the last.

'Stop!'

'Temporarily overloaded,' replied the TV, and suddenly went dark.

One little voice spoke from the darkness. *'Thank you for using our Helpful Librarian tool. From time to time searches on this free service will result in paid-for responses arriving according to your interest.'*

In the silence Mae felt her heart thumping. That was it? That was the great online world, the Net that Mr Wing had talked so long and hard about, that he had yearned for, fought for?

No wonder. No wonder they wanted to replace it.

Mae's eyes swelled with disappointment and anger. What use was it to them, this thing? It was just a way to sell them things, to take money from poor people. What use was it if you had no money, no banks, no way to get Clever Cards or Believability?

Maybe Shen was right. All it did was show us worlds we could never join. We just sit and watch and get soft and fat and bored and talk about Singapore fashion as if we could ever take part. We push our noses against the window and watch other people eat.

'Off,' said Mae. And the TV went as still and ominous as black thunderclouds.

So what was she to do now? Mae plunged her fingers into her hair. Her hair was greasy and needed washing. She had missed a fashion season; she had to find an extra twenty-four riels for the loan.

So what did she have? Make a list, Mae. She listed 'house,' 'three rice terraces.' No orders for dresses?

She had Mrs Tung's memories.

She had sickness, debts, and an idle husband. His hardworking brother. His aging father. She had her own interfering brother, and her overwhelmed mother. If she went to them for help, they would try to take over.

She had Kwan's offer. Would it be so bad, owing Kwan money?

She had Air. She had been inside Air deeper than anyone else. So, what was in Air?

All right. She closed her eyes and tried to find her way back in. 'Air,' she said. Nothing happened. She tried to think her way back to the courtyard. She remembered it, but could not see it.

She did begin to discern something, dimly – an extra weight in her head like a load to be carried. She felt it and tried to describe it to herself. Unlike a headache, it didn't disappear when described. Instead it focused.

If anything Air felt like a turnip. In the rice sometimes a tuber grew. You would pull on what you thought was a weed, but it wouldn't budge, so you would reach deep down into the mud, and follow the root to pull it free. And there, numb, dumb, but salvageable, there would be something you could use.

You just had to haul it out.

Mae seemed to trace this root with her mind, deeper and deeper, but it was held fast, mired. It would not move. It was as if it were rooted by an entire planet rather than its blanket of earth.

And then Mae remembered something. She had an address, and the address was her name.

'Mae, Mae, Mae, Mae, Mae, Mae . . .'

She felt a gentle settling. It was as if she were dust or feathers, in the air during cleaning day. She seemed to swirl in the sunlight like stars, and then to fall gently down.

She settled gently, slowly into place. It was rather calming. She felt a wide smile spread across her face. The loan, the money, the house, her husband, Mr Haseem – all seemed to fall back, up, away into a world that was full of light and dust and settling.

It was as if she were finally, finally going to her bed after a long day in the fields, when your shoulders are sore and knees are full of needles. You settle not so much onto the bed as into yourself.

More and more of Mae fell into place. Gradually, enough of her came together to look up and around.

Mae seemed to stand in the courtyard.

'Welcome,' a voice said. 'You don't have any Airmail messages.'

The stones were blue as if in moonlight. They were made of dust, too. Mae could waft up to and then through them. They were just pictures as on a screen. Did the TV make images out of dust?

She asked for 'Info.'

Air spoke to her, in the voice and accent of her people. 'Right now we have nothing new. We just have some things to show how Air works. You can have a look at some of those.'

The voice was like her own. This is me talking.

'Okay. I want to find out about making money.'

'Okay, but this is the first time you've done this. A lot of things we have here are like movies. They are very familiar because they are made to work like movies. This won't be like that. This will be as if you grew someone else in your head. This will be as if you become someone different. If you don't like it, just say your address.'

'Okay,' said Mae. 'Oh. No. Wait. Does this need my address to work?'

'Airmail and all services but Air movies need your address to work.'

'Am I the only one in the village with an address?'

There was a buzzing. For the first time Mae felt that her brain was made of something. She could feel the ends of it sparkle and fizz, like it was the edge of a tapestry before the ends were tied.

Air said, *'Old Mrs Tung is the only other person with an address. Do you still feel like accessing our Money Expert?'*

Somewhere else, where she was huge like the moon, Mae nodded her head – yes. That was enough for Air.

This courtyard, Mae thought. It is my own courtyard.

Something she could not turn into a voice came at her. It was dim, like talking on her mobile when there was a bad connection. There were no words but she somehow understood. That understanding suddenly ballooned out.

Yes, they want to help poor people and they want to demonstrate this thing, so they needed me.

It was as if she had another Mrs Tung.

It was not quite a whole person. It rattled too quickly and seemed to go a bit in circles. It was a part of person, an attitude to something. It was a thousand things that person knew, matted together like a rug.

So of course I said yes. Money – what do you want to know?

Mae could almost see it, a tiny little overcoming spirit so sure of itself, so amused, and so in love with money and business and investments and trust funds. Trust funds? Suddenly sure, secure, and certain, Mae had knowledge of trust funds. It was not book-learning. It was knowledge like riding a bicycle or how to walk across the spring floodplain by stepping on the tufts of reed.

The banks hold your money and pay you so that they can use it . . .

Stop! Stop! I want to sell people something new.

Well, then, you better find out what they want. One way is to do a 'Koeh so tong ah.' A Question Map.

Mae saw one, all lines of writing on paper, in English. Someone else's memories.

You find people who are like the people you want to know about. Normally that's so tough you need scientists to help you, but in this case you can actually ask all the people. That's a one hundred per cent sample. Just make sure you really have got them all.

Mae saw a series of black balls in a column. This was a list, a way of remembering, called 'Dos and Don'ts.' She saw a name, too, and knew it was the name of the person in her head, and she caught a word. This was Kru. *Kru* in her own language meant 'a great teacher.' This was a Kru word for something she couldn't pronounce but which got turned into 'Mat Unrolling' in Karzistani. 'Mat Unrolling' is what a trader did in the square; they unrolled a mat, laid out their radishes. Mae liked that. It sounded real.

Don't ask leading questions, and that means, a question that puts an idea into people's heads that they might not have had. Don't ask questions that can be answered yes or no. Ask the same question two or three times in different ways to see if you get the same answers . . .

Hold, hold how can I remember this?

The flow of knowledge stumbled. *Who said that?* someone, somewhere, seemed to ask.

The overcoming spirit was frightened.

What's in my head? it seemed to ask.

Nothing, nothing, said Mae, and went still and small. She started thinking in this new train again. How it rattled along this train of thought. Knowledge came intimately as if it were her own. The thoughts felt close and personal.

The thing was eager to share. It felt its life had been vindicated by doing this one great thing. Mae began to see a tiny old white man with bright and shining eyes.

So. They are somehow able to copy Krus, give us Krus in our heads. This Kru was a great and good Mat Unrolling Kru, so great and good that he could afford to give his head for nothing. He gives his wisdom as from Heaven, to help, because he feels pity.

There is a word for that: bodhisattva.

So where else would you expect to find an emanation of the Buddha but in Heaven? But never, never, would you expect the great gift of wisdom to enter you as if from a balloon in reverse, as if the balloon was pumping you up, filling you with air.

This was a very great gift indeed. Mae felt her wide grin and she felt her solid body press both hands together in respect.

And she also had one wicked thought. I have an address. No one else in Kizuldah does.

Mae sat under another desert mountain sky. She sat with hands kept pressed in respect and learned all she could about Question Maps and unrolling her mat.

The stars turned slowly. Mae grew tired, before that bright, enduring, unchanging mind. Somewhere her giant body dipped in respectful farewell. Mae's spirit went back the way she had come. She recited.

'Mae, Mae, Mae, Mae, Mae . . .'

She felt a wind blow and scatter her and spin her. She seemed to spin dancing back into the solid world.

Mae found herself sitting next to the dead and useless mechanical box. Her eyes were wide and streaming with water as if she were weeping from joy. She had not blinked all the time she was in Air.

And she stood up, and she strode forward, and she knew what she would do.

She would make a Question Map and ask all the women in the village what they wanted and that would be what she would make. And she would be one with the Kru to understand how the magic of money really worked, for it seemed clear now that money had come from the gods, was an aspect of them. Until it had been stolen by kings and presidents. Coins should bear the image of the Buddha.

And she would go back and learn more. If the Net were all about greed and gouging then she would learn how to use it to unroll her mat. She would be among the ones who won in this life, through work and virtue.

Air was new, Air was strong, Air would bear her up. She felt the long root go back and she knew now. She was rooted in the world but the world was in rooted in Air.

6

Mae walked back down Lower Street just before three A.M.
She was looking down at her feet, in the moonlight, to avoid stumbling on the old cobbles.

Something happened inside her eyes. It seemed as if the surface of the road swelled up flickering. She felt herself swell, grow larger, but more diffuse, as mist.

Suddenly the road was paved, with yellow light reflected from its smooth asphalt surface.

Mae looked up to see a street lamp, towering over Lower Street on a high concrete pole. When had there been a streetlight on Lower Street? Or a concrete pole?

Mae looked around and saw the town, spilling down the hillside like a necklace, all strings and spangles of light.

Below, in the valley where once there had been a marsh, a neon sign glowed: HOTEL NEARNESS, it said. Next to it was some kind of shop, blazing out blue fluorescent light over its own whitewashed wall and the road. A bright red awning hid the things in its window. Children yelled somewhere, running. Children stayed in the village these days. Why leave? All the world was here now. Because of Air, the children stayed. Mae saw her great-grandchildren every day.

Where am I? Where is this?

The air smelled of car exhaust and was full of noise: televisions, back-firing cars, and an ambulance siren.

Mae was old and irritated by a bad back and she was thinking: *This is where it was: this is where my house once stood. My house with Joe.*

Climbing up this steep hill had cost her. She had fallen months before and her back was still not right. She still tried to walk in a sprightly way, though crumpled, stiff and sore.

It was here, old Mae thought, *here that we met, here it all happened. Here I was reborn.*

A wind rose, carrying with it the sound of blown reeds. The wind seemed to lift Mae up with it.

Mr Ken stood waiting in the courtyard gate.

And the old woman saw Mr Ken. To her, he was a ghost from the past. Old Mae choked, put a hand to her mouth. Everything: heart, eyes, gorge, seemed to swell with panic and love.

There he was, her Mr Ken. He wore a sweatshirt – she remembered it now clear as day – and his good trousers with the spandex band instead of a belt.

The wind blew stronger. The sense of panic and loss were taken with it, along with the streetlights.

And Mae collapsed, not like dust settling, but like a house of cards all at once. And it seemed she pulled the world with her. It had all fallen back into place as she knew it.

What? Mae thought. What was *that*? She clamped a hand to her forehead. It was a gust of madness.

Air, thought Mae.

Air goes into the future as well?

She looked about her. There was no Hotel Nearness. The hills were dark; the rural streets were silent.

Maybe, she thought, maybe I should not go into Air too often.

Mr Ken put a hand to his lips, and paused, questioning, to give her a chance to refuse.

Mae's response was simply to walk towards the valley. He followed. There were no listening lights at three in the morning.

The wind in the reeds was like the sound of a waterfall, like everything tumbling out of her head. They walked in silence. Just outside the village, in the sound of the wind, he felt safe to speak.

'I thought you might not come,' he said. 'Your house was dark. Where have you been?'

'In the future,' she heard herself say. She thought, and then confirmed it: 'I've been into the future.'

'Watching television?'

Mae felt distant. Maybe she was just tired. She shook her head. She didn't want him to talk. She wanted to listen to the world, the wind, and the moon. She could hear the moon move through clouds.

'Mae. What do you mean?'

She was not looking at him; she was looking up, away. 'Kizuldah will become just like everywhere else. We will have stores and streetlights and parking lots.' She turned and looked back at the darkened, silent silhouettes of houses, and already regretted it, mourned her village.

His handsome face was crossed with concern. You are a husband inside, Mae thought: *kind, decent, capable of love.* So why was she not responding?

'I'm very sleepy,' she said, as an excuse, as a lie, as the truth. Mae was feeling suddenly contrary.

He took her hand. 'Are you worried?' he asked. His eyes were searching her face for something.

The woman who had a lover and brandished knives suddenly unsheathed herself.

'What do you think of when you remember Tui?' she demanded.

His head hung for a moment. 'She was my wife.' He struggled. 'She was always frail. She did not like . . .' The rolling of his hand somehow indicated sex. 'It made her shake. I thought that was love, but later I knew it was fear. I don't know what frightened her.'

Mae sighed. 'She was always a frightened little thing. We used to pick on her. It was not right, but we said she had fleas.'

'I remember,' he said, in soft surprise. Had he really forgotten that?

'You never teased her. You were always a good boy,' said Mae. It was not said entirely with respect. But then it is difficult to be bad when your grandmother runs the school.

'I remember the things you would make,' Mr Ken said. 'My grandmother would sometimes show them to me specially. I thought they were beautiful.'

'What things?' she said. People always talked about the things Mae made as a child. It meant they didn't have to say: *You were slow at your letters.*

Mr Ken said, 'You would find old shells, and make a necklace. Once you made peas in their shells, out of library paste. I thought they were wonderful. Grandmother tried to bake them, to save them, and they broke, remember?'

Mae began to understand. He was saying he had wanted her even in those days and had not spoken. The truth was that she had not much noticed him back then. When had Ken Kuei gone from the quiet, staring boy to the broad-shouldered handsome man? Joe had been the one when they were young. Joe was like a knifeblade. Young and sharp, the rebel. Maybe he had been the fashion expert then.

'You married very young,' Ken Kuei said.

He was trying to say that he had been screwing up his courage when the announcement of their wedding had come.

Mae said, 'You should have been quicker.'

'I know,' he said, quietly. He stopped. 'Do you want to do this?' he asked.

Mae shrugged. 'I am here.'

'You don't seem happy.'

Happy? Whoever said life would be happy? His wife had just killed herself. 'No, I'm not, I never am,' she said, her fingers digging into her hair. 'You will have to get used to that.'

They stepped down off a bank, down into reeds. She tried to feel anything at all. Maybe she was just tired.

Maybe I just want to know what it is all for, if everything is to be swallowed up, if we are all reduced like those old photographs of Eloi. History turns us into exposed meat.

Sex, like history, stripped away who you were. You do what everyone else does, overwhelmed by base nature. Sex would blow away their selves, Chung Mae, Ken Kuei, like favorite scarves lost in the wind.

Mae was the one who initiated it. Perhaps she just wanted it over. She pulled his face to hers, they kissed. The ground was damp in patches. The tops of the reeds danced as if in excitement, in honour of the moon. The clouds were strange. They were stippled around the moon, like splattered mud-plaster.

Mae noticed that even while Mr Ken offered the beauty of his flat stomach and round thighs, he was slower this time. He worked himself up through many minutes, while she looked at the moon. Through his endurance, Mae was finally brought once again to the state she had never achieved with Joe. She became no one, just a body.

But she had learned: A lessening of desire in the man makes him work harder, longer, so the woman got more out of it. Joe was always done in an instant.

She said, 'We'd better go, it must be getting late.'

'Or getting early,' he chuckled, and put his forehead on hers again. It was a gesture of – what – relief? gratitude? surrender? It made her smile because already parts of him were becoming familiar.

Mr Shenyalar began to sing from his tower. The sky was already silver as she slipped back into her disordered house.

Inside, it was tiny and dark. The ground floor looked posed, like a museum exhibit, except that it smelled of Joe and was full of his snoring.

It was only then that the love came, the love she had been trying not to feel. It came torn out of her, like a baby ripped raw out of the womb. She missed Mr Ken; she wanted him there, not to screw, but to talk to about the past, the village, and all the things she could never talk about to Joe.

Her marriage was over.

She couldn't bear to get into bed with Joe, so she set about cooking his breakfast. She cooked in hatred, weeping as she oiled the pan and boiled the noodles.

Siao and Old Mr Chung tumbled down out of the loft and she dumped noodles onto their plates and she thought of the ridges of callus on Mr Ken's palms. She remembered his soft voice, the strength of him, the hesitant words.

Joe got up an hour later, hung over and silent. Finally he left to go, he said, to work.

Mae sat in a chair feeling drained and exhausted and baffled by herself. I wasted our night, she thought, as if holding it to herself. And I've got my Question Map to do. How am I to do a Question Map? I can't write.

She was half asleep when the thought came: *It's a manager's job to manage. There's always going to be something you don't know how to do. Just find someone who does.*

It was a beautiful new thought for Mae. Of course, just find someone who can. It warmed and comforted her and made the world seem tranquil and forgiving.

Mae went to sleep and woke up as someone new.

7

The next evening, Mae called on Han An's mother with a proposition.

The house was the last on Marsh Street, down in the floodplain. Even now in summer its courtyard was full of mud, goat turd, and chicken shit. Mae balanced over it on high heels and knocked on the inner door.

An's mother, Kai-hui, opened the door in a haze of fatigue and loose hair. Her eyes widened at Mae's outfit.

Mae bowed. 'Mrs Han-ma'am.'

Mae was wearing her white dress with hearts and over that, her husband's best grey jacket. Her hair was pulled severely back, she wore her huge spectacles, and she carried a clipboard. Mae was well aware: no village woman had ever dressed like that before.

Kai-hui covered surprise in polite responses. She ushered Mae inside and exchanged assurances of well-being.

Formalities over, Mae said, 'I was wondering if I might speak to your daughter. I have a proposition for her.'

An was called, and came in. She was in work clothes, an old flowered dress and an apron. Her hair was in a kerchief, which she quickly pulled off her head. Kai-hui made tea, and served. They talked of the season: It was time to get out into the terraces, but it seemed as if lambing had only just finished.

Mae felt impatience. Dead, dead, this all has died. Perhaps too soon, she launched into the business.

'All our lives,' she said, 'are going to change. Air will come again. We have the television now to help us be more modern, but nothing is really being done to make the village ready.' She explained that she needed the help of a diligent, studious person. She saw a stirring of interest, then excitement, in An's eyes.

Mae continued: 'I have two purposes, I confess. First, it is to help me shape my business. That will change, too. But the second is also to help the village to decide: What do we want to do for the future?'

Also, though Mae did not say so, to write the answers down and read them later.

Kai-hui did not know what to think, coming fresh from floors, the battle against mud, and the trial of boiled socks. 'We are very flattered that you think of my daughter for such an unusual activity,' she said. 'I must confess, I do not understand. Are you offering her a position?'

'Not yet,' admitted Mae. 'I am not yet sure I have a business. People might tell me, "Don't bother, no one wants your fashion." But if I do, then I will need a bright young Talent.'

An's eyes glistened. Oh, she understood, the young one. She could smell the new world, she knew the fragrance of it.

Kai-hui said, 'That is very interesting. But we are talking about time. And my daughter is needed in work here.'

It would not be polite to say: Your daughter will have to leave you one way or another — by marriage or by work. It was not polite, but perhaps politeness had died, too.

So Mae said it. 'An will not always be with you. And like all of us, she faces choices. One choice is to cling to old ways. And end up boiling her husband's underwear. Or, she can use her way with words and her beauty in a new way. A way that will bring cash and not labour into your house.'

An was trying to fight down a smile. Her cheeks clenched, and she was not daring to look at either her mother or Mae.

'May I see the questions?' asked Kai-hui. Her eyes were hard with the mild insult, pained at the truth, and alert.

With a flourish, Mae produced her Question Map. An could not suppress a cry of surprised admiration.

Mae had spoken the questions to Kwan's TV and the TV had printed it out all in lines. It looked like something from the government.

Kai-hui might be stuck boiling socks, but she could read. As she read, she began to look wistful. 'These are indeed questions that need to be asked. I am concerned about modesty. These questions are to be asked of men as well?'

'Mother!' An blurted out, and pulled herself in.

'Indeed, yes,' said Mae, shyly herself. 'The men run the village, and so must be asked. That is one reason why I myself need an assistant, so that there is no misinterpretation. We will always present ourselves together.'

Kai-hui's eyes said something else: *You are no longer a model of propriety.* 'As long as you do not go armed,' she said. An did not move. 'We will consider the offer, its good and bad points.'

Mae bowed as she sat. When she stood to go, An got up and took her arm, and said, 'I will escort our guest.' Her mother decided to relent.

At the courtyard gate, An said fiercely, quickly, 'No matter what she says, I will help you.'

There was no need for rebellion. Kai-hui said yes.

The next day, Mae and An went to work.
Mae had decided that it would flatter people if she made an appointment to see them. It would get them thinking, and it would establish her claim to have done it first. Her secretary, as she called An, wrote a letter to all thirty-four households, asking for a convenient time to visit.

That night, when Mae sat down to consult the TV, Kwan came running down the steps of her four-farm house. She kissed her.

'Mae,' Kwan said, 'you clever, clever lady! Why did you not tell of such a brilliant plan?'

'I felt it might seem stupid,' Mae lied. 'It was unformed, I had no idea what the response would be.'

'But it is just the thing!' exclaimed Kwan, eyes bright and full of pain.

'Oh! It is to help me with my fashion business.'

'It is more than that! It asks us to think about the future,' said Kwan. 'Do you need any help?'

'Oh! You are so kind. No, I have An, Han Kai-hui's daughter, as my secretary. If it works out, she can join me in the business.'

'Ah,' said Kwan. 'Yes, of course. You have that terrible loan to repay.' She paused. 'Our offer of help is always open to you.'

Mae's inner heart groaned. This was difficult. How could she say: you are kind, and a good friend, but I believe you are smarter than I am and would take over my project, make it yours? How can I say that the part of you that hungers, needs to take my project over and make it yours?

Mae replied, 'I may have to take up the offer, indeed. You are so good, such a kind heart.'

Kwan's smile did not change, just her eyes. 'What value is that, in the new world?'

Against her own instructions, Mae had spent some of Sunni's-man's loan on pens and paper and a clipboard for An to write with. This made her feel bad. Her new image made her feel good.

An did not have to be told how to dress. She also wore a jacket of her father's, and suddenly, proudly, wore the big spectacles she had always tried to hide. She looked like a newsreader.

They worked in the evenings, after supper. Their first appointment was with Tsang and her husband Mr Muhammed. The village children lined up outside their gate to watch the arrivals of the Talents.

'Ask her about Kwan's son,' one of the boys bellowed like a bullfrog, to squeals of delight and harsh, unkind laughter.

Tsang had put on her best clothes and made tea, and curtained off the room full of corncobs. Her husband Hasan was a most devout Muslim who wore a black robe and had a copy of the Book ready.

Mae explained her two purposes. She phrased it this way: To ask the man of the house about the coming of Air, and to ask the woman about fashion. But either could speak at any time. Any questions they did not wish to answer were fine. Had they any views about the coming of Air?

'Indeed,' said Mr Muhammed. And spoke for twenty-five solid minutes.

The religion of Peace has always been a friend to science. When the West descended into a dark age, it was Peace that kept alive the teachings of Aristotle and Plato. Peace had no difficulty reconciling God and mathematics, the spirit and the solid world of physical laws.

An nodded and wrote down the odd phrase. Mae said, 'Ah!' and 'Oh!' at each fresh insight and felt her heart dragged down.

Mr Muhammed paused to sip tea. He was all lean neatness, with thin lips going purple with age, and thin fingers. His head was wrapped in white like a bandaged wound that needed to be kept clean.

When she asked her second question – what he felt about the Test – he simply repeated what he had said before. But he added that all information was nothing compared to the word of God. And that if the Air became a channel of godlessness, then it would be a great evil, to be rooted out.

But how had he reacted, what did he himself experience? Mae was surprised. She really wanted to know.

Mr Muhammed denied Air had any effect. It was interesting to see the Beijing opera. But it should not be allowed to drive out the Book.

Tsang, plump, cheerful, and slovenly, agreed with her tidy husband. Everything he said, that was her view. Pressed to say what her activities were, she listed cleaning, cooking, and fieldwork. Fashion – oh, a married woman such as herself needed no fashion.

An's and Mae's eyes caught each other.

They bowed, professed delight, and congratulated Mr Muhammed on his contribution. He seemed pleased and guided them to the door.

'If you need any help, Mrs Chung-ma'am, help teaching the children about this new thing – then come to me. To speak frankly, you have a great enemy. Tuh.' He cast his head back up the hill. 'That animal-worshipping Eloi.'

Mae didn't understand. 'I am sorry, I am just a wife, I do not know who you mean.'

Mr Muhammed's eyes softened, moved by the incompetence and innocence of a woman.

'Teacher Shen,' said Mr Muhammed, gently. 'He hates it. He is very angry with you for what you are doing.'

'What am I doing?' Mae asked.

'Causing trouble,' said Mr Muhammed, still smiling.

Across the bridge from Mr Muhammed was the vast household of Old Mr Doh.

Young Mr Doh was Joe's great friend, and he greeted Mae and An with gusts of hilarity. He tried to pour them rice wine instead of tea, and spoke over his shoulder to his own and his brother's children, who clustered around the door to listen.

Young Mr Doh teased and complimented Mae at the same time. 'Oh! Where are your angel wings? Where are the veils and the bobbles? You are wearing glasses, why did you put on your husband's clothes by mistake?'

The children chorused giggles and hid their mouths.

Mae asked, 'What does Young Mr Doh think of Air?'

'What Air? Where is it? I tell you, it will never happen. How many people died, eh? No one wants it.'

'I want movies,' said his brother, who was a bit simple.

'So do I,' piped up one of the grandsons. 'It is as boring as mud in this village.'

'*Fut-bol!*' roared all the boys in unison, approximating in their language the name of the great international sport.

Mr Doh said, 'We get all of that on TV already. I tell you, nothing will change.'

The two young Doh wives, of course, worked and had no need of fashion. On the other hand, Young Miss Doh was famous for wearing men's clothes and riding a motorcycle. Outside on the street, An and Mae shrugged to each other.

At home, Joe waited for them in the kitchen, still in his undershirt and work trousers. 'So, wife, did you learn anything?'

An bowed, and Joe grunted. Siao and Old Mr Chung watched. Why suddenly, did it seem to Mae that their gaze was insolent?

Mae found she did not want to talk in front of them. Everything was like an egg that she wanted to warm and protect and hide away.

The two women also sat at the table, under the stares of the men. An looked over their Question Sheets. 'Very few of your questions are answered, ma'am.'

'We will need to talk to wives separately.'

'Why do you need to do that?' said Joe, belligerently.

'Because wives do not talk around their husbands.'

'Oh. And you want to encourage them. *Tuh.*' Joe looked to his father and brother for support. Siao grunted, and hid his face.

Mae sighed. 'Joe. I try to make us money. To do that, I need to know what women want clothes for.'

'To cover their nakedness, or else they'd all be whores,' he said.

'Joe, we have a well-brought-up lady guest.'

Joe looked sullenly at both of them.

Mae looked at An. 'Everyone is pretending that nothing has changed. No one will talk about the Test at all.'

An looked a bit tense. 'No one knows what to make of it. Except you.' An hesitated and then decided to push on. 'In your case, ma'am, it was like a doctor prescribing deadly poison as a last resort. You have already gone through it, the worst. Every time people see you, they are reminded. That you were driven mad by it. That it changed you, beyond recognition.' An's eyes were saddened.

'Yes!' said Joe, suddenly fierce. 'Yes! You are not the woman I married.'

An persisted, in a quiet, kindly voice: 'People might become frightened of you.'

'I will walk you home,' said Mae.

Joe forbade it. They had a terrible fight, in front of An. Mae was beside herself. She really had had enough. 'Think, you stupid man – though I know you find it difficult to even recognize your own shoes! I cannot let the village beauty walk home unchaperoned. What would her mother say?'

'Oh, so now you quote tradition at me. You, who walk about in men's jackets!'

'I am not staying here to listen to rubbish or to let you make a greater fool of yourself in front of Miss An.'

Mae stormed out.

She said to An, 'This is going to be harder work than I thought.'

'I think of it,' said An, 'as being like childbirth. I find it is already preparing me for many difficult tasks ahead.' She paused. 'I want to thank you for the opportunity.'

'I want to thank you for all your help.'

'We will find who your friends are, Mrs Chung-ma'am.'

Mae safely delivered An to her mother, and climbed back up to the village square. The Teahouse overlooked the hill, growing out of the side of Joe's cousin's house. It was full of light and smoke and bellowing. Mae walked away from it across their little stream, which was allowed to find its own way across the cobbles. She sat in the dark on the bench in front of Mrs Kosal's house under the great oak. Generations of children had swung from its branches. The people of Kizuldah called it 'the One Tree.' It seemed to reach up into the stars.

Away from her husband, away from everyone, Mae settled back down into Air. She did not have to go far before she felt the wisdom of the Kru come to her.

It was so evident then, what she was doing wrong. She was just talking. She had to explain to people what the rules were, and ask them for quick, simple answers. If people left one question unanswered, it was either irrelevant to them, which told you something, or they had something to hide. Ask questions that had simple objective answers, avoid yes or no. Listen carefully and find a way to characterize the replies so they could be compared.

The Kru was not a voice. It was like bubbles full of answers popping in her head. It did not ask stupid questions like, Why don't you get them to write the answers themselves? (They can't write.) It knew what she knew. It was becoming part of her.

Mae knew nothing, really, about making dresses. She knew nothing, really, of Air or the old Net or what money really was, or even how to get things off this mountain. But she knew one thing. Through Air she could add knowledge to herself in a new way.

From somewhere, from the future, she heard the sound of a siren.

The next day Mae and An interviewed Mr and Mrs Mack.

Musa Mack looked like the other village men except that his hair had a reddish tinge and curled. He was a Christian. So was his wife, who was from across the Valley, a world away, on slopes lost in haze.

Mr Mack was the village's token Westerner, even though his family had lived in the Valley for over a century. He could drink whisky and not get drunk. He was gross in his movements, too large. People watched him for corrupt tendencies, He talked too loudly.

Mr Mack shouted them into his house and both Mae and An blanched as if the sheer force of his shouting could hurl them against the wall. Most gross of all, he had recently grown a long red beard. It was incredibly good fortune to have facial hair, he was like an emblem of good luck, but really, who could bear to kiss such a thing?

There was a picture of Isa, the Christians' God, on the wall, and he, too, had a beardful of good fortune. But why would a god be helping with the lambing?

Tea was served, which was a relief. Mr Mack kept bellowing. He was shouting, Mae suddenly saw, because he was so uncomfortable. All his life, he had been seen as compromised. And so he had become what people thought he was.

'It will be a great thing. It will bring the world in right here,' Mr Mack said. Marginalized, he had a love of foreign things.

'I am very frightened,' whispered his wife, Mariam. 'I did not like that thing in my head.'

'I was spitting terror!' laughed Mr Mack. 'But I reckon that you get used to it after a while.'

It was said his mattress was often seen in his courtyard, draining urine. It was said that he wet his bed.

His wife, when they examined the responses, did most of the talking. Both were frightened of Air, both wanted to learn how to use it.

Mariam spoke at great, sincere length about fashion. Mae was sorry she had never approached her before. It had been unfair thinking on Mae's part. She had supposed the Macks were dirty and uninterested in fashion.

'I would like to have three good dresses; one in white for funerals, and one full of bright colours for festivals, and one very dignified dress for happy ceremonies and for going to my church, which I can only do once a year.'

Mae saw that she was lonely.

'You missed it last year,' said Mr Mack.

Mariam looked sad. 'It was a bad year for farming.'

'What sort of dignified dress? What kind of colours?'

'Simple, very simple, but looking nice, you know? Very modest, please, and easy to keep clean – it must look good after I wash it. But I was thinking, perhaps in blue and white together, if the colours held fast.'

Mariam had a pinched face, and she pressed her hand over her heart.

Blue and white? That was a new colour. Mae saw An write it down.

They said goodbye, and loose Mr Mack had his arm around his wife as though she were a parcel.

Outside, An said. 'They seemed happy enough.'

They visited the Pin tribe. Like the Macks and An's mother, they lived south of the main village, along the river.

The Pins had turned the marsh below Lower Street into a graveyard for cars. Baked tyre-tracks swept round to rows of vehicles of faded green or rusty red. Old taxis and rumpled pickup trucks were missing doors or tyres. Dusty cats and tiny black turkeys called hindis picked their way among them. Under corrugated tin sheds, saws and drills and welding torches were hung with festive abandon.

The core of the family had been two brothers and their wives. When they had stopped farming to become mechanics, Enver Atakoloo, the village blacksmith and a full-blooded Karz, became enraged. Mr Atakoloo shot the elder of the brothers. Pin Xi survived and, it was whispered, lived as husband to both his own and his brother's wife; not to mention, it was whispered in even lower voices, his brother's wife's unmarried sister, who also lived there. The ten children and other homeless relatives meant that no fewer than nineteen people lived among the wrecks of the cars or in the barns that had once sheltered livestock.

The whole house smelled of feet and bedding. The tiny diwan was screened from the rest of the house by drying laundry. Mrs Pin Xi wore trousers and an apron covered in blue and yellow checks. The five daughters peered out from behind the laundry, in awe of the transformation of An.

The five Pin sons considered themselves men to be interviewed. They sat up straight on the diwan cushions and were forthright. Air would be great: the Doh boys were wrong; they could do much more than watch football, there were great games you could play in Air.

Mrs Pin beamed with pride every time one of her huge brood spoke. Fashion? Oh? She needed a new apron. No, lots of aprons, a different one for every day, so she could wash the others. And good dresses? Hmm, it might be nice. Yes, a good dress, nothing fancy.

Nothing fancy, nothing fancy again.

And the daughters. *Come out, girls, come out.* And out poured the girl's hearts, in the direction of An. So An had to do both the wise encouraging nods and the writing.

They wanted to be modern. They did not want to look traditional. They wanted to see what the rest of the world wore. Though (glance at Father) it would be good to show the world that traditional values could still be modern.

They all of them told stories, in turn, of the day of the Test. Mae asked if they were frightened. No, they said, they were not scared at all; no, they were ready. Mr and Mrs Pin shrugged. 'We are old,' they said. 'What do we know?'

Leavetaking took half an hour of shaking hands and bowing. The widow and the spinster sister, who had not spoken at all, now made very formal goodbyes, professing pleasure.

Afterwards, An and Mae stood talking on boards, balancing across the mud of Marsh Street.

'So,' sighed Mae. 'They want work clothes that look good but will wear well. They want lots of cheaper clothes, so they can take them on and off and wash them a lot. The younger women want to be modern but they don't know what "modern" will be. So they will rely on us to show them. And . . . adornment is passing. They like our men's jackets.'

An was smiling. 'Mrs Chung is very wise. I did not see that, but I feel you are right.'

Mae settled under the One Tree on the bench, and called her self, and sank down into Air.

Answers popped again and again.

Numbers sang to the Kru. They showed him their hidden secrets, joyfully. Those secrets shocked Mae. She had planned to buy aprons, oven gloves, blouses, and day shoes cheap in Yeshibozkent. This would cost 125 riels and give her less than 16 profit. The numbers did a dance and showed her: To pay off the interest and only 25 riels' principal each year, she could do nothing that did not make 100 per cent profit. Her situation was impossible.

At least with best dresses there was no risk. You only bought cloth when you had a sale, and it was a luxury, you could charge more. The numbers did a further dance. Mae knew how many girls would graduate next year. There was likely to be only one wedding. Eight dresses, for a profit of about 30.

Doing nothing was not an option. Best dresses it would have to be. If Mae was still going to be in the best-dress business, she would need a seamstress. Cheap.

She stood up from the One Tree and walked to Hatijah Ozdemir's house.

Hatijah sat slumped on the floor.

She looked up piteously at Mae, dark circles under her eyes. Her oldest daughter sat, just as unmoving, but vastly plumper, disconsolately mumbling bread. Forgotten laundry hung crisp and shriveled over the woodbin and the floor was piled with unwashed pots. Another child was wailing in the backyard that Mae had vowed she would never enter. It smelled, specially, of pus.

How, Mae wondered, was such a creature able to sew so skilfully? Maybe she put her heart into that and nothing else.

'How are you, Hatijah?' said Mae, as if she were ill.

'Oh,' said Hatijah, and shook her head.

'Are you unwell?'

'It is all this worry,' said Hatijah. 'Five mouths to feed, and we have no money. And Edrem's joints ache, so he finds it difficult to work, poor man. Sometimes he cannot work for days.'

I've never seen Edrem work at all, thought Mae. 'Would you like some money?'

Hatijah looked back, with a dull and heavy face. Probably not, if it means she has to move, thought Mae. She decided Hatijah's problem was laziness. Hatijah seemed like a woman underwater, too tired even to swim to the surface of her own face. She did not reply.

'Remember, I said back in May, before . . . before the Test' – Mae always faltered finding words for the event – 'I said that I might have some sewing work to offer you.'

Someone else said, 'Only if I get to come, too.' It was Sezen.

By the stars. Everything about Sezen had changed.

Sezen wore grubby black trousers and an old black leather jacket. She glowered. There was no hint of politesse, no smiles, no graces.

Mae herself had grown more blunt. 'What will you bring?' she asked.

'Myself,' said Sezen.

'You can't do anything,' replied Mae. 'Your mother can sew. You would just be a burden.'

'Then my mother won't help you.' Sezen's face was fatter and covered in spots. Her hair had been impulsively chopped back from her face. Her hands were jammed in her pockets. Her posture had changed. Her head leaned to one side; her hips were thrust sideways. Every line of her body was a challenge.

Hatijah just stared.

'Okay,' said Mae with a shrug, 'if this is a house where the daughter rules the mother. Your little brother is half starved and none of you have any clothes. Find money where you can.' Mae started to leave.

'I can tell you what clothes to make.' Sezen stared back at her.

Mae looked at her jacket, her jeans. 'What clothes to rescue from garbage.'

Sezen's plump head wavered on a skinny neck. 'If that's the only place I can find them.' She still challenged: 'Look. You want to make clothes for old women. What does a married woman need a best dress for? I tell you who is most interested in clothes. People my age. And we don't want what you make.'

Mae stopped. She knew what this sensation was. This was the sensation of truth coming from unexpected sources.

'We see on TV. We don't want to look like peasants; we don't want to look like fashion people. This is what we want to look like.'

Sezen had a school notebook tied with string to a post. She opened it and pressed it so it would stay open. She did this slowly with her eyes on Mae, with an air of presenting something outstanding.

Instead of schoolwork, Sezen had been drawing.

She was drawing who she thought she was. This Sezen had long flowing sculpted black tresses, and wore tight jeans, mutton sleeves, pinched wrists. Mae made to hold the book to see better.

'Ah,' said Sezen, and snatched it back. *You will not steal this, fashion expert*, she seemed to say.

Mae shook her head. 'So. Jeans and mutton sleeves. These are new ideas? Many girls waste their time with fashion drawing, there is nothing special in that.'

Sezen's eyes rolled. How annoying when blind people cannot see. She held the book out one last time.

Now the drawings had short, slicked hair pasted up into tiny points. They showed a dream Sezen. She looked like a hoodlum. Everything she wore was black. This was evil fashion, for bad young people, and Mae knew, herself, that, yes, given half a chance, this is what they would buy.

'So. Now you begin to see,' said Sezen.

'The Muslim girls would not be allowed.'

'Hah,' said Sezen, scornfully. 'They are the worst. What they wear under their robes is nobody's business. What they *don't* wear sometimes.'

Mae considered, and on balance this was not what she had planned.

'There is something in what you say, but I don't like to be threatened, and I don't like the way you boss your mother.' Mae shrugged, said goodbye, and walked out.

Mae was out on the street when there was a change in the sound of the air around her and a darkness in the corner of her eye. Sezen had run after her – without giving the impression of having done so.

'I will set up my own business,' said Sezen.

With what, air? Mae blew out air and stopped and looked at her. Mae felt pity for her and dislike at the same time. 'You don't have a bargaining position. Don't you understand that, child?'

Sezen had nothing. Yet she stared back unblinking, determined. That curious wavering of the head. Her mouth was working too, slightly, all the time.

'My mother is useless. My father is useless.'

'Show some respect,' said Mae. Though it was true.

'I have to do everything, my mother just sits there.'

'Not much gets done, does it? Sezen, your house is a disgrace. I would not take credit for that if I were you.'

Sezen suddenly shouted: 'Will you let up on me! All of you! You are always on me.'

'It is because you are rude,' said Mae.

'I hate housework. I will do anything else. I will be very hardworking. And I do know what the young girls want. Look! Look!'

Sezen shook the red book at Mae.

Mae took it from her. Sezen let her. Mae folded it and put it under her arm. Her Kru bubbled in her head. She calculated.

'I will look at these, Sezen, but the problem is that girls your age have no money. Their mothers will spend five riels on a dress. What will the girls spend? One riel? Two?' She shook her head.

'Two riels,' said Sezen. She counted on her fingers. 'You can sell six outfits, and get black denim for them all for five riels in the market. My mother sews them, I sell to the girls, we all make money.'

'I do not count six sales.'

'My boyfriend lives down the hill. He has a motorcycle. There are plenty more modern young people around here than you think. There's one you don't know about.' Sezen waited. 'An.'

That did made Mae pause, and the little minx struck again, hard.

'You see. Your helpful little Talent – An. She wants these clothes.'

'I will think about it, Sezen.'

'So that's six sales for . . . twelve riels total . . . So that's seven riels' profit! I get one, my mother gets one, my boyfriend gets one – that leaves four for you!'

'But I get to spend five riels on cloth?' Mae shook her head. 'You will need to do better than that, Sezen. I agreed to nothing, okay. You understand? Nothing! I will see if this fits in with my business plan.'

'It does!' insisted Sezen.

Mae walked off, still shaking her head.

Still.

What Sezen had said about young people wanting something different was true. A new kind of best-dress business was not an entirely bad idea.

Something bubbled up from the Kru. *You can either be a general*

store and stock cheap standard items. Or you specialize. If you specialize
you have to spread geographically.

If I can sell best dresses to this village and the next, that's not such a
bad idea. Maybe I will need that motorcycle after all.

8

Sunni's-husband announced to the village: he was bringing in a television as well.

'Well, wife, your friend Kwan has a rival,' Joe exclaimed cheerily. He was back from doing business all day at the Teahouse. 'Business' meant sipping tea and playing chess until suppertime.

Mae was ladling soup into Siao's and Old Mr Chung's waiting bowls. She thought a moment. 'I don't know why you say "rival."'

'Tuh. Don't play innocent with me. You know the Wings and the Haseems are rivals.'

'Rivals for stealing their neighbours' farms,' muttered Siao, into his soup.

As if jabbed, Joe snapped his head around in Siao's direction, and then decided this was support. 'Yes, wife. Your friend Kwan is no better or worse than Faysal Haseem.'

Mae served her husband his soup. 'Except that we don't owe the Wings any money.'

Siao said, 'Haseem has to run it off the Wings' account, for which of course, he will pay rent, like water. So Wing still gets richer, at Haseem's expense. That makes Wing more clever.'

Siao was an odd fish. Somehow he knew more than Joe. Mae had long ago noticed that he did all the work, going off every morning with Old Mr Chung to work on the walls. He kept the household's accounts. So why was he content to sleep in the loft?

There was no doubt that two TVs in the village was news. As Mae and An went about their interviewing, they discussed the situation. What, really, would Mr Haseem get out of having a TV? Position, yes, but how would he use it to make money? His only idea would be to charge people for watching it. Since Wing did not, he couldn't, either.

At midnight, Mae went back to Kwan's to work on her TV. She was learning how to use the accounts package. The TV was fine, she had decided, just so long as you didn't go online.

Mae found Mr Doh, Mr Ali, and Mr Ho watching a police thriller. Drug dealers were being rounded up by computer surveillance. Mae found herself thinking: So, they are still loyal to Wing. Who is watching at Sunni's?

Kwan was thinking the same thing. She was serving tea to them, as guests. She had not done that for days. Mae, to show support, began to gather up used cups, and was rewarded by a beautiful smile. Over the plastic tub that was Kwan's sink, they talked.

'I wonder what horrors Mr Sunni shows on his set?'

'How to take over villages, perhaps,' said Kwan.

'I think he wants to be a strongman. Like in the very old days. He wants us all to work for him. If you had daughters he would try to marry one of his sons to them. To form a political alliance.'

Kwan bent from the middle with a silent laugh.

Mae's eyes were narrow and merry. 'He probably thinks that he has the male TV and you have the female.'

Kwan had to put down a cup in order to laugh. 'You have become like a thornbush lately!'

'I hate Mr Sunni's-man,' Mae said with a shrug. 'I wish I had killed him.'

'It will be very interesting when you interview him for your Question Map.'

'On the contrary, I look forward to it. I cannot wait until he tries to do one of his own.'

Kwan was still smiling, but she suddenly, gently, pushed the tip of Mae's nose. 'Do not grow too bold, Mae.'

'I have more than one enemy, I hear.'

'Shen,' said Kwan, her voice suddenly curdling. 'I cannot get over the change in that man.'

'I must talk to him as well,' sighed Mae. She saw she was not just making a Question Map. She was building a party. She realized that, in a sense, it was the party of Mr Wing.

Joe got wind of a construction job in Balshang.
It would take three days to drive there. Siao, Joe, Old Mr Chung, and Mr Doh would drive down in Mr Haseem's van, to join the work gang being recruited in Yeshibozkent. They were to leave that very day.

'It is a good opportunity,' Joe said. 'They are building an industrial farm, many buildings. There is a whole camp for the workmen they are hiring.'

'How much do they pay?' asked Mae.

He blew out air, from stress. 'I don't know.'

'All the men in the country will be going there, hoping for work.'

'But Mr Doh says that it is government work, so they try to spread it to all parts of the country. Who knows? There is a chance, and it is better than sitting around here.'

Mae was glad; it showed her husband had taken on the reality of their problem. 'I will pack your food and your shirts,' she said. It was a proper wifely thing to do. He nodded once, to indicate that this was quite right, too, and drew in smoke from his scrawny cigarette. Mae folded his shirts. Even if it was only four riels a week, if it was four weeks' work, that would be sixteen riels. And if Siao and Old Mr Chung did the same, then their problems were over! Taking into account loss of odd jobs, that was still a total of thirty-two riels overall.

Siao took one final look at the household accounts.

Siao's eyes latched onto Mae's, briefly. 'This comes just in time, eh?'

Mae nodded silently, yes. She could feel her eyes sparkle.

Mr Haseem's van drew up outside their gate and beeped. Mae did not want to be seen by that man, so she pressed the food and the reed box of clothing into her husband's hands. *Farewell, husband, good health, courage, come back a wealthy man* . . . The words tumbled as automatically from her lips as sneezes.

Then came a pause. He stared at her, wanting more; they had been young lovers once, she had borne him three children.

He pulled her to him and kissed her, and she hugged him, pushing her face to the side of his; she would have her freedom after he was gone. Siao called to him from beyond the gate.

Mr Haseem beeped again, she patted him. 'Go, or your good friend will drop you in the shit,' she said.

And unbidden tears came into her eyes. This was very convenient; she made sure he saw them. There were wisps of fear at being left alone, wisps of loss for Joe, who was her domestic companion.

'I will see Lung and our daughter,' he said. 'I will bring back news of Lung.' Joe worshiped his athletic, achieving, military son.

'That will be the best part,' she said. 'Now, hurry, hurry!'

Joe grinned, like a boy again, and broke into a run. He waved at the gate again.

He thinks I love him, she thought. He thinks that in the end we are still man and wife. And she remembered him when he was sixteen, handsome, a leader of the village youth.

Joe never grew up. She heard the car door slam, she heard male exuberance, a chattering, a yelling. She remembered him, his hair greased up, a toothpick never out of his mouth, car insignia stolen from vehicles in the valley pinned to the back of his jacket. She heard the van grind its way down the mountain road.

She listened to the sound of loneliness, the sound of dust. Mr Ken's house was there, like he was – ever present, always close, with a door that could both open and conceal.

Mae was walking before she knew it. I need to be out in the fields by late afternoon, she thought, or people will talk. It was still lunchtime. The children would be napping in Mr Shen's school, Mr Ken's mother might be sleeping before returning to the fields. If not, she could always say: *Who will do your weeding for you, Mr Ken? I and the village women could offer to help.*

She walked into Mr Ken's kitchen. He was sipping soup, his late breakfast. He looked up, still shiny with sweat from weeding his own fields.

'Joe's gone,' she said quietly. 'And his brother.'

'I'll be along,' he said.

She walked back to her own house, shaking. Her body was like Mr Haseem's truck rattling down the road. This is crazy, if anyone comes to call, they will find us. She pinned up the window curtains and drew shut the heavy draught-curtains across the doorway. She took down her sun hat, her jumper, her apron to collect the compost, her high-soled field clogs. She rammed them under the bed. Their absence would signal she was not there. All of that would signal: *Mrs Chung is out at work.* How then did she draw shut the draught-curtains? She opened them again.

She lay down on the bed, still smelling of Joe. It smelled of Joe but that smell would now be driven out by the smell of Mr Ken. That thought alone seemed to loosen the corsets of her belly. I will smell him when I sleep at night.

She heard the latch. Her breath caught. No one called out her name. She heard the latch close. Her heart was pumping. This is mad – if it is not him how will I explain? I will say I caught too much sun and I am ill. The curtains of the alcove were pulled back, rattling on their plastic rings.

It was him and he was smiling. He was shiny no longer. He had bathed.

He was naked under his overalls, which he flung utterly aside, and he was soon on top of her. His skin was as perfect as apricots.

The next day Mae went back out onto her husband's land.
The Chungs had one valley paddy and two long terraces very high up the mountainside. Mae had neglected them since planting the nursery rice. Dock and bindweed were already sprouting between the onions and rice shoots.

She began the long climb up the beaten paths. The swallows swooped about her, scooping insects out of the air. The terraces creaked and buzzed with the sound of crickets. Water lay in puddles, as warm as soup.

On her terrace the air was hot, still, breathless. The heat did a shivering fan-dance in the air. Only the kites circling high overhead looked cool.

Mae went to work hauling out weeds. Her back was soon aching. Tears of sweat wept into the ground. This delicious rice, she thought, it will be seasoned with my own salt.

Her clogged feet sank deep into the creamy soil with every step. The mud sucked and clung like a lover. Her high, broad hat kept the sun off her neck, shoulders, and even her arms. It could not keep away the flies and the midges. Come friend swallow, here is a feast, free me from flies. She waved her hands at the midges but they returned to tickle and stick to her skin that was like cooked rice, glutinous and steaming.

Mae stood up. She could see far below on the plain the livid green paddies of wet rice. The slashes of mirror among them were water reflecting sky. Beyond – hazy, losing all shape in bright sunlight – were the flat yellows, beiges, and greys of the distant mountains.

Was it like this in your day, Old Mrs Tung?'

No.

The voice was like wind.

Suddenly with a lurch Mae fell, growing smaller. The world collapsed around her, deflating. She was somewhere else.

Little Miss Hu was swung up away from the ground and out over the paddies, holding on to a high wooden arm. The arm was part of a pump for transferring water higher up the mountain.

Miss Hu hung for a moment, giggling in a mixture of fear and delight. Boys sat on the other end of the arm, a huge ball of dried mud. Miss Hu drew a breath and let go and dropped down. Her heart rose into her mouth and the mud greeted her like a mother with a plump hug. The little girl stood up coated in wet earth and whooped to the boys in triumph.

She jumped up and down, splashing in the mud, not caring about her old paddy clothes. 'Again! Again!' she demanded. The boys lowered the arm and she ascended again. She looked out across the valley.

The terraces were lined with pumps, dipping their heads like graceful marsh birds. Below, on the hillside, there was no schoolhouse, no mosque.

The opposite mountain was striated like an onion in layers of paddies. The terraces climbed in steps, green and lush, to the village of Aynalar. Its main street zigzagged up the narrow pass between high, fine stone houses with whitewashed walls and stained-glass windows. There was a dome and a minaret.

Hu Ai-ling looked at it with yearning. One day, she promised, I will live in Aynalar.

She let go again and Mae lurched out of the past.

She blinked and that same hill was now beige and featureless, a mass of tumbled grey stone. If you focused, you could see traces – traces only – of the walls.

The flood had washed one terrace down onto another, wiping them all away. One whole side of the valley had gone. No one spoke of it now, no one remembered. It was healed scar tissue. The opposite hillside, once layered with fields, stared back at her like an old blind face.

Mae remembered Old Mrs Tung. She had always sat at her attic window, facing out across the valley, wind in her face, blind. She had been looking in the direction of Aynalar as if, for her, it was still there.

This is worrying, thought Mae. No, this is really worrying, the way the world shrugs, and suddenly there is the past, there is the future. Like I have a sickness in my head.

No one said this would happen. They did not say you would visit the past. They did not say dead friends would not leave. They do not understand what Air is. She felt the wind move, chilling her wet arms like fear.

Where is this? Mrs Tung asked.

All Mae wanted when she got home was a chance to think, but waiting in her kitchen was her brother, Wang Ju-mei.

'Afternoon, sister,' Ju-mei said. He wore his cream-coloured summer suit.

'Hello, brother. Thank you for coming to see me,' she beamed.

Thank you for coming when it will be necessary to make you lunch, thank you for coming so that it will be impossible for me to wash. Thank you for trying, as always, to assert that Joe's house is in some way yours.

'Would you like something to drink?'

'Tea would be excellent,' he nodded.

She put on the kettle and thought: no, I will not miss my bath. She snatched up fresh clothes and draped them over her arm. 'You will not mind, brother, if I wash?' she said, in a little-girl voice.

Or would you rather I stank and dripped sweat into your lunch?

Ju-mei waved his hand as if it were nothing, but he was too choked with his own unsorted emotions to speak. If the kettle boils and he wants to make his own tea, let him.

My brother. He wants this house, and cannot accept it will not be his. He is a grain merchant, he sells insurance, he wears suits, he has to cast his shadow over things.

Anger made her snap shut the curtain closing off the narrow alley between the two houses. She scowled as she peeled off the sweaty T-shirt, all pleasure in her bath gone. She needed to think. Absent-mindedly she scooped cold water over herself from the rain butt.

Ju-mei will want to chaperone me, or even have me move back into his house for propriety. Well, that won't happen. But he will also feel he has the right to drop in and out when he pleases. Joe knows what Ju-mei is up to, that is why my brother never does this when Joe is around. But, oh God, he will be here day and night, with his new baby, and his wife will want me to change its diapers. He'll bring Mother and leave her here and say it's my turn to take care of her.

When I want to sleep in Ken Kuei's arms.

Unless I am so rude that he goes away and doesn't come back.

Necessity in life can have a wonderful, calming effect.

Unless I finally, really tell him what I think is going on. Unless I say it in the way I have always wanted to say it. She began to grin. I am just going to say what I really think. I am a peasant wife used to livestock and hard reality. His little cream suit is no defence against that.

Mae went back into the house, still smiling with anticipation. Ju-mei sat staring at the boiling kettle.

'Ha-ha. Men. You just sit there watching it boil. Can't you make the tea yourself?'

Ju-mei had no answer for that. 'I . . . I was offered tea.'

'Indeed,' said Mae, toweling her hair. 'There it is.' Her hand indicated the earthenware bin, in which the tea leaves kept dry. Briskly she put away the dirty clothes in the wicker basket.

'I hope, brother, you did not come with thoughts of my cooking you lunch. I have my appointments.' She smiled at him. Her teeth had never felt so big.

He was foxed. Nothing was going as he had pictured it.

'You are bold, Mae,' he said.

'Bold? To visit neighbours I have known all my life, what is bold about that? You are bold to wear so much perfume. Pooh! You smell more like a woman than my customers.'

She pulled the alcove curtain shut around her to put on her Talent clothes. 'I'll tell you what else is bold: to drop into another man's house the moment he is gone and expect to be cooked lunch. Or doesn't your wife cook for you anymore?'

'You are a woman alone.'

'No. I am not. Miss An and I always work together, so I do not need a chaperone. I certainly do not need to be chaperoned in my husband's house.' Mae was decent in the heart-patterned dress, so she pulled the curtain back. She wanted to see his face slack with surprise. She stepped into her Talent shoes. 'And there is no need to try to establish any rights to this house. If Joe dies, Siao inherits; if he dies, Old Mr Chung inherits. Either one of them could marry and then it would never fall to the family Wang.'

He shivered in his chair. 'Mae! You are impossible. This is a brotherly call!'

'I know,' replied Mae, flinging up her husband's jacket to open up its arms. She paused. 'And I know exactly what that means. Whatever I've got, Ju-mei, you want. It's been like that for as long as I can remember. You want Joe's cock, too? You want to inherit this house? Maybe you can inherit it if you let Joe fuck you.' She sniffed and made plain she was about to leave. She muttered, 'Both of you would probably enjoy it.'

All blood drained from her brother's face. Abruptly, like a cripple, he stood up, shambling, shivering, having trouble gathering up the cane.

'I don't know what's come over you! You talk like a peasant. A rough farm girl.' He was at the door.

'I am a rough farming girl.'

'I . . . I had come to offer to pay the debt!'

And Mae whooped in triumph. 'I know! I know! And that is how you thought you would get the farm!'

Her sneaky little brother. His face fell. Mae had to laugh. She took his arm and led him towards the door. 'Come, come, brother, it's not so bad, all our fights end this way, only this time I have decided to skip the fight.'

Mae remembered the kettle. She swooped back into the kitchen to take it off the ring, and when she came back, he had gone.

For a few weeks, Mae's days settled into a pattern.
She did her housework in the early morning and worked in her fields until noon. At lunch or during the day, she might snatch some time with Mr Ken. In the early evening Mae and An would visit neighbours with their Question Map and drink tea late into the night.

After escorting An home, Mae worked to master the television. She saw there were hundreds of things she might do with the TV. She could use the television to sell or to Market Call. She could use it like a telephone to talk live or leave voicemail. In a year she would be able to use it to make material for Aircasts.

Aircasts were like films, but they were translated into the Format. They could go then direct to people's heads. So there would be Aircast versions of movies.

And Aircast version of ads, thought Mae. And all the ads, if you looked hard enough, had something called Intimacy Shields. So, Mae began to wonder, how do you do that in Air? When it's inside your head.

She tried to buy bolts of cloth online. But she still needed something called a Believability Card and that was easiest to do when you had a Clever Card.

Kwan rubbed her shoulders. 'The world out there has grown bigger. There are two worlds. There is the one you can see, and another world people have made up, and it is bigger than the real one. They call it "Info." '

And Mae felt lust.

Lust to be part of that world, lust to know how it worked, lust to know how the television worked, and how the Net and how the Air would give all that wings. With a lust that bordered on despair, she wanted to be first, she wanted to know all, she wanted to be mistress of all its secrets.

I will learn, she promised herself.

Kwan would leave to go to bed. Mae would keep learning and relearning how to make the accounts system work. She asked for the wrong things, the machine got stuck on the way she said certain things, she kept forgetting what *fo mu lah* were, and how you entered them, but she knew that it meant the numbers would add themselves up. She thought in passing of Siao, Joe's brother, and how he should see this.

She learned that she could save pictures from the Net or from video. She learned she could change their colour. She learned she could use the tiny camera to copy things from the real world and change them.

Above all else, she learned that she would no longer need to know how to read or write.

And at three A.M., her feet crossing in front of each other as she walked, she would make her way home, as sweaty as if she had been weeding the rice by night as well.

A note on the door might say, in her mother's handwriting: *Your mother called. She wonders where her daughter spends her time and asked if you would be good enough to visit her.* Mae would promise herself that she would. When she had time. She would fall into her bed. Mr Ken might be there, snoring gently. She might kiss him.

More usually, she would sleep alone. She would pull the pillow that smelled of him between her legs.

And she might dream, always of the past, of beautiful thank-you cakes not delivered until stale. Or a prize dress forgotten on a line until the sun bleached it. The sense of unease would persist, as she sat up. The long hot day would begin again.

The next fashion season would not be until after harvest, in October. By then she would know how much Joe and Siao had brought in. She could leave deciding about her fashion business until then.

Mae thought she was doing all that she could.

Then Sunni set herself up in the best-dress business.

Mae arrived at the Kosals to interview them.

'Oh, Mrs Haseem has just visited and asked us all the same questions,' Mrs Kosal told Mae. 'See. She has sent us a leaflet.'

Mrs Kosal went to fetch it and passed it to Mae, her watchful face and smile not entirely sympathetic.

Mae felt sick. The thing she feared most had happened. Her knowledge, her ideas, had been taken and used by her enemy before she had had a chance to complete them.

And Sunni was richer and had more time and she had a television of her own.

Mae stood reading in the street, looking at the professional print job, alarmed and unhappy. An kicked grit beside her.

'I cannot bear to read it,' said Mae, and passed it to her. Did An know she could not read? Perhaps she did. An read it aloud.

TRUE FASHION
FOR TRUE LADIES

NOW THAT CERTAIN PARTIES HAVE BEEN UNCOVERED
AS OFFERING FALSE ADVICE, THE WAY IS NOW OPEN
FOR TRUTH AND BEAUTY.

Mrs Haseem-ma'am sets the new standard for fashion.

With her eye on the world, she sees what the world of fashion really has to offer. Visit her Fashion-Doctor surgery when you have a moment. See what she can offer you as a best dress. It will be

PROFESSIONALLY MADE BY BEST FASHION HOUSES.

She will also visit to listen with clear heart and true vision to what you have to say. Do not waste words like seed grain on barren fields. Only Mrs Haseem-ma'am can make your words grow into green fields.

Sunni was trying to destroy her.

Mae forced herself to be calm in front of An. She looked at the swallows. The swallows still darted, the sky was faithful. Mae took some comfort.

'The village has never had a leaflet before,' she said. 'I have to admit, it is a bold stroke, a great compliment. It says to us: "You are as important as rich city people, to have a leaflet printed for you." '

It was the work of a professional letter-writer. And that, Mae saw, was wrong in many ways.

'She has made a mistake,' Mae said, saving face in front of An. 'She addresses us as an employer would. And who are these fine ladies she writes for? Mrs Wing? Only Mrs Wing, who I think is still my friend.'

'Yes, I see,' said An. But she still kicked grit.

'An, can you help me this evening? Can you stay late?'

An sat at her kitchen table and wrote thirty-three letters in her beautiful handwriting on pages torn from Mae's exercise books. Mae made sure every one of them was different.

> *Dear Mrs Pin,*
> *Your husband feeds his children by fixing cars and vans. How would you feel if a rich man wrote everyone saying, 'Don't use Mr Pin, he can't fix things.'*
> *This would be unkind and untrue. Sunni gives herself airs and calls herself Mrs Haseem-ma'am. She wants you to talk to her like she is your boss.*
> *You can call me Mae, like I am your servant. I will work hard to get you a good best dress.*
> *Your servant,*
> *Mae*

> *Dear Mrs Doh,*
> *I am not rich and do not have the money to pay someone to write letters for me. I can't pay to have them printed in the City.*
> *I am a plain person, who likes beautiful clothes and wants her friends to be beautiful. You do not need to call me ma'am.*
> *I have always made good dresses for my friends and always will.*
> *Your friend,*
> *Mae*

And finally:

> *Dear Sunni,*
> *I may be a servant, but I find I am still a fashion leader.*
> *I start to wear men's jackets and so do you. I do a Question Map, and lo, so do you. Mr Wing brings television. Your husband, so original, does the same.*
> *You follow me and that shows I give true fashion advice. Everyone in the village thinks that, too.*
> *It will be good to have two fashion experts. Because both fashion experts must work harder. It will be fun for me to see you work hard.*
> *Your servant,*
> *Mae.*

Hands shaking with rage, Mae folded up the letters and sealed them with rice paste. 'I will walk you home,' she told An, and then she delivered all the letters to the thirty-three houses, including Sunni's.

Mae looked up at the stars, as bright as the souls of her people. Something inside her thrashed like a fish pulled up onto the shore. At first she thought it was anger. It was the need to do something more. Instead of going home, she marched up the hill to Kwan's house.

Kwan's courtyard was empty, but the television was running an old film with no one watching. Mae sat down to work, speaking to the machine. Kwan's dog started to bark. Finally Kwan came out, saw Mae, and started to laugh.

Kwan sat on her steps in her nightdress, and shook her head. 'Mae! You have just written letters to everyone in the village and now what are you doing?'

'I am setting up a school,' said Mae.

Kwan was still laughing. 'What, tonight?'

'Yes, tonight. I feel like the whole village will be swept away unless we do something now. Come and see.'

Images of the five pens swam up onto the screen. Kwan came up behind her.

'I made these. There are the five pens that Air sets up in your mind. I will make the TV imitate Air and I will show people how to use them, what they will be able to do. What do you think?'

Kwan was quiet. 'That will be a good thing to do.'

'I will call in everyone. I will call in people during those times when they are not busy. I will ask men to come just after breakfast, I will ask women to come after lunch.'

Kwan started to chuckle again. 'You just thought of this.'

'I have been slow,' said Mae. 'We all have to learn, Kwan. Or Air will come and it will use us, not the other way around.' What she felt was akin to panic. What she felt was akin to flying.

'Audio. Poster. Pictures,' she ordered. 'Birds. Swallows. Blue on white.' The words flew onto the screen as if they were swallows. The screen said for her under the silhouette of a bird.

'We have the school here, ah? Okay?'

Kwan nodded yes.

Mae's words became a poster.

SWALLOW SCHOOL
BE LIKE A SWALLOW
LEARN TO FLY IN THE AIR

Mrs Chung Mae has been deep into Air. She has been learning a lot about how the TV works. She wants her friends to know it, too. She will show how Air will work by giving lessons on my television for free.

- *Men come just after breakfast.*
- *Women come just after lunch.*
- *Rowdy unruly young pests come after school and not before.*

Mrs Wing Kwan

(Lady Sunni-ma'am. You do not need a letter writer and a printer to make a leaflet. Mae will do one for you.)

Kwan was, by now, laughing aloud.

'Print,' said Mae, 'thirty-three copies.' Two copies were lined up side by side on one sheet of paper.

There was a whirring sound, and Kwan eased the paper out of her machine.

'Mae,' she said, reading. 'You are a miracle.'

Mae felt triumph.

9

The only man to show up at Mae's first lesson was Mr Ken.
He sat quiet and patient and brought no one else with him. He was
not a leader of the village. 'There is no need to do this just for me,' he
said.

'I need to practise,' said Mae.

Alone, in front of someone who accepted her, she spoke from the
heart.

'We should all be grateful to Mr Wing who brought us this machine
just in time. Finally we can see TV. But not just TV, not just kung fu,
ah, but Info. This is what the rest of the world has had since they were
born. This is what they know like we know how to breathe. Now, this
is where Air starts from. Air thinks everyone knows this. If we don't
know it, we get nowhere in Air. And if we get nowhere in Air, we will
be as far behind the rest of the world as apes are from us.

'You won't believe what Air does. In Air, they don't just give you
TV shows. In Air Krus come and give you their whole head. Their
wisdom enters you; you can use it like it was your own brain. In Air,
children will become wiser than adults. They will have parts of wise
adults in their heads. I know this because I have shared this. I have had
a great Kru in my head, telling me about Mat Unrolling.

'In New York people are already sharing their wisdom, their
dreams in one pool. It becomes like another person that everyone
can use. They call this Collabo. They have Collabo clubs, where
everyone dances to everyone else's music. All of this, all of this will be
on us next year. And half of us have never made a telephone call! That
is why we must move. That is why we must learn now!'

Her hand had become a fist, and she shook it. Mr Ken sat in his
chair as if it were accelerating too quickly.

Sunni came to Mae's first afternoon lesson. She wore a black gown with gold leaf, and a floating chiffon scarf, and she was pink and white, and her hair was in a glossy sweep. Her nails were painted, her shoes were white.

She made Mae look as if she had come direct from the fields. Who was more of a fashion expert now?

Sunni's face was a mask of a smile, and she gazed at each of the women, and gave them a nod.

'I assume it is all right for me to come as well, Mrs Wing-ma'am.' She did not even look at Mae.

Kwan smiled and said that all were welcome. 'Mae is doing helpful work for all of us.'

Sunni sauntered among the rows of cushions, nodding gracefully to each of the women. 'I will be round later with the fabric I promised you.' She folded herself neatly onto a cushion and sat next to her ally, Mrs Ali. Elegant, dignified, they gazed about them as if from a great height.

Sezen showed up with her boyfriend, to whom Mae took an instant dislike. His face was frozen into a sneer and there was a tattoo on his neck. Mae had Sezen's notebook ready to give back to her. 'I'll talk to you about it later,' said Mae, and Sezen, for no very good reason, turned to her boyfriend with her mouth open as if aghast at bad behaviour.

More women came in clumps of friends, chattering and laughing. Mrs Mack came alone. All the Pins came together. Mae's sister Soong Se came with Ju-mei's wife, who had been born a Soong. As they arrived, misgiving-doubts overtook Mae. Could she really talk to so many people?

Mae was torn between different impulses: one towards elegance, one towards directness.

'Hello. I am very pleased to see you all here.'

The women murmured hello back. Exactly as if they were in school and Mae was teacher. This surprised her, made her shy, made her retreat into peasant bluntness.

She tried to start as she had started with Mr Ken, but it came out muted and flat. 'When we go on Air, this is what they all know. So we need to know it too, to keep up with them, okay?'

The TV would not go on. Mae realized that the TV had always been on when she arrived. Here she was, a teacher, and she could not switch it on.

'It's asleep,' said Kwan. The ladies laughed, not knowing that it was an actual word.

'Wake,' said Mae, shyly.

Up came the five pens of Air.

Mae felt Sunni behind her, looking for every mistake. 'What the Test did is change everybody's mind. It made the inside of your head look like the inside of a TV.'

Mae was taken aback when the women laughed again. 'So. You have these five pens inside your head now. Air imitates TV. So learning how to use the TV will help learning how to use the Air.'

'I use it to breathe,' said Mrs Ali. She was looking in a conspiratorial way at Mrs Sunni-ma'am. More chuckles.

They wanted this to be jolly, like a ladies' tea party. Mae found she was too shy in front of so many people to be relaxed enough for that. She was exposed to an enemy who had perhaps brought allies.

'Now you will also use it to think,' Mae said to Mrs Ali. It sounded like a rebuke. Sezen's boyfriend gave an ugly squawk, and he whispered something rude that made Sezen giggle and hiss at him to be quiet. Sunni's eyes were on Mrs Ali, and very slightly she shook her head.

Mae pointed to the screen, which was showing the familiar Air Format. 'You will see that you already know how Air works.'

'Oh good, we can go now,' said Sezen's boyfriend. Sezen hid her mouth and laughed.

'Each of these four areas contains different things. The section called "Help" is the one we cover today, because this is where information about "Info" is kept. Open "Help."'

Up came a list of options. Mae could not read it, but she knew it by heart. 'This shows all the things the television can do, how to make the TV work, how to find things that we want to know, what to do when things do not work.'

Mae turned to them. 'Is there something any of you want to know?' They sat. Sunni sat looking down at her new dress, adjusting the scarf into a perfect position.

'Mrs Haseem-ma'am, perhaps you would like to learn how to print a leaflet.'

'I have already printed a leaflet,' replied Sunni, her face a mask of a smile.

'Good, then we need not do that,' said Mae. Her eyes said: *That is what I wanted; you will not learn it from me.*

Mae wanted to humiliate Sunni in public. Her gut moved her forward. 'There are many things the TV can do. Perhaps I can show you how to use it to design special clothes in a special way. Sezen? May I use your drawings?'

Sezen sat up and blinked. 'Uh. Ah. Okay?' Her boyfriend laughed at her, and she hit him. Mae trotted forward, feeling short-legged, and took the notebook.

'Scan,' Mae said, and held up the book in front of the little camera eye sitting on top of the TV. It took a moment. 'If this was an egg, I would now go and wash the bowls and come back later.' The homely touch made most of her audience laugh.

Then Mae pulled the camera round. 'Now, please scan Mrs Haseem-ma'am.'

The audience was onscreen, and Mae touched the screen image of Mrs Haseem, to select her.

'You see, we live in new ways already. Sezen has been looking at new kinds of clothes for modern people. What the TV can do is show us what such clothes will look like on real people. So they can see themselves if the fashion suits them. We will show modern fashion on Mrs Haseem.'

The young people spurted laughter. Mae had seen a department store in Tokyo do this. If they could, she could.

The machine whirred. Kwan's face was held still, but its smile was spreading. Slowly.

'What the machine is doing is building an image of Mrs Sunni-ma'am. This image will be complete and can do many things. Though it might take some time to make.' She glanced at the screen. The TV whirred to itself.

Mae was stuck for something to say. 'So. Let's start to make our new clothes for new people.' She murmured to the TV, 'Multitask.' The machine did not understand. 'Multitask,' Mae said again.

Sunni raised her voice, very slightly: 'Not everybody follows your orders, Mae.'

'Indeed not, Mrs Haseem-ma'am. I am not in a position to give orders.'

A new window opened with the image of Sezen's jacket. Mae told the machine it was to be a jacket and Sunni's size, which she knew from ordering her dresses. Mae called up textures, she called up colours.

'Oh!' gasped Mrs Pin, as the drawing of the jacket suddenly inflated into something that looked almost real.

Mae stuck in the knife and twisted. 'The advantage is that you do not need to visit the City to see fashion. You do not need to have Talents come and visit to parade clothes that look good on them. You can see what clothes look like on you.'

'It might have been better manners,' said Sunni, looking pained. 'To try it on yourself.'

Mae sniffed. 'I have just come from working in fields. I no longer care what I wear.'

She started on the jeans. Black jeans with handcuffs at the belt.

'Every business will have to change. Even farming, even water, all of it will change because of "Info." That is why I want you to be ready.'

The jeans were made, in Sunni's size.

'A different hairstyle for you, Mrs Sunni-ma'am?'

Beautiful, spiky, cropped, slicked.

'We can give you a whole new look.'

Mae went back to the newly computed image of Sunni. You could paste on the designs, and the person could stand up and turn and see the clothes as if they really wore them.

Mae did not know the command. She knew how to paste images, but the images were flat and dead.

The command she needed was an English word. Mae could not remember it. She searched her Air-scarred mind. She felt what she called the root, the thing that was reached back into Air. 'What is the thing I need?' she demanded.

The whisper was slight, as slight as the moment when you remember. Mae saw a sign that looked like it was made of red and yellow blocks: 3-D. Mae remembered the funny seesaw sound of English. She really did not know if this was going to work, but if it did, the village would talk about nothing else.

'Tree dee com poo tay shon.'

Pause.

The screen went dark. Mae heard, very faintly, a grinding, she heard the sound of wind. Please, wind, please air, please sky, I am of the earth. Help me.

Pink, said the lines of the screen, awakening.

Sezen roared. She stood up and covered her mouth and hopped up and down, beset by hilarity, hope, all manner of feelings, including hatred of the rich:

For, on the screen, Mrs Haseem-ma'am was sitting on her chair, dressed as Sezen had dreamed. Spiky hair, black leather, black jeans, everything black. Mrs Haseem looked down in shame, she tried to look up in pity. She saw herself as too old, too plump, squeezed into jeans, and looking like a drug dealer.

'I use clothes to flatter friends, not to make fun of people,' Sunni said.

Bad Girl Sunni said it, too, an echo on the screen. She stood up with maximum dignity.

Onscreen, the effect was hilarious, for she walked off like a fashion model on a catwalk, as in a video. She looked proud to be Bad Girl Sunni.

Mrs Pin and Mrs Doh grinned, eyes goggling, pleased at her defeat.

Mrs Ali stood up suddenly, straight and fierce, and walked off to join Mrs Haseem. So I know who my friends are, thought Mae.

And I am somewhat in Sezen's debt.

'Now,' she said, 'for those who are left: Let's go back to looking at this thing.'

In the afternoon, the children came to the Swallow School.
Their clothes were ragged, their stripy T-shirts brown with age and dust. They clutched notebooks to their chests.

'We want to see the games!' they chorused.

Mae remembered Teacher Shen. 'I think we had better look at education,' she said.

She saw a little girl called Dawn wince. 'It's not so bad, Dawn,' said Mae. ' "Education," ' Mae told the machine.

And an owl flew onto the screen.

Maybe an owl meant education in America, but in Karzistan owls were birds of death, not of wisdom. This owl wore glasses, which was especially terrifying. The children went silent.

'Hiya!' It began to parrot and prance.

Dawn covered her eyes.

'See? It's a friendly owl,' Mae said. It began to recite all the options. 'It can help you with schoolwork.'

The children stayed silent, but became accepting. They accepted it might be useful to know this, and none of them had opened up the owl before.

'Call me "Owl," ' said Mae.

The children giggled, nervously.

'I am old. I am wise. I am friendly. You call on me, and I will help you.'

'Ow-ow-ow-owll-l' wheedled Dawn, twisting in her chair, and they all broke into giggles. It was extremely rude to call an adult 'Owl.' Mae let them laugh.

Mae decided to show them a symphony from Paris. There was more than one of them. A list of choices offered things Mae had never heard of. 'Explain,' she said.

The television spoke. They were names of people who had made music.

'Who is Bay Toh Vang?' she asked.

And the television told them about the man, his life, and a world that was unfamiliar, strange, gone. The world was a big place, and history made it even bigger, showing different worlds at different times. It was like looking down a huge chasm. Mae even felt a bit dizzy.

The children wanted to see the nest of singing Talents called the Pink and Gold Girls instead. Up they came, breasts sparkled with sequins, but with positive messages about learning being 'the Way' for both boys and girls.

Mae found Hindu raga, and Indian musical movies; she showed them Muslim music from the Arab league. Half her audience sat forward, for they yearned with all their hearts for a Muslim world.

She showed them Puccini. A voice explained that opera was about love and action, stabbings and vows and disguises. Mae showed them Collabo from New York, the music from a hundred American minds pouring into one mix. It bounced, jagged, strange, brave, bold, stupid, smart.

The children of Karzistan saw the careless faces of New York and they saw themselves. Dawn leaned forward wide-eyed, the light of the future dancing in her eyes. When they left, they made a sound Mae had not heard before. Thirty children left talking, as loudly and seriously as adults.

When Mae got back home, she found that Mr Ken had cooked her a meal. He stood, slim and broad at the same time, wearing an apron and grinning at himself.

'What are you doing? What? What?' she asked.

'I cook for you,' he said, pleased. God, he was beautiful.

'That is my job.' She was chuckling.

'Oh! And you've been working. Sit. Tea is made. Then we eat.'

Mae looked at her good man. Sometimes life was a miracle. Sometimes you found a good man to love you. Sometimes he lived next door. The only foolishness was to expect it.

Mae took off her field hat, and gave Ken Kuei a kiss. Looking at his face, Mae thought: No, true foolishness would be not to know it when you got it – and take it.

'Noodles and pig bowel,' he said, proudly, of his supper.

The size, the beauty, the miracle of the world. Fields of butterflies, thousand-year-old fields, children's faces, drifting clouds of life.

Mae dropped down onto a chair, and took her bowl of tea. Under her arm, she still had Sezen's notebook. Mae opened it again. She saw the immaculate clothes, the lean hard faces, sheet after sheet, one dream after another.

All clean, all hard, getting darker, meaner, and angrier.

Amid all that filth, she dreams of this, with that useless mother, the dirty babies. No wonder she is angry. Angry and hard as nails, and she wants, and she wants. Mae recognized that hunger. It was Info Lust.

The thought came as simply as the bursting of a bubble. Sezen wants me as a mother. How touching do I find that?

I am going to have to do something different, now that Sunni takes half my business. Do I say yes to Sezen, and do these bad-girl best clothes?

The food arrived, borne by beautiful arms, crowned by a beautiful smile.

Bubbling up from inside her came a chuckle. She pulled him to her and kissed his shirt with its slightly rounded belly. 'Where is your mother? Where are your children?'

'Didn't you hear? No, you were gone this morning, working as always. They are all visiting the other grandparents.' He smiled. 'We are truly alone.'

'Oh!' Her voice trailed away in delight.

After supper, in the alley between the houses, Mae stood nude before him.

Kuei poured cold delicious water over her. He soaped her, washing her back. She poured water over him, and washed him. Then, soapy and nude, they made love. She had never even dreamed of doing this with a man. Kuei knelt and with gentle, puppy-dog lapping, kissed her most-secret places. It was animal, doglike. A year before, shame would have overcome her. Instead she felt as though another layer of clothing had been flung free.

Mae held herself even more open for him, and soft, warm, wet, he explored her. And she saw the swollen head of his penis, round and the colour of a peach, and she knelt then, and ate. 'Oh, I am sorry,' he gasped, and the fruit burst in her mouth, and the strongest possible taste of masculinity pumped into her. He pulled her to her feet and most shocking of all, he plunged both of them into a kiss. He poured water over them, cooling, purifying. And it was her turn to crumple in the middle, and she pressed the back of her own hand against herself, as if to quell the trembling. He kissed her cheek, and stepped out to dry himself. She looked down and saw her hand was bloody.

She was menstruating. She poured water over it.

She explained she had not known. She was worried; some men were terrified that menstrual blood would weaken them.

'Then we both have the most each other has to give,' he said, and kissed her again, and she went wet again, and they made love again, this time more conventionally. I have blood and semen inside my belly, she thought. They washed again, the water like a cool, loving tongue of some creature that cared for both of them.

Dust, stickiness, their everyday selves were all washed away. Both of them tumbled into bed, darkness settling over their minds like night.

'Kuei,' she whispered. Finally, she had called him by his first name.

They were awakened by a pounding on the door.

A man was calling her name in rage.

'Joe!' gasped Mae.

Kuei was naked beside her in bed, and his clothes were in the small shed with the drain. Between the drawn curtains it was night.

'Stay here!' she whispered, pleading.

'Mae! Chung Mae!' someone bellowed.

Could it be that it was not Joe? Her heart shuddered. Anyone else would be a relief.

'I must talk with you. Open this door. I want words!'

Mae fluttered into her morning robe, her mind clearing, as if a strong wind had blown through it. She snapped the curtains shut around the alcove, and turned on the kitchen light.

Mae shouted back: 'I am coming. Who are you to be shouting so?' The kitchen was covered with unwashed pans, but betrayed no other sign of a male presence. 'Patience, patience!'

She opened the door and something was thrown in her face. It was lightweight, it fluttered, it did not hurt, but it made her turn her head. When she looked back, she was dismayed.

It was Teacher Shen.

His lean and handsome face was hard with tension; his eyes were wide with anger.

Mae was temporarily undone. She had been a friend.

Shen demanded, 'What are you about? What are you trying to *do*?' He was beside himself.

'I ask the same question of you. Have you gone mad, Shen, to shout at me? What is this about?'

'You know what this is about.'

'The TV.'

'You. Setting up a school!'

So that was it. This was going to be tiring, and there would be no resolution.

'Come in,' she said wearily. Mr Ken would be trapped in her alcove. 'I was in bed, I have been at work all day.'

'At that school.'

'I call it a school because that's what it is, but it is not a school-school. Everyone knows that. It is a way of teaching people.'

He glowered at her. 'Teach them to watch bad movies. Teach them that it is better to live in Beijing or Bombay or any other place than here.'

I have made a mistake, thought Mae. I should have spoken to him, and got him to agree. This mistake will take time to undo. Her fingers were burrowed into her uncombed hair.

'Teacher Shen. We have always been friends.'

'Yes!' he insisted.

'I am an impulsive person. I see something needs doing, I do it. I should have talked to you first and explained.'

'You should not set yourself up. You let your rivalry with Sunni carry you too far.'

Ow. That was true.

'Teacher Shen. Do you know any thing about Info?'

He resented that, though his expression did not change.

'We all need to learn about it. We need to learn about it, because soon we will spend half our lives in Info. And no one, not one of us, knows a thing about it. We will all become like little children again. We will all be lost unless we learn.'

His expression had not changed, but there was something helpless, frozen, about him. A poor peasant boy who fought and fought to learn, who gave everything to be allowed to be a Teacher.

And he was her friend – kind Shen, wise Shen, poor Shen. She saw in his face that he feared he had lost everything. He lived in a hovel in a village on a hill; he had given his life to trying to teach the children.

'You are right about Sunni,' she said softly. 'Sunni tries to take my farm, my business. She wants to take everything I have.'

His chin started to tremble. He knew the feeling well. 'They can't even read most of them,' he said, finally, and looked up at the ceiling. 'What did you show them today?'

'Bay Toh Vang. We heard a part of a symphony, and we had "Info" on him. I knew nothing about Bay Toh Vang.'

'They do not know their multiplication tables! And you are telling them, everything will be easy, just wish into the machine. You don't have to work. You don't have to learn.' Teacher Shen glared at her. 'You will make slaves of them.'

'No,' Mae said quietly. 'I will do the reverse of that.'

'Who puts Air into their heads? Who controls it? Who makes the things they see there? Do they? No. The great, huge, powerful things in the world do. You know how computers work, woman? By numbers. In the end, all those pictures, all those words, are just numbers. And these children cannot even add.'

Shen got up to go, sick at heart and unable to bear her and what she was bringing. 'Do you think any of my children went home and learned their arithmetic last night? Or were they humming the songs that Yu Op Pah wanted them to hum?' He had an old socialist hatred for the West.

'Tell them that, Shen,' said Mae. 'Tell them they must learn their numbers to control the machine.'

'When you call up Bay Toh Vang by toggling your right ear, by calling yourself "Madam Owl"?' He looked hunted, destroyed, and powerless. 'You talk about Sunni to get my sympathy. You have done what Sunni would do. That's what you have done to me, Teacher Owl.'

Shen stood up. Mae thought: I have lost a good friend.

'I don't want us to be enemies,' she called after him.

He was already in the courtyard.

She went after him. 'Shen, Teacher Shen, we are on the same side! We both want the same things!' She ran across the courtyard. 'Shen, please. Come to my school, use it yourself. You must find out about it, too!'

That was of course entirely the wrong thing to say. He spun on his heel and snarled at her like a dog, baring fangs, beyond words.

Mae stopped, her breath halted by the shock. And suddenly he was gone, down the street.

Stumbling back into her kitchen, she saw what he had flung at her. Her leaflet, of which she had been so proud.

Kuei was by the table, towel around his waist.

'That sounded terrible,' he said.

'Oh! I should have talked to him. But there wasn't time. There never seems to be enough time!' She was near to weeping. She went to her Kuei, and leaned against him, and he put an arm around her. Her head turned around and looked at her room.

Then she saw. She had not pulled the curtain fully shut behind her. Mr Ken's shoes were beside the bed, fully visible, and the pillow with two head marks. Mr Ken had hidden behind the curtain, but the curtain had a gap on either side of it.

Had he seen? Teacher Shen was both a friend and an enemy. Would he say anything? When and why would he say it?

Later that night, asleep in bed, Mae heard applause.

She lifted up her head. The sound came from all around the house, as if the hills were a theatre thronged with people. She got up and, half asleep, stepped out her front door.

Bam.

Mae was shaking with terror and up to her thighs in mud in her own courtyard. She was wringing with sweat and panic. Mud and water were pouring through the open gate. Part of her had to pause to check: Yes, this is my house, my house in a flood.

Everything else in her danced – fingers, knees, bladder. For some reason her first thought was for Ken Kuei's mother.

Somehow this Mae was carrying a flashlight. She shone light across the courtyard at the battened windows and the closed doorway. Mae had to fight through the mud towards Mr Ken's house. The mud was a heavy, slow evil, and there were sharp rocks inside it. *What . . . when?*

Flood, said a voice. It was Old Mrs Tung.

Mae could see shelves of water moving over the surface of the mud, each one a millimetre deeper than the last.

I told you there would be a flood.

'Mrs Ken!' Mae called again. If there were no one left in the old house, she would run. Where was Mr Ken? Where was anyone?

Behind her, outside, she heard the entire hillside move.

'The terraces are going!' Mae screeched.

Then she dropped back again, to some version of now. Sweat trickled from her, and she knew she had seen the future.

The Flood was coming again.

10

Sunni hired a minibus with rows of seats to take her customers to Green Valley City.
Mae was in her terraces working and saw the van drive out of the village. It stopped on the road below her.

Mae's eyes were sharp. So were Sunni's. Sunni leaned out of the window and stared up at Mae over the top of sunglasses. Sunni's hair was perfect under a blue scarf. She said something. Inside the van, Mrs Ali looked around Sunni to see Madam Owl at work in her fields. Mrs Nan, Miss Ping . . . all peered up at her.

This is stupid, thought Mae. She keeps trying to poop on me in such tiny ways.

Mae grinned and smiled and waved as if at friends. She felt like turning and pointing her arse at them. Did they really take such delight in knowing that she had to work?

Mrs Ali said something and patted Sunni on the shoulder. Having exposed Madam Death as a mere peasant, the van of the other party drove off towards the City.

Mae found she really didn't care. She chuckled and went back to work. Her hills were beautiful.

Her husband had found work; whatever happened, she would have some kind of business; her school was a success. Joe would come home, and then, perhaps like childbirth or mourning, the thing with Mr Ken would have to end.

The rice whispered in the wind as it had done for two thousand years. At times the world seemed good and at peace and happy. Mae knew this was only a respite, for life was a constant struggle. Bird eats worm, bird has its eggs, and those eggs are eaten. The rice is beautiful and then cut down. People melt into the earth while yearning for the sky.

In the afternoon, Mae taught her school. At sunset, walking home from teaching the children, Mae saw a van come jostling up Lower Street.

Oh, this is Sunni's circus, she thought. Well, I can wave just as prettily again.

The van squealed to a halt at the tight corner. The driver did not know the road. The sunset light made everything look golden, but his van actually was a beautiful flaked metallic gold.

'Excuse me,' said the driver. Balshang face, Balshang accent. 'Can you tell me where lives Mr Wing?'

Mae thought quickly. 'Yes, indeed, but it will be easier if I show you. May I?'

The man's face did not change. For a moment, he was silent, and then said, 'Please.' He pushed open the door for her.

The back of the van was jammed with tools, books, a suitcase, and a hastily rolled-up blue tent. The metal pegs had earth jammed into their grooves.

He asked her, 'How soon to harvest here?' He was young – very young indeed, to own such a fine van. He was incredibly skinny. The biggest thing about him was his hair: young, thick, springy, and forced under a hat. It was a completely useless hat. It was soft and khaki-green and had no brim. It would not keep off the sun, but it would make the head hot. He wore tiny glasses and smiled benignly. There was a gentle air about him that made Mae want to warn him: Be careful where you choose to sleep alone in that tent.

'It is just under a month,' said Mae. 'The men will be back soon.'

'They try to find work. Ah,' he said. His mouth jerked in a strange downward motion.

The van revved up the sudden steep slope towards Mr Wing's house. 'Why – is there a problem with work?' Mae asked.

'Huh,' said the man. It was a kind of a laugh. 'Haven't you heard?'

'We get no news up here,' said Mae.

'Ho. Just that there is none. The entire country is moving, looking for work.'

He eased the van into Mr Wing's courtyard. Dashboard lights flashed and he flipped something off and swung himself out of the van. Mae followed. He stood, hands on hips, regarding the house.

'These old mountain houses are very fine,' he said. 'It is lovely to be so cool. Mr Wing keeps his television outside?'

'That is so the village can use it. I teach on it.'

He turned. He was very young, but with a crease down either side of his mouth that only skinny men get. 'What do you teach?'

'How to use the TV. What Air will be like. I call it Swallow School. So people can fly in the Air.'

'Hmm,' he said. 'What's your name?'

'Mae,' she said.

'No,' he said. 'Your full name.' He paused. 'I'm from the government.' He seemed to think this would reassure her.

Mae did not answer. 'There is Mrs Wing.'

Kwan was coming down her steps, a question on her face.

'He's from the government,' warned Mae, wincing.

'Mrs Wing? Is your husband here?' the man asked.

'My husband is visiting his many farms, to see how things progress,' said Kwan.

'I . . .' he began and thought better of it. *I did not expect an Eloi,* is what he wanted to say. 'I am from the Central Bureau of Information Technology,' he announced. 'We are very concerned to see how the Test went.'

Kwan maintained a faultless exterior. 'That was some months ago.'

'Yes. There are many villages. I am visiting them all, to inspect the damage, and to help prepare people for what is coming next year.'

'We are doing that for ourselves,' said Mrs Kwan. She inclined her head towards Mae. 'Mae has been helping us all.'

'So I hear,' said the Central Man. He beamed and nodded approval. 'It is not so in other places.'

'It is so here,' said Kwan.

'Good. And your TV. It works well?'

'Oh, very well,' said Kwan, not sounding like herself at all. Her smile stiffened and her eyes glistened with meaning at Mae. She wants him away from her TV, thought Mae.

'Good. The Central Bureau of Information Technology gave him a grant, no?'

Kwan fluttered. 'I am afraid I know nothing of my husband's business.'

Mae changed the subject as if it were a rug under his feet. 'Do you need a place to stay? You see, my neighbour has spare rooms now. You could park your van in my courtyard.'

Kwan waved another flag of distraction at him. 'Oh yes, poor Mr Ken. You might like to talk to him. It is so sad. His wife was driven mad by the Test and drowned herself, and his grandmother died of shock.'

The Central Man looked stricken. He shook his head. 'Such foolishness,' he said.

'We are not educated people,' said Kwan, casting her eyes down.

'That's not what I meant,' he said. 'I mean it was foolish to have that Test.'

A Central Man, saying the government was wrong? Either he was young and foolish, or very dangerous. Kwan and Mae exchanged further anxious glances.

The Central Man looked pained. 'Were . . . I am sorry to have to ask, Mrs Wing-ma'am: Did anyone else in this village die in the Test?'

'No, no, those were the only people.'

'Such a terrible thing, two in one house.'

Kwan's eyes were on Mae's again.

Child voices sounded outside the gate, whispering in wonder. Mae said, 'Sir, the children have seen your van. If you want to drive anywhere, we'd better go now.'

The truth of it made Kwan and Mae laugh, as water does on a skillet. 'She's right,' said Kwan.

The Central Man made the same, embarrassed-looking downward jerk of the mouth. He nodded, put on his useless hat again, and said, 'May I come back to talk to you tonight?'

'Of course,' Kwan replied. 'But it is Mae you really need to talk to.'

'Ah,' said Mae. 'The rough little monkeys have seen us.' Dawn and Zaynab peered grinning out at them from behind the gate, and the Pins crowded behind them.

'Oops,' the man said, and broke into an ungainly hobble.

As the van bumped back down Lower Street, the perfect thing happened.

Sunni and her busload heaved up over the hill into the little square. The Central Man swerved his golden car to miss them.

Mae stuck her head out the window and grinned and waved. Ms Haseem, Mrs Ali, Miss Ping: Their faces fell to see Chung Mae in a golden car of her own. 'Hello! Hello!' she called, smiling and nodding.

The Central Man was grinning, too.

'So those are the opposition, are they?'

Mae felt endangered. 'What do you mean?'

He changed gear and his van inched forward. 'Oh. The Test has created much trouble in villages like this one. You'll have to tell me where to drive.'

How about back to Balshang? Mae thought to herself.

The government van fitted neatly through the gate of Mae's courtyard.

Mr Ken's hens scattered, the dog started to bark, and his youngest daughter came running out to stare at the golden van.

Old Mrs Ken emerged, wiping her hands.

Mae bowed to her lover's mother. She exchanged formulaic greetings and then Mae explained: *This gentleman needs a spare room.* Old Mrs Ken looked doubtful.

Then the Central Man said, 'I can pay you five riels a night.'

Mae was dumbfounded. My God, I could have paid back the interest on the loan!

Mae had to endure Old Mrs Ken's sunburst of a smile. She bowed and bowed again to Mae, delighted at receiving such bounty from a neighbour. 'It will be an honour and privilege!' she exclaimed. 'It will bring happiness into our house again. Dear Mrs Chung, you think of your neighbours too much, you are too kind. Oh, no, sir, let us carry your things. Kuei! Kuei!' She called her son's name.

Ken Kuei emerged, having just bathed. He puts the city man to shame, thought Mae, as Mr Ken lifted up the Central Man's case. Kuei was round like ripe fruit; the Central Man was stricken bushes on a plain.

The Central Man said, 'Mrs Chung, I must talk to you some more, once I am settled in.'

'Of course,' said Mae.

Her house was dark inside. She drank water, ate cold rice, and felt suddenly alone. It was strange having Old Mrs Ken smile on her. If Kuei's mother had known the truth, she would have beaten her breast and called down scandal from the village all around.

The thought was as cold as the rice, as the silence: how am I going to find my way out of all of this?

And then the government spy came back in.

'Excuse me,' he said.

'You are the government,' she said, and shrugged, meaning, *How am I to stop the government?* His golden vehicle was the colour of sunlight through her one tiny window. Poverty was shabby around her shoulders, like a moth-eaten shawl.

'I'm not the government,' he said. 'Well . . . I come from it, but we are all Karzistanis. We care for our country. May I?'

He indicated a chair. What would you say, Central Man, if I denied the chair to you? Probably, Mae decided, nothing.

He finally remembered formalities and offered Mae his name. It made Mae close her eyes and smile, embarrassed for him.

His name was Oz Oz.

Last names had been adopted only in the last century. People chose their own for good luck. *Oz* in the Turkic language of the Karz meant 'real' and 'genuine,' and sometimes, 'naive.' The Central Man's name meant 'Mr Genuinely Sincere.'

Mr Sincere tapped the top of the table. 'The Test was far too soon,' he said. 'And Karzistan is not a powerful enough country to stop it. And,' he sighed, 'it would have been wrong to stop it, because the Test would have come, but it would have been run by big companies.'

She stared back at him.

'Big companies, owned by very rich people. They would have run the Test instead. You have heard of the Yu En? United Nations?'

She shook her head. I am an ignorant peasant.

'They decided to have the Test. The world's governments. I know: governments are not people. But they are better than big companies. Do you now how the Air works?'

'It depends what you mean.'

'All right. In a computer, there is a plate. And that plate holds Info.' He took one of her dishes as an example. 'Now, to hold any Info, it must be patterned.'

'Like embroidery?'

'It must be divided into circles, Like this. And sections, like a pie, like this, and then certain kinds of areas must be created.'

'Like the pens,' she said. 'You mean the Format.'

'Exactly!' he said. 'The Format. So. The question was this: Did we want big companies, rich men, making the shapes of people's minds?'

Mae grew solemn. 'I see,' she said, sitting forward.

His strange long monk's face looked at hers. Did she?

'The Yu En felt it had to prevent that. So it came up with a different Format. It was a Format that . . . that would allow more companies, more countries to join.'

'You didn't want the big companies to run people's brains,' said Mae.

'Yah,' he nodded.

'So you pushed through the Yu En Test to be first.' And, Mae thought, that's what killed people.

'I didn't push it,' he said quietly.

All you Central Men. You never say anything is your fault.

'Tuh. The big men behave like the little villages,' said Mae.

They walked back to Kwan's house.

Mae tried to delay the Central Man as long as she could, by talking about the deaths of Mrs Ken Tui and Old Mrs Tung, until he began to show signs of exasperation. As they walked, the village children, out well past bedtime, flocked around him.

Pin Soon yelped, 'You work for the government?' He gazed up at the Central Man in something like admiration.

'Yes.'

'Are you rich?'

'No.' Mr Oz chuckled. 'No one who works for the government is rich.'

'My brother is in the army and he is rich.'

'Ah. The army. That is a different thing. What rank is he?'

Pin Soon looked blank, a bit ashamed. He didn't know. 'He drives a truck!' he announced proudly.

The Central Man asked, 'Do you go to Mrs Chung's school?'

'Yes, yes,' he piped. ' "Old Madam Death," we call her.'

The Central Man looked uncertain. 'Why is that?'

'Because the "Education" sign is an owl!' giggled Dawn, who still could not believe the stupidity of such a thing.

Mae watched for it, and saw the quick downward jerk of the mouth. An embarrassment at a certain kind of awkwardness in the world. It reminds him of himself, Mae thought.

'I asked them to call me Madam Owl, so that they would come to think in a different way about the owl.'

'Let's hope it helps,' he replied. He stopped at Kwan's gate, and turned towards the children. 'Okay. I am now visiting with Mrs Kwan, and she will not want to be bothered with so many children. So you all go home now.'

'We want to ask you more questions,' said Dawn, and put her hand experimentally into his pocket. He pulled it out, but did not slap it.

'No candy,' he said, his smile going thin. 'I have none.'

Dawn giggled. 'I was looking for money.'

He was useless. 'Dawn. I will box your ears,' warned Mae.

Dawn was laughing too hard, twisting in the Central Man's grip.

'Dawn,' said Mae, her voice darkening.

'Okay, okay,' Dawn chuckled, and pulled back.

Mae said, in her best Madam Owl voice, 'All of you go home and go to bed. Go on!'

'It is the same everywhere,' the Central Man smiled.

Then why haven't you learned how to handle it? Mae thought. She pulled the gate shut and barred it.

Then the Central Man said an unexpected thing: 'Would you say that the opposition here falls along religious lines?'

Mae's eyes boggled in the dark. You had to be very careful raising questions like that, even with no one around.

' "Religious lines?" ' she asked.

He laughed aloud. 'All right. It has in many places. Some of the minority tribes are very superstitious about it. They think the voices are ghosts or demons or something. Some of the Muslims are very welcoming.'

'We have had no trouble like that,' said Mae.

'Hmm. Well, this village is one of the best I've seen,' said Mr Oz.

Kwan was settled on her floor, sitting cross-legged. It looked as though she was writing letters. She gathered them up quickly. Mae caught her gaze and Kwan's eyes twinkled. She had done whatever it was needed doing to the TV. She went to make tea, cheerful and expansive.

The Central Man asked questions, one after another after another. They were as many as grains of rice in a terrace. Kwan yawned.

'Look, you want answers to all of these things, Mae has done a Question Map.'

'What?' He sat forward.

Oh, many thanks, Kwan.

'It was nothing,' said Mae, and she glared at Kwan.

'What do you mean, it was nothing? What did you do?' the Central Man asked.

Kwan realized her mistake: 'Oh it was a trifle.'

'A Question Map means that you go and ask everyone in the village the same questions. Is that what you did?'

Mae still could not lie. 'Yes,' she admitted. 'But it was about fashion.'

'But did it deal at all with the Test? What people felt about it? Can I see it?'

Mae's eyes narrowed and she let them drill into Kwan's. Unseen behind him, Kwan did a quick, abject bow of apology.

'I gave it to Kwan,' said Mae, still angry.

'Oh, that's right. Now, where did I put it? You know, I think Luk must have thrown it out. He thought it was just useless paper.'

The Central Man begged. 'Please let me see it, please!' The young man was very earnest. 'You don't know how important it is. No one talks to me, I am supposed to do research, but if I do it the way they want, no one will talk to me. But we need to know. We need to know, if we are to help you!'

He looked back and forth between them. I almost think I should believe you, thought Mae. But you are a government spy.

He was in despair, he ran his hand across his forehead. 'Most people are pretending it did not happen,' he said. 'They are learning nothing. They are not making ready. It will come again, as sure as winter comes. It will come next April.'

He twisted in his chair. 'And I have to be able to tell the government. They must spend money; they must send teachers out into the villages to prepare. The Test was a disaster. A disaster, but going on Air will be an even bigger one!' His fists clumsily punctured the air in frustration.

All right, so I believe you, thought Mae. You are a nice, sad, powerless boy. Why should I trust the government?

He was a boy, but not a stupid one. 'I won't tell anyone you showed it to me. I know, I know, your neighbours will think you betrayed them to a government spy. But let me see it, so I know how it affected them, I don't need their names. But I do need to be able to go back and say to the government: "They need help." We need to listen to people to find out how to help them!'

His two fists were bunched together.

Mae relented. 'We feel the same way, you and I.'

He breathed out in relief.

'But governments never help the likes of us, we are too far away from everything.'

'That is why I need to see what you have done! Look, the people in government have sons in the army. You all have sons in the army. Do you think our sons wish the people harm? Or do they want the Karzistani people to succeed?'

'Not all of us are Karzistani,' said Kwan. Her face and voice were pinched.

Mr Oz had no argument against that. He slumped slightly. 'A terrible mistake has been made. If the government won't help you, who will?'

'We help ourselves,' said Kwan.

'You're about the only ones who have,' he muttered, more to himself than to them.

'My Question Map was about fashion,' said Mae. The very idea now struck her as absurd, silly. 'I did it to find out how the Air would change my business.'

'What did you find out?' he asked quietly.

'That the village has died,' Mae said, equally quietly.

Mae realized that she had been hearing a clock ticking for some time. What clock, where?

'How do you mean?' he asked.

'I mean . . . I mean our children will become like children everywhere else. They will play computer games and learn everything and the very last of the old ways will go. Absolutely everything we know and love will go. They will have supermarkets here, and streetlights, and the men will drive Fords, not vans or tractors.'

Mae looked around Kwan's room. There definitely was no clock. But it ticked.

Mae heard the sirens again. She turned slowly and looked and saw that outside Kwan's window the air was full of orange light as if their village life were burning. She knew she was staring at the future again. She stood and walked, as if on a ship at sea, and stared out from Kwan's high window.

There was a blimp with neon lights advertising an electronic address, tethered to the courtyard gate. There were tables full of people in the courtyard. This house was now a restaurant. The streetlights were yellow and they fell far away, all across the valley and up the other side, and there were moving lights of cars all over the valley, and drifting music, from everywhere.

'Mae?' Kwan's voice was anxious. 'Mae!' Her hand was on Mae's shoulder.

Mae started to speak, in a voice that was not entirely her own. It was partly Old Mrs Tung's.

'All the old songs,' she said, 'and the old good manners – all that will go.'

From down below, in the restaurant, a drunk laughed loudly.

'We used to work all together in Circles, and take turns to bring the lunches, and all of us who could read, we'd recite the poems for the ladies. Not . . . not pop songs . . . not some song in English, but our own great, great poetry, words that had meaning. We would read the Mevlana.'

And Mae or Mrs Tung or someone started to cry. ' "Listen to the reed, how it tells a tale . . ." '

'Mae, Mae!' Kwan was saying over and over. 'Mae, come back.'

'We made our own clothes, we smoked our own tobacco, we didn't worry about hairspray and makeup. What counted was how strong a woman was, how much she could lift. In winter, wives cooked in teams, one set of wives making the soup all day, another set of wives making the goulash all day, everybody ate, no one was lonesome. On the first day, the Muerain would call on God and give us wisdom, and the next day the priest in his robes would bless the food, and on the third day, the Communist read from his little red book. And in Kizuldah all three were the same man!'

Mae watched her hands wringing a tea towel over and over. 'And we're destroying it! We have to destroy it to live!'

Kwan was speaking quietly, but she was turned towards the Central Man. 'You asked me if anyone else died during the Test. Mae did. She was in someone else's head and they died, and Mae came back a different person. She gets like this, she joins the dead, she loses herself. She was always so beautiful. Your Test did that to my friend. I'm very angry at your Test. I'm very angry at all you people.'

And Mae saw on Kwan's stern face a single, slow tear.

The Central Man sat with a hand covering his mouth.

Was that true, what Kwan had said? Was she – Mae – in that condition?

'I'm sorry,' the Central Man managed to whisper.

'Huh,' said Kwan. *A lot of use that is.*

The noise from the restaurant below faded. This room became clearer, as if someone had turned on many extra lights.

Mae decided something. 'I will let you see my Question Map,' she said.

Back in Mae's house, Mr Oz read the Question Map, shaking his head over and over.

Mae said, 'I will let you have it to take away, if you tell me everything you know about Air.'

Mr Oz read the Question Map, shaking his head over and over.

Mae kept on: 'Yu En. Gates. All that stuff.'

He looked up at her. 'How?' he said. 'The quantitative data has been entered into a spreadsheet and computed. The qualitative material . . . How did you know how to do this? This is a structured piece of research.'

'In Air. There is a Kru in Air.'

The Central Man went very still indeed. 'You go back into Air? You are not supposed to be able to do that.'

'When . . . I had my accident. To get out, I made myself an Airmail address.'

'How did you do that?'

'It's my name.'

'They're not still Aircasting,' he said, perplexed.

'The Kru is still there.'

'He shouldn't be. He's copyright, he agreed to do it only for the Test.' His mouth did its downward twist.

'You people,' said Mae, 'you don't really know what Air is, do you?'

'You're right,' said the Central Man. 'We don't.'

He explained. The Kru was a great businessman, a rival of the company that made the Gates Format. He had donated his expertise as a demonstration for the Test of the Yu En Format. The deal *wasn't* that he would go on forever, giving away everything he knew for free. Everyone had assumed it would end with the Test.

'Mrs Tung is always with me,' said Mae.

Mr Oz left, going across the courtyard. Mae heard Old Mrs Ken greet him with all the gusto that five riels a night could purchase. Mae smelt chicken cooking for the generous guest. She sat down and wondered if Kuei would be able to visit her now, with all of his house in an uproar.

I am like someone in mourning.

Of course you are in mourning, said Old Mrs Tung.

It was a dull, kind voice.

We all want an anchor, we all want to turn the corner to go home. But home always goes away. Home leaves us. And we get older and then older again, and farther away from home. From ourselves. We die before we die, my dear. We go from village beauties to old crones; from mischievous children to weary adults; from ripe maidens full of love to embittered, used women full of bile. And all we have is love. With nothing to love. Just the love, aching out, reaching out and never clasping love in return.

Just the reeds, just the swallows, just the mist in the air, the sunlight in the air, just the sound of the wind. That never changes. That is all the home we have.

Dear Old Mrs Tung.

Sleep, my dear.

For all the beauty we have lost, and all the beauty we will lose.

11

The next morning Mr Oz and Mae found two groups of armed men in Mrs Wing's courtyard.

On one side were Mr Shen, Mr Koi, and Mr Masud. They were all either Eloi or old-fashioned Muslims.

Against them stood Mr Mack, Mr Pin, Mr Ali, and Old Mr Doh.

Shen said, 'We are bringing this to a stop.'

Mae read the two sides: Mr Ali was of Sunni's party. He was here to help save Kwan's machine. An alliance against Shen, so quickly? Mr Ali had brought his own gun: that would mean Shen had already threatened Mr Haseem. There was a clicking sound. Lean, brown, hard, Mr Wing stood on his steps. He held a Russian rifle with the hammer pulled back. He said, 'That does not belong to you, Shen.' From out behind him stepped Enver Atakoloo. He also had a gun.

Mae stepped forward and gave both parties a bow of respect. She said quietly, to Shen, 'Bring what to a stop, Teacher?'

Shen pointed at the TV. 'We don't want *that* in our village.'

'I am sure it is for you men to decide,' Mae said, sweetly. Like a cat with humans, she had a voice she only ever used with men. 'But, Teacher. Consider. You won't be able to keep out the Air when it comes.'

The Central Man felt the time had come for him to intervene with his full authority. 'Mrs Chung is right. The TV will help you prepare for April.'

Mae wanted to smile at him and weep at the same time. Poor boy, this is happening because you have arrived. You will be invisible to them, like an angel. Untouchable, but also invisible.

Mr Shen's answer was simply to walk to the TV with his rifle-butt raised to smash it.

The sky ripped open. Guns had always sounded like firecrackers to Mae, a pop, and a snap. She had always been surprised by how small they seemed.

Now, trapped within the courtyard, the sound of a gunblast battered around the enclosed space. Mae jumped, covered her ears. *Please, God, no one has been hurt.* She looked up. The guns were pointed at the sky. From all around the village, birdcalls billowed up into the air: screeching, shrieking, and cawing.

Everything in the courtyard was frozen. No one moved.

Mae said, 'At least that got the birds off the rice.' It was the first thing she thought.

Mr Doh, Mr Ali, and Mr Mack burst into laughter.

'It's true,' said Mae, confused. Mr Mack nodded – yes it was.

Shen stood trembling, rifle still raised.

Mr Wing warned him: 'Don't be a vandal, Shen. The government man is here to see it, you will end up in court, and it will not be because anyone betrayed you to them. Eh? Don't be foolish.'

Shen was pointing. It was hard to tell if he pointed at Wing or Kwan. 'You . . . stay . . . away from my wife!' he demanded.

All the laughter stopped. *What?*

Wing looked perplexed. 'What madness now, Schoolteacher?'

Silence. From the western reaches of the village came the roaring of a motorcycle.

Kwan stepped out from her diwan, onto the landing. 'He means me,' she said. 'Suloi and I are working together on a project.'

Mae felt a stirring of misgiving. Kwan and Shen's wife? When? What were they doing?

There is something my friend Kwan has chosen not to tell me.

The roar of the motorcycle grew louder. Sezen's boyfriend came through the open gate, on his cycle, Sezen riding behind. Another Bad Boy from the Desiccated Village Kurulmushkoy followed, his machine black with grease. Sezen's boyfriend hopped off, pudgy and carrying a length of pipe.

Sezen's boyfriend said, 'The machine stays.'

Shen was helpless. He looked to the old men of his party. 'You see the elements who will triumph from this thing.' Shen started to weep. 'Look at them! They think this is a Hong Kong movie. Guns and motorcycles! This is how the world will now be. With women running rampant with foolish ideas. Bad children, running wild.'

A division seemed to break inside Mae's head, as if blood had found a fresh way to flow. She suddenly remembered the angry driven child within Teacher Shen. She saw him as a little soul, to be protected. Her eyes blurred over as if milk were inside them, and her throat felt gnarled, rumbly.

'It has always been thus,' Mae heard herself say, as if she were sitting back and listening to someone else.

The voice from inside her spoke. 'There has always been one big change after another. But we always think our first world was permanent. Shen, my little bright boy. Your world came just after the Russians drove out the Chinese. Before you were born, the Eloi were fighting a war against the Chinese. Guerrillas would take over our houses. Our husbands were shot as rebels for sheltering them. We had to give our grain to the Red Guards. Before that it was the village strongman. There is no old way to go back to, Shen. My brightest little boy, are you still too young to see that?'

Shen was looking at a ghost. The tears seemed to have frozen on his face, going creamy with salt in the sunlight.

Mae began to feel giddy, divorced from her own body. Her fingers were numb. 'You cannot bring back the old world. Which old world do you want?'

The Central Man was staring at her. Mack, Doh, they all looked at their shoes.

Mae's forehead was covered in thick sweat. The corner of her vision went dark and gritty. 'I have to sit down,' she said, and fainted.

Mae woke up in Kwan's guest room, lined with cushions.
Grim-faced, Kwan was mopping her brow.

'We saved the TV,' she said.

There was business at hand. Mae responded: 'We had Sunni's people on our side.'

Kwan nodded briskly. 'I fight against my brother, until my cousin attacks him.'

'The Central Man frightened them.'

'Everything frightens them,' said Kwan, with real scorn. 'I never had any respect for Teachers.'

Mae chuckled. 'You hid it well at school.'

Kwan shrugged. 'They held the keys.'

'What are you and Mrs Shen up to?'

Kwan paused, worked her mouth. 'I should have told you,' she said.

Mae was ready. Info Lust. It made people hide things.

Kwan sighed. 'Suloi and I have put screens on the Net.'

Mae didn't know what she meant.

'We put screens about our people. On TV.'

Mae sat up in wonder.

'You did what?'

Kwan stared back at her, a little bleary with guilt, a little obstreperous: What business was it of Mae's? 'You sit up, you're well enough now to see,' she said. She stood up, not waiting for Mae to follow.

Mae walked through the shuttered room, following Kwan out into the porch. The TV had been moved up from the courtyard to the landing. Something had scratched its side. Below on the courtyard stones a dark stain sweltered. Blood? Grease?

Kwan's fingers danced on a keyboard. Words in English rattled on the screen.

'Audio. Karz output, Eloic input,' Kwan ordered. 'Volume down.'

Then she gave orders in the language of her people. Her language flapped and cawed like a raven and seemed to make Kwan into a different person, less considered, more urgent.

Up came a photograph of Eloi embroidery.

The television murmured as if it had a secret. *'The Eloi people are an ancient race, now living in the mountainous region of Karzistan. Karzistan is on the borders of China, Tibet, and Khazakstan. These screens have been created by the Eloi people themselves.'*

The screens offered 'Arts.' Under 'Arts,' Suloi and Kwan sang in high straining voices. In video, they told old stories, while English words danced around them. There were screens of tattoo patterns. Kwan's patient voice explained their meaning. Mae recognized the neatness and complexity of the tattoo outlines. Kwan had drawn them. The patterns, like Kwan, were restrained and somehow private.

Next, the meaning of the embroidered Eloi breastplates was explained. These collars were worn by courting men and their betrothed. Note, the television said, that the beads all form straight parallel lines symbolizing two lives in conjunction.

Photographs of the old forts, tales of Eloi heroes against the Cossacks, the Turks, and the Chinese. A history of war.

A section on the 'Heroes,' meaning the men who fought against the Communists.

'Few people in the West even knew of the conflict. It lasted for generations and ended in defeat for the Communists and the creation of

a new republic. We thought it would be for all the people, not just the Karzistani majority.'

Behind Kwan's voice, shepherds began to sing. They sang of heroism, about living in the hills and praying to all their various gods, smoking thin cigarettes in freezing winds under clear stars. Heroes rolled rocks down onto the heads of troops, only to find that the crushed bodies were those of their cousins conscripted into the Communist armies.

Photographs, in smeared black-and-white, were shown. Handsome young Eloi dead stared up at the sky, their chins missing. Handsome young Eloi, alive around fires, their eyes burning with this message: *I may die, but it will be worth it. We are the people who stopped the Chinese, who stopped the Arabs. The Eloi are the world's great secret force against tyrants.*

Where did Kwan get these photos?

Then Mae remembered: Kwan's father, dear Old Mr Kowoloia.

Dear Old Mr Kowoloia must have been a terrorist. Kwan had these photos. She has kept them secret from all of us.

So this is why she wanted the Central Man gone.

'Kwan, is this wise?' Mae asked.

'The site is locked against any instructions in Karzistani. Only in Eloi or in English.'

On came the video of the Karzistani woman in her new Balshang apartment. Kwan's recorded voice grew harsher.

'Listen closely to the Eloi woman, torn away from her people, praising refrigerators. Her voice is rehearsed, her eyes fearful. For she knows: Her people are being destroyed.'

Mae looked over her shoulder. What if the government man should hear? She looked back, and saw: Kwan's hands were two pale fists, the skin over the knuckles dead white. With rage.

'We appeal to the world. Do not let this great and graceful people disappear from history. All you need do is show that you are interested in us, as you once were when we controlled the passes through which wound the Silk Road to China.'

'Sleep,' ordered Kwan.

Mae breathed out. 'I'll keep that spy away.' No wonder you had not told me. Tell the truth, Mae.

'I am jealous,' said Mae. 'I had vague plans to learn how to do that. You went and did it. How?'

'After you left,' said Kwan.

'From four A.M. to seven A.M., every day?'

Kwan nodded. 'Suloi and me together.'

'Wing did not know?'

'He did not care,' said Kwan, and stood up, graceful, dignified. *Eloi*, thought Mae. *Every particle of her soul is Eloi, and I did not know that, so I did not know her. Like her screens, she is locked away. You must speak Eloi, to have the key.*

'Will . . . Will you teach me how to do that?' Mae burned to know.

Kwan looked bleary now from confession and the exhaustion that follows. 'The TV will do a better job of that than I can,' she said. She took Mae's hand and slapped it as if in apology. *Do not be surprised – you are my dear Mae, but you are also Chinese in the end: the enemy.*

Kwan lit a cigarette. She pulled a bit of stray tobacco from the tip of her tongue. 'The real question is: What is the nature of our alliance with Sunni?'

Mae shook her head. This was all moving very quickly. 'Not very strong,' she replied.

Kwan turned to Mae. 'Do you want to destroy Sunni?'

'She tries to destroy me,' said Mae.

'Do you wish to see her destitute?'

Mae shrugged. 'No. I don't wish anyone in the village to be destitute. Why?'

Kwan was really very strange. She seemed to uncoil like a serpent, pushing herself away from the TV box.

Kwan sighed. 'TV does not come free, you know.'

Mae waited.

'It comes like calls on a mobile phone. Every time you choose something, you pay. Our government subsidy pays Mr Wing's telephone bills so the TV gets used for the entire village. But the telephone company will charge everyone else. We administer for them.'

Kwan unfolded a blue, official-looking piece of paper. 'I told Faysal Haseem that. But you know how he is: "Uh, you charge twice, you try to trick me, I no pay you!"' Kwan did a remarkably good job of imitating him. 'So I didn't tell him again. The first month's bill is fifty riels.'

Mae felt nothing; or rather, she felt a balancing that left the scales at zero. 'We need him as an ally.'

'What I was going to do, was let it get to one hundred and twenty-five riels, and then say: "My husband's company will cover these costs. Even though we warned you. We will do this if you write off the loan to Chung Mae."'

'That was very kind,' said Mae. She could imagine it: Sunni's face held like it was fragile porcelain as Mae kept the money without paying it back. She could see Faysal Haseem glower.

And she could see herself in debt to Wing Kwan in other ways.

'We will drop all this rivalry,' said Mae. In the end you had to support your own against the government, or even the telephone company.

Kwan smiled, pleased, 'I thought so.'

Sunni's TV set was on even at eleven at night.

It flickered in Mr Haseem's courtyard, showing a fashion parade. Mae hid her smile. Is that as far as Sunni had got with it? To choose picture shows?

Only one person was watching. Mrs Ali turned in her chair, saw Mae, and blinked.

'Good evening, Mrs Chung,' Mrs Ali said after a moment.

'Mrs Ali.' Mae bowed. 'I wish to speak to Mrs Haseem-ma'am.'

Mrs Ali considered. 'I will tell her you are here.'

'I will need to talk to her alone,' said Mae.

Mrs Ali did not respond, except to push her chair back and walk into Sunni's kitchen.

In the courtyard, the Talent chattered. *It would seem that bright colours once again adorn fashion in the West. Could it be our own local Green Valley designers are in the lead?*

Mae heard real voices murmuring in the kitchen. She heard the rumble of Mr Haseem, but she judged he would stay out of this unless there was some kind of argument. If there were some kind of argument, it would give him an excuse to be abusive. He would not wish to take part without that chance.

Mae was not here to apologize. She was here to get both sides to see sense. And out of that sense, to get advantage for herself.

Mrs Ali was in the kitchen doorway, outlined in electric light. 'Please come in,' she said in a quiet voice. She stood away from the door, and reassured Sunni's whining dog as Mae approached. Mae gave her a polite nod, and entered Sunni's room.

A modern stove had replaced the old brazier. It seeped raw gas.

There were new white curtains in the tiny windows and a new metal top to the sink. All of these things meant fresh expense. Sunni sat behind her table, perfect as always, her hair a motorcycle helmet of crisp, hard shellac. She looked tense, insecure and arrogant. Mae found in herself a strain of pity for her, and brought that to the surface.

'Hello, Sunni,' she said.

'I hope it will be more of a pleasure to have you in my house than it was the last time.'

Mae gestured: *May I sit?* Sunni nodded yes, dismissively.

'Last time, both of us were angry. Both of us said things. I find life moves quickly these days. That night seems years ago now.'

Sunni made no reply. She certainly did not agree.

'I find after the events of this morning, that we have more in common than the disagreements which divide us.'

A brief moue flickered across Sunni's face; it was true, but it did not please her.

'We could cooperate for the common good. We both need the village to be prepared for what is to come. A possible agreement is this. We both do all we can to help our neighbours learn to use this new thing. In the meantime, both of us are free to pursue our commercial interests.'

Sunni was not really up to this kind of bargaining. Mae was well aware that she was talking like a man. It was the only way to avoid the pits of emotion on either side and keep all the issues separate.

'You speak as if we were in politics,' said Sunni, finally.

'Do you not think that we are? You and I both value the future. We are rivals, yes. But we certainly do not want the TVs destroyed. Both of us are intelligent women from the same village, and we do not want our village to fall behind.'

'That is true,' agreed Sunni.

'There is something else,' said Mae. 'Something I did not know until today.'

'And what might that be?' Sunni sounded unimpressed. She perhaps thought Mae was trying to be mysterious.

'There are telephone charges for using that thing.' Mae pointed into the courtyard.

From the courtyard, breathless commentary in a piping female voice continued: *'Again we see a new trend towards colour. Modern women have found time for joyful expression.'*

'I know,' said Sunni.

'Do you know how much?'

Sunni's face was blank. 'I am sure my husband does.'

'They are always on the lookout for special touches, something new which makes even the simplest dress different, expressing a new facet of their personality.'

'After a year, it could be as much as six hundred riels.' Mae paused, waited.

Sunni was very good. She did not flinch, she gave no sign. She began to sweep nonexistent crumbs of food from the table into her cupped hand. Still in silence, she raised her eyebrows as if to say: *So? What is your proposition?*

'For example, this dress expresses the model's interest in Third World issues.'

Mae took the plunge. 'Mr Wing can ensure that you do not have to pay them. He can arrange things so that they go to his account and the government will pay them.'

Sunni's visage did not alter in any respect.

'In exchange he wants the warfare between us to stop.'

'There is no warfare.'

'Sunni,' warned Mae.

'No, there is none.'

Mae quoted Sunni's leaflet. ' "Now that certain parties have been uncovered as offering false advice . . ." That is what you wrote about me, Sunni. It is one thing to set yourself up in business. It is another to call me a fraud and to invite your friends to mock me.'

'I will remind you of a certain incident on your screen,' said Sunni, darkening.

'Indeed. I have not forgotten. That is part of the war. It must stop, Sunni. While we play village games, the world is beating down our door. While we try to destroy each other, it will destroy us.'

'I will demand a full public apology,' said Sunni.

'I will demand that we both apologize to each other in public. At the same time. That way everyone knows: The TV people are united.'

'And I will need individual assessment of what you say about charges.'

Mae nodded. 'I can bring the government man here. No, Sunni, not to make trouble, please hear me out. I can make it look like a friendly visit. And you can ask him yourself: "The TV is new." I will say you have just bought it. "What kind of charges would I pay?" '

More crumb-sweeping. There was hurt behind Sunni's eyes.

'There is one more thing, Sunni. The loan. The terms of the loan will change. It becomes interest-free.'

And this was something Mae was keeping from Kwan. She did not want to be beholden to Kwan.

Sunni went still altogether. 'You know I cannot agree to that by myself.'

'You can perhaps talk to your husband.'

'I will see.'

'Just remember, Sunni, the bills mount up, all the time that thing is on.'

Sunni sighed. Oh, it was like wearing the wrong-size shoe, for her to be in a weak position. She was not used to cutting losses.

Sunni said, 'I could always have a word with the Central Man and mention to him whatever it is Mrs Wing and Mrs Shen are making.'

'Oh!' groaned Mae, in utter weariness. 'I am talking about an alliance that will benefit everyone. And you threaten me! Sunni, how can the village learn, if it has to ration the TV? Two machines will be much better than one. Can't you see? We both win, if we agree to this. Or, yes, we can both lose. Badly, very badly. Perhaps one of us will go to jail. But which one of us will be beloved in the village, Sunni, if you are known to have betrayed Mr Wing to the government?'

Sunni's gaze was not direct. 'I did not say that.'

'You said you would tell the Central Man, Sunni. You meant that you could betray Kwan and get the Wings into trouble. Didn't you?'

She was silent.

'Sunni. From the beginning, I have not wanted to be your enemy. If you tell yourself the tale of what has happened, you will see that the first hostile move was your husband's. And I am not always the most pleasant person in the world when I am angry. So, yes, I behaved badly.'

All Sunni wanted was to be first, and Mae was always ahead of her. Even now she had lost, for Mae was the first to propose peace *and* in such a way as to garner advantage.

Curiously enough, that was sufficient revenge.

'Talk to your husband, Sunni. That is necessary. The terms are simple. We are friendly rivals in business. We both work to teach the village. We both work against the party that wants the TVs off. And as a gesture, the loan becomes interest-free.'

It was all a bit of pretence. Mae was being clear, not for Sunni, but for Mr Haseem, whom she was reasonably certain could hear every word. Mae sat and waited.

Sunni's face was closed, not exactly in shame, but in hurt. How she wanted to be the village leader, the 'ma'am' of the village. But Kwan would always be that. Sunni would never be free, not until Kwan died. And by then it would probably be the turn of An, or someone like her. Mae found she did indeed pity Sunni. All that time with nothing to do because her husband would not let her work. Mae pitied her lack of application. Sunni, Mae knew, was not as smart as others.

Sunni said, 'I have the better fashion sense.'

Mae pondered this for a moment. 'I think you are probably right, Sunni.' For rich ladies, with money to spend, you are probably right. But you know, I think I will be the one to make the money. Mae chuckled to herself. 'You are certainly younger and better looking too.'

Sunni wasn't laughing. Sunni was not loved by a beautiful man, who cooked dinner for her, who had wanted her since he had been sixteen. Could Sunni stand to sleep with that harsh husband?

To be jealous is futile; we are all human, we all live in pain, and Sunni lives in more than most.

That does not give her the right to steal my shoes or stand on my toes.

'Sunni, I know you are very busy. Mrs Ali sometimes visits my lessons at Mrs Wing's. Perhaps she could tell me what you decide.'

Since you will not want to visit my hovel, or risk coming to Mrs Wing's.

'Is it really as much money as you say?' Sunni asked. Ah, money, the juice of life. At least yours. Their eyes finally met.

'Yes, Sunni, it is.' Mae stood up to go.

They exchanged polite greetings and Mae left.

Outside in the street, Mae felt a wild joy swing out of her, like when she had been a schoolgirl and flung her bag of books into the air. She was free of the interest on that loan! They would pay back twenty-five riels a year, and use the money as capital! She could use it to buy cloth or Joe could invest in the farm. Joe would bring back more money; they would be comfortable and happy.

She thought again that she must put distance between herself and Mr Ken. Otherwise the fabric of her life would be torn. She would tell Kuei that she would always love him, but that it was impossible to continue. She would hold the memory of him always to her, like pressed flowers hidden in schoolbooks, like clever old Mrs Tung and her secret love. And she would teach the TV and she would pick the brains of the Central Man.

Mae would learn to put up a screen, too, just like Kwan, only Kwan would wonder how she had learned so quickly.

A screen of what?

Of fashion? Of course, the whole world would want fashion from a mountaintop in mid-Asia. That was the very thing they lacked. Mae laughed at herself, and went, 'Wheeeeeee!' And spun, and saw Kwan's screens, of Eloi embroidery.

And suddenly she saw the screen slightly different. It offered Eloi embroidery for sale. The year's most unusual fashion statement. *Expressing the model's interest in Third World issues.*

Mae's smile was fading. Instead, excitement seemed to grip her stomach.

Native Eloi embroidery, unavailable except through these treasured outlets.

Either broaden what you make, or extend your geography, the Kru had whispered.

Videos could be sent for free to the big stores. She could tell the big stores about her Eloi fashion, and if they liked it, fine. *Then* she could buy the cloth and the bead.

Reduce your risk at every opportunity.

So she only makes them when she is paid.

Individually tailored to meet your requirements.

Oh! Oh, oh, oh, oh, oh! Her effrontery made her giggle. Sell to Singapore, Tokyo, Taiwan. Maybe even Paris or New York. The calls would be free, from Wing's magic free TV. Mae will send her offer with her pretty pictures, but it will not be fashion she is offering. She will offer something real, something from the mountain, something from a long-forgotten, beautiful people.

Love and ideas, how she loved her life now!

Visions of her screens danced in her head. She saw Kwan and Shen Suloi twirl in their embroideries; she heard the words: *Native Eloi beauties model the traditional wear of their people.*

This is the traditional wedding pattern. The yellow signs promise fidelity, the blue, understanding of foibles.

Mae's head seemed to swim, as if the air itself were a river, with currents. She felt herself picked up as if flying only a few inches above the road, and suddenly she saw her screens, very clearly indeed.

Mae saw her screens in fact. She was looking at the TV in a room at Kwan's house, not far into the future. Sunlight came through the window; her new screens glowed. In a video, Wing Kwan turned, modeling an Eloi collar.

This future would happen.

Why, then, sitting in that room in the future, did Mae feel sick in her stomach with loss? Why was she living with the Wings?

Mae shivered, and it was gone, this future full of promise and loss.

She went into her courtyard.

There were two men outside her doorway. A flashlight shone in her face. 'There she is,' said a voice.

'Who is it?' Mae asked, blinking. She saw movement, and she knew who it was from the way both bodies moved.

Joe was back. Shen stood with him.

'What is all this?' Joe demanded. 'What is all this about a man?'

12

The world stopped, like a truck.
'What is what?' babbled Mae, looking back and forth between the two
men. What do I do, what do I say, do I deny it, do I act like I have no
idea?

Shen, the serpent, looked at her with eyes that seemed green. He
seemed to be made of stained green copper like the statues in town of
forgotten generals. She hated him; she knew why he had done it. Shen
had decided to destroy her.

'You know, woman,' said Joe, and strode forward and hit Mae in
the face.

The flesh of her cheek was like a pond into which a rock is hurled. It
rose and rippled and washed about her eyes. Mae felt her nose give,
just to the point of breaking.

Mae allowed herself to be knocked backwards. She landed and lay
still to buy time for thinking.

'Joe, Joe,' she heard Shen say, gently restraining.

'Wake up, woman!' Joe demanded. He was leaning over her, she
could feel his breath. 'You cannot pretend with me!' His voice broke.
He shook her. Mae kept her head limp.

'That . . . uh . . . That was premature,' said Shen. 'She can answer
nothing now.'

'She is pretending. I know the vixen,' said Joe.

'Look at that bruise,' said Shen.

Mae's mind raced. Shen had seen only shoes and a shadow through
the curtains in her room. Can I undermine his story? He is a feeble
man; he will hate it that I have been hit. Can I make him retract
through guilt?

And Joe? Joe is weak as well, but he will be full of pain. I bet he's
come back with no money.

Mae groaned. She let the broken flesh and its black swelling speak
for her. She moaned and started to cry and held her cheek. She sat up,

on the cobbles of the yard, streaked with mud, and wept. The two men stood over her, one now constraining the other.

Joe was shouting. 'Well might you weep! Well might you weep!'

She was weeping for the happiness, the happiness that had been hers just a minute before. Mae wept for her marriage, her love of Mr Ken, her business. In the end, Mae wept for death. Many things would now die, little baby possibilities that she had been nursing. It was life. Dog eat dog.

'Joe, she's not up to answering much,' said Shen. He turned and tried to help her up. 'Come on, Mae. This has to be gone through.'

How was she going to play it? She could lie, try to disguise it, play the wounded and confused wife, but there was one problem. Shen had truth on his side and knew it. She saw that in his eyes. Fashion expert that she was, her powers of dissimulation were not up to it. She did not have the heart for it. She felt a gathering presence in her breast, a tension. She had decided to draw power by telling the truth.

She did not take Shen's hand. So, Shen, so you expected my poor farmer of a husband to react like a schoolteacher, did you? Ruin lives, but avoid making a mess. Is that what you thought you could do?

Mae rolled over and sat on the cobbles, near the ground, as if the ground could nurture her. She looked at Shen only. 'What you are doing is very evil,' she told him.

Shen warned her: 'I am not the one who has done harm here.'

'You are doing this because you want to stop the machine.' Mae said it wearily. 'You do not care about Joe. You will destroy him, destroy me.'

So be it.

'It is true, Joe,' she said, turning.

A throb of silence. 'Whore,' whispered Joe.

'Whores do it for money. I did it for love.' She still sat on the ground.

'You are not ashamed?' Joe was failing.

'A bit. Ashamed to be caught. I am the only woman in the village who has been caught.' She nursed her jaw. She would be a sight.

The two men rocked slightly.

She held forth while she still had the chance. 'What do you do when you are away, Joe? Eh? When you are drunk and looking like a comedian. You go with women.'

He looked comic now, hair askew, eyes bugged with both shock and sadness. He would not easily forgive being made to look so foolish. 'No,' he said in a wan voice. 'I . . . do . . . *not*.' His voice became fierce on the last line.

Oh, Joe. It was probably true. You probably did not. More fool, you.

'Who was it?' Joe demanded.

Shen said, 'That does not matter,' restraining Joe again.

Mae spoke. 'Oh no, you don't want *the man* to get into trouble, do you, Shen? You feel for the man. And more mess would weigh on your conscience.'

'Who is he?' demanded Joe; her foolish Joe going dark, fists clenched.

Shen sighed. 'Does it make a difference?' Which was exactly what Mae was going to say.

'I was so happy.' Joe was weeping. He pushed the palms of his hands into his eye sockets. 'I had looked all over for work, it took weeks, finally I found it, and there was this stupid thing and I had to go home. All I wanted to do was go home!'

'I was happy, too,' whispered Mae.

'Oh, yes,' said Joe, snatching away his hands. 'You were skipping. Back from your cock, you whore!'

The listening lights of the village were on. They reflected on the walls, on the clouds.

Mae's eyes were on the Teacher. 'Who do you think you have made more unhappy, Shen? Me or him?'

Shen did not answer.

'It was me,' said a male voice.

And that was Ken Kuei.

Oh, fine. Oh, good. You come in to take your share, to take your part of the blame. To protect me. Just when it all was quieting down, when Joe and I might have talked.

Why is goodness so stupid?

There he was, her handsome stupid man against her comic sad one, ranged in orange light, like fire, to burn. Joe's face said, in horror (Mae could see his thoughts): *My neighbour, Ken Kuei?*

Mae could see Joe think: *We will meet each other every day.*

Shen had covered his mouth in shock. Of course he would not have known who it was.

Mae said, 'Feeling proud, Shen?'

'I am sorry, Joe,' said Kuei. 'I have always loved your wife.'

Oh, even better.

'How long!' yelped Joe. He looked in horror between them. 'How long have you two done this?'

'Not long,' said Mae, shaking her head, in a quiet voice.

'Is Lung my son?' squealed Joe.

Oh, best yet! – better than anything she could have dreamed. The one thing right in Joe's life was his boy.

'Of course,' she said, but she could not speak loudly. She had begun to tremble, deeply, inside. She felt like being sick again. 'Lung is your son,' she tried to say again.

'You pig,' wailed Joe, and launched himself at Mr Ken.

'No!' said Shen, and tried to stop Joe, and, to Mae's immense pleasure, Joe hit Shen full in the face with his fist. Shen spun, holding his nose, blood spurting from it.

Mae found that part of her wanted to laugh.

There will be news enough in this night to keep the village going for a year. We will be destroyed, will all lose station, dignity, voice.

Joe tried to hit Mr Ken. Kuei caught his fist.

'I don't want to fight you, Joe.' Oh, don't you? thought Mae. You will not have much choice.

Joe swung again, and connected.

'Joe, we could not help . . .' Mr Ken did not finish as a second blow was struck.

It is like a toy that you let go, and watch whizzing off until its batteries run down.

Joe wanted to fight. Joe wanted to die. Mr Ken wanted to talk. The two agendas were not compatible.

Joe swung again, and this time Kuei swung back.

'You're good at hitting women,' said Kuei, and swung again.

Joe was going to get beaten up.

Oh well, thought Mae, here we go.

Mae started to scream. She did it quite deliberately, almost without emotion, to rouse the village to the point of being desperate to see what was happening. They would stop the fight. The scandal would be immense.

'Stop it, you're killing him!' she wailed, choosing her words carefully.

That truly did it. Beyond her gates, doors bashed open, footsteps clattered, men shouted, women cried aloud. Old Mrs Ken came running out of her house, clutching at her bathrobe. Mr Oz came running out hopping into his trousers, panic-stricken. He trampolined towards his golden van to make sure it was safe. The gate boomed back against the wall, and there stood Mr Kemal, with a pitchfork.

'What is going on here!' Mr Kemal demanded.

There was Shen, bloodied, Kuei and Joe fighting, and a beaten woman on the ground.

'What is this brawl?' demanded Mr Kemal. 'Teacher Shen, I am surprised to see you involved in this!'

The dismayed expression on Shen's face almost made it worthwhile. Almost.

You should have stayed unconscious, advised Old Mrs Tung.

Mae had to leave her house and go to live with Kwan.
It would have been impossible to stay with Joe and even more impossible that she move in with Mr Ken. Joe would have murdered them in their bed.

Mae's brother arrived about a half hour after the fight, demanding she move in with him. 'I do not wish to do that,' said Mae. She was flinging her clothes into a bag as Joe was comforted by Young Mr Doh.

'You have no choice,' said her brother. Ju-mei followed her all the way up the hill, making demands. He did not even offer to help Mae with her bags. 'It is all right, brother, I got myself into this mess, I certainly did not expect any help from my family!' She turned and left him standing openmouthed.

'My god,' whispered Kwan, when she saw Mae's bruised face.

Kwan let her sleep late. About midday she came up to Mae's attic room with tea, and sat with her.

'Will you leave the village?' Kwan asked.

Normally, that would have been the answer. Mae and Ken would have packed up and gone away, to live in the city. Balshang, probably. God, what a fate, to bake in those sweltering tower blocks, with no money, no air, no friends. Until they ended up hating each other, as was normal.

Mae shook her head. 'I have to help here.'

Kwan held her hand. 'You are not in a good position to help.'

Mae shrugged. 'I will still have my school.'

'No one would come to it,' said Kwan. Her eyes were sad, her mouth firm. She held her friend's hand.

So Mae had lost the school, too. She looked at Kwan's hand. The hand was the village, all she had left of it. Mae loved the village.

The fields she had worked in all summer were her husband's. They were not hers to work any longer. The rice she had nurtured, watered with her sweat, was hers no longer.

The house she had cleaned was no longer hers, the pans, the brazier, all the old spoons. That house had seen her through three children. She had stirred the laundry and the soup alike as the babies fought and wailed around her ankles.

Her home.

She nearly lost even the rough old sewing machine. Mr Wing fetched it for her, and had to remind Joe that legally it belonged to Kwan.

The sewing machine now sat in the corner, next to Mae's suitcases. They looked small in the empty loft room. The only furniture was a couch that Kwan and Wing had wrestled into the space. The roof had a window through which sunlight streamed. Wing had taped clear plastic where panes of glass had been. Everything was coated in a fine white dust.

At midday, just under the tiles, it sweltered. In winter, she would freeze. Swallows cried urgently to be fed from nests under the eaves.

'Bloody Shen,' said Mae. 'Joe's come back with no money and who will buy dresses from me now? I don't even have the loan to pay for any cloth.' Mae sighed and shook herself. 'Still – nothing broke. I kept all my teeth.' Such was peasant luck.

'Joe has been getting drunk with Young Mr Doh,' said Kwan. 'People say that he lost his job through drinking. Siao and Old Mr Chung will work on the construction.'

Mae groaned for him. He had come back with nothing, to find nothing. 'What are they saying about Shen?'

'To me? Nothing. My dear, I am your champion. There are people who will walk past me as if I am not there.'

Mae pondered this for a moment. What was her position in this house? She would have to make some kind of contribution, both in money and in attention and gratitude. How long could she stay? She needed to stay, but every friendship can wear out.

'God, I hate being poor,' said Mae. Poverty afflicts everything, in the end, everything that should be sacrosanct. Love, friendship, the chance to dream, how you live, with whom you live.

'You can stay here as long as you like,' said Kwan, quickly, to get it out of the way.

'If I get my business back together, can I run it from here?'

Kwan faltered ever so slightly. She saw cloth, sewing machines, strangers coming into her house.

'I can work from one of the barns. I know it's difficult.'

Kwan fought her way to honesty. 'I have to ask Mr Wing.'

If not . . . Well, things would be bad if not. Well, things had always been bad and a dishonoured woman in a village had to settle for what she could get.

'Could you tell Joe for me about the TV charges? How I bargained with Sunni? And that the interest on the loan has been waived? That should ease his mind a bit.'

Kwan nodded and worked Mae's fingers in her own.

'You are still fond of Joe.'

'Of course. I lived with him for thirty years.'

'And Mr Ken?'

'The saddest thing of all is that I had decided to end it.'

Kwan sighed, and patted her arm. 'You rest,' she said.

Mae fought her way to honesty as well. 'There is something else,' she said.

Kwan could not help putting her hand on her forehead. What now?

'I think I am pregnant,' said Mae.

Sezen came to call, still blinking, with black hair in her eyes.
Sezen said, 'You sit in bed? You have work to do.'

Mae was not in a position to admonish her for rudeness. Merely visiting Mae had put Sezen in the position of being owed. 'I will start work again, soon,' said Mae.

'Your face is a mess, but no one has to see it,' said Sezen. 'Musa and I can get the cloth for you. No problem.'

'I'm not doing bad-girl clothes,' said Mae.

'Of course not,' said Sezen. 'Just whatever you need the cloth for.'

Mae adjusted to this in silence.

Sezen added, 'Aprons, oven gloves. Things people really use.'

What is it with you, Sezen? Why can't I understand what you want? Why, in a word, are you sticking by me?

Sezen jerked sideways in an angry, harnessed way that was entirely new. 'I have bad news,' she said, and her jerking body expressed impatience with herself for not knowing how to begin. 'Han An has gone off to work for Sunni. I saw the two of them still going around with clipboards, trying to look as if you had not done it first.'

Mae judged the seriousness of the blow. Finally she said, 'That is the least of my worries.'

'She's a traitor,' said Sezen, pouting with scorn.

Mae thought she was going to defend An, but found she could not be bothered. 'Yes.'

'Hmm! She'd better stay clear of me or I will pull out all her hair. Musa and I can go this afternoon to buy your cloth. But we will need the money to do that.'

Her hard brown face, her demanding dark eyes.

Mae felt her deadened face strain towards a smile. 'There is no money, Sezen,' she said.

The girl blinked.

Mae kept explaining: 'The loan was to my husband. It's his money.'

'We will do something else, then,' Sezen said, her jaw thrusting out.

'*We?*' wondered Mae.

'That government man, he must be good for money,' said Sezen.

'You mean I should ask the government man for money!' Mae felt outdone in audacity.

Sezen shrugged. 'He keeps saying how advanced we are. Meaning you. So. Ask.' She sniffed and then said, 'I can't have you going soft, like my mother.'

'I won't do that' said Mae. It was a promise.

In the evening, Mr Oz called.

His eyes said: *How could you do this to me?* 'This is a serious setback to our programme,' he said. He tutted. Light caught his spectacles. 'I was relying on you to be our model.'

'If only I'd known,' replied Mae. 'I would not have fallen in love.'

'I have to write my report.' Mr Oz swayed, as if under a burden. 'I have nothing to say. Except to tell them it is all a mess, everywhere.'

'When hasn't it been?' said Mae, and thought: *How could they send a boy like you out on his own?*

Down below, on Kwan's landing, the men were gathered around

the box. Mae could hear the barking announcer and a sighing crowd: the sound of *fut-bol* on TV.

'Can you continue your school?' Mr Oz demanded. 'Can you still teach others?'

Mae pondered just how much she needed this young man. She wanted to tell him off. 'My main worry now, Mr Oz, is my own life. I have lost a home and a husband.'

He understood that, and winced and rubbed the back of his neck.

'Mr Oz. Do you want to help?'

He looked up as eagerly as a puppy. 'That's what I'm here to do!'

'Then teach me how to make screens, so I can sell my goods.' Mae sat up on her bed. 'I want to specialize and spread my geography. I want to make things to sell abroad to specialist markets that will express the buyer's interest in Third World issues. I want to sell my goods to New York, Singapore, Tokyo . . .'

The government man was in love. His pulse had quickened, his eyes gleamed, this was what he yearned to report. 'Yes, yes, I can do that for you . . . I can set them up, I can show you how. I can show you how to tell people how to find your screens . . .'

Mae nodded. 'But I am now a poor woman on my own, with no money to invest. You are from the government. Do you have any way the government can help me?'

He paused to think. 'Not by myself. But . . . But I can help, yes, I can help. I can find forms, yes, I can help you fill them in. But you know, we will have to make a case to get the grant.'

'I have a case,' said Mae.

The Central Man, to his credit, was ready to move. 'Let's go now,' he said, beaming.

He really was fresh from the cradle. 'Mr Oz. I am a fallen woman. I cannot go out to those men, and chase them away from the machine!'

Down below, the crowd sounds roared towards a crescendo. 'No!' shouted one of the men. Their team was losing. They would be in a bad mood.

'That's okay, we can use mine,' said the government man, enthusiastic and oblivious. 'My van has a computer.'

They would have to walk out through the landing. The sound of the men, drunken below, rose up like the odour of a stew.

Mae climbed down the ladder from the loft, to the staircase and from there into the carpeted diwan that led to the landing. Her stomach was a knot of nerves. She felt as if a layer of skin had been stripped from her.

Just past the stone arch, the men were crowded onto the narrow landing. The barking voice finished and there was a swelling of jolly music. The game had just ended.

Allah! Please make them all decide to go home!

The men yawned. Chairs scraped on stone. Mr Oz started to walk. Mae grabbed his sleeve and he looked back at her in surprise. He finally understood that she was afraid.

'Okay, now a movie?' someone said. Chairs scraped again, and suddenly there was Bollywood music. Mae gave in and nodded yes to Mr Oz. She tried to be invisible. She tried to waft forward like a ghost onto the landing.

Men were crowded around the TV. Mae glimpsed among them Mr Ali, Mr Pin, and both Old and Young Mr Dohs. Joe was not there. Mae tried to slip around the backs of the chairs. The air seemed full of thick, half-cooked bread to delay her.

'Tuh,' chortled Mr Doh, in something like disgust. Mae did not look around.

'There's a funny smell,' said Mr Ali. ' Kwan should not keep pigs in her house.'

Mr Pin agreed. 'Ah. You should keep pigs in the basement. They like rolling in shit.'

The men chuckled. Mae was nearly at the head of the stairs. It would be easy to push her down them.

'The heat of their bodies warms the house,' said Mr Ali.

'It seems hot pigs fuck even government men.'

'Hot pigs must be killed,' said Old Mr Doh.

The very air seemed to shudder. Mae had to glance back then, in case the time had come to run.

Young Mr Doh had a hand on his father's arm. He looked at Mae in alarm and jerked his head towards the gate: *Get out of here quick!* Mae thought: You are Joe's best friend, and yet it is you who still treats me like a human being.

Mae scurried forward, her feet bouncing down the steps like a ball.

'Gentlemen,' said Mr Oz, Mr Sincere. 'Good evening. I am glad to see that you make such good use of the TV.'

Mr Oz stood with his legs planted apart and across the top of the stairs.

Mae ran.

Mae waited in her old courtyard, trembling in the dark.
She had bolted her gate and crouched behind it. She had to hope that Joe did not come outside. Or Mr Ken.

There was a knock. 'It is me,' murmured Mr Oz.

'Ssh!' said Mae, and lifted the latch more gently than if it had been a blanket over a baby.

They tiptoed to the barn and closed the door.

Inside his van, Mr Oz said, 'I will drive you back home. If those dolts are still there, you can sleep here in the van.'

Mae slumped into the seat. She felt a weakness in her belly and had to hold her head for a moment as nausea passed over her.

She knew the signs. Yes, she was pregnant.

'Are you all right?' Mr Oz asked.

Mae was outraged. This . . . This *youngster* had only just noticed that she had been beaten, bruised, and cast out. 'No! I am not all right!' she said, angry.

Oz was used to kindness being returned, and was confused. He scowled.

'Oh, for heaven's sake, stop being such a child and help me if you are going to!'

He jerked somewhere just under his lungs, and leaned forward. He plugged in wires, and something whined to life. There was a tiny box with a flip-up screen, a kind of mini-TV.

'Go to "Info," ask for "Government,"' he said.

Mr Oz took Mae into new provinces of Info. There were rules, regulations, advice, offers of service, all from her own government. Up came a voiceform.

The voiceform kept asking impertinent questions. Are you over forty? How many children do you have? All over twenty years old? Any dependants? What is your annual income? 10,000 riels! 1,000 riels? It offered no figure that was low enough. Mae murmured: 500 riels.

'Is that true?' asked Mr Oz, quietly. 'If you say too much, you may be disqualified for some things.'

So she told the truth: One hundred riels a year. The Central Man looked sad, but his eyes did not catch hers.

'Okay, let me take over here,' he said. 'What do you want the money for?'

And Mae told him: To buy modern oatmeal cloth that rich people like, and to pay others to embroider it with Eloi patterns and then tell the West and the Big East that the cloth was a statement about Third World issues. Mr Oz chuckled at that, and looked around at her face.

Then he spoke into the machine, translating what she had told him into official talk. It sounded to Mae like a news item, terribly important, like the way rich people talked about themselves. But it didn't move or excite her.

'That's boring,' she said.

He shrugged. Mae imagined someone at the other end, listening bored to her answers.

And she reached into the patterns, reached into the new glowing links inside her head, and spoke with the knowledge of the Kru, without being the Kru.

'The proposal is to use the power of the Net to extend the reach of local crafts skills to specialist niche markets, most especially America, Singapore, and Japan.'

Mr Oz turned around and blinked at her.

'This will not be traditional direct marketing. Efforts will be focused on information finders of various types, particularly fashion or craft networks . . .'

He warned her. 'Don't use the word "Eloi." "Traditional local crafts," that's what these are. Do you have a Horseman?'

Horsemen in Karzistan had traded for centuries in the most mobile currency of all: horseflesh. They used their commodity also to bear news, where there were shortages of horses or any other goods. Other traders paid them for such news.

Horsemen, like fashion experts, had always been in the information business.

Now they were people who were paid to sell and sort Info. They were called something else in English, but in Karz, they were called Info Horsemen.

Mr Oz had names and addresses ready. 'You have to give an address for a Horseman. They don't think you've done your homework otherwise.'

He added an official report to her application. It was a separate file attached to her application. His voice validated his identity.

'This is a core project for the Green Valley/Red Mountain area,' he said. 'Its proponent has taken a lead in instructing the village people on the Net and the coming of the Air. She has founded the Swallow School, a project to train locals in Info skills. She has also used a well-constructed Question Map to determine the views of local people on Air. The proposed scheme will demonstrate to this community the value of the Net. It will be the best possible advancement for the aims of both the Yu En Air project and the Central Bureau of Information Technology/Ministry of Development's Joint Declaration of the Taking Wing Initiative.'

Then he sent the form.

'I think we'll get it,' Mr Oz said. 'I cannot imagine a better case.'

He looked calm, sated, knowing how fine it would look on his own record.

So you get something, too. Just as well.

'How do I become an Info Horseman?' Mae asked.

He looked around at her and for once, his eyes were adult. 'You would need to know very much more than you do now,' he replied.

'Can I learn it?'

He sighed. 'You would need to know how wires work. And money. And banking.'

Mae thrust out her chin. 'I have my Kru.'

'And the people – most of all you need to know the people, the people in those worlds. It is not for me to say that you can learn.'

We are who we are.

'Thank you,' she said. The Central Man had said no in a way that she could understand and accept.

'Right,' she said. 'Now, teach me how to make screens.'

Mr Oz crumpled. 'It is late—'

Mae cut him off: 'And I risked my life to come here, and I cannot do it often. You say you want to help, then fine. *Help*. Helping people costs; you've got to do it when you're tired. Go on! Do your job!'

Mr Oz paused. The muscles in his face worked like biceps. His face seemed to swim up through anger to the placid surface of a smile. 'This is very good for me,' he said. Then he grinned.

'Right. You make screens with something old called HTML. XML makes it work on TV and AML will even make it work on Air.'

'That means nothing to me.'

'You'll have to learn the words,' said Mr Oz. In the realm of Info, he could command.

The next day Mr Ken came to ask Mae to live with him.

Mae was sweeping Kwan's diwan, the carpets rolled up. The men were already at the television, already there were sports results. A voice behind her said, 'Shouldn't you rest?'

Mae turned and saw Mr Ken. He looked terrible, abject and sleepless.

'Did *they* say anything to you?' Mae asked jerking her head down towards the landing. Ken Kuei would have had to walk past all the men.

'Some things,' Kuei said.

'I can imagine,' she said. 'When you leave they will ask if your dick is wet.'

'I have come for a serious discussion,' he said.

Kuei's wonderful good behaviour disguised a lack of intelligence. He was diligent, kind, silent, and sympathetic. Just not very bright. Or were all men stupid? Or only the ones she knew?

His ballooning broad shoulders, his round face like a peach, his lips like something soft and chewable. If he were to start on her now, here in the sun-drenched guest room on the swept flagstones, pulling down her trousers, she would dampen, open, admit him.

But no, he wanted a serious discussion.

Mae sniffed. 'Okay. We talk.'

'It is impossible for us to stay in the village,' he said.

'It is impossible for me to go,' she said, very quietly.

He coughed, gently. 'I . . . propose,' he said. 'That we leave. Together. Take my children with us. We would go wherever you like. But I would suggest Green Valley City.' He looked helpless, proud. 'I would hate Balshang,' he said.

'I want to stay here,' she repeated.

He nodded. 'Okay. Okay,' he said, trying to absorb what she meant. 'I will need to find us a new house. It would not be possible to live so close to Joe.'

'Which house? Whose, Mr Ken? Is there an empty house here? I thought they were all crowded with too many children, and children's children. And oh, such a difference, Mr Ken, to be two minutes away from one's husband. Passing him every day in the fields. Weeding his fields instead of yours by mistake.'

'I know, I know,' Kuei nodded.

'I want this to stop,' Mae said.

'It has not been good,' he admitted. He looked at her, his eyes that wanted to stay a child and that wanted her. 'But it could be good. If we just say, "Yes, it is true, but now we will live together, open." We could do that, and in a year they will get used to it.'

'You don't understand,' she said. 'That night – huh! The night before last, it seems a year ago. That night, as I walked home, I had made up my mind. That this would stop. I decided then.'

She heard the men and their laughter, the birds in the fields, and the very slight noise of the river that flowed right across the heart of the village. She looked into his dark eyes.

'I have been doing too much. I know what I want to do. I have to do just that, if I am to do it at all. And I cannot bear to give up.'

'Info,' he said, almost in scorn.

'This village,' she answered him. 'What your grandmother showed me is that everything dies. It is not good enough just to live. You have to know that death is certain. Not . . . Not just of the person, but of whole worlds. Ours is going to die. It is dead now. The only thing I can do is help it be reborn, so we can survive.'

Kuei was picking at something on the windowsill next to her. 'Mother to us all,' he said, in some bitterness.

'If it were a different time . . .' she said.

'If we were younger . . .' he said.

'If it were as it should be . . .'

'If we were as we once were . . .'

He shook himself like a dog, shivered. '*Urggh*,' he said, partly in anger, partly in casting anger off. 'Will you go back to Joe?'

She paused in order to think, but found she did not have to. 'No,' she answered. 'No, I will concentrate on this.'

'On what?' Mr Ken yelped. 'You will concentrate on loneliness, Mae? On an empty house? A room in someone else's house, working like a servant in order to say thank you?'

Mae sucked in air through her nose, in a thin, focused stream that hissed, but was not a sigh. It was a gathering of strength.

'On clearing the floor for work.'

Kuei stared back at her, helpless. 'What work?' he asked again. He really didn't know. She wanted to hug him then, hold him, comfort him, for he was one of the dead. But it would be misinterpreted.

'Teaching us how to use that thing,' she said. Each word was like a brick that she could barely carry.

'You can do both!'

She held up her hands. 'No. I can't. I don't sleep, I hardly eat, I work in the house, I work in the fields, and then I work on that, and there is almost nothing left of me.' Suddenly she was shouting, 'I'm tired!'

The only thing in his face was sympathy for her.

'Maybe when all of this is done,' she said, more quietly, relenting.

'I will be waiting,' Kuei said helplessly. 'I waited before.'

A year from now? Maybe the change would come, and after that a time of calm. After the massacre, stillness?

Mae nodded yes, but said nothing further, to avoid giving him too much hope. He nodded yes as well, and made no move to kiss her, for both of them had agreed to end, not to begin. He turned and went down the stairs to the kitchen. The diwan seemed full of fine white dust.

And she ran up the wooden stairs to look out of a high window through bleached-blue sunlight over bleached-blue rooftops. Mae looked down and saw Kuei as if through a mist. He walked tall, straight, holding his jacket against the heat, the back of his T-shirt stained with sweat and nerves, past the men, who ignored him. They turned, grinning, to look at his back.

There goes my young man, thought Mae.

You only get one, said someone else's voice.

Remember him, remember his broad back, for he is walking into the past, into the Land of the Dead. Even if you meet again, you will both be different again, strangers or friends. Say goodbye now, for you will have no other chance; say goodbye for every moment to come without him. But at least you had him. For once you had him.

And again, that old question: Granny, Teacher, why is love pain? Why such a sweet sad sick hurt, a dragging-down in the belly, an ache, a yearning?

Because it always goes away.

Mr Ken paused at the gate and looked both ways, left and right, as if considering, though he had no choice. Then he walked on. Mae permitted herself to weep.

13

Mae got her money.

She was working at three A.M., on Kwan's TV, when it announced that she had mail.

'*I will read it for you,*' the machine said. By now it knew that Mae avoided reading herself.

'*The Republic of Karzistan, Ministry of Development, under the terms of the Taking Wing Initiative, is pleased to inform you that it will grant funding in full as requested in your recent application, under the following conditions . . .*'

Mae was numb. The government was talking to her. The government knew who she was. They had just given her the money?

What conditions? Her mind went dark, ready to be hurt.

First, they wanted her to keep records of both sales and replies.

'*The Taking Wing Initiative needs to know how successfully you have unrolled your mat. Please save the attached suite of Customer Care software. It will automatically record the data we need . . .*'

It was a Question Map. The same information was recorded over and over – any letters she got, any orders she fulfilled, would be analyzed by country, referral, and type of business.

Mae kept listening for serious conditions. But there were none. No interest? No percentage?

Mae was enraged. What kind of foolish government was that, to arrange its business so badly? How could it prosper? Were they all children, like Mr Oz?

But praise the gods – Luck, Happiness, whatever – for giving them masters who were so naive. She had her money; she had her business back. Oh, could she ride this life like a leaf bobbing up and down on the river in a storm!

Mae needed to tell someone, but who could she tell at three in the morning? Poor Kwan who had nursed her but was now asleep? The

Central Man, yes, but that would mean going back to her old house, to Joe, to Mr Ken . . . Who?

Mae went to Sezen's house. She knocked on the door. Then, beyond politesse, Mae pummelled it. This was good news.

There were hissed voices, shuffling, a child's cry, a shushing, slippers on the floor.

Sezen answered. She wore a little girl's nightdress and the spots on her cheeks had gone blue-black from merciless squeezing.

May seized her hands. 'I got the money!' she whispered. 'Sezen. It was as you said, the government gave us the cash!'

'This is a joke. This is madness,' said Sezen.

'They gave me every last riel of it. I asked for too much!'

'You mean we are going to do it?'

'Yes, yes, they loved it!'

Sezen squealed and hugged her, spun on her heel, and said, 'Let's get drunk. You have any booze?'

Mae shook her head.

'Rich woman, you will have whisky. You will have silks.'

You will build your mother a new house.'

'Tuh!' said Sezen. 'No. I will buy a motorcycle. Of my own.'

Mae pronounced her, 'Wild girl.'

'Look who is calling people wild. Eh? You? Adventuress. Madam Death. The man in her family. All these things people call you.'

Sezen bundled Mae into her own poor house. She threw cushions in abandon into a heap. In the middle of the night at the end of summer, the fleas were at their hungriest. They nipped about Mae's ankles in a mist.

Sezen knelt in front of a small keep in the wall. 'Here,' she said, pulling out a bottle. 'This is disgusting, but strong. Father made it. It is the only thing he does well.' Its creator snored behind the curtain, like a boozehouse accordion.

Rice wine. Amid the filth of Sezen's house, Mae sat and drank, and told Sezen everything about the grant application and the answer.

'Who needs the village?' Mae said. The rice wine was milky and tasted like chalk, but it seemed to creep up her spine, numbing it vertebra by vertebra.

'*Ptoo!* to the village,' said Sezen, and pretended to spit. 'Only their clothing holds them together.'

'Are we naked, then?' asked Mae.

'The naked are brave,' said Sezen, and raised her glass.

'To the naked!' said Mae, and raised her glass.

'To Mr Ken,' added Sezen. 'Oh! I want to be fucked.'

Mae was too drunk to be shocked. 'Musa,' she managed to say.

Sezen held out a graphic little finger. 'All you Chinese . . .' she said. 'He's a Muslim, but Chinese father.' She shook her head, and then suddenly laughed, and shook her head again. Still laughing, Sezen put down the glass suddenly, as if it were a great weight she could no longer bear.

'I am a pig and my family are pigs. All the men I meet are pigs and I shall have piggy children.' She picked up the glass and toasted her helplessness, or the house, or her fate.

The fleas around Mae's ankles rose and fell like flames. Abstracted by the wine, Mae hazily swatted and scratched. She watched helplessly, as she realized Sezen was no longer laughing.

'You only come to me because you are fallen,' accused Sezen, grumpy.

'If you want more people to come, just . . . clean up,' Mae said.

Sezen looked back at her bleakly. 'This *is* cleaned up.' She sputtered into laughter. 'I have just cleaned up, this is as clean as it gets! Listen, even the fleas are disgusted with this place.' Laughter ached out of her. A string of sticky spittle clung between her lips. 'I am such a lady, you see, I get bored cleaning. It is beneath me.' Sezen was not really ashamed.

In the future, there will be no ladies, thought Mae. All of the old channels we pour down will be blocked. Ladies, peasants, men, women, children, rich, poor, clean, dirty, we will all be churned up together. We will be churning clouds in the air, blown by wind, pierced by swallows . . .

'I'm drunk,' Mae managed to say.

'Poisoned, more like,' said Sezen, looking at the milky wine. She poured it onto the beaten-dirt floor. 'Maybe it will kill the fleas.'

'Welcome to the Mae-Sezen Fashion Emporium,' said Mae.

'New York . . . Paris . . . Singapore . . . Tokyo . . . Kizul-duh.' Hazily, Sezen stood up and did a model's turn. Her nightrobe was eaten at the hem and knees. 'Sezen-ma'am displays the fine cut and design features of her latest creation.' Sezen held up the rotten hem. 'Air ventilation for summer wear, illustrates the holes in Miss

Ozdemir-ma'am's head through which Air seeps.' She grinned like a tigerish Talent, and batted her eyes. 'This year's fashion adventure.'

Mae was chuckling. Calmly, she noticed that she had knocked over her glass.

'That will burn a hole in your heart,' said Sezen, of her father's wine.

'Holes in the heart are this year's fashion adventure,' said Mae.

Sezen stopped. 'You're crying,' she accused, suddenly young and let-down.

Am I? wondered Mae. She felt her cheeks. They were wet. 'Just from laughter,' she promised Sezen, who only wanted escape. 'Just from laughter,' Mae said again, and reached forward and patted Sezen's hand.

'Uh! We need a radio,' said Sezen. 'Then we could dance.'

'When the Air comes,' said Mae. 'We will have music whenever we want it. Any kind of music.'

'When the Air comes!' sighed Sezen, with sudden feeling. 'Oh, when Air comes I shall put the music in my head on Air so everyone can hear it.' Sezen sat and closed her eyes, and Mae realized she was seeing something new.

Sezen was someone who wanted Air. Mae was afraid of it. She regarded it as Flood, Fire, Avalanche, something to be faced up to and controlled. This was different.

Sezen sat with her eyes closed and whispered. 'When the Air comes, we can sing to each other, only we will sound like the biggest band in the world.' She swayed, as if to music.

Mae joined in: 'When the Air comes, we can dress each other in Air clothes.'

'Light as spiderwebs . . .'

'When the Air comes, we can see all the naked men we want . . .'

Mae expected Sezen to give a wicked, wild-girl chuckle; instead she whispered, 'So many beautiful men, that it will grow as normal as birds.'

'When the Air comes . . .' Mae began.

'We will all be birds, we will all be naked, all be brave.'

Sezen said that?

Sezen kept speaking, in a trance. 'The clothes will drop away, the fleas and the fur, and we'll jump out of our bodies and fly, and the world will all be dream, and dream will be all of the world.'

Her voice trailed away. She was asleep. Mae felt a curtain descend behind her forehead, a curtain of sadness and exhaustion. I will sleep here amid the fleas, she thought. Because I have just seen a miracle. A miracle comes when someone speaks, really speaks, because when someone does that, you also hear God.

Air will be wonderful. I didn't know that.

Mae leaned her head down onto the earthern floor. It smelled of spice and corn, not garbage. Sezen was snoring. Mae took her hand and managed to blow out the candle. Anaesthetized, Mae fell asleep.

It was still dark when the smells of the filthy house woke her up – stale vegetation, drying shitcakes, and sour old rice in the bins. The voracious fleas were sticking needles into her. There was slippery, queasy stirring below, in addition to a blinding hangover headache.

Mae was bleeding, below.

She felt her breath like a candle flame. Blood means I am not pregnant. I can't be pregnant. She needed to check, to be sure. She would not risk feeling her female wound with dirty hands. She could not do that here. She could not sleep here now either, sober. The house did stink.

Forgive me, Sezen, I did keep you company for a while.

Sezen stirred, murmuring. 'Good night,' Mae whispered.

Mae stumbled out onto the cobbles, and looked up at the mountain sky, a river of stars across it as milky as Sezen's father's wine. The air was sweet, it cleared everything. Yes, Sezen was right, the Air was wonderful. She, Mae, was not pregnant. Good things were still to come, good things to do.

She listened again to her village – to the far dogs, the wind in reeds, and the sounds of their river leaping over stones.

Pregnant? demanded a voice in her head.

The nausea came again, in a wave.

In the morning, Mae was still nauseous, but told herself it was the wine.

If she was bleeding, she could not be pregnant. And if she were ill, badly ill, she found, she did not mind.

All that she asked was that she lived long enough to get the village on Air.

Downstairs, in the kitchen, Kwan was worried. 'Where did you go?' Kwan asked her.

'I went drinking with Sezen,' said Mae, abstracted by hangover.

Kwan looked horrified.

'She is very bright, brighter than you would think.'

'She would have to be. Perhaps you could teach her to wash.'

Mae felt like a truck on a bad road. There was need of repair. 'We all need to improve in some ways,' she said.

Kwan rumpled her lips, as if to say: *Don't be so mealymouthed and pious.*

'I'm not pregnant,' Mae said.

Kwan blinked, for a moment. 'That at least is a blessing.'

'In some ways. Who is to say what is a blessing these days?' Mae sat up. 'I need to see my government man.'

Things were still too bad for her to walk in daylight through the village. Certainly not to be seen returning to the home of Mr Ken.

Kwan sighed.

Mae said, 'I fear I am proving to be a trouble to you.'

Kwan gave her head a dismissive twitch. 'I will send a child with a message.'

It was only after Kwan had gone that Mae realized: I did not tell her about the government money. She will think I am hiding it from her. Maybe I was.

Mae washed. She was still bleeding. The blood smelled of woman. She pushed a clean rag up herself, and went downstairs. She told Kwan about the government money, after giving an apologetic dip at the knees. 'I was more relieved at the other news.'

'Both are good,' said Kwan, blandly.

The government man came, Mae told him about the grant. He smiled, but he did not look overjoyed. 'That quick.' He shook his head. 'That means there have been few applications. They have spare funding; they need to use it.' Mae tried to read the hand across his forehead, the distracted look.

'You are worried?' she asked.

'It means no one else is finding anything,' he said. 'It's not working.'

From down below came the sound of the men and the TV. Do women and children ever get to watch it now? They were watching snooker. Of all the pointless things to waste a morning on.

'Stay here,' Mr Oz told her.

He turned and went down Kwan's whitewashed steps. Mae listened, hidden behind the doorway. The staircase smiled white in the sunlight.

Suddenly there were howls from the men, protests.

'Quiet,' demanded Mr Oz. 'This is more important than sports.'

A roar of protest from the men.

Mr Oz continued: 'What do you care about snooker scores in Balshang? Balshang doesn't care that you burn shit for fuel. Balshang doesn't even know you exist!'

Mae blinked. Fighting words from such a frail boy. Who would have thought it? The men suddenly fell silent. The screen made a trumpeting sound, the sound of government. Humbled, silent, made small by the weight of society above them, the village men waited. Mae could feel them wait.

Then she heard a spreading mumble.

They know, she realized. They know about the money. He's shown them on TV.

'Thank you, gentlemen,' said Mr Oz.

Naked but brave. A harlot funded by the government to make herself richer than the men. That's what they will call me. I will have to have a face of stone, now. I will have to be as enduring as the mountain. Mountains hold up air.

Oblivious as always, the Central Man bustled back in with paper. Kwan emerged, concerned, curious, wiping her hands. The paper had printed out all the terms and conditions.

'Right,' he explained. 'The funding is in the form of bank credits. Do you know what those are?'

Mae shook her head. 'Believability Card?'

'Better than that. But I need to go with you to ratify them. That will set up a business account in the bank. We then need to set up a Question Mark account, so that you can use it on the Net. Then . . . you are in business.'

'That means going to Green Valley City,' said Mae. Her heart leapt. The City! She had not seen it since spring.

'Mmm-hmm,' Mr Oz said, oblivious again to what that meant for her. 'And that is good, too, because there is a big seminar there this week. For people in the Taking Wing Initiative. It will be good. The Wings have also been invited.'

'Can we take Sunni with us?' asked Mae.

Sunni ran out of her house to the government van.

She was immaculate in city-woman oatmeal, with a beige scarf on her head. She darted down the hill to the bridge, quickly so that no one would see her. She squashed into the backseat next to Mae, and greeted Mae, Mr Oz, and Mr Wing. Plainly, she wanted to be away.

'Hello, Mrs Sunni-ma'am.' Sezen beamed at her. *Pleased to see me?* Sezen's eyes were spiked with merriment like a dog's collar against wolves. Mae gave Sezen a little warning with her eyes.

'Good morning, Sezen,' Sunni managed. She flinched at Sezen's graduation dress, mounds of shiny lemon-yellow. Sunni put on her sunglasses as if against the glare.

'Mrs Haseem-ma'am,' Mr Wing replied with dignity from the front seat. Mr Oz nodded and backed the van back into Upper Street.

Sunni turned to Mae, and her smile was from the old days. 'It was very kind of you to ask me,' she said to Mae.

Mae said, 'I felt it would be good for old friends in the party of progress to go together to see what they are doing in the City.'

'And it is such a beautiful morning!' said Sezen, reaching around Mae to touch Sunni on the shoulder. 'We can stop and wave to all your friends, working in the fields.'

'If those who are friends of progress are not friends of each other, then disaster awaits,' said Mae, and glared.

'Indeed,' murmured Sunni. 'Those are my feelings.' Protected by sunglasses, Sunni looked fragile in defeat, uncertain and frightened by the need for trust.

Impulsively, Mae took her hand. 'It is good to be with friends.'

'Where is the Lady An?' chirped Sezen.

Sunni found enough heart to reply. 'An is studying for a qualification in fashion studies. She does this through the Net on my TV. She is enjoying it. Perhaps you should talk to her, Sezen, and see if the course interests you. You could study together.'

'I would love to do that!' enthused Sezen, so brightly that it was plain she could think of nothing worse. 'She would teach me how to improve my pronunciation.'

And improve your manners, thought Mae. She gave Sunni's hand a little squeeze. To her surprise, Sunni squeezed back.

Sunni persisted. 'Such a terrible thing that people do not understand the uses of the TV. To think! There are people who want it turned off!'

'People who try to destroy others,' said Sezen, her voice now simple, hard and dark.

'Indeed,' said Sunni, simply. Mae twisted around and her eyes said to Sezen: *Enough*.

Sezen's smile was one of contentment. She gave Mae a little salute and looked away, honour satisfied.

Already their little village was gone. Just alongside Mr Oz's window, there was a brutal falling-away of stone. 'Music?' Mr Wing asked, and turned on the radio.

Full of echo and sounds of machinery was something like a song for Sezen's generation. She was drawn, silenced by what to her was a mating call, a cry to be joined with the modern. The old folk fell silent.

Fluttering past like insubstantial scarves went rice fields, misty terraces, fat men riding donkeys, women in broad straw hats considering harvest.

They went down into the Desiccated Village. Mae was shocked to see grey dishes and wires on most of the houses.

'They've had those since summer,' said Sunni, turning. 'Perhaps we are not so advanced in Kizuldah.'

'Installing *sat ho lih tuh*,' said Mr Oz, shaking his head, as if they all shared his amusement. 'Still, it's reliable old technology.'

Mae felt unable to ask: *What is a satellite?*

'Look,' said Sunni, suddenly pointing. 'They are already threshing!'

Going down the hill was like plunging into their future. On the burnished-yellow threshing ground were big rented machines and wagons loaded with chickpeas. The men were pitchforking them raw into the threshers. The jets of straw, the waiting reed baskets to collect the peas, the women and boys bearing them off to plastic matting, the little girls herding the geese away from the mats – it was all as it always had been.

The vision was withdrawn behind a flurry of fencing and gates. A good harvest.

'Ah!' sighed Sunni, as if the relief were her own. 'They will have a good party, then.'

'High feasting,' agreed Mae. 'It is useful that they are so dry compared to us. We grow rice, they grow chickpeas.'

'Mmm, we can just exchange,' Sunni agreed. It was what they always said.

Suddenly the road stopped complaining under them. Suddenly it was smooth, humming like a song. The clouds of white dust died away in trails behind them, like the silver tracks of aircraft.

Sunni and Mae looked at each other in wonder: *Paved? Our road is paved?*

Then they both broke out in laughter.

Sunni held her plump belly. 'Who . . . Who thought it was worthwhile paving a city road here?'

'Make it easier for the donkey!' chuckled Mae.

They thought of all the fat old farmers, their bewildered wives, the barefoot children, the brown-toothed brigands with ancient rifles. Oh, indeed, how they needed a highway.

'You need it for motorcycles,' said Sezen, sharply. The radio played another Balshang song. 'We will all have motorcycles.'

Mae placated her. 'I know, Sezen, but it just seems strange.'

'Remember when grass grew between the wheel tracks?' Sunni said.

'Yes! I'd forgotten that.'

'And the first time down each year, there was no track at all.'

'Yes, yes, the wheels spun on the spring grass, and you were always frightened the tractor would slide off the road!'

'My father always made us get out and walk. He would cast lye behind him to kill the grass.'

Mae turned to tell Sezen. 'You went to the town, oh, only if your father was buying a horse . . .'

'. . . or parts for the tractor . . .'

'And we would pile all of us, oh, six or seven children, in the trailer behind. It would take all day to get down. We would sleep in the trailer overnight.'

'You remember the fires?'

'Everyone set up camp in the market square.'

'You would cook soup over the fires.'

'And the lutes . . .'

'The lutes came out, particularly the Horsemen, and they would sing. Remember the Cossacks! So handsome with their moustaches, they would sing . . .'

The truck seemed to lurch and sway as if on green grass. Mae turned to warn Mr Oz about his driving, but as she leaned forward, everything lurched, swayed, and suddenly she smelled smoke . . .

. . . and saw the fires.

The Cossacks wore spotless white shirts, with high collars.
They smelled of smoke. It clung to their huge moustaches. Like

thieves, they had wicked faces but they were lit up with kindly smiles, and the little girl was sitting on the knee of one of them. His face was lit up with love, tender love.

'I . . . have . . . a . . . little . . . girl,' the Cossack said, slowly, in Karz. 'She is pretty. Like you.' His truck full of horses sweltered even though it was night. His mates smoked pipes, and her father sat drinking with them, ramrod straight and slightly twitchy. He was frightened of Cossacks.

It was not Mae's father. The little girl was not Mae.

The Cossack said, 'I send presents to my little girl. She does not always get them. Things are so bad, the postmen take them.' The Cossack shrugged. 'Oh, I miss my little girl. You are happy to live with your father. You are far from the war.'

What war?

The Cossack patted little Miss Hu on her head and let her run back to her father. Her father was plump, smooth-skinned, beardless. He smelled of chives and garlic, not smoke. Miss Hu climbed onto his lap and was covered in kisses as hot and damp as new leaves on tender shoots.

'Ai-ling,' breathed out Mr Hu.

World War Two. This would be, say, 1941.

The town square was dark, except for one streetlight, and there were no tall buildings. Indeed, the square was a terrace of shacks, with men sitting out front, in worn, torn, dusty clothes. Barbershops, bars, spare-parts shops, teahouses. There was a traffic light, and Mae remembered. There was only one traffic light in the whole town.

The Cossack grinned, picked up his viola: It was tiny, unvarnished, with loose wood holding up the strings. The bow was made of horsetail hairs. 'For pretty little girls,' he said.

He played something high, sweet, sad, simple.

'Song says, "*Red children, Red children, play . . .*"' he explained, and began to sing.

It was a jolly song that made Ai-ling want to dance, jolly but somehow sad. She thought it was the most beautiful thing she had ever heard. She wanted to remember it forever and ever. She beamed up in delight, wonder, at her father, who smiled down indulgently.

And little Ai-ling began to dance. She held out her arms, and spun, wearing her best town dress, a stiff froth of lace, her hair in ribbons, so pretty, little princess, spinning and spinning. The Cossacks, as hard as the roads, melted as if in rain. 'Ahhhh!' they sighed, for all things homely and beautiful. The moment came that Miss Hu loved, when she ceased to be shy. Then she could really dance.

So she really danced, knowing herself to be little and pretty and sweet. All the Cossacks began to sing the song together, enraptured by the sight of a pretty little girl, of home. Some of them came from other fires, with mandolins. The music mounted. Little Ai-ling fell back into shyness, and stopped, and hid her head in her father's trousers. The Horsemen laughed with love.

Mae was rocked like a little paper boat cast out onto the ocean.

The music changed. It rattled. It was Balshang music on the radio, with a roar of engine and harsh sunlight.

Mae was sick again, waves of nausea. She wanted to say: Stop, I need to be sick.

See? See? said Old Mrs Tung. *See what you are destroying?*

A young person was crowded close to her with concern. Mae did not know who she was at first. 'Are you all right?' Sezen asked, an arm on hers.

'Hmm,' said Mae, not quite saying yes. 'I was sleeping.'

'You were singing,' corrected Sunni, her eyes hidden in the sunglasses. 'In another language.'

They roared down into Green Valley City.

Yeshibozkent was flung like a soiled handkerchief onto the lie of the land. There was much new building now on the outskirts. Raw concrete in irregular frames held panels of barely mortared brick. They would fall in the next earthquake. The air was blue and grey. They were lowered into it, and heat enveloped them like a blanket, smelling of old automobiles.

Dust and fumes and Toyota jeeps that would not stay in their lanes, and old women that walked right out onto the road.

Mr Oz did not slow down, but beeped frantically, continually, forcing people to jump back, or taxis to veer out of his way. Mr Wing chuckled at his driving courage. 'I always wondered how you people got through so fast,' he said.

The city people in sharp clothes walked unconcerned as the van seared the air, passing them by inches. A light turned red and the van lurched to a halt. Pedestrians poured across the intersection.

Sezen laughed, suddenly raucous, and pointed. 'What is that?'

A young man walked in front of the windscreen. He wore soiled, fruit-bowl colours and long braided hair, died blond streaks amid his natural black. Some sort of glasses marred his face, like an eye test or camera lenses. He turned almost blind and looked inside the van. Light flicked, inside the lenses, inside his eyes. His skinny, starveling face bared fangs at them. His teeth were bright yellow like a row of embers.

Sezen rolled down the window. She leaned out and yelled at him, 'What are you?'

Sunni seemed to melt with shame beside Mae.

He yelled back, answering another agenda: 'I just took your photograph.' He staggered slightly, for no reason. *'Dih zee toh el.'*

Mr Oz spoke: 'He's an *Ay oh het.'*

Mr Wing jerked with a superior grin. 'Or he thinks he is.'

The man still yelled at them. 'It is a photograph of peasants!' The smile was nasty. 'You are all dead!'

'It means Airhead,' continued Mr Oz. 'He can't be an Airhead – the Air has not come here yet – but he has read about it in some magazine.'

'You are a fool,' Sezen shouted back, laughing at him. 'The Air is not here yet.'

'My eyes are cameras!' he shouted, as the van pulled away.

Sezen was agog with both scorn and excitement. 'Did you see what he was wearing! What did he have on his eyes?'

'A computer,' said Mr Oz. 'Part of it is embedded in his head.'

The two older women hissed in pain.

'No wonder he was such a mess,' said Sunni, shaking her head.

'Yah, but imagine if it was someone handsome and clever and not a fool,' said Sezen.

'Imagine clean streets,' said Mae. The town was richer, but that just generated drifts of crushed tin and old papers in the gutters.

'Yeshibozkent? Clean?' Sezen was scornful. 'We still think garbage rots. We will never be clean.'

'We are a very clean people,' said Sunni, in outrage. 'There are only two dirty families in our village!' One of them was Sezen's.

Sezen just laughed. 'To someone from the West, we all look like pigs.'

The van beeped furiously. A donkey had suddenly swerved from the side of the road into its path. The van screeched and slid helplessly, shifting sideways as the wheels locked. The van slammed into the animal.

Mae could feel the donkey's ribs, its fur, the knobby knees, all communicated through the front of the truck.

'Oh!'

Mr Wing jumped out. The animal, dazed, kicked itself back up onto its feet and blinked.

'Who owns this animal?' Mr Wing demanded of the street. Plump ladies in shiny purple pantsuits looked mildly surprised.

Sezen was helpless with laughter. 'Does it have cameras for eyes, too? Airhead donkey?'

Mae was not sure why Sezen found it so funny.

No one answered. No one claimed the donkey. It twitched its ears and wandered off as if nothing were wrong. Perhaps, like them, it was dead and didn't know.

The main market square no longer had a public-address system.
The familiar sound of town-coming had been silenced. The smells were the same; vegetables in sunlight laced with city drains. The gabble of trading seemed strangely muted and the square curiously spacious.

'There aren't the people,' said Sunni, mystified.

Mae looked around. 'It is a Saturday. Where are they all?'

'At the hypermarket,' said Sezen, sniffing, collecting her volumes of lime-yellow cloth.

'What's that?'

'The big new store, outside town. "Just-in-Time Rescue." '

The name alone made Sunni and Mae chuckle as they stepped out of the van, braving public view and the eyes that dismissed them as peasants.

'It sounds like a newspaper headline . . .'

'A cheap romance . . .'

Sezen was not to have her modernity fazed. She shrugged and managed to step down from the van like a princess.

Sezen belonged.

'They call it that because they know everything that is bought, and can predict exactly what is needed. They sell out every day.'

'So does a good trader here,' sniffed Sunni.

Perhaps no longer. There were grannies, some middle-aged women, some potbellied men come to sit on folding deck-chairs and chat with friends who stayed by their unrolled mats. There were few customers to distract them from their open tins of beers. Mae felt disappointment. She had always loved stepping out into the market, the heart of the town.

No fires or spangled trucks, no drunken Cossacks dancing.

Around the square a forest of bright new plastic signs danced, opening and closing like flowers.

Akai. Sony. Yeshiboz Sistemlar . . .

A far cry from the dingy restaurants, the boys running with trays bearing glasses of tea.

You are dead, the Airhead said.

'Right, what is the plan?' Sunni asked.

'Mr Oz and I will go to the bank . . .' began Mae.

'Me too,' said Sezen, and the hunger in her eyes said: *I want to learn about money.*

Sunni adjusted her sunglasses. 'I have some errands.' Fashion work she did not want Mae to know about.

Fair enough, thought Mae.

Mae suggested, 'Shall we meet by the van at, oh, two hours from now? For lunch?'

'That will be lovely!' exclaimed Sunni. 'We can go to the temple gardens.'

'Ugh,' said Sezen.

Mr Oz intervened. 'We don't have time, if we are to get to the congress. I'll just order lunch now.'

He keyed in the address of Just-in-Time Rescue.

The Central Man escorted Mae to the bank.
They were welcomed with great politesse. Mae had expected to feel uncomfortable, but found herself immune to feeling inferior. She found that money made her as good as anyone else.

They sipped tea in the Director's office, and he was friendly and polite in white shirt and tie. He was full-blooded Karz, big, with hairy arms and a moustache like a trimmed broom and he had a full-blooded Karz name: Mr Saatchi Saatchi.

I am here, thought Mae. I am where I always wanted to be. I am a businesswoman, modern, respected. Sezen sat clenched like a fist with admiration. Mae felt her eyes swell. Don't cry, she warned herself.

'Madam Chung will need a cellular account. She will be doing business with you always through mobile services.'

'We have had such facilities for over ten years, so it is good to see them in more general use,' the Director said, determined the government should know how advanced they were. Mr Oz had enough wisdom to nod approval.

'Under the terms, you will notice that Madam Chung has the full backing of the TW Initiative, with extendable credit. If she verifies any overdrafts are for the Initiative-sponsored business, then the government will made good any losses.' Mr Oz paused. 'The credit is therefore to be extended when she asks.'

The director's eyes widened slightly, then he nodded. 'Hmm,' he said, the implications sinking in.

'Uh. This means the government will also have full and regular access to Info on this funded, guaranteed account.'

'Of course,' said the Director, arms held open.

'We will need to discuss security and coding.'

'I have a full report,' replied the Director. He had a copy for Mae. He strolled with them to the front door.

'An honour, Madam,' Mr Saatchi Saatchi said. 'Such enterprise gladdens the hearts of all.' He shook hands with all of them. He smelled of pine, and through the white shirt was the brighter outline of his perfumed vest.

When he had gone, Sezen seized Mae's hand. 'Oh, Mae,' she said, lost for words.

Mae felt like chuckling. 'If only he knew who we were!'

Sezen shrugged. 'Did you notice,' she said, 'the Director was not wearing a wedding ring? Perhaps I can marry him if you cannot.'

Mr Oz and Mr Wing went off together to admire computers. Mae wanted to get her hair done. She went to Halat's. The little hussy was even busier and ruder than ever. She snapped her fingers and sent Mae and Sezen to her assistants. The young girls showed them on screens how Mae and Sezen would look with their new hair. The young girls looked very smug, expecting Mae to be knocked sideways by science. 'Tuh,' said Mae. 'I do that on the top of Red Mountain.'

As the girls cut and trimmed, they looked all the while at the screens for instructions.

'How can Halat be so foolish?' wondered Mae as they left.

'How do you mean?' Sezen asked.

Mae shook her head. 'She makes it too plain that she herself adds nothing.'

Fashion had shifted again. There was more garish colour, not less, particularly on the young women. Fashion had gone crazy, in all different directions at once.

But the ice cream shop was there, and the old streaked cinema showing Hong Kong movies, and the tiny shops offering acupuncture, healing herbs, fortune-telling. Lined up outside the tiled wall of a butcher's shop was a row of severed goat's-heads.

The shop of the disabled seamstress was closed. Mae had wanted to buy her stock of oatmeal cloth. Its green door had a hastily hammered board across it.

Mae went into the next shop, which sold various sweets, walnuts on thread in dried fruit juice. A rather sour, slumped-looking woman ran it.

'What happened to Miss Soo?' asked Mae.

'Oh! She left to be with her boyfriend.'

Mae was silent. She remembered the girl's staring eyes, the twisted limbs, and she wanted to know: how did she get the money, what did she find when she got there?

The woman was blunt. 'They didn't stay together, but she found a job anyway and stayed in Balshang. Tuh. I had to board her shop up myself to keep out the vermin.'

'What happened to her stock?'

The woman was not that interested. 'I think it was sold at auction.'

Mae paused. The oatmeal cloth. She saw it now with different eyes. It had been finely woven, with white mixed in, tight warp and weft, and it would hang so well, so well when weighted down with fine embroidery.

'Was anything left over?'

'Oh! You will have to ask around. Hold on. Hakan? Hakan?' The woman called her husband, a Karzistani. 'A lady here wants to know if Miss Soo had any stock left over.'

There was a bellow from behind the curtain, and a murmur from a TV. 'How should I know?'

The woman did not like to be shown to be lower-class, poor. She felt herself to be showed up by her husband's response. 'You are a man in business, I assumed you knew.'

Mae was surprised how sorry she was not to see Miss Soo, sorry not to be able to follow her story. She looked at the boarded-up shop, and its closed and shuttered windows. The plywood was already streaked and cracked. Mae discovered that she had liked Miss Soo very much, and admired her. And it would have been useful to have a friend in the Balshang fashion business.

'If she ever comes back,' said Mae. 'Do tell her that Mrs Chung sends affectionate regards.'

Sezen asked as they walked back to the van. 'So what now?'

Mae sniffed. 'I have credit now. I will order cloth online.'

Everything ends, said Old Mrs Tung.

The meeting was held in the Mudharet, the Town Hall, with its cracked tiles and filthy toilets.

The meeting room was laid out like a theatre, with a stage and rows of seats. It was crowded, unbearably hot, and roaring with sustained talk. On the wall was a blank panel of patterned teak with some twist of black iron pinned to it, like an ugly brooch. Sculpture.

There were no seats left except in the very front row, as if the participants were schoolchildren wanting to avoid the teacher's gaze.

Mae walked down the aisle and along the front row and saw faces. A young, sharp eagle of a man sat in a suit that looked expensive and cheap at the same time. He smiled slightly while his eyes glared. He is a shark, thought Mae. He eats people.

Beside the Shark, a masculine-looking woman with no makeup, short hair, a sleeping-bag jacket, and army boots was talking to herself into some kind of microphone.

A fat man with pink hair was blowing his nose. The boy next to him provocatively pulled up his T-shirt to display tattoos.

All these people, Mae realized, have new faces. I can only just read them. She began to feel a tremor again, the tremor of fear.

The Talent who read the local news walked onto the stage, to a mixture of polite applause and boos. She was immaculate in fire-engine red. She was prettier than she looked on TV, and far more steely. She gave a television smile and welcomed them, but there was no polite silence. If anything, the noise from the crowd got worse.

'Good afternoon. I am pleased to welcome you to the afternoon session of today's important discussions . . .' She explained that they had been enlightened and enthralled by the first set of speakers. They were now to usefully discuss and come to some conclusions about the use that the Green Valley should make of new technology.

Someone shouted at her, 'Don't bother with all of that. Why has the government accepted an outmoded Format for Air?' Mae looked around to see a scrawny middle-aged man.

The Talent's smile did not falter. 'The UN Format is the agreed international standard. Karzistan is not in a position to choose a different Format than everyone else.'

There was a groan of protest mingled with raucous laughter.

A scrawny man who was all white city teeth grinned. 'Not in Tokyo.'

'This is not Tokyo,' said the Talent with icy forbearance.

'In Tokyo they use both!'

'Just don't make it practically illegal!' shouted the Army Boot Woman.

'Please,' said the Talent, holding up her hands. 'This meeting can do nothing about the UN Format!'

'They are running the Gates Format at the same time, in New York!' another Head shouted.

'Look. This meeting is to review local efforts here in the Happy Province.'

'What efforts?' the fat man yelled, still eating. He was enjoying the atmosphere.

'This, among them—' began the Talent.

'This is supposed to be a discussion, give us Focus!'

'Focus!' someone else yelled.

The Talent turned and snapped her fingers. Mae found herself admiring her. The Talent's voice was suddenly louder. 'Okay, we each have the Focus in turn, but please stand up and say who you are. You first, sir.'

The fat pink-haired man stood up. 'Ali Bey Turkoman. I ask again, what efforts? There is only one Taking Wing officer for all of the Red Mountain area. Is there a single e-mail address for all those villages yet? Is this a concerted government effort?'

He wants to sell us things, thought Mae.

'It is precisely the lack of e-mail that Air and related technologies are meant to address. Next question!'

The Talent, tense, pointed to someone else. A scholarly looking man, bow-backed, spectacles, unfolded upwards from his chair. 'Professor Li Ho, Department of Medical-Computer Interface.'

He took out a written statement, and there was another squawk of laughter.

He droned. Mae wanted to understand. It was the first time she had heard a professor talk, and she expected wisdom, and it was no surprise to her that she could not follow what was said.

But she did begin to find it difficult to breathe.

There was something called Juh-ee Em. Another English word. Was all the world English? GM was something about very small things. It was about growing things. It was also, somehow, about making people smarter. The professor wanted to change things in people.

He started talking about children who could read after six months, who were doing advanced mathematical work at thirteen. That, she could understand. That, she could picture. He was saying that people were stupid, but they could be cured.

He was having to raise his voice. 'GM is one area in which Karzistan could push ahead, becoming a new centre of advancement for the world.'

'More like a playground for crooks!' someone shouted.

'Karzistan is not a garbage pail for the rest of the world!'

The professor was shouted down.

'We're here to talk about Air. Go play with your own Juh Nee Sus!'

An Airhead got overexcited. He leapt up, like a dancer, and he didn't need the Focus. He yelled, voice breaking, 'Air can do anything GM could do! In New York, they merge minds for a hobby to make new music! We are still talking about it as if it were television! We still use the word "screens"!'

'The blind could see!' roared the Army Boot Woman next to Mae.

'School's out. No more need for Teachers!'

'Or Talents! That's her real problem.'

Is this a war? Mae wondered. The shouting was so unlike the Karzistani way. It was ugly, showed lack of control, lack of harmony, even lack of Islamic discipline. Lack of everything. Who were these . . . these . . . children? In their goggles and crazy clothes?

And were people so very stupid that they all were to be erased, made better?

The Shark stood up. He smiled slightly and flicked a finger toward the Talent. The air around him seemed to brighten.

'Hikmet Tunch, Green Valley Systems.' His voice, typically Karz, was gravelly, but surprisingly high, almost like a woman's. He said nothing else, but immediately the noise in the hall reduced.

'Professor Li Ho is correct, of course. GM is a technology with immense potential and one that Karzistan must not ignore. At Green Valley Systems we are looking at all aspects of Medical Interface. We have a programme to see how the Gates Format could be used in our cultural setting, perhaps alongside the UN Format. One of the applications we are looking at is the use of Air to artificially augment intelligence, which does avoid some of the ethical issues surrounding GM.'

There was an admiring murmur and a scattering of applause.

The next question was respectful, from a colourless young man in a loose grey shirt and not a trace of Airhead finery. 'I would like to ask Mr Tunch-sir what is he finding out about the Gates Format and the ways it differs from the UN Format.'

That, thought Mae, is someone who was told to ask him that question. Sharks have little fish that follow them for scraps.

For some reason people chuckled. The Army Boot Woman gave a kung fu kick of joy.

'The Gates Format is very . . . confusing,' began Mr Tunch-sir, and there was a fresh wave of comment as if there had been some kind of admission. The Talent gave the same embarrassed grimace as Mr Oz.

Mr Tunch seemed very aware of the effect he was having. His face became hooded, hazy somehow, smiling like a mask, his eyes screened. 'Once you are beyond the Gates, everything merges, with no neat divisions. It is a little bit slower than the UN Format, but once the Gates are open, it becomes very intuitive. For all of those reasons we hope that augmented functions will be able to merge invisibly with the user's own functions.' He smiled again and Mae saw teeth.

Mae felt vertigo. She understood none of it, not the words, not the disputes, not what people wore, or even how they moved. Her future had seemed settled and in order. It had felt like a staircase up to a door that was clearly labelled: Air. You only had to make that climb once.

Instead the future was a pit. It went down in layers, each layer stranger than the next. And there was no bottom to it.

The Talent intervened, smiling, embarrassed, heightened in the Focus. 'I am sure that we are very interested in Mr Tunch's insights into the Gates Format. Which, of course, he has never entered himself, as the creation of second imprints is illegal.'

A murmur of laughter and collusion. Panic gripped Mae. Here, a scant thirty miles from Red Mountain, people were talking a new language, about things she had never heard of, dreamed of. All of them were lazily familiar with it. It was a whole Way of which she knew nothing. Nothing except that it was death to her village. Death not only to her village, but to all human beings, as they once had been. Blood seemed to drain from Mae's head.

Did none of them love being human? Did they all so badly want to become machines, to be measured? Mae's fingers and knees buzzed.

'Why do you want us all to die?'

Mae was suddenly aware that she had spoken aloud. She had spoken aloud without willing it. She tried to say, to Sunni, I did not say that. I shouted but it was not me.

And she couldn't. She, Mae, couldn't speak.

She sat frozen in her chair, unable to move, everything numbed except her mouth. Her mouth seemed to snap by itself, like a turtle's. She heard herself shout.

'We built you! We built this City, we put in the drains, we nurtured you. And now you want us to die? You want us to put ourselves to the knife? Fade back into the earth, to be despised by you . . . you automobiles. You, you, streetlamps. You, you radios, you parrot radios!'

'It's happening again,' Sunni said quickly.

'It's never been anything like this,' said Sezen, sitting up in alarm. 'Look, she's fighting it. She's trying to stop it. Mae, Mae, it's not you talking, is it?'

Mae managed to make her body nod once: *Yes.*

Mr Oz looked appalled, embarrassed. Mr Wing crouched around out of his chair and knelt in front of Mae and looked deep into her eyes.

'We will not go without a fight! Humankind will not go without a fight!'

'Stop it, Mae!' pleaded Sunni.

Mae's wide eyes tried to say, mutely, *I can't!'*

And Sezen suddenly stood up, jaw thrust out, and signalled the Talent. The Talent saw they were peasants, saw it was an emergency, and yearned for order. The Talent acquiesced and passed the Focus.

'All you city people,' said Sezen.

Mae kept shouting. *'In the olden days, ancestors were worshipped!'*

'You talk as if most of your own people do not exist. I am a peasant.

I live on the top of Red Mountain. My mother keeps a goat in the living room and we sit on the corncobs we eat for furniture!'

'I want to go home! I want my home!'

Fighting made it worse. Fighting made the thing resist. Mae decided to try to calm it. Sssh, Mrs Tung, dear Old Mrs Tung. Quiet, my love. I am sorry you are dead, but all things die. How many times has our village died, one people after another? You said that yourself.

Something was halted and grew confused. *'Where is this? What is this?'* it asked in miserable confusion. The hall itself had fallen silent.

Sezen had turned to the room and was pointing at Mae. 'That woman, my boss, was in your Air, when you tried your Test. And another woman died in her arms because of your Test. And the other woman's mind still lives in her! Are you happy! Are you proud of Juh-ee Em now?!'

The Talent grew concerned in a professional voice: 'How . . . How was this not reported?'

Sezen answered. 'We live thirty miles up a mountain! There is no one to report to!' There was an unreadable noise of reaction in the hall. Sezen kept shouting:

'We here are the party of progress in our village. Ah? But there is another party. It goes around destroying the TV sets. My brave boss Mrs Chung Mae tries to teach our children, our women, our men, how to use Air when it comes, she teaches us on the TV. And the Schoolteacher prevents her! The Schoolteacher actually tries to stop us learning. He breaks the TV! That is what we face! While all of you are going to the moon!'

Sezen stood enraged, quivering, and there was not a sound in the hall. None of them had any answer to that at all.

Helpless in her own body, Mae felt back deep inside herself with her mind. Once more she reached back to some heavy, mighty, implacable thing in which she was rooted. And she felt herself there, felt this root, and it was gnarled, twisted, confounded. Two of us, she realized. There are two of us there, entwined like a ginger root. Mae was nearly at the point of understanding. Then she was called back.

'Mae?' It was Mr Wing. 'Mae? Someone is here. He wants to help you.'

The Shark in the suit, the man with the gravelly voice, was kneeling over her. His pinched face and his coiffeured hair seemed to shift inside Mae's eyes as if a membrane had descended over them. His face seemed to turn green and twist into a sardonic grimace. She saw him suddenly as the Devil.

Or someone did. And that person roused herself and rose up to her feet and saw in him everything that was destroying her world.

Mae felt her own body seized from her. She felt herself pushed away and then drift upwards like a boat no longer moored. Mae floated free of herself. Everything went dim and still and calm, and she had no fear or anger. It was suddenly clear that none of this really meant anything. She viewed it all with the detachment with which she would one day view her own death.

Mae saw her body strike the predator in the face, a tiny dogged woman hitting a City operator. She could even smile at it. It amused her. The smile was metaphoric, because she was no longer in touch with her body.

Mr Wing held her by the arms and was pulling her back. The body started to sing. It bellowed an old war song, loud and defiant, a song of war against the Communists. Sezen and Sunni stood between her and the man, who held his bruised face. They stroked Mae's hair. Distracted, wild-eyed, the face continued to sing, the old songs, the dead songs, the songs her beloved warrior had taught her fifty years before.

Old Mrs Tung was fighting to live. The only life she had was Mae's.

14

Mae woke up in a strange bed.

The walls were pale blue with white cornices. Sitting patiently at the foot of her bed was a man. His face was familiar.

It was Mr Tunch. The name meant 'Bronze.' He seemed to be made of something burnished. He was wearing a different suit, zigzag black on beige. Like the other one, it was shiny.

'Good morning,' he said pleasantly.

Mae sat up. The hotel room had flowers, a TV and a chest of drawers made of polished red wood.

'Where are my friends?' asked Mae.

'They have gone home. You have been somewhere else for many days.'

'What do you mean, "somewhere else?"'

'Ah.' He shrugged. 'Mrs Tung has been here instead.'

'For what? Days? *Days?*'

Mr Tunch nodded. He tried to look sorry, but instead looked rather excited.

Mae was prickled with terror. 'How did I come back?' It was the most urgent thing to know.

'She wandered off,' said Mr Tunch. 'Or rather, she simply could not understand what she was doing here. She couldn't remember where she was, so she kept trying to leave. And finally she did.'

He chuckled. 'She got very frustrated.'

Mae murmured, 'They do.'

After Mae's father was killed, her family moved, along with the bloodstained diwan cushions, to the house of the Iron Aunt, Wang Cro. At first Mae did not understand what was wrong or why the adults whispered. The Iron Aunt was nearly eighty and strong enough to move oil jars, but she always thought it was Thursday, cooked dinner at nine in the morning, and could not remember that Mae was not her mother. The children could tease her into a fury.

Mr Tunch explained: 'Your friends thought it was best if we did what we could here.'

'Yes. Yes, I can see that,' murmured Mae. Yes, I can see you now, in your Bronze suit playing the big man. You even soothed Sezen into leaving me.

'Can you do anything?' Mae demanded.

Mr Tunch leaned towards her and put a hand on her shoulder and made a slight gesture of helplessness. 'We need to know more.'

'You can't help.' In some ways, Mae was relieved.

Mr Tunch smiled. 'Not yet.'

'In that case,' said Mae, 'I want to go home. I have business to do.'

'What business?' chuckled Mr Tunch, with something too much like scorn. 'Look. There is nowhere else in Karzistan that has as much knowledge about the Air Formats as my company. We are experts in Human-Computer Interface Medicine. Do you know what that is?'

With a sudden chill, Mae knew. 'You put cameras in Airheads' eyes.'

Tunch blinked. Gotcha, thought Mae. I don't like you.

He recovered. 'Right now we are far more concerned about the damage the Test did. We are very concerned about the Format that was used in that Test, and we are horrified at what happened to you. Mrs Chung, we all have business interests, but your health is more important. Forgive me, but you did not do much business these last three days.'

You oil your words like Dr Bauschu, thought Mae. You do everything for reasons of your own. But perhaps, just perhaps, I need you.

Mae was driven to Yeshiboz Sistemlar along a new empty road.
Suddenly there was a wire mesh fence, with what looked like a white airport hangar beyond. Mae noted that it was built just outside the jurisdiction of the city.

Gates were raised and lowered. Bright young people, the brightest Mae had yet seen in Yeshibozkent, looked as scrubbed as the painted metal walls of the hangar and somehow just as cheap. They performed the function of people without the solidity or the beauty. They would age badly.

Mr Bronze was king. Inside the front lobby, girls smiled and, modern as they were, dipped their heads in traditional respect.

'This is Madam Chung Mae. Our patient,' he said to a woman at the first desk, with a quick grin.

No covered heads here. No broad straw hats with the rims white from dried sweat. The people looked as though they had come from Florida. Disney World, thought Mae. I bet the offices at Disney World look just like this.

'You'll excuse me, Mrs Chung. Like you, I have business to attend to. But Madam Akurgal will take excellent care of you.'

Madam Akurgal was not yet thirty and dressed like a nurse with a rubber tube around her neck. She kept calling Mae by her first name, as if she were a servant.

'Just come through here, Mae. We need to disinfect you,' she said, with a winning smile and a TV-Talent accent that came from nowhere specific. She led Mae into a corridor and there was a blast of air, and a sound like vacuum cleaners, and purple lights that made the white nurse's uniform glow white.

She sat Mae in a chair and told her to relax and lowered a kind of metal hat on her head. Mae waited for a sensation. None came. They sucked blood from her arm. Like at the hairdresser's, Mae was given a magazine to read.

Doctors looked at paper being printed and shook their heads and called each other over to look. They ignored both Mae and the nurse. Finally one of them tore off a sheet of the paper and showed it to Mae.

He was a Chinese gentleman, one of her own, probably a Buddhist, and she hoped for understanding. 'We have found nothing,' he said, beaming, pointing.

The paper was printed with jagged lines.

'So Mrs Tung is not here.' He jabbed a finger at the paper. 'Everything is working as usual. Except see, here, this line covers activity in the area of the cortex we think corresponds to communication with Air. We think you are constantly checking for Airmail.'

He was rather pleased. 'This is very encouraging. It means we speedily learn to use Air even without realizing it.'

'What does it mean for me?'

He shrugged. 'It means that things are basically okay in your physical brain. It confirms what we had all thought, that the problem is with your imprint in Air. Somehow yours is linked with another imprint.'

'Well, okay then, just wipe out those imprints in Air.'

'Ah,' he said, delighted with the beauty of the thing. 'Everything in Air is permanent.'

Another doctor entered, and the first greeted him effusively, waving the paper. Then he turned back, nodding politely.

'Oh, and one thing to cheer you up. Your blood test shows that you are expecting a joyful event. It will be a son. Good day.'

Madam Akurgal shook her head. 'Stupid men,' she hissed, and looked, stricken, into Mae's eyes.

'What does he mean, I'm pregnant? I can't be pregnant.'

The woman looked serious. 'Oh, yes you can.'

'I've had my period.' Mae was whispering frantically but even so, the male doctors turned. 'Do you understand? I had a normal period!'

The woman shook her head. 'Then there must be real problems. Is the bleeding just today, recently?'

'I have not miscarried! It was just a period and now it's over!'

The woman stroked her forehead. 'Then there may be something really wrong. We can have you tested.'

'I don't want to be tested again, I have had too many tests!'

'Just give yourself time to think. My name is Fatimah. Fatimah Akurgal. I will always be nearby.'

'What does it mean that they found nothing wrong with my head?'

Fatimah sagged under the weight of so much evidence of things gone awry. 'It means that you are the first of a kind. There is little that we know.'

'I don't want her taking over!' Mae was nearly in tears. 'She is trying to take over!'

'We will be looking at the Format to see if there is a way we can control it, even stop its communicating with you.' Fatimah paused. 'I am so sorry. I wish I had better news.'

Mae did begin to weep then. She hid her eyes. The doctors kept talking about her.

Mae spent the rest of the morning having magazines passed to her. She could not read them. She thought about what these people had said, and the way they had said it.

Fatimah took her to the bright noisy canteen and bought her a lunch of spicy red leaves that Mae had never seen before. 'We'll see about getting a car to drive you back to the hotel,' Fatimah said.

'Be sure to tell Mr Tunch for me,' Mae said, 'that I will be going straight back home to Kizuldah.'

Fatimah protested.

'Just ask Mr Tunch to talk to me,' said Mae.

Mr Tunch drove Mae back to the hotel himself.

The car was bronze-coloured and inside it smelled like a toilet, all false pine.

'You are going to have to give me something else to keep me,' said Mae.

'I beg your pardon!' coughed Mr Tunch.

'You can't cure me, why should I stay?'

'Why should I want you to stay?' Mr Tunch's eyes twinkled. It was cool in the car, air-conditioned. People outside squinted against the sun, walking on empty, baking streets.

'You want information from me. And information is like sugar, it is to be sold.'

'How very wise,' replied Mr Tunch, sounding very pleased, as if she were a clever pupil.

'You always sound surprised when I am not stupid. That's insulting.'

He dipped his head in respect. 'I'm sorry. But I would have thought that a possibility of a cure was reason enough for you to stay.'

'*Possibility* of a cure. That's not a lot. What do you get?'

'I get to understand your unusual situation. That will tell me a lot about how Air works.'

'Then,' she sighed, 'I am afraid this is not a fair trade. I do not want to spend time here being explored by you, only to find that there is no cure. I have work to do.'

'What else do you want?' he asked blandly.

'To learn everything you know,' she said. 'About what is coming.'

He chuckled. 'My dear woman, why would you want to know that?'

'So I can prepare my people.' Mae paused. 'Not your people. My people. There is a difference.'

His face did not lose a mote of its benevolence. 'You could not possibly learn all the things I know.'

'I want to know about this "Juh-ee" stuff. And what these Gates are. And what will really happen inside people's heads. What the great powers are using Air for, what they are going to get out of it.'

Mr Tunch smiled. 'Is that all?' he said, his irony losing its airy touch.

'One other thing. What is your full name?'

She almost saw his tongue flick. 'Surely a modern woman such as yourself does not believe in the Wisdom of Names?'

You do, Mae realized. That's why you don't want to give it to me.

'I am just a peasant,' she said. 'It is not good to do business without knowing your client's name.'

He shook his head slightly. 'I am your client, am I? In your professional hands?' He relented. 'My full name is Mr Hikmet Tunch.'

Mr Wisdom Bronze. A wise criminal has no need to soil his hands and so stays shiny. People mistake the polished bronze for gold. A wise criminal can sometimes even help his people, but always for a price.

Mae, you are flying with hawks. Watch out for their talons.

'So. Okay. The deal is this. I stay here one week. Not one day longer. We spend three hours a day finding out what you want, and three hours a day finding out what I want. Okay?'

'Agreed,' he said after a moment.

'I have the mornings,' she said.

Doors bleeped and blew and said hello to Mr Tunch.
'Sorry about all this, but we try to get rid of all the dust,' he said.

His office walls were covered in wood, and it was cool, without windows, and the electric lights were phony, made of bronze to look old-fashioned.

The surface of his desk was covered in glass. Mr Tunch touched it and spoke to it and it came alive with the familiar Interface.

'In order,' he said. ' "Intro background briefing on genetics, cosmology, and Air history." "Resistance to GM and its relevance to the development of Air." "The nature of the UN Format and background history." "The nature of the Gates Format and background history." "Speculative futures." ' He paused. 'Is that what you want to know?'

'I will check my list.'

'Good. I will be back here at lunchtime.' He caught her scowl. 'I did not agree to teach you myself. That machine is far more used to teaching than I am. And much more patient. But please let me know if there is anything it cannot tell you.'

'I don't know how it works.'

'No. But it knows how you work. Good morning, Mrs Chung-ma'am.'

And he was gone, through another jet of air.

The machine began to speak and show pictures.

They had, apparently, unthreaded humanity like a carpet.

Inside the beautiful white semen, nestled inside the warm home of the womb, were threads, one from the male, one from the female. They now knew what made the threads, and the meaning of each stitch, as if it were Eloi embroidery.

They could place each stitch. Or replace it with better ones.

This was miraculous stuff to learn. Mae could imagine the souls of the unborn blossoming in new forms like flowers bred for new colours or perfumes.

They could make people prettier, stronger, and smarter. Mr Tunch's desk repeated the arguments against doing this. Favourable modifications would be available only for the rich. An even greater gap would open up between Haves and Have-nots.

Air, however, would make everyone a Have. So they said.

These Everyone-Haves would have their memory, their knowledge, and their skills increased. Their ability to calculate figures and link previously unrelated information would all be enhanced by using Info through Air.

It all sounded so calm and clear and reasonable, a briefing for the Disney people of Yeshiboz Sistemlar.

Mae knew when she was being sold something. You are trying to scare me with all this talk of rich people buying smarter babies. You want me to buy Air instead.

She sat forward. Already the bland neutral voice was slipping in warnings. Like old village gossips trying to get their way. Unplugged security problems that might mean the UN Format may not be controllable.

Like her Kru. They put him in Air and they can't turn him off, and all that knowledge goes away for free.

No money to be made. What you need me for, Mr Tunch, is to learn how to turn off Mrs Tung and turn off my Kru.

There was a tickle somewhere. The tickle was a way of looking at the world, a narrative. It was impatient.

'The benefits of Air for social inclusion are evident,' said Mr Tunch's desk. *'But questions of safety for users must be paramount. And intellectual property must be protected.'*

The tickling grew as insistent as a headache. It was fear. It was hopelessness. It was a dread of the world beyond Kizuldah.

The desk said, *'Liberal economists wanted to open up Air to the competitive marketplace. Others argued that there could only be one Air, and that it would be wrong to grant a monopoly to any purely business interest. With two competing Formats, users could choose.'*

They want to own our souls.

You see! You see?

Her. She's here.

The desk said, *'An international consortium of software houses agreed to set standards. The anti-monopolists soon claimed that the consortium was in fact controlled by the Company.'*

It's always the same with these people.

Showdown, thought Mae. It's you or me.

'Tension increased when the Director of the International Air Consortium resigned, charging the Company with bad faith.' The Desk still spoke.

Before there was time for conscious thought to signal what she was doing, Mae said, 'It is so sad about your daughter-in-law's death.'

What? The old one did not like surprises.

'It was then that the director-general of the UN founded a new consortium to continue development of Air.'

'Tui. She died. The same day you did.'

Someone answered Mae aloud: 'What? That's a horrible thing to say!'

Mae replied, 'She threw herself down a well, don't you remember? I know you're dead, but you have been told about it many times. The day of the Air Test – it was months ago. She died. By the way, who are you speaking to?'

The desk said, *'But the new consortium struggled for lack of funds.'*

'This is a terrible thing to do, to try to scare an old lady this way!'

'Scare? All I asked was, who are you talking to?'

'I . . . I . . . Well, Mae, of course!'

Mae remembered Aunt Wang Cro. She would pretend and pretend that everything was fine. There were no mirrors in the room. 'Mae? Where is Mae? Can you see her in this room?'

Mae leaned back in case the old one could see her reflection in the desk.

The desk stopped teaching. *'Excuse me, was that an instruction? I do not understand.'*

Mae pushed again. 'Okay. Who are you?'

'I am . . .' The thing stopped. For a moment, it had no identity. 'I am . . . I am Madam Tung Ai-ling!'

'Then who are you talking to?' Mae thrust words like a knife.

'Excuse me, was that an instruction?'

'I don't know! I can't see! I'm blind. This is terrible to do to an old blind lady – make fun of her! Why are you doing this?'

The thing tried to stand up. It tried to look about. Mae could feel a twitching in the nerves of her legs and neck and eyes. She needs my body to live, Mae thought. She wants it.

'So,' Mae asked airily. 'Do you like being in Yeshiboz Sistemlar?'

'Excuse me, was that an instruction?'

'No!' Mae told the desk. 'Please continue lesson.'

'Who are *you* talking to?' Mrs Tung demanded in triumph.

'An intelligent desk. They make them these days. It's giving me a lesson in the UN Format.'

'I don't know what you mean.'

'Of course you don't; you can't remember anything from one minute to the next. You are here in Karzistan's most important medical-computer complex. Where did you think you were?'

'I don't . . . It's of no importance!'

'When international fundraising efforts failed, the major Company offered to pay for both Formats, promising to keep both workstreams entirely independent.'

On the screen, important people shook hands, and half the UN General Assembly rose to its feet applauding. Others notably stayed seated.

'See this desk? The whole thing is a screen, yes? See the people applauding?'

'Yes, of course!'

'So, who in Kizuldah has such a thing?'

Mrs Tung fought to keep her equilibrium as had the Iron Aunt, by disguise and improvisation. 'Kwan? Kwan. We are in Kwan's house! Everyone says she has made her house very modern!'

'You see the desk?'

'Yes, of course I see the desk!'

'How? You are blind!'

'I . . . I my eyes have got better.'

'How long have they been better?'

'Since yesterday! Since yesterday!'

'Oh! There was a miracle yesterday! What else happened yesterday?' Mae was shouting.

'The Consortium proved to be short-lived. Amid technical disagreements and charges that the Company was rigging Air structures that would only work with its other solutions.'

Old Mrs Tung faltered. 'I . . . I . . . You came to see me?'

'Who? Who came to see you? Who are you talking to?'

She chuckled, embarrassed. 'It's so silly . . . I can't . . .'

'There's no one here! Where are you?'

'I don't know!' Mrs Tung wailed aloud.

Mae bellowed: 'I just told you! Why can't you remember?'

Old Mrs Tung broke down into desperate tears. 'I can't . . . I can't . . .' She shook Mae's head.

Revulsion flooded through Mae's body like a case of food poisoning. Something was sickeningly out of place, wrong. I am like a ghost, I am invisible, I have no body.

'I can't move!' wailed Old Mrs Tung.

Mae began to weep for her, for the neat dead system of responses on the other side of the screen of the world. Mae felt the terror and the sadness and the horror of being dead.

And so the thing gained strength. It spoke as if Mae and she were one. *'We'll lose everything! This is a terrible place. We must get away!'*

Mae struggled back, her voice more feeble: 'What place is this?'

'I don't know. Don't start that again.'

'Where are you? What day?'

'Stop pestering me! Who are you to come at me with impertinent questions?'

'Work began on the new Format. From the beginning, some engineers felt the schedule was too ambitious.'

Mrs Tung barked, 'What is that thing talking about?'

'I told you. The UN Format. But you can't remember. Shall I explain it again to you?'

'No, I don't want to hear about it!'

'Of course you don't, because you're scared of it and you're scared of it because you know you wouldn't be able to remember it. You can remember nothing! Where are we? Can't remember? I just told you where we are but you can't remember, can you? *Can* you? You can't remember what day it is or where you are or even who you are!'

The thing howled and stood up and Mae stood up with it. The thing was in a rage. Mae felt it thrash inside her with frustration. If the thing had carried an old walking stick, she would have beaten Mae with it. The thing spun in confusion and anger and disgust and terror around and around the desk, and it threw Mae against the imprisoning walls. Mae felt a buzzing in her brain and her body, as if there was a great numb abscess in all of her being.

Suddenly Mae's hand reached up and slapped her own face.

Mae clenched and fought, her hand shook in midair, wavered as if pulled by magnets.

Mae shouted, 'Whose face did you slap? You slapped and you felt it yourself! How could you slap someone's face and feel it yourself?'

'I don't know! Let me go! Let me go!'

'Excuse me, I am hearing sounds of distress. Do wish me to call for help?'

The hand slapped Mae again, even harder.

Mae fought with words. 'You slapped a body. Whose body?'

The thing howled in terror and struck Mae's face again and again. Left hand, right hand, left hand, beating her about the face.

Mae pushed: 'You're sick, you're old, you're mad, you're crazy!'

The thing stumbled, wounded and disorientated. 'I don't know! I don't know-ho!-ho!' The thing wailed in complete despair

'You can't remember, you're senile, you're dead! You're dead and senile and sick; you have no hands; you have no eyes; you are nowhere; you do not exist!'

'Let me go!' The thing heaved with sobs. It could no longer speak, for grief and despair and horror. Its voice rose to a despairing shriek, and it picked Mae up and flung her across the desk.

And like the passing of a tornado, suddenly everything was still.

Mae was left panting, alone in Mr Tunch's office.

'Do you need me to call for help?' the desk asked.

'No,' Mae was able to croak. Her throat was raw from shouting. She had been speaking for both of them.

Tears and spit were smeared all over her face and splattered over the desktop. The cheeks and the palms of her hands stung. She sat up and looked at her own reflection in the glass-topped desk. A fresh bruise was coming up on her cheek.

Suspicion made Mae look up, and she saw a camera in the corner of the room. Tunch will have seen all that, she thought. He'll have been spying.

Well, if he's seen all that, then that's all he's going to get from me.

Mae pulled in deep, shuddering breaths. She stood up and wiped her face and tried to straighten her hair.

I've seen her off. I know how to see her off and I don't need Mr Tunch.

Time, she thought, to get down to work.

'Continue with lecture,' she told the desk.

Mr Tunch joined her for lunch.
'I thought you might like to try the new food,' he said.

Because of her lecture, Mae knew what that meant. New proteins, new tastes, grown from new organisms.

'They are designed to be delicious,' he said.

The soup was bracing and solid, like lentils laced with lemon, and made hearty with something like tomatoes and pork. It was sour and sweet, with a bitter undertow like coffee.

'You see?' he said, chuckling. 'Good, isn't it?'

'Yes,' Mae had to admit. 'Yes. I wonder if I will be happy to go back to cold rice?'

He laughed again, and said. 'Maybe you won't have to.'

I am, in part, a Question Map for his future.

'You are experimenting on me,' she told Tunch, coldly.

'The food is specially formulated for expectant mothers,' he told her. 'Its nutrients pass within seconds into the bloodstream through any tissue layer. In effect, it is being digested the moment it enters the mouth.'

'Does that mean it's shit by the time I've swallowed it?'

Mr Tunch only chuckled. He touched Mae's bruised face. 'Mae. We're trying to help you.'

For a moment, she almost believed him.

In the afternoon Fatimah led Mae to what looked like a flying saucer. Mae lay down in it, and again, there was no physical pain. Fatimah clucked once with her tongue. She turned the scan off, helped Mae down.

'What, what?' Mae said.

'The child,' said Fatimah, dazed. 'The pregnancy is in your stomach.'

Mae blinked. In Karz, the words *belly* or *womb* and *stomach* could be confused.

'Your food belly,' said Fatimah.

How? Mae knew what she knew. That was not possible. 'Your machine is wrong,' she said.

'No chance,' said Fatimah. 'Here.'

She replayed the file of the sounding. The screen showed a shifting mass of what looked like translucent grey porridge. Shapes seemed to bubble out of it.

Pumping and alive, something sighed and shrugged inside her. Fleetingly Mae even saw something like a head.

'That's the child. It has grown the usual protective sac, and appears to be healthy for now.' Fatimah turned back and looked at her. The downward slope of her head crumpled her chin and neck and made her look older, sad-fleshed, like Mae. 'It is in your stomach.'

'So how could it happen?' Mae's voice was raised.

Fatimah's deep-brown eyes kept staring down into hers, as if to offer her a stable place. 'Pregnancies can take root anywhere in the body, once the egg has been kissed. The question is, how would an egg and the male part meet in your stomach?'

And Mae knew how. '*Ilahe Illallah*,' she gasped, though nominally a Buddhist, and covered her mouth. She had swallowed Ken; she had swallowed her own menstrual blood. She felt like a flurry of scarves, all fears and horrors. She was stripped and bare, her sexuality exposed, her private secret bedroom found to have one wall missing. The whole village could look in. Scientists peered over Mr Ken's shoulder, prying into her strange habits.

'Has this ever happened before?' Mae whispered.

Fatimah shrugged. 'If it has, it would miscarry by now.'

'What will happen?' Mae was following the consequences of this monstrosity. Birth through the throat? Surgery?

'The child cannot be healthy,' said Fatimah. 'As for birth, it should be by surgery, but I cannot recommend that. We . . . We can help you quietly, telling no one . . .' Her voice trailed away, a warm hand on Mae's chilled arm.

In the raw villages of Karzistan, unwanted winter babies were left to crystallize in the snows. Third daughters were whisked away and dispatched before the mother could see them and love them.

Fatimah seemed alarmed by something. Her voice was still low. 'There can be no question of your keeping it.'

Mae felt as though she were clutching a cloth over herself to hide naked breasts.

If the village knew this, what would they do? She was already a monster for simply falling out of marriage. A woman who talked too much and then gave birth to a monster through her mouth? They might drive her away with stones.

'You must understand. The stomach is full of strong acid. To dissolve food? We don't know what that will do to the child.'

Mae was seeing Mr Ken's face. Her young man . . . Young? Either one of them?

Yes, at heart they were young. At heart and in memory, they would always be in school together, longing and shy. They would always be the lovers who found each other late in life.

That heart and memory would only be as real as long as they lived. But if there were a child, that meant that love would outlive both of them.

And that was what love was for, all the waste and the pain and the inconvenience and the awkwardness and the ugliness. It was to draw together and build an island of love, in which children could grow, and love can be passed on.

'Mae? Mae you cannot be thinking . . .'

Mae was thinking of redemption. In Karz the phrase for it was 'Unexpected Flower.' It was seen as late Indian summer, surprising the world with roses. My Unexpected Flower, she called the child. The machines were silent and blue around them.

'I need to think,' was all that Mae could say.

'You won't be given much of a chance for that,' said Fatimah.

The rest of the afternoon session consisted of qualitative research. Mae was introduced to a bald, eager stranger with spectacles. *This is Mr Pakansir, he will ask you questions. Hello, Mrs Chung-ma'am. Please answer the questions quickly, no need for deep consideration.*

The name Pakan meant 'Real Man.' Mae sat, legs crossed, arms crossed trying to find cover. The questions began easily enough: occupation . . . marriage . . . was she a happy woman? How did things change after Formatting? After the Test, how did things change?

'Would you say that your sexual habits changed after Formatting?'

'No,' said Mae.

'But . . . uh . . . you are pregnant. In an unusual way.'

'No one knows how such a thing is possible,' replied Mae.

'We understand, however, that your marriage broke down.'

Mae sat silent.

'Is that true? You have just said that you were happily married. How did it become unhappy?'

Mae smiled silently.

Mr Real Man's grin went a bit fierce. 'Mr Tunch has said to remind you, perhaps, of your bargain. That you will help us understand, in return for training. Your mind was interfered with by the UN Format. We are trying to understand what happened. To help others.'

Mr Real Man went back to his sheet of papers. They were printed, but not entirely square on the paper. 'Did you find yourself perform-ing sexual acts that were not part of your previous repertoire?'

Silence.

'Please, Mrs Chung. These are medical questions.'

Poor man. You do not know who you are dealing with, thought Mae.

'Had you ever heard of or known about oral sex before the Format-ting?'

Mae couldn't help but answer, 'How on earth do you think peasant women avoid being pregnant all the time?'

He looked disappointed. 'Oh. So you knew about sex with the mouth before the Formatting. There is no chance that the Formatting planted the idea?'

Mae did not answer. Her heart was growing as tight as her masklike little smile.

'Was it something that you practised frequently?'

Mr Pakan slouched forward, groin thrust out. Unconsciously he began to rock back and forth as if having sex with the tip of his long tie. Mae stood up, thinking of Mr Haseem, and kicked Mr Real Man between the legs.

He groaned and doubled over. She struck him in the face. His glasses slipped lopsided, and he slumped forward on his knees. He crawled out of the room. Mae kicked him on the bottom and sent him sprawling over the polished padded floor outside the room and then she slammed the door behind him.

She waited, her breath quivering as though it were fire.

She was not an ignorant peasant or some farm animal made to

reproduce as they wished. They were going to have to learn to treat her as a person of consequence.

Mr Tunch came early. He looked amused. 'You are confirming important data for us.'

'Am I really?' said Mae. She felt as though her teeth had been filed into a saw.

'You were not violent before the Formatting, were you?'

Mae paused. 'I never met such bastards until the Formatting.'

Mr Tunch was still smiling. He was amused. 'I wish I could have seen it – poor old Mr Real Man. Asking his neat little machine questions, and meeting Real Life by mistake.'

Mae was unmoved, unfooled. 'He was doing your bidding.'

'Are you going to hit me?' Tunch asked in mock alarm.

Mae considered. 'I might kill you if you go too far.'

Even Mr Tunch blinked. 'Oh,' he said, darkening.

'I am a direct person. Are you going to blame that on the UN as well?' Mae batted her eyelashes at him.

It was his turn to grin, masklike.

Mae sat back, feeling hearty, like she was surrounded by friends and picking on an enemy. 'That's why you do this, Mr Tunch. You want to sell the Gates Format. You have to say the UN Format is bad. It is bad because it gives away too much to people like me. Is the Gates Format paying you?'

Mr Tunch closed his eyes and his smile went gentler, amused, and rueful. He looked at her in something like affection and said, 'Unexpected Flower.'

Mae felt a chill. Just how much had Mr Wisdom Bronze penetrated, with his machines and Question Maps?

He sighed. 'Whenever I despair for our people and think there is no hope, with the ignorance, the poverty, the deep divisions, the lack of resources, someone like you surprises me, and I know, I *know* Karzistan could take on the world.'

The two looked at each other, both surprised.

'You are very damaged, you know,' he added.

You want to rifle through the pages of my life, hold my underwear in the sun to show stains.

Mae gathered herself up and asked brightly, 'Did you make the money for all of this from drugs?'

His face hung suspended.

She shrugged. 'Look, you can't shock me. A wise man makes money where he can. You are not from Yeshibozkent. I can tell that from your accent. You are from far down the valley, where soil, sun, everything is hard. The poppies grow there.'

He was staring at her, almost wary.

'Am I still your Unexpected Flower?' she asked.

His face had recovered, but at least he no longer looked amused by her. 'Even more so,' he said.

'You see, I know you. You are Wise Gangster. Godfather.' Mae mimed a *rat-a-tat-tat*. 'So. Yes. I am afraid of you. I know what you could do to me.'

'I do what I have to do,' he said, then he added hastily, 'That was not a threat to you. I meant: I do what I have to do to help our people.'

Mae was considering.

Wisdom Bronze said, 'How else was I to build this?'

She believed him. 'How else. And you hate the foreigners even more than you hate us.'

He looked uncertain.

'After all, we are ignorant, poor, deeply divided.' Mae sighed. 'So many of us must get in your way.'

'I am trying to be your friend,' he said softly.

'Ah,' said Mae, looking at the floor. 'Do you know how terrifying that idea is?'

He smiled one last smile before leaving her. But he also pointed a warning finger.

Mae found that she knew his story. She could see it.

Fate and his father's seed, his mother's egg, conspired to give birth to someone very smart indeed.

Hikmet Tunch would have been a clever clownish farm boy, wickedly sharp and sometimes brutal. She could see him scowling with thought as he forked chickpeas into the mill, or kicked geese away from the grain.

This is for fools, he would have thought, seeing the hard work that produced only pennies a day. He saw the daredevil thugs in their shiny track suits and heavy jewellery. He joined them. Volunteering, asking for the most dangerous jobs. He carried the stuff across borders. He did this so he could see how the rest of the world worked.

Hikmet Tunch at seventeen would have looked like a truck driver, stumpy, hard, unshaven, smiling ingratiatingly to the guards at the borders. All the time he spoke to them, his merry eyes would be innocent, even though he knew the gas tank was half full of white paste.

Hikmet would have seen Berlin, Prague, and St Petersburg. He would have studied the world by screwing its women, to discover from them their languages, how they thought, what they valued.

He would have come back and hated the way the buildings in Karzistan did not sit straight, the way the dust gathered in the road. He would have hated the peasant clothes, and the paintings on the trucks, and the old wooden houses.

Wise Gangster would have built up friends, loyal men from his village – big, hefty, criminal men nowhere near as bright, but who followed him and threatened others.

He would have killed people. Not often. But you do not take over the drug trade from a position of mere carrier without knowing when to strike, and to strike so hard that the enemy can never recover.

Wisdom Bronze was a man who would have burned fields, whole villages, killed male heirs who were only five years old.

And yet, thought Mae, underneath it all, our aim is the same. To help the people.

What Wise Gangster knew was that Info was the new drug.

Fatimah came into Mae's room, looking only slightly shifty.

'Have you thought about the pregnancy?' Fatimah began. She was genuinely concerned, but she had been told, Mae could see, to get the same information as Mr Real Man.

I have become an Unexpected Poppy to be milked for juice.

'Could this have happened to you before?'

Mae decided to lie. They want answers, so I'll fuck them up by giving wrong ones. 'Oh. Yes. Of course. We all suck in my village.'

That meant Fatimah could say she had done her job. To her credit, the thing that most concerned her was Mae's plight.

'I have something that will resolve the problem for you,' she murmured.

Do you really think I would do anything here, in your clutches, to be entered into your records?

'What is it?' Mae asked. If it was a pill, she could pocket it.

But Fatimah took out a needle. 'Very quick. One injection, then it is gone, with no chemical traces, a natural dropping. Especially given where the pregnancy is.'

'No.' said Mae.

'Look, Mae,' said Fatimah, 'the earlier, the better – the easier. In all ways: physically, emotionally.'

Mae looked at Fatimah and found she knew her, too. A pretty woman, very smart. She had a rich father. Good education, but where could she use her skills in Karzistan? Where else but here? Where Shytan himself rules. A kind woman, too, as rich women often are. But small. Being rich inflates smallness like a balloon. Being rich stretches it thinner.

'Don't you believe in love?' Mae asked her.

'I . . . I . . .' Fatimah fluttered.

That brought you up smartly, city woman.

'You don't think love is of no concern in medicine, do you?'

'No,' said Fatimah, hurt. 'No, no, of course not.' She prided herself on her care, her concern, and her sensitivity.

'Then why are you so blind and deaf to the simple fact that a mother might love a late and unexpected flower?'

Mae waited, and then added, 'Especially when the father is the only man she has ever loved.'

Mae knew somehow that Fatimah had never been loved, and part of Mae wanted to hurt her.

Fatimah seemed to wilt. 'I . . . I did not understand the situation.'

'Perhaps you would care to help me, instead.'

Fatimah looked thoroughly chastised. Her eyes were downcast. 'If you'll let me. I have to know what you feel, to help.'

'So,' sighed Mae. 'Is it the case that I am supposed to let you question-map me, and only then you will care?'

Fatimah looked chilled to the bone.

'You want to be a good woman,' said Mae, smiling ruefully. 'Perhaps it is not possible to be good here.'

Fatimah rallied: 'Is it possible to be good anywhere?'

Okay, so we get down to something true. 'We all do the best we can,' said Mae. 'So. You tell me. How do we save my baby?'

Fatimah considered. 'It might not be possible. If the child is small, some kind of birth might be possible, otherwise it will be surgery.'

'When would you say it is due?'

'Its development is strange. Say, May or June. Would you be able to come back here?' Fatimah's eyes were pained, askance. 'I am sure that this place would help you have it. It has the most advanced medical and scientific equipment in Karzistan.'

'What would they get out of it?'

'Probably nothing further. They will have gotten enough for them to be generous.'

'What will they get out of me?'

Fatimah sighed. 'Scientific fame? A high profile in the industry?' She smiled sideways. 'Medical-IT Interface.' In Karzistani, the word for *interface* was 'two-face,' which had an implication of betrayal.

Neither of them needed to comment on the appropriateness of that.

'You must not do physical work,' said Fatimah. 'If you do miscarry – vomit . . . make yourself vomit all you can. Do not let anything stay in your stomach. And call me. I will do what I can to come to you.'

There were no windows in the room, and no clocks, but Mae felt it was late. 'I would like to go back to my hotel now.'

It was as she had feared. Fatimah's face went still with shame.

'I'm sorry,' Fatimah began. 'But given your condition, it is felt best that you spend the night here.'

'I want to spend it in my hotel.'

Fatimah's eyes were sorry indeed. 'It is very comfortable for our guests here.'

'I know too much,' said Mae. 'I said too much.'

Very quietly indeed, Mae had become a prisoner.

The rooms are very comfortable in the palace of the devil, considering there are no windows.

A guard brought Mae her dinner. He was huge, so tall his bulging belly did not look fat. He had hairy hands and eyes like camera lenses. Mae knew him, too. She saw him as big farm boy, playing in the same stubble fields as Wisdom Bronze.

'Did you know Mr Tunch when he was a boy?' she asked.

Nothing in his face moved. He watched her eat and took back the plate and the knives.

Mae saw the tiny blinking red light that watched her. She waited until all the lights were off and they could not see her. She whispered to herself without even moving her lips. 'Mae Mae Mae Mae Mae . . .'

She traced the gnarled root of herself back down deep. She felt the settling peace, the calm, and the end of fear and terror. As she fell away from it, the white walls of Yeshiboz Sistemlar looked as thin and frail as eggshells.

Mae settled as gently as an angel into the courtyard. Her clothes seemed to trail after her in ribbons, like silk underwater. The courtyard now looked more like Kwan's grand house. Instead of pens, the blue walls were lined with beautiful new businesses all glowing golden with light. They had modern plastic shop-signs that looked like poppies opening and closing. INFO . . . HELP . . . THAT'S ENTERTAINMENT . . .

Mae entered HELP, and there was Mae herself, dressed as a Talent. Assistant-Mae knew what she wanted. She wanted to see the Gates Format for herself. *'I am afraid there is no programming that allows communication between the UN and the Gates Formats. You will not be able to find any Gates Format imprints.'*

Mae asked the mask, 'Does this system contain any information about the Gates Format?'

Mae-assistant smiled like a shop sign. *'The "Help" function contains information about functions in this Format only.'*

'Is there anything in "Info"?'

I want to know what imprints are and how they work. I want to know what the UN Format is and how it translates thoughts. I don't want to owe Tunch for anything.

The assistant-Mae replied smoothly: *'The "Info" section was developed for the pilot project and contains only examples of proposed kinds of content.'*

Mae regarded her own face. Is my smile so unhelpful when I turn it on my customers? 'Why doesn't Air contain anything?'

Was the smile more broad? *'It is a common failing of IT projects to underestimate the difficulty of providing content and the time scales required.'*

Air was pig-ignorant. Mae was not fooled, either, by her own face. These things – the courtyard, the shop fronts – they are just for show, this is not Air itself, they are the traffic signs towards it.

So Mae turned without another word and walked into Air. Air, she knew, was eternal. Mae walked, deliberately this time, into the blue of information.

She merged with the blue walls, as if they were glowing blue fog. She kept on walking. The walls faded into night. She stood in chaos, and kept feeling the gnarled root, deeper and deeper until even the sound of her own thinking was hushed and she felt even herself fade.

The root seemed to get thicker and thicker, as if it had become the trunk of a tree. It would eventually become Everything. It would become the world; and all the worlds in which the world sat. Mae herself was the thinnest possible little trail back towards the fiction of the world.

She could no longer remember what she was looking for.

I don't want to go on, she managed to think.

Blindly she felt her way back. The blue light shone, her fingernails glowed as white as her hospital gown as if everything were smiling.

Mae stepped back into the courtyard. She walked quietly into That's Entertainment. There were games machines, and radios all along the walls. There was soaring operatic music. In front of a TV set, Old Mrs Tung sat watching *Turandot*.

'Hello, Granny,' said Mae gently.

Mrs Tung turned and smiled, eyes twinkling. She could not remember the last time she and Mae met. All she remembered was the love, deeply imprinted.

There you are, dear. I was just thinking, I hope Mae comes to pay a visit. Isn't it marvellous, the TV? How I've yearned to see Turandot. *They say it happens in Karzistan, you know.*

And you have seen it over and over and over, because it is the only thing on TV in Air. But you can't remember that. Heaven is the place where you cannot change and nothing can ever happen, so the things you love are always eternal. Hell is exactly the same.

The hero Kalaf was singing. *'No one's sleeping. No one's sleeping.'*

'I just wanted to make sure,' said Mae. 'I just wanted to make sure that you were well. I just wanted to make sure that you were as beautiful as I remember.'

Oh-hoo-hoo. The hooting laugh. Now eternal.

And Old Mrs Tung reached across and took Mae's hand. Mrs Tung thought she still had a hand. *Is the beaning going well this year? I used to so love it. All of us on blankets doing the shelling together.*

'Yes,' said Mae. 'It is still going well.'

Then Mae said, though she knew Mrs Tung could not understand: 'I know it is not you who does these things to me. It is the error they made, whatever mistake it was. I just wanted to make sure of that.'

And Old Mrs Tung hooted again, as if she knew what Mae was talking about.

And Mae began to repeat her own name over and over. Her and Mrs Tung's metaphorical hands disentangled like roots.

In the morning, the guard served Mae breakfast on a tray.
The food iridesced like a rainbow, and the flavours veered between pork and jam and all the flavours of breakfast at once. It was delicious. She threw it up into the wastebasket. It continued to shift colours in the bin.

Mae covered her eyes and wept, and then cast off the water from her cheeks. She was led out through all the Disney World people, all spanking new and polished. Do you know they keep prisoners here? she asked their pristine smiles. She was led to the desk. Time, she told herself, to learn.

The desk began by showing her the inside of an eye. Early efforts at interface had beamed coded light signals onto the retina and recorded differences in pathways. Residual patterns of neural activity appeared that were nothing to do with the light. Other information appeared to be passed.

The brain was responding to low levels of electrical charges from outside the body.

Animals were given sudden peak charges that stimulated all areas of their brain. Every neural pathway was stimulated at once. The mystery was that, once stimulated, the charge continued. The brain entered a new state, always charged, always open. The charge continued to exist without any further source of energy.

How could this be? There could be no perpetual motion, no undying source of unreplenished energy.

Unless the brain existed in a realm with no time. Once imprinted, it stayed charged. It was like a radio switched on forever, but not in our world.

There was another world, of seven other dimensions beyond time, and Air existed in those. Air had no spatial dimension. In Air, one mind occupied the same space as another. Stimulation of one imprinted brain correlated to increased activity in another.

But attempts at shared thinking resulted in disorder and discomfort. One brain works in a way very different from another.

What was needed to make Air work was a uniform Format for information.

In theory at least, this Format would simply be information, too. It could be added to the imprints, providing a shared mechanism for making messages compatible and so able to be shared.

The first Formats were crude mathematical formulae that made only the simplest kinds of neural impulses to be communicated.

The first successfully shared Air message was '2 plus 2 equals 4.' It took the form of nervous jolts: two jolts, two jolts, and then four in succession.

If Air were to be used for any commercial purpose, it would have to do more than that.

Synaesthesia was a phenomenon long known and little understood. Some people saw sound, tasted colour, felt words in their fingertips. The brain, so delicate, so responsive, was responding to minute charge differences caused by other phenomena. Infants experienced them – then learned how to block them.

From synaesthesia, a means of stimulating images, sounds, and even tastes was developed. A means of translating this system into first protocols, and then encoding for those protocols, was some years in development.

End of lesson.

Lunch came. Again it was the silent guard who brought it. And Mae knew then, that despite all his smiles, Hikmet Tunch was frightened of her.

Lunch moved. It was delicious new organisms that could talk.

Bits of lunch piped up, in merry little voices: 'We are designed to provide full vitamin and other protein content undiminished by death or cooking. Think of us as the perfect form of happy nutrition.'

Then they sang a happy little song waiting to be eaten. They looked like limbless prawns without shells, with little carbon crystals perched on top like jewels.

'Take that foulness away. Tell Mr Tunch that I will starve myself rather than eat anything other than normal food.'

The silent giant nodded once and left the room, with the lunch still pointedly on the table, still singing like little intelligent bells. He came back with a bowl of ordinary soup. He sat and watched Mae eat it, as if making sure she did. He looked at his watch.

It was only after several mouthfuls that Mae realized the soup had an aftertaste. 'Is there something in this?' she asked. The giant left.

Colours began to sharpen. Mae felt her unease with a new razor-sharpness.

The door opened, and Mr Pakan came in with a dog.

The dog's head was shaved, and a neat little metal cap was bolted to its skull. The cap had a speaker in it.

'Mae, hello, Mae,' the dog slobbered in affection. 'I have a job. People trust me with a job. They have made me much smarter, and taught me how to talk. There may be a future for dogs, if we can tell jokes and love our masters.'

It came toward Mae, backing her into a corner.

'Please let me lick your hand. I only want to lick your hand.'

Mae's head was beginning to buzz, and there was a kind of gathering tension, as if a bubble had swollen and was about to burst.

'You bastards,' she managed to say. They were doing this deliberately, to bring Mrs Tung back.

'Don't you like me? Please like me,' the dog was pleading, wanting to whimper, but the whimper was given a voice. 'Who will feed me if I am not loved?'

Where are we, dear?

Mae heard oxygen rustle in her ear, and she understood so clearly everything that Mrs Tung was feeling. The floor was shifting underfoot, the room was melting.

Let's go home. Do you know the way?

Mae settled onto the floor. Mr Pakan nipped forward and began to wrap Velcro around Mae's arm.

The last thing Mae saw before losing her body was the dog, eating the singing food. 'Gosh, this is good,' said the dog.

Mae was buzzed all the way to the back of her body.

Mrs Tung stood up and sat in a chair, and asked Mr Pakan, 'Would you be good enough to find a blanket for me, dear?'

Who is that man? Mae tried to ask her. You don't know who he is, do you?

The colours chuckled and Mae fell silent.

But oh, Mrs Tung thought, *it's so good to have joints free from pain! And to see so clearly! My books! I shall be able to read my books again.* Mrs Tung hooted with pleasure.

Now, she thought, *if only Mae were here.*

Mae awoke feeling limp, as if every bone were broken.
She was in bed in a room that was like a hospital, but it was a room for

one. SICK BAY RULES, said a notice on a bulletin board. She was still being held.

A kind of ringing went off.

A young male nurse put his head through the door. His eyes skittered over machines.

'How do you feel?' he asked in a high, quiet voice. He might have been Hikmet Tunch's brother.

How do you think I feel? Mae thought. 'Not too good,' she replied. 'Do I still have my baby?'

He paused for a beat. 'I think so.' He wasn't sure. 'Someone will see you soon.' He turned and left.

Somewhere music was playing. The buzzing strings, the slight wheedling flatness of the flute, marked it as Karzistani. The melody was in a European scale, sad and measured. With its wavering Muerain singing and electronic sounds, the music was perched exactly between Asia and Europe, the old and the new. Like us, thought Mae. How like us it is. It was yet another song of lost love.

I am missing the harvest, thought Mae. The valley floor will be cleared and Mr Wing will hire the green machines and the rice will be separated from the stalks. The rice will be piled high in mounds. Someone's car will be running with the radio on to make music. This song perhaps. Mae saw them in her mind, the yellow-blue-green of the old ladies' aprons over their blue trousers, all faded with washing, age, and dust.

Fatimah was back in the room.

'You did this to me,' Mae said. She knew. They had deliberately provoked Old Mrs Tung to return.

Fatimah blinked. 'I'm sorry.'

'Do I still have my baby? Have you taken my baby?'

Fatimah was getting weary of this. 'No, we haven't,' she said quietly.

'Did you learn what you had to?'

Fatimah sat on the bed. 'We now know what happens when the other imprinted personality takes over. It requires emotional synergy, when both personalities feel the same thing. For example, when you both feel fear . . .'

Tell me something new, thought Mae.

Something in the way Mae shifted on the bed made Fatimah stop.

'We have given you a drug that will help you keep the . . . other personality under control.' Fatimah was holding a foil in her hand.

Her eyes said, *See? We are trying to help*. She was amused by something at the same time. 'These pills are so new, the paste is still drying.'

'What does the drug do?' Mae asked.

'It reduces emotional synergy.' Fatimah shrugged. The only words she had were big ones. Either she didn't want to or couldn't say clearly what it did.

But Mae knew. She could feel it. 'It scatters me like leaves,' she said.

Fatimah sighed and breathed out once, hard: *That's it*. 'It might have side effects like that.'

I would not be part of the harvest anyway. The village would shut me out. I have no rice to harvest; it is all Joe's rice. So I would hang around outside the threshing field. Like a ghost.

If I try to tell people what I have seen here, the drug will make me vague. Or Mrs Tung and I will rise up together, in front of them, mad.

Then I will give birth out of my mouth. And be a monster.

'You rest,' said Fatimah, and patted her arm.

Part of Mae wanted to weep and say: I want to go home. But she was blocked from that. Strong emotion or clear thought melted away.

At some point Fatimah had gone, and Mae was alone.

Where is my good dress? she wondered. I took my good dress to the city and my Talent jacket. She looked around the room and saw nothing that was hers.

The good dress and the Talent jacket faded in importance. Mae swung her feet out from the bed. She stood in a surgical shift.

There was nothing in Mae's mind as clear as a decision to escape. She simply left. She did not consciously say: Leave the drugs; better the war, the pain, and the clarity. The foil of pills remained on the table by the bed.

Mae opened the door and walked out into the corridor, and the dog was there.

'Go,' growled the dog, ears alert, teeth bared, rising up. 'Back.'

Mae assumed that for all practical purposes she was talking to Mr Tunch. 'We've completed our bargain,' she said, in a faded, weepy voice. It wasn't fair, she'd done what she said. 'Fair trade.'

'You are supposed to stay there.' His voice was even, mechanical, with strange jumps of tone and texture.

'Why?' Mae asked.

The dog cocked his head to one side. 'Because you are sick.'

'Now I'm well.'

The dog loped forward and snuffled her, and licked her hand.

'Sorry I bit you,' he said. He looked up at her, needing direction.

Mae touched the box on his head, too scattered to feel disgust. The drugs made her feel wonder. She thought of her Kru. It is like this for the dog. They imprinted him and plugged him into the skill of language. Or maybe the skills of a whole person. Maybe it was Tunch. 'You can understand things now. Do you remember what it was like before?'

'A little bit,' said the dog. 'There were only smells. I remember smells. Now I remember other things.'

'You can choose,' said Mae. 'You can decide things.'

She thought of getting back. The world swam around her; the task of leaving the building, walking across the town, finding her way back up the mountainside – it was all impossible without help.

'You can help me get back home.'

The dog cocked his head. His tail wagged suddenly, twice.

'What he's doing,' said Mae, to no one in particular, 'is things that would not be allowed in any other country. That's why they're paying him. So he can do things for them, and find things out.'

'Like me,' said the dog.

'He had to make you as smart as he could. There would only ever be one.'

The dog stepped forward, head lowered, tail still wagging.

'You can't get out that way,' the dog said. 'They will see you. This is the way.'

He put his nose to the floor and snuffled. He was following a scent.

All Mae was aware of was that it was pleasant to have a companion. When she was a child, her Iron Aunt had had a big rangy dog called Mo, who was a bit crazy.

Mo peed everywhere. He would come up and join Mae, and walk with her for a time, but only at his own choice. It felt like that now.

They turned down corridors. The dog's ears pricked up, and he spun around once and tried to bark. 'Who?' the mechanical voice said.

A man in white came up, chuckling, and scratched the dog's ears. Not Mr Pakan. 'Hello, Ling,' he said. 'Where are you going, boy?'

Mae still swam on tides of herself, and it was in both innocence and a bit of cunning that she replied: 'Ling is taking me where I am supposed to be going.'

'Oh, Very good. Wonderful isn't it? Have you talked to him about smells? It is like entering another world.'

'I have, a bit,' said Mae. 'And it is wonderful.'

'How are you feeling?'

'The drugs have taken very powerful effect,' said Mae.

His smile went a bit steely. Perhaps it was the drug, but his teeth seemed to glint. 'That's good,' he said. He bowed and left.

'We did not tell the truth,' said Ling. The mechanical voice could convey no emotion.

'We're learning,' said Mae.

There was a booming and a bashing ahead of them. Mae thought of thunder, then drums. Ling stopped and waited and inclined his head in a universal, cross-species sign: *Scratch my ears*. Mae unconsciously obeyed.

The sound came from huge metal barrels. Men in blue overalls rolled them past Mae. Ling growled, establishing he was a loyal guard dog.

'Good boy,' chuckled the deliverymen, gazing in blank lust, even at a middle-aged woman in a shift. 'Rather you than me, Ling,' they said, deciding Mae's lack of erotic charm made her an object of scorn.

Ling sat panting patiently. He lifted up his nose, tasting the air, lapped Mae's hand, and walked on, his claws clicking, slipping on the polished floor.

He led her to a blue door. He nudged the long metal handle with his nose.

Mae was numbly grateful. 'Thank you.'

She pushed the door and stepped out into a full parking lot in blazing sunlight, full of burnished company buses and three limousines.

Ling followed.

There was a fence. It was high and made of crisscrossed metal, and was crowned all along the top with barbed wire.

Mae was dim and detached. She felt her root into Air. It was easier to do on drugs, for she was as a calm as if she were in Air.

'This is all a joke,' she said, and suddenly smiled.

It was true. The world was a joke. It was a story, twisted by gravity out of nothing. It was an accidental by-product of Air, of the eternity where Air was.

She could feel this eternity. She could take the story into her hands. She could feel the metal fence. The fence was mere fiction.

So she tore it.

Reaching into Air, Mae seized reality, as she herself had been seized, and very simply, very easily, Mae's mind ripped the metal of the fence apart. She giggled at how funny it was that everyone should take the fence so seriously. She tore the mesh like a strip of cloth.

'This season,' she said, 'Air-aware young ladies will wear the fences they have torn down as sign of their strength.'

The torn edges of the fence danced, as if in wind.

'Sing,' she told the fence, and started to chuckle. 'Why not?'

And the snapped, sharp edges of the torn wire began to tinkle, just as lunch had done. Anything was possible.

Wind blew the dust, the fence danced and sang, and Mae stepped out, into the desert, followed by a talking dog.

Beyond the fence was hot valley scrubland, full of bracken and thorns grown to Mae's height. The thorns and bracken parted and bowed before her. She walked barefoot through them. They rose up again behind her to shield her. She heard Ling's feet behind her in the dust. Overhead was sky, unchanging, clouds as they had been in the time of the Buddha.

'You're coming with me,' she said.

'Yes,' said Ling. 'It is my job to stay with you.'

'How will we get home?'

'I will follow you there.'

A lizard scuttled across their path into shadow and froze, watchful, its throat pumping.

'What do you see?' Mae asked him.

'Many corridors,' said the dog. 'No ceiling.'

'That is called the sky,' said Mae.

The dog paused and then was pumped with Info. 'Oh, yes,' he said. 'I see it is the sky now.'

They walked. Overhead hawks circled looking for desert mice.

'I want to hunt,' said Ling.

'No. Not yet. Later. You have a job,' said Mae.

Ahead of them were the mountains, soft and rounded in the nearer layers, then rising up, one after another, back into the hills, back to the sharply folded crags, the snow. Mae had a vague plan, to walk through the undeveloped plain around the town.

Already they were pushing their way through a hedge, into a dust track leading to the outskirts of a village. A handsome green mosque rose up above mud huts, and there was a smell of billy goat. Two women were making dungcakes. They turned leathery desert-plain faces to her, not quite believing what they saw.

A naked Chinese woman, they would later say, *with a dog wearing a metal hat.*

Mae pushed her way through another hedge, and walked across a field of straw.

'When do we eat?' Ling asked.

'I don't know,' said Mae. Something seemed to go pop in her head. Her thinking was clearing.

'Ling feels unloved if he is not fed,' warned the computer on his head. *'He becomes anxious and unreliable.'*

'There is a big juicy steak at home and a bowl of water,' promised Mae.

Water dripped from Ling's panting tongue. 'That sounds good,' he said. 'I can see the steak,' he said. 'I can smell it.' The computer was feeding him.

'Good dog. Good boy,' said Mae, feeling sorry for him – for being fooled, for being possessed. It made her feel they had things in common.

The city had spread beyond its old boundaries. Mae paused at the edge of a road. There was nothing for it but for Mae to keep walking. The streets were bright, broken. Traffic idled past her, heads turned. A woman shouted something about covering herself up, drunken woman.

The dog turned and growled, baring teeth in black jaws.

Why are they all so worried? wondered Mae. My shift is as long as my knees, and some of us are still so poor we wander barefoot. A teenage boy, all in sleeping-bag clothes stepped out, then stepped back into a small bookshop and called to his friends. A man helpless in a barber's chair stared at her as she passed, his face going slack and open.

'The world is so big,' said Ling. A man in old, stiff clothes and a peasant's cap dropped a bag of tools.

'These are all houses for people,' said Mae.

'Where does the world stop?' asked Ling.

The man began to follow.

'It never stops,' said Mae.

'Your . . . Your dog is talking,' said the man.

Ling thought he was being praised and turned back to sniff the man.

He was a hard Karz villager with a face that looked as though someone had smashed it with a plank of wood, stubble-black chin merging with huge moustache. He backed away in alarm.

'They do it in the Air,' said Mae, explaining, wanting him to know it was nothing extraordinary. 'It is like a radio in his head and in his throat.'

The man began to shake his head over and over. He wiped away the world with his hand. 'I fix cars,' he said. He turned back. 'The dog understands?'

'I want to,' said Ling.

The man gazed into the dog's soft black eyes, as if he could fall into them and disappear. '*Tuh,*' was all he said, the sound of his world changing, suddenly, for real. He picked up his bag of tools. Ling sniffed them experimentally. Dazed, the man scratched his head and turned away.

The boys from the bookshop stared.

Mae gave them a little wave and walked on.

The streets began to climb steeply.

'How far to the steak?' Ling asked.

'Oh, perfect boy, lovely fellow,' said Mae. 'It is a long way but we will talk.'

'What is the world like to you?' Ling asked her.

'Right now, I am drugged. So everything is very strange. Like it is for you.'

A woman came up to her and wordlessly pressed into Mae's hands a pair of plastic sandals. The plastic was clear and full of silvery flakes that reflected and caught the sunlight. The woman's eyes were ringed with mascara, full of outrage and pity. She wore a purple jacket and Western-woman working boots.

'May I suggest a light mauve scarf with a such a strongly coloured jacket?' said Mae.

Mae, she told herself, your mind. Your mind is not working properly yet.

The woman's face did not change, but she walked away quickly.

Mae walked on in her silver shoes to where the road turned off, towards the sign for home, and she looked back over the city with its trees and light. Shadows were slightly longer, sunlight and shadow were balanced in the foul blue air. It looked cooler, golden, mauve. Rising up out of the light was the Great Saudi mosque, made of frosted crystal, dancing quotes from the Koran catching the sunlight to be illuminated from within.

A long bronze-reflecting limousine coasted to a halt beside her. A window slid open like the protective lens of a lizard's eye, and Mr Tunch leaned out.

Mae felt terror, only the terror could not fight its way to the surface of her face, her limbs, or down into the pit of her stomach.

I'm caught, she thought blandly.

'Hello, Mae,' said Wisdom Bronze. They both waited. He pushed open the door on the other side of the car. 'Let me drive you home.'

Mae could not move. Part of her wanted to cry. Her eyes tried to cry, but the drugs prevented it.

Ling looked back and forth, back and forth.

'Mae?' he pleaded for direction.

'Get in,' she said, in a voice so soft only a dog could hear.

'He said we're going home,' said the dog. He climbed into the backseat, next to Mae's old best dress.

Mr Tunch was doing his own driving. 'I meant what I said, Mae.' His eyes were blanked out by glasses. 'There's something I want to explain.'

Something seemed to pop in Mae's head again. Something told her the walking had been good, it had made the drugs worse, but they'd be over with sooner. The thought meant she had not yet got into the car.

'Don't be silly, Mae, you are not important enough to me to hurt you.'

She got in the front seat.

'Me,' whimpered Ling, and, claws clattering, climbed onto Mae's lap. His feet dug in for something to grab.

'Ouch,' said Mae.

'Hold me,' said Ling, and she realized he was afraid. He ached for the window, where there were smells, the world he truly believed in.

Mae hoisted him around so that he sat on her lap comfortably.

'All in?' asked Tunch, as if they were a family on an outing.

The car went in the right direction.

'What will happen to you back home?' Tunch asked.

Mae considered. 'I will be an outcast. It will make helping the village very difficult, for they will not listen to me.' *Pop*, went her head, clearing again. She began to be aware of the light breeze of fear blowing through her.

'You won't take the drugs?' he asked.

Mae shook her head.

He had to change gear, glancing in the mirror at the future behind them. 'That is probably wise. It will leave you with a clearer head. But when you and Mrs Tung feel the same thing, she will emerge.'

'I can beat her off,' said Mae. 'Except when people interfere.'

'Sorry,' said Tunch.

Mae could have said a lot of things. Do you say 'Sorry' to the wives of men you kill? Or do you just threaten? How do you keep all your separate selves apart? I hope you manage to keep the small-time assassin separate from the man who wants to rule.

Pop.

Tunch went on: 'One of the side effects as the drug wears off will be a period of, uh, greater sensitivity. Someone needs to be with you.'

Pop. 'You know my address in Air. Will you be recording that, too?'

Pop. 'And sell the information to the foreigners? Or have they already paid for anything you might find out?'

'It depends,' murmured Tunch, 'on the information.'

'Ling,' said Mae, 'he may try to kill you. Too many people have seen you, boy. And you are not supposed to exist. Do you understand me, boy?'

'Yes,' said the unreadable mechanical voice. Mae buried her face against his furry cheek, and the bare, shaved forehead.

'I'm sorry. I didn't understand. I should have left you in the compound. Watch him, Ling. He has masters, too, like you do. He has to be loyal to them or he does not eat. You and he are the same.'

'I understand,' said Ling.

'Good boy, Ling,' said Tunch. 'Just be a good boy.'

'I always am,' said Ling.

Mae said, 'You will turn Karzistan into the garbage pail of the world.'

'Karzistan has to make a living,' he said.

The car drove on, grasses blurring by. What was close was lost in speed.

'You do not understand me, Mae,' said Tunch. 'I am slightly relying on the drug to help you accept what I will say. What I am about to say, is said using very carefully chosen words, used in a very precise way.'

'I'm ready,' said Mae.

'I am a hero,' said Tunch.

Ling's nose was pushed out of the window. 'This world smells different,' he said.

Mae was unimpressed. 'I am waiting for the precise meaning of the word,' said Mae.

'A hero mediates,' said Tunch. 'He brings together good and evil. He uses the tools of evil, may even *be* evil, to do something constructive. People need heroes. They yearn for them. That is because people who are not heroes think that heroes are good. And evil is done by people who think they are good. Good people do harm by being gentle and not stopping things. Good people fight wars out of love. They need heroes to break that cycle. To defend them, to build things.'

Black shadows danced inside Mae's eyes, and Mrs Tung tried to gather her thoughts.

'It is terrible, but it is the only way forward. Heroes are not like in stories, where they wear a mask of nobility. All heroes do evil, terrible things. Robin Hood was a thief and murderer. John Kennedy ordered invasions and wars. So did Lawrence, who fought like a wolf for the Arabs. Ataturk destroyed the mosques and killed the clergy. Wonderful, terrible people are both good and evil.'

The drug made it difficult for anyone to gather their thoughts. 'You are trying to tell me why you will never do me harm,' she said, 'now that you have learned from the harm you have already done me.'

'Exactly. You are too valuable. I want you home in your village. You know why?'

'Yes,' Mae said meekly. 'You think I am a hero, too.'

Tunch simply gave a thin, satisfied grin.

'How did you tear the fence?' he asked.

Mae told him. 'Air is real and we are not.'

Wisdom nodded once, something confirmed.

Mae told herself what she did not tell him. What they have done is make an artificial soul. You and your Format want to sell our souls back to us. You are about to find out that we have always had them.

They drove on, into the night.

Ling rode with his head out of the window.

Halfway up the hill the dog asked, 'Why are there stars? They don't smell.'

Tunch replied, 'They smell of heat, so fierce it burns away the ability to smell.'

'Are we getting closer to them?' said Ling, looking around.

'Not yet. Not for a good few many years,' said Tunch.

Mae suddenly understood that Tunch intended to stand on the stars, however many centuries it took.

Tunch asked the dog, 'Do you want to know how the universe began?'

'Oh. That would be good to know,' said the dog, looking around.

'Dreadful pride,' said Mae.

Tunch was very pleased with that, and grinned.

'When there is nothingness,' he said, 'gravity does not attract. It becomes repulsive. Ask what those words mean.'

Obediently the dog consulted Air, sweat dripping off his panting tongue. After a moment Ling said, 'Gravity pulls everything together. It makes us heavy so we stay on the ground. Otherwise we would float off to the stars.'

'Good,' said Tunch.

'So, my nose won't burn out.'

'No.'

The dog seemed to grin, panting.

Tunch continued: 'Before anything existed, gravity had nothing to do – except pull apart. It pulled, and nothingness stretched, like a rubber band, until it broke. When it broke there was a burst of light and heat. So energy was created, and out of energy, things were made.'

'So far so good,' said the dog.

'So with something there instead of nothing, gravity then became an attractive force. It pulled together. As the universe exploded, it also pulled and twisted things into shapes. Clouds of gas, then balls of gas, then stars.'

'Is gravity a hero, too?' asked the dog.

'Yes,' said Tunch, pleased.

'How?' asked Mae.

'We know that, mathematically, there must be eleven dimensions. Like height and width, except these other dimensions were not affected by the explosion at the beginning. They are still the same size, coiled at the heart of the universe. Where nothing really changes. Think of the point right at the centre of a wheel. The wheel turns, but the point does not.'

'What's a wheel?' asked Ling.

'We're riding on wheels. Access the mathematical definition of a point.'

'Okay, boss.'

'In those coiled dimensions, we know that the same equations that describe electromagnetism, describe gravity. In the timeless realms outside our universe, they are one. Now, ask again, what is thought?'

Ling had the answer ready. 'An electromagnetic phenomenon. Differences in charges produced by chemical reactions.'

'Gravity is like thought. It has power over everything in this universe, but it is not *in* this universe. There is no gravity wave, no gravity particle. It exists outside time. It makes things. It loves things. It tears things apart.'

He let the car speak for a while, the roaring of its wheels on the rough surface, the hum of the engine.

'You know what we're going to do, people like you and me, Mae?' Again the disembodied grin, adrift from the sunglasses, lit from underneath now by the dash panel lights. 'We're going to prove God exists. We'll send it messages.'

Mae thought:

I am trapped in a car with a madman who happens to tell the truth. I am trapped in a car with someone driven so crazy by a big opinion of himself that he thinks he will live forever. He thinks he will shake God's hand by machines. The truly awful thing is that he might just do it.

Mae saw clearly that his system was so greedy it would eat anything. Anything she did or said – kick Mr Pakan, befriend Ling, argue with Tunch, or agree – would be wound into his Bronze madness, feed it.

The only thing she could do that would not help him would be to stay silent. Staying silent would prevent him from wanting to know anything more about her. If he felt there was more Info to be derived, he would imprison her again until he had it.

Mae pretended to go to sleep.

The car crackled to a halt over loose gravel.

Mae blinked around her. 'This is it,' she said. She petted Ling. 'Treat him well,' she told Mr Tunch. 'He has been promised steak.'

Ling looked up into her eyes. 'I want this box taken off my head,' he said. 'I want this voice taken out.'

Mae looked at Tunch. Would he?

'We can do that,' Mr Tunch said, and gave Ling's head a casual scratch.

Mae said curtly, 'Thank you for driving me.'

She got out, stepping out of the smell of luxury, leather, and polish. She smelled drains, the little river, and the mud.

'The future will be wonderful, Mae.' He passed her her best dress, covered in hearts.

She simply smiled and nodded, as enigmatically as possible.

'Work towards it,' he told her. And closed the door. Mae waited as the car turned. Ling's nose was pressed against the gap in the window.

'I will be a dog again,' he said.

The car sighed back down the road and was gone. Mae turned and began to walk and realized that her knees were shaking, weak.

He talks of God. So would the Devil.

Mae was halfway up the slope to Kwan's when she realized that the silver shoes were gone.

15

---

e-mail from: Miss Soo Ling
15 September

Of course I remember you, Mrs Chung-ma'am. You were always so appreciative of my work, and so generous in payment. It is good to know I have such good friends back home. I am enjoying my job in Balshang very much. I contribute to designs now, but cutting and sewing are my secret weapons. No one thinks I can, so then I do and people's eyes widen.

You are kind to enquire after Bulent. I am afraid we are no longer together though we are still good chums. We advise each other on how to survive working with all these Foxes and Otters and talk about the Green Valley and all the people we left behind.

Regarding your appreciated offer to purchase my stocks of cloth: The cloth is stored in Yeshibozkent with my mother, Mrs Soo Tung. I have written to her to ask her to arrange the shipping of the cloth via your bank.

Thank you also for the fascinating review of your work under the Taking Wing Initiative. I am not a follower of technology, and you opened new windows for me on this new world. Do stay in touch. Will you be visiting Balshang?

---

e-mail from: Lieutenant Chung Lung
6 October

Mrs Chung Mae,

Is my mother really on e-mail? Dad told me that you work on the Wings' machine. My sister is thrilled, too. The army allows us an allocation of personal correspondence. They assume most of us have no e-mail addresses to write to! Please let me know if I have the wrong Mrs Chung.

---

audio file from: Mrs Chung Mae
6 October

My son

You cannot know the joy getting your message has given me. You are being so discreet about all that has passed and so sweet not to mention it and so I am even happier to hear from you because no one in the village talks to me and I must talk to people because, Lung, the future is not just coming, it is here now and no one at Kizuldah is ready for it. They are all like quivering mice, trying to pretend there is no hawk, no cat. I have learned many things, my son. I took a Question Map of the village. At first I thought to find out about what clothes people wanted, but I began to ask what they felt about the Test. This is what I learned: They think the Air will be like TV. They do not want to see that it will be in their heads, will change their heads. They just think it will be all football and games. They are frightened of what is coming and that means they will not face up to all they have to learn. I tried to start a school to teach them, Lung, and they came for a while. Then, to stop the school, Shen told your father what I have done. So the school ended. Oh, Lung, I am so sorry for you, and how confused you must be by what has happened. I fell in love, a silly thing for an old woman to do, but I ask you who are still young and can still grab life, to try to understand that when you are old you can suddenly see that there is something you have missed, and that you must have now or get used to never having it. I mean love, Lung. I know how much you respect your father, and how, as an officer in the President's army, you value good behaviour. I behaved badly. Now I am a fallen woman. You know what that means in a little village. Let me know if this is embarrassing, and I will not call again like this. I must go. Oh, I have a business on the Net; look at www.native/fashion/wing.htvl. Give your sister all my love.

EYE OF THE BEHOLDER

Around the world, nothing is more beautiful than authentic expression of native culture combined with simple elegance.

Here you will see beautiful native embroidery incorporated in modern designs. Please choose the item that most appeals, to see it modelled by the native women who produced these magnificent clothings.

But the beauty that exists will have been produced in your own beautiful eyes, for you wish to see what a forgotten part of the world can produce.

FRIENDS IN NEW PLACES

If you have visited us before, we can show you new things that might interest you especially. So please do leave a Calling Card, so we can be friends. Please tell us what you think, for we are ignorant peasants in the hills and yearn to hear from you.

OUR FASHION TAKES WING

'TAKING WING' SUIT

This simple trouser suit in oatmeal cloth has authentic Karzistani embroidered panels. No designer thought of them. This ancient 'Swallow' pattern means good luck in marriage. This would make excellent wedding outfit or a present to hopeful, happy bride. The suit is modelled by tribal craftswoman Shen Suloi, she of the happy smile. Her husband is our schoolteacher.

I AM A JOYFUL PERSON WORKWEAR

This is whole native coat and hood, meant to be worn in fields and in sun or rain. It banishes resentment. One chooses what one is in life, and so it is foolish to resent the need to work. Wearing this shows that one is brave to face real life.

Worn by Sezen Ozdemir, who is not a native woman. She is a good girl who goes a bit wild sometimes. Buy this, and she will save the money for a motorcycle.

LISTEN TO GOD SPECIAL DRESS

Let this special pattern speak secretly to your heart on important days. This is special dress for big occasion, say if your son marries or you go to high school prom. What this panel does is tell the gods that you listen to them. It is not for mankind to understand what the gods say. We just must keep listening. So this is a most noble panel.

Wing Kwan, a four-farm wife, wears this dress and she made all the panels.

Native people have many gods in shamanistic tradition. Chinese folk in Karzistan are Buddhist, but trueblood Karz tend to be Muslim. We even have Christian family living in our village! All are welcome here.

SEE OUR HOUSE

KIZULDAH – OUR VILLAGE

We held the TV's camera from the roof to show our village and terraces. We are lucky to live in such beauty. It is more beautiful now that so many people can see it. We plant rice on the terraces. They are 2000 years old.

THIS IS US

The models all stand in front of Mr Wing's machine in his courtyard. He is four-farm owner. Videos from this screen show us and the house of our business. We work in the barn, all us ladies together. We are very happy, and you will see us all, even me.

I am wicked Madam Chung Mae. I am not popular in the village. I try to tell our people about the future. Also, I am a fallen woman, but my friends forgive that. My nickname is Madam Owl, which is not respectful at all!

---

e-mail from: Lieutenant Chung Lung
8 October

Thank you for such a long letter. At first I was going to give you short note only. But then I realized that it would look as though I was angry with you.

I feel many conflicting things hard to put into words. I know my father and I respect him, but he is human and I can see his failings. I take no sides. I wish that both of you had behaved properly and stayed together. I regard this love as a kind of disaster, but you cannot be angry with the victim of a flood.

I see you alone, living in Kwan's attic with no position, and I grieve for you. Then I see your screens and feel that you are also in some way happy, and I have to ask: What has happened to my mother? How is she able to do this?

I showed the screens to some of my fellow officers who thought them very impressive. Some of their wives were also impressed and thought the clothes looked very modern. Others said that it made Karzistan look undeveloped and uncivilized. I noticed it was the more intelligent ladies who said that, no, it was like Americans talking about their Indian Heritage. One woman said you know when you love something that you have truly bested it and are mature. They regard our peasant days as something to be overcome.

Are the clothes selling?

---

audio file from: Miss Soo Ling
10 October

Mrs Chung-ma'am

I must say I was enthralled by your screens, both the content and the fashion ideas they display. So original and of the moment. Really. Congratulations. It was good to see my oatmeal cloth put to such fine use.

You are quite right, Horsemen do get you listings, but they charge you, and magpies do not. Our fashion house will only work through magpies. They harvest opportunities for enterprises and build up lists of people with particular interests. Magpies charge distributors and not you. I attach a list of excellent magpies to contact. I hope this is helpful.

With fond memories of a good friend.

---

videomail from: bugs@nouvelles
27 October

Hiya! People call me Bugsy and I run the Nouvelles fashion magpie for Media, Inc., and I just want to say that I love your screens and I love the things you sell, and I think they are just right for the people we have built up relations with, and that therefore we would be delighted to sell information about you to stores here in the US, and to tell our magpie about you. I know my people and they will love you just as much as I do. Also, you might like to note that I've pegged myself one of your 'Listening to the Gods' special dresses. Believe me, I could use a little spiritual refreshment here in the middle of New York.

Your,

Bugsy (Adele) Harris

Editor, Nouvelles Magpie

---

audio file from: Mrs Chung Mae
28 October

Dear Bugsy Nouvelles-ma'am

Our hearts are singing after so kind a missive. A link with such a prestigious entity gives us as much joy as a marriage in the family, for like all marriages it will bring both love and money. And middle-aged ladies in Karzistan need both! Please be kind and send us terms and conditions. Kindness and blessings.

---

videomail from: bugs@nouvelles
2 November

Hiya! No terms and conditions except one. Let us know if any stores get in touch with you, and tell them to go through us. We charge them a finder's fee and take a cut on sales to our people. We started out, believe it or not, running the software that found people the TV shows they wanted to see. We got real big, and started different kinds of TV interest groups like fashion. We then realized we could use our software to find anything, not just TV shows. We got the idea of selling information to suppliers and then telling our groups how to buy the stuff. So you pay us nothing.

audio file from: Chung Mae
4 November

Lung, Please tell your officers' wives that Nouvelles Magpie in New York lists us as an important fashion resource. Tell them that we are big news in the New York fashion world. Tell them they are undeveloped for not knowing the future is upon them and that they should have shame for not doing something about it. I have clipped onto this record our Ahk Sess numbers and addresses and you can see that we are a great success. Show that to the officers' wives. Tell them that humble wild girl Sezen learned to tell the computer to produce new instructions to send special messages to each of our customers.

Thank you for your kind words. Your sister sent me a very kind and informative card a few weeks ago.

audio file from: Lieutenant Chung Lung
4 November

Are you angry? I meant to say I was proud of your site and that I forgive what you have done.

videomail from: bugs@nouvelles
10 November

Hiya! I just wanted to let you know that we are getting plenty of comments in our newsgroup about you guys. Can I make a few suggestions? Put who you are and your address on each screen. Incredible as it may seem, some people still print out screens. Usually they give them to other people, but if the address doesn't show, then people can't find you. Second, people love you. They want to know more about how you live, how things are going in your lives. Really! So more hot gossip. Also, forgive our ignorance, but people here know absolutely nothing about Karzistan. Your President looks like a lovely man, but we have one of those ourselves. So, a few more links to other sites about Karzistan would be go down well. Finally, do you have any music you can put on the site? The Collaborationist movement here is desperate for new sounds to share and build on and something from the roof of the world (are you guys in Tibet?) would be very popular. And remember, we love you, so give us more news.

videomail from: Mrs Chung Mae
15 November

Dear Mrs Bugsy-ma'am

It is very strange because I am speaking Karz and my lips are doing one thing and the voice is coming out in English! I do this for the first time because this is a special occasion. We have a deal from big New York store and they say Nouvelles drives people crazy for Eye of the Beholder screens. This plays our hearts like a harp. We do feel you are family, and Mrs Wing Kwan offers suggestion for a special token. Native women make a circle of friends. A circle of women all work together. They spin, wash, crack nuts, sort beans, beat old tough lamb, sew, do everything but clean house together. So they can sing and tell stories and smoke pipes. Each woman wears a special collar for that Circle, which they all embroider together. It is a small sign of belonging among friends. Would readers of Nouvelles like to join our Circle and have a collar? We promise special low price, to cover cost. Available only to friends of Nouvelles through big New York store. Oh, and we clip on a file of our access statistics, which show how powerful Nouvelles is as a way to make new friends in many lands. One final request: Can you send me any information you have on Air and the difference between the Formats?

voicemail from: bugs@nouvelles
16 November

Mae-honey. It'll drive 'em wild. No sooner said than done, but I need a shot of the design. I have to say, despite the mismatched lips, you look and sound great. You should get on TV more often. But hey, where's my News from Kizuldah screens? Like I said: gossip, girlfriend, gossip. But hey, I've been speaking English to you, what language have you been hearing?

SIZZLING SEZEN'S POP PICKS

Hello, young people, this is hair-in-eyes Sezen who is impatient with everything, except my Auntie Mae. We may not be having Madonna sixtieth birthday parties, but we are full of music here in Karzistan and it is great mix of modern and old. We got Arabesque, we got Lectro, we got Traditional, many different musics, and this is where you can hear what we sound like and use it in Collab.

GIVE US MONEY

You can listen, but don't keep the music unless you pay. Our musicians are poor, okay? So try to send us something. We are starving up here – well, not starving, but my mother keeps corncobs in our chic diwan, and our neighbour keeps a pig in her kitchen. And it is very bad-tempered. So don't steal these poor people's music or you are dried shitcake!

That noise was Auntie Mae telling me off for being rude. I talk too much anyway. So here are my 'Pop Picks.'

'BALSHANG' BY CHEN TUI

Start with my favourite. Tui is Chinese girl who writes all her own stuff. She plays Karz flute and the violin, she used to do Lectro dance, but this is both real and Air music at once, and it's so beautiful, about girl who falls in love with a married man and his city at the same time. So she talks about the city and the man using the same words at the same time. They say there is an Air version full of pictures and memories as well. I want to see what her beautiful beau looks like!

'KISH MASHALI' BY ERCHAN PEKER

How is it that fools can make good music? This guy thinks he is pretty, and pastes his face all over everything. He is good-looking, but we should discover that for ourselves. This is a fun song about school, the words are really good, and he wrote them but he is a Balshang Otter, which means he is small, smooth, and vicious. Listen to the rhythm and the way his voice jumps about. That is pure Karz, like he is.

'KLASIKLERI' BY MUSA

Just how smart are you? This word comes to us from Europe, it is your word, you should just say it and you will know what it means. This is new song but played in completely Traditional way and it is about all things classical and Karz that are going away, like Musa himself – soon, I hope. Musa is how all Karz men would like to be: big, fat, hairy, full of bristle and moustache, and everyone says how handsome he is, but I think he is old and ugly, and he says some very dull things about new music. But everyone loves him and so do I, in a way, like a good father. One of his other songs is called 'Yorgun,' which means 'Tired,' and that is very appropriate.

'MUT' BY YULDUZ

'Mut' means 'Destiny,' and the singer's name means Stars, so she has high opinion of herself. She used to be backup singer with Chen Tui and she would like to be Chen Tui, but Chen mixes Chinese, Karz, and New York Air. Yulduz is just another Balshang Fox. Most of her stuff doesn't work, but this is really good, nearly as good as Chen she imitates. It is about our country and how it mixes things and how it is lost now, but will find itself.

'HARP HATAMAHLARI' BY BULENT DO-UDAN

War memories. This is the story of our country in the 1980s when there was a terrible war. My Auntie Mae's father was murdered. She has to run from the room whenever this song is played. So the song is harsh, big, it roars at you.

Now, look at the picture, the only one on this page. Isn't the singer beautiful, all makeup, polished hair, lipstick, a woman as shiny as the front of a new car? You will get a shock when you hear the voice, because that person used to look like Musa. And one day, Bulent suddenly looked like that instead, no explanation. The voice stayed the same. The name didn't have to change either. Nobody cared. Don't you find our country is surprising place?

GOODBYE, AND REMEMBER TO PAY

So that is some of our music. We don't have many books, our television is all kung fu. All our heart and soul is in our music. It's where all our brains are, too, in the little tapes. They play around our heads like swallows even here in a dump like Kizuldah.

----

audio file from: bugs@nouvelles
18 November

Just thought you'd like to know that there's a Collab sharemind base called the Sezen Drop. You can't go into any New York club without hearing Karz music. Your little girl's a fashion leader. Oh, brace yourselves. Got the collar offer up on my home. And thanks again for telling us about the store. Attached to this you should find an article about the difference between the Formats and who's behind it. You may be interested to know how hard the cable people fought against all this! That's my old industry!

e-mail from: Lieutenant Chung Lung
20 November
Mother,

It pains me to write to you like this, but I feel I must point out that the things you put on your machine are open to the world. Sezen Ozdemir recalls my grandfather's murder. There are people here who misread the site as being full of backsliding minority nationalism.

I urge you to have a care and to be less of a wild woman.

audio file from: Mrs Chung Mae
20 November
Son, it pains me to write to you like this, but I am not entirely cut off like a thread from the world and news does reach me. You married and did not invite me or even tell me. I would have understood that you could not have your mother there, and that only your father would be invited. If only you had explained, I am adult enough to understand. You chose not to tell me at all. I am open before the world, you are hidden even within the family. So, is that the difference between good and wild behaviour? So go fuck yourself. Is that wild woman enough for you? By the way, all my mail is private, unless you have been using army decoders to read it. Have you? Are you a spy as well? Tell your army friends that they will find a world they cannot control, and that I am glad that they are all asleep.

audio file from: Mrs Chung Mae
28 November
Bugsy, you are the only one who can help us. Bugsy, we have over five hundred orders for the collar. We make our embroidery special, we cannot make five hundred collars, not at special deal price. We were very foolish not to think of this and apologize humbly for causing our good family friend such difficulties. It is not our way to make native designs by machine, it is not what our business is for. What can we do? Also, why is your name Bugsy?

audio file from: bugs@nouvelles
28 November
First things first. Bugsy is a gangster's name and people call me that as a joke, because they say I remind them of a gangster. Second, I attach info about a

machine that embroiders to order. Yes, it's a machine, but listen, you give it the ID files of your guests, and it will weave their names and or a message into the collar. It won't be handmade, but it will still be special, and the design will still say a Circle of friends.

Now, on the distribution. I've talked to the store, and hey, live the changes! Nouvelles is now a distribution centre. What you do is send all the collars once to us and we'll send them out. But. We need our own customer's barcode on each one to be read and shipped. Attached is a file with all the customers with our barcode details for each. If you can get the machine I suggest, it will also weave in the barcode in the back of the collar just where we need it. Now listen up. If you get the machine, it's so smart that you will be able to do individual things for your customers. Customize! Live that change! You're in business, not a museum. Don't apologize for not making everything by hand. Love the new screens.

---

audio file from: Chung Mae
29 November

Bugsy-ma'am, I will not lie, I need a friend. Kwan has been better to me than a mother would be. But even a mother can tire. My business is in her barn, and she lets me live with her. There are people in the village who want to stop the future, and so they tried to stop me. They stopped me with the truth. They told my husband I was in love with another man. It was true. And so I became a fallen woman, and only my little tribe of women will talk to me. They suffer too, especially brave Shen Suloi. It was her husband who tried to stop us, and who told my husband about me. Mrs Shen is Eloi and is loyal to me because I show the traditions of her people to the world. She believes that the soul of her people is growing in the world through me. Her husband is Chinese and does not understand.

Many of the husbands think this thing with all the women is strange. So Shen Suloi and I work and laugh and help each other and there are things we cannot say. We all have to put our feelings in little boxes in this village, or we would end up killing each other. Kwan tells me I should go out. I do not have the heart. People treat me like I am a ghost. They try to walk through me. All I try to do is help them, but they are so suspicious now and fear even to be seen with me. So I stay in and talk to the machine. I am lost to the machine, I spend all my time on it.

I am trying to find out about the Gates Format, I am trying to find out about the Air before it kills me. I can see why the UN Format was tried, but I agree with those who want the Gates opened. UN imitates the machine, the Gates open like our own heads. Also, I have personal reason that I will not unburden to you, to hate the UN Format. I am become its opponent. Can you help me by telling your powerful friends that those who are as dependent on you as children, should at least be asked what we want done to our heads? The Test killed people in Kizuldah. Can you please get them to understand that we are real, that we are here? We are frightened, and ignorant, and we are trying to catch up. I hope opening the door to all this misery does not lose me friendship.

_____

audio file from: bugs@nouvelles
30 November
Every time you write me, I wonder what have we done to the world. Three billion of us live in a world with lights, cameras, action; the other four billion can't get clean water, let alone bandwidth. There are times when I want to do an article: 'Mae's Story.' Then I think what a nasty thing to do, turn a friend into copy. But Mae, you got me jumping, wanting to tell people: 'Look, look over there, look what you've forgotten.' But what I want to show them is too big. I can't do it, only you could. Only you could tell them. If it's not too much to ask, could you do a talk about your life and let me magpie it? Bugsy.

_____

audio file from: Mrs Chung Mae
1 December
Listen Western woman all painted in finery, we survived the Japanese, who at least look human. We survived a war of liberation that cut off our men's heads and left them in a row by the roadside. We survived childbirth, disease, joints, worms, hunger, winter winds, drought, the Red Guards who ate everything, the guerrillas who made us pay them tax, as well as the government. We ate rotten seed rice, we boiled up grass, we pulled out our own teeth, sewed up our own wounds with thread. Do you really think you can obliterate us with your lights cameras action, your shows, your wires? We who are rooted in the earth like trees? Who do you really think is stronger? Who will be dead in one hundred years, you or us? I hope you die like vermin, all of you.

_____

audio file from: Mrs Chung Mae
1 December
Bugsy, that last mail was not from me. I heard it with horror. But I see I must explain at last. I said that the Air Test killed. The Air Test killed my neighbour

Mrs Tung who was ninety. I saw her every day and I loved her, for she was kind and gentle and was my teacher from earliest days. She always saw something special in me because she loved pretty things and I was good at making things pretty. We talked every day, as if I had a good angel of a mother. When the Air Test came, she was visiting me. We were all in panic and in terror, and the shock killed my friend, my dear Old Mrs Tung, and I called her, called her, and the mail put me inside her, and I died with her, and when I woke up she was copied inside me. At first it was like having a well-wisher inside my soul. But it is not wholesome, and she has curdled like goat's milk into hatred. She wants a separate life. I have been studied. I have been told such a thing could not happen if Air came by the open Gates; that is why I hate the UN Format, why I study it, why I try to find ways to undo it. It turned my beautiful friend into a monster. It turned me into someone who can be surprised by a dragon erupting out of her own mouth. The past talks out of me, instead of the future. I am fighting for the future, she fights for restoration of the past. Please, please, do not think I am mad, sick in the head. If you do not believe me, talk to Yeshiboz Sistemlar in Yeshibozkent. They did the study on me. Beware, for that place does things that would be illegal in the West. But Satan sometimes tells the truth, while goodness hides itself in soft lies. It was not me who said those things.

---

audio file from: bugs@nouvelles
2 December

That does it, Mae. I am writing my article. I don't do it to embarrass you or your country, but because my own people must know what is happening. Your Old Mrs Tung was right, we are so far from the soil. Mae, I don't know what to say to you, except I'm on your side, too, kid. I'll let you see the article before I send it out. Any news about the machine?

---

audio file from: Mrs Chung Mae
3 December

Wise criminal, you recall me to business. No, we do not have the machine. I have sent repeated messages to Mr Saatchi Saatchi at the bank and I believe the thing has been ordered and even paid for. I fear the worst. The worst is that in this country someone has paid someone else to lose it on the road. So we cannot deliver collars as planned. Our Circle is sewing day and night; even I am sewing day and night, which means I have less time for miserable reflection.

----

e-mail from: Mr Oz Oz
4 December

Mae,

Many thanks for your voicemail. I am very sorry not to have replied to your others, but I have not been in a position to help anyone until just a few days ago. You were so worried about brigands in hills; so was I. But I felt secure in the main pass down from Yeshibozkent. I pulled over to sleep late at night on the road, and woke up with a gun in my face. Mae, they took everything – the van, the computer, all my clothes, even the beautiful coat you gave me. I was left barefoot by the side of the road. I walked into Sogan (Dilapidated) which lived up to its name and did not open a single door, except for the police, who put me in jail. I am young, Mae, and like a child I wondered why they treated me like a thief. I found out soon enough, for I was going to be treated like a thief by everyone.

I didn't know, but it is a racket: government officials go out, and come back shoeless, saying everything is stolen, when in fact they've sold everything, especially the computer. I was the third Taking Wing operative that had come back that way, and the government was sick of it. They held me under house arrest until the computer was sold to a foreigner in Balshang. The thieves were so dumb they did not even know about the hard-disk watermark, and, thank heaven, it was an honest bumpkin of a thief who said that, yes, they had stolen it from me. He was so foolish, he even said that he had been the one to persuade the others not to kill me, thinking it would save his neck. It saved mine. The government expects its operatives to be killed defending its property, or spend time in jail. It was Allah's will – all my material on your village, including both your and Sunni's question maps had been sent online, and were received as a model of what the operatives were supposed to achieve. So, having been a thief and in serious trouble, I was restored to my former favoured position as the only operative who had succeeded in doing anything.

Thanks to God who sent you to me. Mae, it is all your work, and I have tried to tell my boss that it is so and he waves it away. After all, you are an ignorant peasant woman as far as he is concerned. Still, I have written a further report on you and I have not been short of wind in describing what Teacher Shen did to you. I expect that there will be a result there. This is not cheap revenge, Mae, for truly we cannot have teachers who block the education of our people.

It also means I am back in a position to chase your machine. As an honest victim of theft, I am in a strong position to denounce corruption. So I am making a big stink. We have traced your machine to a depot in Balshang where we have a signature. Naturally the signature matches no one who works there, so we arrested the shipping agent. Now I know why the government arrested me. The shipper is a tough but civilized man. He keeps saying he knows nothing, and probably does not. But we keep him in jail, and have seized all his goods and thrown all his people out of work so they have no money. The idea is simple. With no job, one of the employees will rat on the one who did it. All we can do is wait.

Your site makes full use of audio, video, and customer database, so everyone at Taking Wing is proud of you. But, a suggestion: Perhaps you could have something more about how much the government has done for all the united peoples of Karzistan? I know your simple heart bubbles with gratitude for the government, for I heard your words and saw your face when we opened the bank account. But some people here do not know you, and are concerned that people abroad might get an unbalanced picture of the variety of peoples in the Happy Province.

Your friend in waiting,

Mr Oz

---

audio file from: Mrs Chung Mae
4 December

Mr Oz-sir

My heart delights in news from you, and I add to the chorus of voices that can confirm your innocent youth and innate honesty. I am overwhelmed that the government makes such efforts to restore my machine to me. I really am not worthy. Do make sure they know how much I owe to you and how I would not have known what to do without you. Your coming was like an angel from the Lord for us. I knelt and praised Allah, for I saw that the government of Karzistan had given me hope. I did not feel it was the place of humble fashion expert to describe the work of government, which passes my understanding. But your just admonition has shown me that however embarrassing my crude efforts would be to myself, I must add my voice to the chorus of earned praise. Please see the new addition to my site and please express my gratitude. I attach a letter for your boss, and if it is worthy, please show it to him.

---

e-mail from: Lieutenant Chung Lung
7 December

I am not a son to choose to lose a mother, even when she is lost to herself. Your material at your home site has recently much improved. I trust that it was because you listened to your son's advice. Encouraged, I write again.

Yes, I married, and in confusion did not tell my mother. And my honest sister in an innocent card told the truth for me, and that is humbling. I've clipped on a picture of your new daughter. Her name is Sarah. You see perhaps why it was a bit more difficult to tell you?

Sarah is from Canada, and has chosen to cast her lot with your son, though I cannot think why. She is beautiful and intelligent, and regards your son as an educated man because of Army College. She stayed in the American Institute here while studying the history of Attila the Wonderful. She is not a model of Karzistani femininity, but she opens a world for me. She is very good with the other officers' wives, who tell me they find her delightful. She has seen your screens and your last letter and likes both very much!

I did decode your personal mail. Either I did it, or someone else would. Your friendship with the fashion magpie is well regarded by officials here. I thought I would set your mind at rest.

Your son,

Lung

---

audio file from: Mr Oz Oz
9 December

Mae

Your letter was well received here. All our hearts were warmed by such simple, truthful words from a good Karzistani woman who works so hard for her people. We know what happened to your machine. You will not get that one again, but we have arrested your Mr Saatchi Saatchi. He will be executed next month. The warehouse boss who I thought was innocent, was not. My boss has personally approved a repurchase for your business. It will be delivered by the army!

---

audio file from: Mr Hikmet Tunch
9 December

Mae,

I am sorry to slip back into your life, perhaps unexpectedly. Don't worry, you will not need to escape me again – though you should know that I have watched the development of your fashion screens with interest. Do you really intend to become part of a romance for Americans? They do so like foreign pets. And how is your little inner friend? Both of them. A file is attached. It is a scientific paper about you. It is about to appear in the *Journal of Medical-Computer Interface*. It shows that no physical change has happened to you. It shows instead that a mangled imprint of two selves have been united in Air. It shows how this could happen, due to real flaws in the UN Format. It also proves that such a catastrophe could not have occurred if the Formatting process had been achieved by opening the Gates. It suggests that elements of the Gates Format be copied across and made part of the UN system.

One further thing I meant to tell you when I drove you back. You are in the Information business, Mae. That means everyone you know will betray you. You can relax with me. I already have done that.

Your guardian angel,

Hikmet Tunch

---

audio file from: Mrs Chung Mae
12 December

Bugsy, I was pleased to hear about your new apartment. I understand how lovely it is to have a place of your own and how living even with best friends produces sadness. I was so happy for you, to think of my good friend in her own place. Please send me pictures of your apartment. It *will* ease my heart. Oh, woman, I am avoiding telling my news because I do not know how to begin. It is so strange, the workings of life. I do not say the workings of God, because I am not sure He would do anything like this! Last night, the electricity was shining in Kwan's barn. The Circle has been sewing our beautiful collars late into the night. Naughty girl Sezen brought in some rice wine from her boyfriend's village. Why not? Her mother Hatijah, who was frightened to join the Circle at first, is becoming lively and outgoing. It is now Hatijah who warms up the wine, and it warms us, and soon we are all singing. Then the door is thrown back with a loud bang, and in comes Mr Hasan Muhammed. He is strict Muslim gentleman, white lace cap and long beautiful beard, but he is carrying a whip. He strikes the whip against the walls of the barn, and we all scream and clutch our work, for we never lose our embroidery place. There could be an earthquake and none us would lose a stitch. So we all are pressed against the wall and he prowls and curses us as wicked women all – little singing old women who sip a bit of wine.

Well, Kwan is courageous and she arrives and says, 'Mr Muhammed, have you left your brain behind? Why do you frighten guests in my barn as they work so hard?' And he says, 'This all the work of Shytan, all of the women have gone mad since this thing has come, most especially that bride of Shytan,' and he points at me. I hardly need say that this is not an amusing thing. But listen to how destiny plays like a cat with your friend Mae. Mr

Muhammed still jabs his finger like a knife towards me and says: 'That devil woman leaves her husband, and now my wife has left me to live with him.' And he cracks his whip. And all us women try hard not to laugh, even Kwan. For you see, we all know his wife Tsang. Tsang is a pincushion, she has had every man she can get. She is plump, ripe, shameless, lots of fun, and about as devoted a wife, and devout a woman, as a gerbil. In my fashion-expert days, I was always giving Tsang a makeover for her latest paramour. Poor old Mr Muhammed has finally discovered what the rest of the village knows. So there is now a closing of Tsang's always-welcoming doorway. That Tsang finally should have taken wing with my dull old husband strikes our humble peasant sense of humour like a blow to the elbow. Poor Mr Muhammed yells like a character in an old play, 'They have run off to live together in Balshang!' It is terrible but we all have to fight not to laugh, though the poor man is in agony. Kwan says kindly, 'It is not Mae's fault that your wife strayed, we are all scandalized by such behaviour.' And Mr Muhammed points again at me and says, 'Why, then, do you welcome that viper into your midst?' And Kwan answers him: 'Because though she strayed, she helps the whole village build business.' He screams back, 'She is the mother of all whores! My sweet and faithful wife has had her mind poisoned by that creature and her machine!' And Kwan puts her hand on his shoulder and says, gently, 'It was not Mae who corrupted her. Your wife just this spring lured my young son and had sex with him until I asked her to stop, for my son was growing confused. And she had both Mr Alis before that, and before that, Mr Pin's eldest boy, just before his marriage. Tsang corrupted herself. Mae had nothing to do with it.'

And poor old Mr Muhammed's face melts like candlewax. 'You all knew?' he says, and drops his whip. 'Didn't you?' asks Kwan. He does not answer but, hollow like an old crisp pinecone, he goes out of the barn. So we all wonder, Did he know as well?

But oh, woman, there was further news to come. Joe has sold our house. He has sold it to Mr Haseem and taken the money to live with Tsang in Balshang. The house and lands I fought all this year to pay for and save, those are deserted. The kitchen I cleaned for years, it is dark, with only moonlight for lighting. The brazier I kept alight for thirty years is now cold and full of dust. The chairs and tables are lonely, the cupboard hastily emptied, as if by thieves. I sit wearing all my clothes in Kwan's unheated attic, listening alone to the happiest time of year, to the harvest, the parties, and the various Circles. I hear life waft up like smoke from the village below. My life has been unstitched, cousin, like embroidery needing to be reworked. Oh, Joe, Joe. You always thought money was quick, because you were slow. So you have quick money to make new life in the city with Tsang. That old mattress, she will be bouncing with other men the instant your back is turned. You will be a dolt in the city. You will lose tools, you will not get work. And you will come back here, and be surprised when your friend Mr Haseem does not give you back your house. And your father and your brother Siao – what of them, Joe? They now have the indignity of living with your first wife's brother, Mr Wang Ju-mei. Oh, Joe, what will you tell the spirits of your fathers? You sold their land? For how much, Joe? Would your good friend Mr Haseem, knowing you were desperate to be away, be so generous as to give you half of what it is worth? Oh, Joe, you will go to live near your beloved and clever son Lung. You should love and honour him, for the son is far wiser than the father. But you do not understand him. Your son is Army Officer. Your son is Balshang Fox, who has married the Western world. He does not want a dolt of a country father embarrassing him, staying all weekend long when he has to be entertaining the Colonel and his lady wife. Oh, Joe. You will return lost and befuddled with no money, no woman, no son, and wondering, wondering where it all went. Now I know what a man's chin feels like. It gets shaved clean, everything scraped away, with everything needing to grow back. What else, I wonder, can happen in this year of shaving away? To speak of business: Eye of the Beholder is getting fewer visitors. We have no new orders for the collars, which is great relief and worry at the same time. What can I do to speak to my friends in the world?

_____

e-mail from: Mr Ken Kuei
13 December
Hello.

I am very proud, for I have sent you a message like this. You see, I am learning. I have taken your words to heart, and so I learn on Sunni's machine. I have had to learn without you.

I am good at learning. And good at waiting.
Your friend,
Mr Ken Kuei

_____

e-mail from: Miss Soo Ling
13 December
Mae,

I hear that many houses here are imitating your success, selling collars, etc. In any case, all fashions come and go. Have you been thinking what you will do next? There is a Western phrase used by all: Live the change. It means, 'Get in first and get out first.'

———————

e-mail/videomail: no sender
They have found the Eloi site. They will raid. Get your business off Kwan's machine now. Move it onto Mr Haseem's if you can – now, tonight – but move it in any case.

16

Who would send her such a message?
Mae's mind raced as her slippered feet slid in the dark on Kwan's polished wooden floors. Mr Oz? Hikmet Tunch?

She went into Kwan's bedroom and smelled the savour of husband and wife and sleep.

'Kwan,' she whispered. 'Kwan, wake up.'

There was a groan.

'Kwan, please, this is urgent, it must be done. Please wake up.'

The movement, the sound, ceased and a calm, alert voice said: 'What is it, Mae?'

'I just got an audio file. Came on looking like a packet from America, only it was just a scramble of, you know, symbols. Then it started to wake up as words. It said it was a self-decoding cipher. So whoever sent it would have to know the watermark on your hard disk.'

'What did it say?'

'That they know about the Eloi home, that they will raid. It said, "Get your business off Kwan's machine."'

'Can I see the message?'

'No, it burned itself up.'

There was quiet. Outside, a nightjar was singing.

Mr Wing spoke next: 'If they know about the minority site, there is not much point removing it now,' he said, with the same cool voice he used when repairing plumbing. 'What does it say, Kwan?'

'It tells what is being done to my people,' said Kwan.

Wing breathed heavily, once, in and out. 'You are a woman. Perhaps they will treat you gently. Pretend you are foolish and emotional. Mae, whoever your friend is, they are clever, and you must upload all your data to Sunni's machine, and wipe it from ours.'

'Do you know how to do that?'

'Not if you don't.'

The TV was now kept in the diwan. Already secretive, they did not turn on the lights, but huddled in quilted coats around the screen.

Mae tried to copy her business onto Sunni's machine. She kept repeating different, likely instructions. Finally she found one that worked.

The TV said, *'Making contact with htvl/sunni/takingwing.htvl.'*

Mae told it, 'Volume down! Can you make it look as if the files have always been on her machine?'

The TV made noises like mice were at work inside it. Then it murmured, *'I can make it look as if your site has an alias on htvl/sunni.'*

Mr Wing told Mae, 'Do that. You can say you had it on two machines in case one of them went down.'

'Okay, go ahead,' said Mae. The machine made nibbling noises as if mice were at work. Mae turned to Kwan. 'After this, we wipe the Eloi site.'

'The site stays up,' said Kwan.

Mae protested. 'Kwan! The site will be wiped anyway. But perhaps if it's not here when they arrive, we can have some story ready!'

Kwan's face shone as white and cold as the moon. 'It is too late, Mae. I have e-mail from professors about the site; I have answered them. If the government are reading my e-mail, they will have all that, too. They have me, Mae.'

The two women stared at each other in silence. Blows are like this, thought Mae. At first you are dazed and do not feel the pain. Mae found she was listening for the stealthy rumble of an army truck.

The TV murmured low: *'Permission denied.'*

'Mae,' said Mr Wing, 'let's at least save your business. We'd better go and ask Sunni for permission now.'

'Right, okay, I do that. But both of you go, get away!'

'Where to, Mae?' demanded Kwan. 'You think we should hide?'

'We'll take care of ourselves, but first we will go with you,' said Mr Wing. 'Mr Haseem may not talk to you.'

They threw stones against Mr Haseem's shutters to wake him. He threw the window open and they heard the click of a safety catch. Mr Haseem had a gun.

Mr Haseem rumbled, 'Get away from my house, Mae. I bought your husband's place fairly.'

'Of course you did,' Wing intervened. 'This is trouble with the government. Let us in, Faysal.'

They were allowed only as far as the kitchen. Sunni automatically bowed to Kwan, sleepily mistaking this for a social call.

'The government has found our Eloi site,' said Kwan.

Mr Haseem looked unmoved. That was their problem, raising stuff like that. Sunni looked alert, and watchful.

Mae spoke: 'I need to copy my business site onto your machine.'

'Tuh!' said Haseem. 'After all that has passed between us?' His heavy face assumed its most natural expression of scorn.

And Sunni? Her eyes met Mae's and something passed between them. Sunni turned to her husband and shrugged. 'It will cost us nothing. And Mae told us about the wire charges and saved us much money. It is a simple favour to return.'

'I don't want trouble with the government,' grunted Haseem.

'Have you seen Mae's screens? She has a link to one government office, and another government office, and there is a part on it in which Mae sings gratitude to the government. Having such a site on our machine will be protection against the government.'

Mae and Sunni exchanged a long look: *Now you are repaid*, Sunni seemed to say.

Mae pressed her advantage. 'Your server is running, but my machine needs permission to download.'

Sunni nodded once. 'Who sent you the message?'

'Someone who masters privacy. Either Mr Oz or my friend Mr Tunch.'

'We better move, Mr Haseem, Sunni-ma'am,' said Mr Wing.

Mr Haseem's leaden face looked up at him, appraising, challenging, but not triumphing. 'What will happen to you?' he asked Wing. Haseem regarded himself as a man, and men were serious. The villagers were seriously against the government, as they were against blight on crops.

Wing's eyes brows flickered and he gave a brief, buccaneer's smile. *'Inshallah,'* he said. Men were also brave.

'Many thanks, Sunni-ma'am,' said Mae.

Kwan spoke: 'We'd better leave. We have enemies who might say they saw us conspiring.'

Later, Kwan's TV spoke: *'Permission extended. Uploading begins.'*

They waited, listening to the very faint sounds of moving heads inside the machine. The wind and the future whispered in shadow.

Kwan was calm. 'I could move into the hills. Go visit Suloi's relatives until all this is past.' She turned to Mr Wing and smiled. 'You could say I became a wild woman and left you.'

Mr Wing shrugged. 'You are allowed three books in prison,' he said. 'The Koran, the Buddhist texts, and the Mathnawi of the Mevlana. I have been saving myself for them. I will do a comparison of all three and learn thereby the truth.'

'They are long enough for a life sentence,' said Kwan, with grim humour.

'Then I hope my life will be long enough,' said Wing. 'I would prefer a life sentence to death.'

'Swear,' said Mae, suddenly swept up in superstition. 'Swear now that if you are not sent to prison, you will begin to read them now anyway.'

'I would swear to do that, Mae,' chuckled Wing, 'if I thought it would do any good.'

Mae felt a gathering in her mind as if a tree had sent down roots into it, and then bloomed. She had an idea.

She asked the television, 'Can you do the same thing as that message? Arrive and then disappear?'

There was a whisper inside. *'Huh?'* the TV replied. A technical term, meaning it did not understand the request.

Mr Wing shook his head. 'They would be able to see through such doctoring, Mae.'

'What I want to do is send the whole site to Bugsy and get her to host it. That way it stays up, but off your machine. So we can wipe it, yes?'

'Thank you,' said Kwan. 'But Bugsy does business with you. That will get you into trouble. And Mae, you do not have the encryption code, so that is that.'

Mae kept on: 'Look, at least wipe the site! Maybe it will be enough for them if you take the site down.'

Mr Wing started to rub her back. 'Mae, Mae.'

'I would only put it back up, after they left,' said Kwan. 'The world has to know about the Eloi.'

'So, you've had the site up and now the world does know!'

'Not enough of them.'

Mr Wing was smiling with quiet pride. 'Mae, Kwan will never give up fighting. She will never rest until justice is done.'

'Why must it be you who fights?'

Wing's smile extended slightly. 'Because we cannot let the goons who run this country stop us telling the truth. What are we supposed to do? Run and hide and say, "Oh, wondrous masters, we owe you so much for letting us live and battle the land for grain which you take from us as tax"?'

Mae had never heard such talk. She recognized the constriction around her chest for what it was: fear. This was genuinely dangerous talk.

'They are destroying an entire people, only because their own ancestors failed to conquer them. The Eloi show it is a lie to say that this country can be called Karzistan, that it is a Muslim country of Turkic peoples. So they try to make the Eloi disappear.'

Mae felt a little bit sick. She thought she was brave, but she did not have that kind of courage. To face the men who controlled the torturers, the lists, the surveillance, and say: I am going to do the very thing you say I must not do.

And yet they were right. How were things to get better if no one fought?

She looked at Mr Wing and thought: this man could become a terrorist. If there were more of him, my son Lung might be sent to fight him. They might kill each other through a screen of dust and smoke.

And Mae felt a dull buzz inside the core of her head. The echoing. All this had triggered another attack. 'It's coming on again,' said Mae.

'The old lady feels the same way?' he said, still looking amused.

'She has strong memories of the war . . .'

Mae took a grip.

She began to chant to herself things Mrs Tung would never believe: Thank heavens for the machines, they give us an ear of the world and then save us from our masters . . .

Something in her head opened up, a bit like a flower, a bit like a radio tuning.

If this is starting up again, you must hide! If you fight them directly, they send in their soldiers!

And Mae told it: The government will change itself; its very soul will be blown by the Air . . .

They come and cart you off in the middle of the night, or pay the neighbours to turn on you!

We will be a world of people beyond governing . . .

Both sides end up eating their dead.

The rice wine when it came was as transparent as water, but it burned. They sipped in silence. Mae could think of nothing to say.

From the television came a sound like a rooster, faint and faraway.

'Mae,' said Kwan. 'Something's coming up on the screen.'

Words on the screen read, *EMAIL/VIDEOMAIL: NO SENDER.*

There was an Egyptian dance of hieroglyphs which suddenly resolved into letters and words and sideways V signs.

'That's computer code,' said Kwan.

Mae sat forward. She knew what it was. Someone had sent her the encryption code. She told the machine to save it, use it, and kept talking to send a message.

'Audio file to bugsy@nouvelles. Bugsy, sorry to arrive in this way, but this is no laughing matter. Clipped to this message is an entire site. It is very political, very dangerous, about the Eloi people. The world must know what is happening to them, but it is too dangerous to hold here. Please find a machine other than your own, and put the site up there. Do not – do not – put it on your machine, okay? And never talk of it, and do not reply to this e-mail in any way, okay? Sometimes you will get encrypted message like this. It will be an update for the site. Like this message, it will then eat itself. And please, do not put anything about this in an article! And don't reply! Your chum. Okay endmail.'

Mae turned and looked up. 'Kwan? Will that be okay? Can we wipe the site, if this works?'

Kwan hauled in a thick breath through thin nostrils. 'Okay,' she whispered, nodding. 'Okay.'

The sun rose.

Mae tried to sleep, despite sunshine blazing through the windows.

Kwan's warm wine had been a mistake. It burned her stomach. The acids churned like the fear of the soldiers, fear for Kwan, fear of Mrs Tung, fear of everything. Her stomach was as panicked as her soul.

And she began to gag. She felt something tear.

My baby. My strangely nested, new-as-Air, born-from-Air child.

I'm trying to kill it.

Her stomach rose up like a fist. She could feel something heavy but alive bunch up and cram against the top of her belly.

No, no, I don't need this now!

Mae saw Mr Ken's handsome face. It will be such a beautiful child, she thought. She struggled to pull in a breath. The flesh pushed harder against her oesophagus; she felt something gulp open inside her.

As if Kwan's wine were fire, a blast of juices burned her throat and seared tender nasal tissues.

Her child slammed up against her again. Her breath was knocked away.

No!

Mae's face twisted like a rag. She wrenched herself and also something else deep in the world. She twisted and dragged and wrung it. The world felt like silk, ripping in ragged line.

From all around her came the sound of tiny bells. Was that blood in her ears?

Mae remembered the fence, the fence she had torn when she escaped Mr Tunch. The fence had sung when she tore it.

Sing! she told the air. It did. The air around her crinkled like tin foil.

And light seemed to come from the singing. Light wavered in patterns on the walls, as if reflecting from water. The light was confused with the thin tinkling sound from nowhere.

Mae thought of all of them – Tunch, Old Mrs Tung, Fatimah, the village women. No! You will not take my child from me. Soldiers, armies, people who will not learn, people who hate the future, no you will not get him, my last late Unexpected Flower. He is going to live.

Mae swallowed, and swallowed again. The room went dark. Mae's fingers went numb. Mrs Tung was coming, drawn by the fear.

Mae felt her arrive. Mrs Tung seemed to come into the room and sit on the bed next to her.

The old woman was charmed by the homeliness of babies and indigestion. Old Mrs Tung offered advice.

Yogurt is always good for an upset tummy.

The voice was as kindly and as sweet as pear drops.

Mrs Tung had always been kind. Mae remembered her sweet, blind face.

Yogurt it is, thought Mae, and remembered the tang of it. Yogurt she thought, remembering its creamy sting, and the yogurt sheds with their smell of wood smoke.

Suddenly the light and the singing smelled of yogurt. The whole room smelled like those old sheds. Mae swallowed again.

And was soothed. Like a storm at sea when the wind suddenly dropped, the acids in her stomach seemed to calm. They burned no longer.

Like a barque, clumsy on the waves, the separate flesh inside her settled calmly down into the waters of her stomach. Mae could even feel the foam of the waves.

Mrs Tung was smug. *The old remedies are always the best. Now I think we should all just get some sleep, don't you?* She seemed to toddle off to bed.

Everything went still.

Suddenly Kwan's attic was just a room, quiet and full of sunshine, a room full of peace, even joy. Mae cradled her stomach. I will build you a safe harbour, little boat. I will fence you in with docks and sea walls. They won't frighten you out of me. If I have to call on all of Air, you will stay.

Mae felt her face stretch with a relieved smile. She slept.

The army did not come. That day.

Mae still had to find a place to work.
She and Sunni had made amends, but Mae would hardly be welcome working on Sunni's machine day and night as she needed to. And it would be better if the Circle did not operate out of Kwan's premises. So where, how?

---

audio file from: Mrs Chung Mae
14 December
Dear Mr Oz-sir
It is plain that my business has reached the point at which it is necessary to run it from our own machine. The grant has been more than generous, especially as regards our beautiful knitting machine. Would money be available for me to operate a service centre of my own?

---

audio file from: Mr Oz Oz
14 December
Dear Mrs Chung-ma'am
It is possible. Form for grant is attached, partially filled in for you, but do not submit it until I can take soundings here. Your course of action is wise.

Mae scanned the message and pondered its every word for any sign that Mr Oz had sent the two encrypted mails.

She decided that he had. The soundings he spoke of were to find out how the government viewed Mae's controversial connection with the Wings. Mae felt like a traitor to Kwan. 'Your course of action is wise,' meant simply that she had done as she was warned, and moved her site.

Mae stared at the form, filled in completely by Mr Oz, except for a white box which read: *'Reason for Expense/Benefits for Community.'*

She could say that she was running a service centre for the whole valley, so more commercial sites could be implanted. She could say that she was offering her own expertise in building sites, and publicizing them.

In fact, that was not just an excuse. In fact that was a very good idea indeed.

Mae sat pondering it, seeing it clearly. Mounting sites for Mr Ah's car repair, setting up an electronic voting station, providing a link for Mrs Mack to her Christian church. She saw specifically, Sunni's Valley Fashion Service. She saw again, the Swallow School, now on the Web itself, giving advice, explaining terms, trading Info with other Net traders.

She sat staring into another new branch of the future, happy.

The machine made a noise like a rooster. *'You have follow-up message,'* said the screen.

'Mae,' said Mr Oz in video mode. 'My friend, the most amazing thing has happened. Open a second window, and I will transmit.'

She did so. The window was full of writing in the Roman alphabet and a photograph of the Circle: Kwan, Mae, Sezen, Suloi, Mrs Doh, Hatijah.

We look so happy, Mae thought. We look like the kindest people in the world, and the happiest.

Mr Genuinely Sincere kept talking: 'Mae. It is an article that has appeared in the *New York Times*, both online and in disk. It is called "Mae's Story," and it is by one of your customers – you know her, an editor of a New York magpie. Mae, it is all about your life and how you fight for info, and how Mrs Tung was copied into your mind by overhasty Formats. It quotes your friend Mr Tunch. It quotes you saying you hate the UN Format. But Mae! It is a perfect reflection of the government line! How the West must not take us for granted, but must consult on Info. It could not be better. Everyone here is so pleased! They are calling it a diplomatic coup for Karzistan!'

Mae looked at the photograph of Kwan's beautiful face. Have I managed, accidentally, to save my friend?

'Does this mean I get my own machine?' Mae asked.

Mr Oz laughed. 'I expect so.'

And suddenly Mae was sure: Oz was not the one who had warned her. He would never be so cunning or so quick. She was relieved she had been so discreet in her mail to him.

It was Tunch, she realized, Tunch who had intervened.

'Let me complete the form and send it to you.'

And that meant the encryption equations came from Tunch as well. That means Tunch watches me, in Air. Guardian angel indeed.

Oz jerked with pleasure like a colt. Mae thought: Being robbed and thrown in jail by his bosses has not made him older. He will always be a boy.

He asked her. 'You okay on what to say on the form?'

'I know exactly what I want to do with it, but you advise me, okay?'

'Okay. You want to save the article? Your machine can read it.'

Mae paused and reflected. 'No,' she said quietly. 'I would rather not.'

He looked a bit perplexed. Then the windows closed. Mae completed her application and sent it to him.

Then she asked the television to write a proper letter to Sunni.

My old friend,
How strange is life. I keep saying that these days, especially thinking over the last few months. Now, here comes something just as strange as everything else that has happened.

Can I rent my old house from you? Consider: The real value of what you have purchased resides in the land, and there are plenty of farmers hereabouts to whom you can rent the land. That is very good business for you, especially as you do not need to give accommodation as part of the deal. It is pure land rental. So what do you do with the house? Rent it to Mr Ken for his hens? How much is he going to pay you for a barn?

Ah, but, Sunni, a workshop for my Circle, now that is a business premise, and you can charge far more for that. And I will have the money to pay, once my machinery arrives.

I make a proposition to you. I offer 10 riels a month rental. That is in place of given-away accommodation on which you make nothing, or 5 riels a year for a ham – 120 riels a year.

Do we need to talk further?

And, Sunni, for me the old days are dead, forgotten. Forgiven. My hope now is that you can forgive me the wrongs I did to you.

Your friend

Mae

Mae sat back and looked at the letter. So, she thought, my battle for the future begins again. I'm doing it for my baby. New song new life.

17

Mae looked out of her attic window and saw snow was falling.
Winter is here, she thought with excitement. Winter was dark, enfolding, and safe. She saw her new winter very clearly: long happy hours alone in her old house, with her own glowing screen.

In the grey morning, snow blew like feathers. It nestled along the top of the stone wall, and on the roof tiles. This was good heavy snow that fell with a gentle hissing sound and mounted up quickly, as if the town were being padded with thick white pillows.

It had been so long since Mae had been outside. In winter, everyone stayed inside; no one would see her. The snow would be a veil.

Mae threw a scarf over her head, and wrapped round one of Kwan's Eloi sheepskins. It sat slightly askew around her shoulders, bulky and still smelling of lanolin.

Outside on the landing, she snapped on a light. The staircase stayed dark. Kwan called up through the darkness. 'There's a power failure!'

Mae felt her way down the staircase. The main room had its front door open to let in grey light.

'I'm going out in the snow!' Mae announced. 'Come along!'

Kwan's answering chuckle was both affectionate and edgy. There had been no sign of the army, but Kwan was still cautious. 'I'll stay here,' said Kwan.

Mae eased herself down Kwan's slippery stone steps. The snow was already sealing over the dungheap next to the barn. Mae's own breath was a sheltering scarf of fog.

All sounds were muted. On the chilly stones of the courtyard the snow looked like lace, its delicate patterns refrigerated from underneath. Mae pushed the courtyard gate, and for the first time in weeks stepped back out into her village.

Everything was being tucked into a bed of snow, as if by a mother. The houses and terraces were all outlined in white. From the high hillside came the tuneless clanking of twenty or thirty sheep bells.

Someone had left his flock out to pasture too long. Mae smiled. The same happened every year. Was it Old Mr Pin? Lazy Mr Mack? Who would sit in a corner of the Teahouse, smoking a hubbly-bubbly and grinning with embarrassment?

Mae walked up and over the bridge. The invulnerable ducks still paddled in snow-rimmed water. Mae passed the door of Mrs Doh and her fearsome dog. Mae heard its breath, and the scratching of its giant claws against the other side of the doorway. She caught a gasp of food odours from Mrs Doh's kitchen window: garlic, bean sauce, rice.

The next door opened just as Mae was beside it.

Out came Sunni's friend, Mrs Ali. 'Oh!' she said startled. Then she saw it was Mae. Her face faltered and then recovered.

'Hello,' she said. 'It snows.'

This was awkward. Village manners would not allow them to part without talking. Mrs Ali slammed her door twice with her customary thoroughness. She was bundled up against the chill, tall, skinny, regal and slightly absurd, like a walking telephone pole.

'It is very beautiful,' said Mae. 'It makes me feel like I have come home.'

Then the old rake did not know what to say, for Mae plainly had lost her home several times over. She was discomfited, but not hostile.

'Well, we all have fond memories of snow.' Mrs Ali paused. 'I hear your business does well.'

They both started to walk down the hill together.

'Yes. We have orders from America for five hundred collars. I don't know how we will do all the work!'

That was so far beyond Mrs Ali's imagination that she could not be sure she had heard correctly.

'Successful indeed!' she said, and her smile froze. 'That brings in money?'

'It is a special deal. We have a good relationship with a New York fashion magpie. So we said, join our Circle and wear our collar for only ten dollars each.'

Yes, thought Mae, that does make five thousand dollars. 'So amidst all the terrible things that have happened, there has been some good. The ladies of the Circle share the money. Sunni and I are friends again.' Mae shrugged with her eyebrows, a kind of peace offering. Don't forget that I have been hurt too.

They were at the Okans', the last house on Upper Street. Mrs Ali paused.

'I have noticed,' said Mrs Ali, 'that your friends tend to benefit.' She looked back at Mae, and there was something completely unexpected: a rueful humour, as if Mae were one of life's bitter jokes.

'Good day,' said Mrs Ali. 'I have no lard, and winter is upon us, and I go to beg some from Sunni.' She turned and began to trudge uphill towards Sunni's big house.

There was a rumble, as if from the sky. Mae scowled. Something shifted gears and roared and suddenly, a truck came round the hill and up Upper Street, straight towards her.

A big green truck with huge devouring tyres.

Army! Mae thought, and it was a though a fist had seized hold of her heart and stopped it pumping. She ducked to the side of the Okans' house.

Army, army, army, army, struggled her heart as if to breathe.

The truck roared past, green canvas over camouflaged sides, lashed down, bolted, huge. Army, army, army roaring up the hill, slowing to shoulder their way over the bridge.

Towards Kwan's house.

Mae ran without thinking. Her feet slipped on the snowy cobbles; the cold reached down like deep roots into her lungs. Please! Please! It was a prayer.

She had to be there to tell her story, to explain. I am *New York Times*! I am *New York Times*! Mae ran out of breath and had to lean forward onto her knees. Fire from her pregnancy shot up her gorge into her mouth. She swallowed, pushed herself upright and struggled on up the hill. Kwan's gates gaped defencelessly. The courtyard was already full of truck. Mae stumbled into the yard.

There was a bloodcurdling yell, and the green door of the cab swung open. A bull of a man burst out of it in piebald camouflage. Before Mae could think, he was running towards her, full pelt, male, huge, fast, young, and strong. She managed to skid to a halt, and was about to turn and run.

He grabbed hold of her.

And then swung her round and round and round. Her string shoes with their slippery leather soles left the ground. She flew. Kwan's courtyard became a merry-go-round, spinning around her, and the man was laughing. Mae wanted to be sick.

He kissed her.

'Surprise!' he called, as if out of a nightmare. Mae's feet were helpless as flippers as she fought to find footing.

She looked up at him. She saw his teeth grinning. 'It's me!' he said.

The world shifted gears like a truck. Her breath left her, she clutched at her chest, all was confusion.

'Lung?' she asked. 'Lung!' For one further terrible moment she thought her own son had come to arrest her best friend.

He laughed. 'Not expecting me were you?'

'No,' she said weakly. 'What are you doing here?'

He laughed again. 'We are bringing you your knitting machine!' As big as a tree branch, his arm was flung towards the cargo under the canvas.

'Oh!' she called out, clutching herself in relief. 'Oh! Oh!'

'Your Mr Oz told me the machine was going, and said, it would be a good chance for me to see you again. Also we have the new TV for you! Did no one tell you?'

Relief spilled over, sloppily, loosely into other emotions. 'Oh Lung!' she said again, and hugged him, held onto him as if he were a new village tree to root things in place. Suddenly it was joyful to see him. Out of confusion, relief, and love her eyes were suddenly full of tears. He chuckled and patted her back. 'Meet my colleagues,' he said.

Two more soldiers lurched out of the cab. One was small and wiry with bad teeth in a cheerful grin. The other looked uncomfortable smiling. He was slim in the hips but fat in the face. Fat and brutal was how he would swell into the future. Both bowed slightly in politeness.

'This is Private Ozer, and Sergeant Alkanuh,' said Lung. 'This is my mother, Mrs Chung Mae.'

Mae was shivering with cold and nerves but managed to bow to each of them. She looked back at her son. The cold was bringing a beautiful pink to her cheeks. The two soldiers were chuckling, the tears and emotion were what they expected from a homecoming. Mae saw Kwan, pale, grey at a window.

'Kwan!' Mae called. 'It is my son Lung. He has brought our knitting machine.' She pushed the tear out of her face and smiled, smiled as wide as she could so that Kwan would see everything was all right.

'Kwan, come out and see my huge, new son! I mean, machine!'

They all laughed because it was true.

Lung was a monster. He had left home as a skinny, spotty seventeen-year-old, off to Army College and refusing to admit that he was shy of the future. Army food and training had made him tall and broad and fit. And he was handsome, oh how handsome Lung had become! She stared in wonder at his perfect face, his perfect teeth, his perfect combed jet black hair.

'Why didn't you tell me?' she said and hit him, lightly on the arm.

His colleagues chuckled again.

'I thought Mr Oz would tell you,' he said, coyly, charmingly.

The skinny one spoke. 'Lung wanted to surprise you.'

'He surprised me all right, I thought I would die!' Her eyes betrayed her again, she wept again. 'It has been three years since I have seen him!'

Shaking like fine china on an unsteady shelf, Kwan crept down the stone steps of her house, clutching her coat. Kwan looked as though she had been punched in the belly.

'Mrs Wing-ma'am,' said Lung, with a practised adult politeness that would have been beyond him when he left home. He bowed, and beamed, and enveloped Kwan's frail hand in his own. 'It is so good to see old friends.' He smiled. He held onto Kwan's hand and said to Mae, 'Come, quick, see your beautiful machine.' He escorted them both to the back of the truck and flung back the tarpaulin with one huge gesture.

The weaving machine like her son was huge, brown and khaki.

Lung chuckled. 'Mrs Wing-ma'am,' he asked the owner of the barns. 'Where do you want it?'

Mae spoke instead. 'Oh not here. I have rented our old house. It needs to go there.'

Lung's smile faltered; he did not look at her, but he managed not to look sad, or ashamed.

The beefy one with the dark chin said, 'We better get it there, Lieutenant,' said the Sergeant. 'Before the snow settles too badly.'

'And there's a power failure,' warned Mae.

Lung barked with laughter. 'Of course! There always is the first snow of winter! Come on, let's get this in!' He bowed again, quickly to Kwan, and was striding back to the cab on legs as thick as prize hams. 'Come on, Mama!'

'We need to stop at Sunni's.' said Mae. He pulled her into the cab, and for lack of space sat her on his lap. It was strange to be so supported by your baby.

'I remember when I used to hold you like this,' she said. He looked like a barrel full of apples, all round, red. She knew she was looking with a mother's eyes, but there was no doubt. He was so much better looking than the other two. They were invisible next to him, as if you were blinded from looking at the sun.

No wonder a Western girl fell in love with you, Mae thought. They must all fall in love with you. She felt herself fall in love with him, all over again. So this is what my son grew up into. Lieutenant Chung.

Mae realized that her son was the best looking man she had ever seen. Better looking than a movie star. But he smelled different from those pretty boys, there was nothing wispy about him. This was someone, you could tell, who jumped from aeroplanes, who built rope bridges across ravines.

Mae thought of Joe. No wonder he had been so proud, so amazed at what had stepped out from his own loins. No wonder he wanted to talk about nothing else. Lung was the one good thing he had done.

'We stop here,' Lung told the skinny driver, and the truck whined to a professional halt, not skidding in the snow.

Sunni greeted Lung graciously, just as if the family Chung had not been shattered by scandal. Her kitchen still smelled of gas and was lit with a gas lamp.

Mae murmured to her about housing the machine in the old house. Sunni waved a hand, in a grand ladylike way that was also slightly crabby. Mae suddenly saw how she would be when she was old. Saw that Sunni was already getting old, but that somehow, getting old would be good for her.

'Oh!' Sunni said. 'I already told that man of mine, I said we will get nothing else for that old place, it's only good for giving to tenants and who needs tenants? They are trouble, you have to give them the house for free with the land. Pshaw! Fifteen riels a month.'

'Twelve,' said Mae.

'Twelve,' said Sunni. 'But only because I want to see to see the machine loaded.'

Both ladies got to sit on Lung's lap, one thigh each.

The snow still fell, shooting past the windscreen as the truck moved through it. The snow looked like shooting stars, as if they were travelling through outer space.

Their old house turned as if to greet them, grey as a ghost.

'I'll get the gate,' Mae said, and stepped down from the truck. She lifted up the ground bolts, and wondered why she did not feel more. Snow, power failure, Lung, machine, there was too much going on to feel the pain and the loss of what had happened. That was good.

As the gate opened amid a spangle of illuminated snow, it was more like a festival.

The huge green van bounced into the courtyard, just missing taking off the lintel from the gate. All Mr Ken's hens were inside out of the cold or surely some of them would have been crushed. The great truck swung around and backed up. Mae saw Mr Ken's house, darkened as if deserted.

Her washing line was folded, her kitchen door was locked, and the stump for chopping wood lay sideways. Mae went to open up the barn.

The bolts were cold on her hands; the old doors groaned as if in protest at being awakened. The earthen floor had been beaten flat as polished flagstone.

The floor sloped down, as did the entire courtyard.

Lung stepped out of the truck, holding what looked like a remote control. Sunni hung back behind him as if afraid. Mae walked out then.

'We've got to put it on something first,' she said.

'Why?'

'There are floods,' said Mae.

Mae felt as if elastic braces were drawing in around her heart as she knocked on Mr Ken's door.

She looked at the old grey wood of the door, and waited unable to breathe, feeling Lung's eyes on her back. She heard footsteps; the door opened.

There he was. Mr Ken. He looked older than she remembered, more rumpled, but then she had seen Hikmet Tunch, and her son Lung, since. His eyes quickened when he first saw her, widened, darted over her face, then looked behind and saw the truck. He tried to straighten his hair; he looked embarrassed, befuddled.

'Hello, Mae,' he said. 'What's going on?'

There was no time for yearning, remembrance, or even any sign of what happened. Not with Joe's son looking on.

'Hello,' she said with restraint. 'I am sorry to bother you like this. But we are putting a new machine in the barn . . .'

'My mother needs to talk to you about this . . .'

Mae cut him off. 'It is actually Sunni's barn and I rent it. You once said that you had no use for the stone drinking troughs. Can I have them?'

He looked at her with an expression that was impossible to read. *You and I meet again and we talk about this?*

'I'm moving back in,' she told him. 'I've only just decided.'

Behind her, Sunni said to Lung, 'I have the keys. Let's get the TV inside.'

Kuei's hands did a helpless little wave. 'Have them if you want. They are very old. What do want them for?'

It would not be right not to warn him.

'There will be a flood. Everything will be washed away. I need to have my machine on a platform, to save it.'

His whole face was wary. 'This is Grandmother talking,' he said. 'Every winter, she would always warn us about the flood.'

'This time it's true.' All right, don't believe me, she thought. I have no time to argue. The truck's engine is running and so is Lung's. She glanced behind and saw her TV lowered from the back of the van. 'May I have the use of the troughs? I can pay you for them, whatever you ask.'

Mr Ken held up a hand. 'Take them, take them.'

Mae nodded, smiling, hoping her eyes were also able to jam into such snatched time, a form of remembrance.

'I'll have them back when the flood does not come,' he said darkly, and shut the door on her.

Mae blinked, for that had been too sudden. She turned slowly, followed her TV as it was huffed and sighed into her old house.

'Here, here, into its new home!' enthused Sunni, too bright, too glowing. She was covering for Mae. The house was small and dark and smelled of dust. Noodles had stiffened on plates left on the table. Some of Mae's old dresses still hung from the wall, as if preserved by the cold. Lung glanced down, ashamed.

'Does it convert to Aircast?' Sunni asked tapping the top of the TV.

'Oh yes, I expect Sezen will use it to serve Collabo.'

'Can I rent it?' Sunni asked. Mae hesitated. 'I want to serve high fashion. We can split the market.'

'It has possibilities,' said Mae. 'We'll talk tomorrow.'

The two fashion experts nodded, eyes hooded. Then something

happened. Listen to us both, they seemed to say, and both burst out laughing at themselves.

'Captains of industry,' said Lung, but he was smiling.

The truck roared back into Kwan's courtyard to find it full of preparations for a party.
A tractor ran its engine and its lights, and Mr Wing and Mr Atakoloo were moving tables. Children stuck their heads through the gate and turned to run back home. There always was a party with the first snow, this year it would be at the Big House.

The forecourt quickly filled with people. Hot wine was left on braziers that smoked as much as most people's mouths steamed.

Men took cups of warm wine and stood on Mr Wing's steps. Lung strode into their midst, shaking hands, remembering names. Mae, as his mother, accompanied him.

'Ah, you've grown!' said men snatching hats from heads, out of politeness.

Mr Ali squared up to Lung. 'Your father tells us much of your doings. You are a lieutenant now, I hear.'

'Yes, luckily enough, I had early promotion.'

'Your father is very proud of you,' said Mr Ali, glancing in Mae's direction, the fallen mother.

'That is good to hear. He lives in Balshang now, so I see him every day.' Lung smiled and plainly moved on.

'Good evening Mr Ali,' said Mae, deliberately sounding pleased. 'Lung has bought me a huge weaving machine. It is automatic, and intelligent. It will help the Ladies Circle meet all its orders.'

Mr Ali was as heavy as lead. He glowered at her and did not answer. 'And you are looking so well Mr Ali,' said Mae in a little bell-like voice. 'So plump. If you don't mind me saying.' Mr Ali pushed past her as if to go for more red wine.

Mae saw her own family arrive. Ju-mei, his wife, Mae's mother and, after some deliberation no doubt, Siao and Old Mr Chung.

'Lung! Lung!' called Ju-mei.

'Uncle!'

Mae deliberated too and decided to let Lung greet his uncle without her. The two men hugged, and clapped each other's backs. Ju-mei wore a heavy Russian coat and pork pie hat. He looked like a Party chairman. Lung paused when he saw his Uncle Siao, and blinked in some surprise that the two families were friends. Siao shook his hand and winked. He and Lung hugged too, but the hug was gentler, less showy. Lung had grown up with Siao, who was more of a big brother to him than an uncle. Siao looked up. His eyes caught Mae's, and he gestured for her to come near them.

Very well, thought Mae. For your sake, Siao. She remembered: Siao has never fought me or called me bad names. She was surprised; she realized that she knew in her heart that Siao would keep things calm and good.

Mae saw her mother's plump face close up like a purse as she approached. Old Mrs Wang retreated from Mae behind Ju-mei's Russian back. His face looked like polished soapstone. Siao spoke first. 'Mae, how are things with you?'

'I am happy to say the business goes well.'

'And happy to see Lung,' said Siao.

'Indeed!' chuckled Mae.

Old Mr Chung blinked like an ancient tortoise, and bowed sweetly to Mae, out of respect or mere good form.

'We are *all* happy to see you, Lung.' Ju-mei grinned awkwardly and jabbed his upper body up and down like a crow pecking at road kill. He was trying to bow with respect to his officer nephew.

None of them were comfortable. Mae glanced up and saw a tight little knot of Alis and Dohs, peering at them over their shoulders. They were a spectacle: the family of the deserted husband in company with the adulterous wife and her brother.

'People are staring,' said Mae's mother miserably.

Mae felt sorry for her, so small and worried. 'Pay them no mind, Mama.'

'It is easy for you to say, you are a woman who has no face left to lose,' said her mother. 'You do not even come to call on us.'

So which is it Mama, are you ashamed of me or mad because I do not call, or are you just looking for another reason to be miserable?

Siao intervened. 'Perhaps it is because Mae is embarrassed that her husband's family are staying there with you, Mrs Wang-ma'am.'

'You credit her with delicacy,' said Mae's mother. 'Ju-mei, I cannot bear this. I am on show. I have been an object of show all my life. I thought all that had ended. But there is always something. I so look forward to the first winter party, but I must . . . I must . . .' Mama had stared to quaver again.

'You stay here, Mama,' said Mae. 'I was just going back into the kitchen.'

Lung looked dismayed. 'I'll be down in a while, Mama,' he said.

Mae smiled with gratitude at Lung and said goodbye to them all in turn. Standing as straight as she could, Mae turned sideways to slip through the crowd and down the stairs to Kwan's kitchen.

Kwan was at work, wearing her best dress. The tables were already full of food. 'It's a good thing I guessed the party would be here,' Kwan said. Whenever there was a power failure, there would be a party in someone's courtyard.

Mae's stomach suddenly felt heavy and she had to sit down. They were alone so Mae said quickly, 'I don't know what else these soldiers know, so it will be good to stay cautious.' In the half-darkness, the two women looked at each other. It was plain where Mae's loyalties lay. From outside there came a swelling of laughter. Lung had finished a story.

'Can I help?' asked Sunni.

Without missing a beat, Kwan smiled. 'Sunni! Hello. Yes, I am sure there is much to do.'

So there they were, the three of them, in Kwan's kitchen, with the ropes of garlic around the wall and the pile of round village bread.

'Shall I restore the bread for you?' Sunni asked. Village bread was dry and needed to be moistened.

Mae offered, 'I could string the beans.'

'Oh, it will be fun with just us three,' said Kwan, kneeling. She hoisted out a bucket of water and a tray for soaking bread.

'Yes, it will be good to sit and be convivial,' said Sunni, and smiled at Mae. The kitchen smelled of pork and rice. 'Oh! Soy and lard on boiled rice. Oh, that takes me home.' Sunni, though Muslim, had grown up in a liberal household.

Mae strung and snapped the beans. Sunni took out her corncob pipe and so did Kwan. 'Look at us, we look like old grannies!' said Sunni.

'We are, nearly,' said Mae.

'Oh! You talk!' said Sunni.

'Lung is to be married soon,' said Mae, not quite telling the truth. How could she admit that she had not been asked to the wedding?

'You bet,' said Sunni, 'He is a prince, and any girl with brains would get him as fast as she could.'

'She is a Western girl,' said Mae. 'She is very pretty, educated, and says she likes me. This is because of my screens. How can you like someone for their screens?'

'Oh,' said Sunni and looked sad. 'Then we will lose him?'

Mae let this sink in. 'Yes,' she said. 'I am sure he will stay in Balshang at least. And who knows, he may even go back to Canada with his wife.'

'Has he talked about what has happened?' Kwan asked. She meant the end of Mae's marriage.

'Yes.' Mae played with the beans and with the truth of the situation. 'Mostly he tells me he forgives me for what has happened. But I don't think he really has.'

'Ah,' said Sunni, getting down to the meat of it.

'I don't think he really understands it,' said Mae.

'I don't think I do,' said Sunni.

Kwan said nothing. Her back as she worked listened and was tense.

'It was love,' murmured Mae.

'Oh I understand that. I understand why you married Joe and I understand why you would tire of him. Speaking frankly.'

'Indeed,' said Kwan, for Sunni was being very frank.

'There is no other way to talk about these things. What I don't understand, now that Joe has gone off with the Pincushion, is why you are not with Mr Ken.'

'Ah,' said Mae. She had no immediate answer.

Sunni patted Mae's hand. 'Joe has left you. That evens things up. Go live with your Mr Ken. The rest of us will get used to things in the end.'

'I'm not scared of the village,' said Mae. 'But I do sometimes wonder if I love Mr Ken because his grandmother does.'

'Ah,' said Sunni, and her hand shuddered.

'I think I see him sometimes through Old Mrs Tung's eyes.'

The room seemed to hold its breath with the cold.

Lung strode in, booming, 'And what good things are you ladies cooking?'

Back to work.

The ladies carried out vats of quick-fried beans, swollen wet bread, and pots of rice with tiny chillies burning within it. The army truck played Lectro on its Balshang radio. Its vast army antennae could pull in signals from the capital. Kizuldah heard advertisements for hypermarkets, toilet paper, and clubs that could play Airfiles on giant TV screens.

The villagers hated the music. A cable was strung from the army van's battery to a cassette player, and more traditional music was played for the adults.

All four hundred people were crowded into the courtyard and barn despite the snow that was still falling, as if the stars had given up clinging to heaven.

They chuckled and sipped tea from mugs. The mugs were then filled with rice and beans. Kwan, Sunni, and Mae moved among the people passing out the food.

The men had to take beans from Mae. The situation allowed no other response. They looked at her, said nothing, were grumpy out of loyalty to Joe. But Joe was not here. And Joe had gone off with Mr Muhammed's wife.

They took the winter food in silence and Mae's presence was made more normal if unwelcome.

Some of the younger men, overcome by the cold, by energy, by the end of the year's work, began to dance. The girls squealed and pretended to be overcome with embarrassment, hiding their cheeks, turning their backs. And turning again to look.

The married women smiled ruefully and shook their heads. The older men held their hands over their ears as if hating the music and wavered and wobbled in secret rivalry.

'I always knew men were more interested in each other,' said Mrs Mack. Mrs Mack? Mae laughed and touched her arm. Mrs Mack, less aloof towards Mae than others, responded with a chuckle at herself. 'Did I say that?'

'I am afraid so. You are wild Western woman,' joked Mae.

'Oh!' said Mrs Mack, not so pleased with the stale view of her Christianity. 'Yes. I look like the motorcycle girl.'

'I'm sorry. I am the village fallen woman, remember?'

'Tuh. These villagers,' said Mrs Mack. 'They forgive murder faster.'

Mrs Pin said, 'Pay no attention to them, Mae.'

Mrs Mack leaned forward. 'I understand that you are shorthanded in the Circle. I sew well . . .'

Mae still needed allies. 'Yah, sure, you want to join? Please! Why did you not say so before?'

Mrs Mack was too Christian not to be blunt. 'I didn't know you were making all that money.'

There was not much to say in reply to that.

'And they say money can't buy friendship,' said Mae.

'It can't,' replied Mrs Mack, blunt again.

Mrs Doh, who could practise tact, ballooned out her eyes at the behaviour of her two friends.

Mae paused. 'I'll take that to mean we are friends beyond the money.'

Mrs Mack paused. 'If you like. But you have not previously regarded me much. No one in this village does.' Her eyes were sad.

'We will be at work tomorrow, in my old house,' said Mae. 'Come and join us. All of you.'

'You are kind to extend such a valuable invitation,' said Mrs Doh, the fine lines on her eyes and forehead wincing at Mrs Mack's Christian manners.

There was a sudden involuntary stir amid the people. Oh! said one of the girls.

Lung had joined the dancers. He hopped in, no embarrassment, looking incredibly pleased to be there. And began to dance as a village dance should be done, broadly, happily, rolling his shoulders, hips, and arms in one great sinewy motion. It was what was needed, to finally make the party warm.

Some of the women ululated, in high warbling warrior tones. The men joined in. The slower and fatter men finally hopped into the middle. White beards mocked themselves, or showed that once, they could dance with the best. But no one could compete with Lung.

He began to clap his hands high over his head, he spun around on his heels. The other younger men in the village began to gather round him, to dance just as vigorously. In the cab, Ozer snapped off the Lectro. The flutes, the violins, the tablas of the traditional music flooded the courtyard.

Lung began to sing along. He could sing too, and his voice when lifted up was not that of a Balshang Otter, or a Karzistani Soldier. It was the voice of a happy peasant who had eaten his fill and was dancing to keep warm in the winter.

Every village had one, a Tatlises, a Sweet Voice. Lung's voice slipped around notes as if escaping them, escaping order, to follow the flow of blood of the heart.

'*Gel, gel, goomooleh gel,*' he sang. Come, come, to a house of welcome. They all danced, they all clapped, even the women began to dance in the snow, amid the sound of who they were.

And Mae's heart that had been starved of company was suddenly stuffed full. She could feel it strain, like a belly, with the light, the noise, her people, and her son.

Joe was a village hero, too, Mae suddenly thought. When he was young.

The air's warmer. It always is after the snow comes.

Too warm, warned Mrs Tung. That's all she could say, too warm, over and over.

Finally people left late, bustling children to bed.
Discipline drilled into them, the soldiers did all the clearing up, gathering up the basins, mugs, spoons. The women were helpless before their speed. Kwan shook their heads. 'We are surplus, ladies,' she joked.

'Why can't we have the army all the time?' Mrs Nan said.

In the kitchen the three soldiers scrubbed the cutlery and boiled water in the pans, scalding off the fats and oils and congealing beans.

'We'll sleep in the truck,' said Lung. Kwan insisted that she had spare rooms. The soldiers nodded in polite gratitude, shaking hands before going to get their bags.

'I will walk you upstairs,' said Lung to Mae.

'I am unlikely to come to harm,' said Mae, smiling. But all understood. He needed to talk.

The joy of the evening fell away behind them as they climbed the stairs. He carried a candle. Mae had to take his arm in the dark. She began to remember their recent unpleasant exchanges by voicemail.

He helped her fold away her scarf and sheepskin.

'You got my warning then,' he said.

In the dark, it was as though Mae could see the steam of her breath glowing. 'It was you?'

Her mind raced: if it was Lung, not Tunch, then the army knows. Did he send the second encryption as well? If so, was he a friend? If not, she must not tell him anything else.

Lung whispered, 'Yes, ssh.'

Mae began to calculate. 'You know about Kwan?'

'Yes,' he said simply.

'Is she in danger?' Mae asked. She began to feel sick.

Lung sighed, 'I don't think so, now. Those screens have gone. She should be all right. After all, you have made Kizuldah famous. What you might ask her to do, which would be even better, is for her to put up some new screens that tell both sides of the story.'

Like milk, the very air seemed to curdle, go sour.

Lung elaborated. 'You know. How the government houses the Eloi, gives them homes . . .'

'Refrigerators in Balshang,' murmured Mae.

'Yes.' He sounded pleased; she could almost see the teeth in his smile.

'That way, the world does not puzzle over where the site has gone,' Mae added.

'You are very wise,' said Lung. 'But then, you always were wise, Mama.'

She was thinking: You came here to accomplish this. To get Kwan's site to do the government's work.

No. You came here to protect your own career in the army.

Lung relaxed; he felt he had done his job. 'Who would have thought you could do all this? The site, the business? Where did you learn all this?'

Mae was narrow-eyed in the darkness. What was he trying to find out now? 'Oh,' she said airily. 'Your mother is not so stupid. It is all available on the TV.'

'And from Hikmet Tunch,' said Lung, lightly.

'Indeed.'

'How did you find him?'

'He found me.'

It was strange being interrogated by her own son, in a dark and unheated room, as if they had both died and come back as Evil Dead.

Her dead son gave a short, slightly edged laugh. 'No. I mean, what did you think of him?'

'What do you think of him?'

'I think you should stay away from him.'

Mae decided not to ask him: Is that what the army thinks? She decided to deceive him, to protect Kwan, herself, her Circle. 'Why?' she asked in innocence.

'Look. The government likes him being here, he brings in money, but he does things in that place that are illegal everywhere else. You know how he started?'

'As a computer student?'

'Oh, Mother, he was the country's biggest drug smuggler. They let him off because he runs a computer business.'

'Our government would do such a thing?' Mae sounded shocked.

'Our government does many things,' said Lung, quietly.

And you are its servant, thought Mae. You look at what you do full in the face, and you still serve it so that you can be a lieutenant. And Kwan will never put up a site to do what you want.

We could all end up looking at you, my son, from the wrong end of a gun.

Come, Air, and blow governments away.

Then her son said, 'What are you going to do about the pregnancy?'

Mae's whole face pulled back until it was as tight as a mask. 'The usual things.'

'It is not a usual pregnancy.'

Mae watched the wreathing of her icy breath. 'Who told you that?'

Lung blew out. 'That man Tunch. Well . . .'

'A nurse called Fatimah.'

Lung jerked with a chuckle, amused by his mother's quickness. 'Yes. She at least seems very concerned for you.'

'Yes she is. Perhaps we should both avoid that man Tunch.'

She couldn't read Lung's reaction. He shrugged and laughed and nodded. 'No disagreement there.' Then concern. 'Are you okay, well?'

Mae decided not to let him off the hook. 'No. I feel sick and as you can see I am not welcome many places in the village.'

His eyes could not meet hers. He ducked and ran a hand over his hair.

Mae asked him, 'How is your father?'

'Ugh,' said Lung, involuntarily.

'Seeing a lot of him? He visits you often?' she asked.

'I can't hide from you, Mama. He is there all weekend, every weekend. Sometimes I have to say to him, look, Dad, I am having all the officers over for dinner.'

Dark, dark, and cold, in this attic room not her own.

'And the officers, do they find him interesting?'

'Don't, Mama. No, they don't find him interesting. He gets drunk, and tries to talk up what he has done, and pretends to be a businessman.'

And Tsang, thought Mae, I wonder how you like the overripe peach that people must mistake for your mother.

'But he also visits your sister Ying.'

'Yes, yes, he bounces between the two of us. But she is married to an officer too.'

Mae saw it all: poor Joe, desperate, helplessly in love with his son, yearning only to see Lung and how strong and smart he was, and trying, also desperately, to avoid seeing that he was in his son's way, his daughter's way.

You are not so smart, Lung. You are enough of your father's son, I saw that somehow tonight. This is as far as you will go, and then you too will start, unaccountably, to fade.

'You want some advice, son?' Mae moved through the winter silk of the night. She took the hard band of muscle beside his neck and worked it. 'The army will not like it that you have a Western wife. They will be disappointed in your father. You know what you should do? Though this pains me, I cannot think only of myself. You should be your wife's husband, and go back with her to Canada.'

Lung sighed. 'I know.'

And then, thought Mae, you will not be a spy on all of us.

18

---

audio file from: Mr Hikmet Tunch
16 December

New York Times? How useful. For whom? For me, certainly. Thank you for making such an emotional case against the UN. The government will also be pleased to be shown in such a good light. And your friend Bugsy. How do you serve her? You bring visitors to her superficial and decadent magpie. Do you really think American ladies – for whom a shift from chiffon pastel to black cotton is big news – are capable of being one with your Circle? Remember, Mae, that 2020 is an election year. Your friend is a Democratic journalist. She is using you and your praise of government subsidy to attack the Republican president. You are not a stupid woman, Mae, so it interests me to find that you allow yourself to be acted upon. Finally, you may be wondering who supplied that interesting code that arrived so happily a few nights ago. You should avoid thanking anyone else for it. So who is watching whom?

Breakfast was late and boisterous and prolonged.
Lung was still pumped full of love from the night before and didn't want to go. He joked and kicked his big-booted feet, and accepted one cup of tea after another. He and his men had gone out before anyone was up, and repaired the powerline.

'We found a frame for the wires just hanging in midair. The wires were holding it up and not the other way around. We just stared!' Lung mimed a village dolt scratching his head. 'Then we saw burn marks. Some old farmer had been burning off straw and burned the pole as well!'

Kwan scraped dishes, her lips drawn. There was a vertical grey line down the middle of her cheeks and her hands suddenly looked thin, frail and veined.

'I'll do that,' said Mae. Lung was merry, and oblivious. His cheeks still glowed from freezing morning air. He looked like a polished apple. Kwan sat arms folded, her eyes dim and small.

Finally Mr Wing came in, bundled in sheepskin, his eyes measuring like lasers. 'It's started to snow,' he said.

The little private looked anxious. 'We could get snowed in.'

Lung moved slowly, regretfully. Kwan stood up and delicately shook his hand and could not look him in the face. She was scared.

The sergeant and the private flew up to their rooms and hopped back down, swinging khaki bags. Mae speeded things along by getting Lung's bag for him.

In the courtyard, Lung recovered his poise. Sergeant Albankuh already had the engine running, and Lung had begun to understand that he was not quite at home. He spent time thanking the Wings handsomely for their hospitality, and also – his hand covering Kwan's- – for their kindnesses to his mother.

Kwan had recovered as well. She replied with exquisite politeness, knowing that he had come to warn her off and, perhaps, to report on her.

Mae marvelled at them all, the maintenance of form and the retention of humanity.

It is the village that allows us to do this, she thought. We know each other, and we all hope that that knowledge keeps us each in balance, within limits.

Then Lung turned to Mae and both of them seemed to relent. They collapsed into a hug. For Mae it was like hugging some huge stranger. He kissed her forehead, called her his Clever Little Mama. Then he stepped back from her. He shoved on his army hat, and that was somehow heartbreaking. It was a boy's gesture, innocent and eternal. All the soldiers throughout history had pushed on some kind of boot or glove just before they left their mothers to die or to come back for ever changed.

This was the last of her boy. He would swell even bigger, like a great fat boil, and she saw how he would coarsen as he aged until his astounding beauty could not be credited.

'You remember what I told you,' he said, suddenly serious, pointing a finger at her.

'You remember what I told you,' she said, equally serious.

He nodded and hopped into the cab, and nodded to the sergeant to release the brake with – it seemed to Mae – a kind of relief. The truck crept forward, and suddenly Lung's face was flooded with a grin, wide and white between two cheeks like peaches. It was how both of them wanted him to be remembered.

Snow clung to Mae's hair. It seemed to be wrapping the village in lace. Lace was wrapped tightly around things in drawers, to preserve them.

Mae stood in the courtyard for many minutes listening to the rumble of the truck as the snow fell. She heard each acceleration, braking, or change of gears. The sound trailed away, away, farther into the valley, step by step, deeper and deeper down, away from her.

Mae turned to Kwan and said, 'I'm going, too.'

Kwan blinked. 'What? Why?'

Mae said, 'I'm renting my own house from Sunni. I'll move my business there. I don't want to be a nuisance.'

'You're not a nuisance,' said Kwan, and took her hand.

'Then I want to go before I become one.'

She went up the long staircase to the freezing attic room, and packed her bags again. She redirected her mail to the new TV of her own. She went back down to the kitchen. Kwan was putting together an evening meal from the remains of last night's feast.

'You won't have any food in the house,' explained Kwan. 'I thought you might like to have this. We have kindling and shitcakes in the barn. Take some of those, too, to warm the house.'

'You have been so kind.'

Kwan looked sombre. 'We have been through a lot together.'

'Oh! You could say that ten times and it would still not be enough!'

'But we came through.'

'We came through.'

Kwan hugged her. 'You can still stay, you know.'

Mae touched her arm. 'I really do not know what I would have done if my friend Wing Kwan had not been so kind. There would have been nowhere else for me to go. But the time comes, even with family, when one must leave.'

Kwan nodded.

So Mae took her one carpetbag, and another bag of food and fuel, and set out across the courtyard. Her slippers scrunched on the snow, and her breath rose up as vaporous as a fading memory. She knew Kwan would be watching from her diwan. Mae held up a hand and waved goodbye without looking back.

The Wang household was the first door she passed, on the corner of upper and lower streets.

It had been her home through most of her childhood. Mae stopped and looked at the doorstep. The single step would always get muddy and she and her older sister did not want anyone to think of them as dirty, so every day for ten years they had scrubbed it. The water in the plastic bucket was always cold.

Mae now brushed the snow off the step with her slipper. Here, in this house, Mae had slept in one tiny bedroom with two sisters. Their mother had slept on cushions on the diwan. Her brother and an uncle shared a room. The Iron Aunt kept the main bedchamber for herself. It was a fatherless house full of work and worry.

Mae realized she felt guilty for neglecting her mother. She felt a sullen resentment that her mother had not been to see her. She felt awkwardness and she felt a kind of twist of triumph. She felt many things she did not like herself feeling.

Come on Mae, she told herself. She knocked on the front door.

Her sister-in-law opened it, to a sudden swelling sound from within of a baby wailing. Her sister-in-law's face drooped and then froze, mouth open.

'Li-liang, may I come in?' Mae heard herself ringing a sweet little bell voice, which was designed to put rude people in the wrong.

'Uh . . . Mae. Hello.' Her sister-in-law was not an independent person. If there was a surprise, she could take no action without Ju-mei. 'Ju-mei!' she shouted. 'Your sister is here!'

And still outside in the snow, Mae thought, smiling like a row of tinkling windchimes.

My family really is as bad as I think they are, she decided.

The sister-in-law stepped back out of view, leaving the door hanging open and Mae standing outside. Mae heard steps.

Her brother Ju-mei's voice was dim. 'Why is the door open?'

Mae was not in a tolerant mood. 'Because your wife does not want to invite me in and does not have the courage to slam it in my face,' said Mae.

'I had my baby to look after!' said Young Mrs Wang.

Ju-mei swelled suddenly into the doorway. He needed a shave, his shirt was untucked, and Mae knew: They did not want me to see them as ordinary, scruffy, and so hated answering the door. That is the

Wang family way: to be rude in order to preserve good appearances. I am probably the same.

'I am moving back into my old house,' Mae announced. 'I can afford to rent it from my friend Sunni Haseem.'

Ju-mei snorted. Friend? Haseem? And yet there was doubt. What if they *were* friends again?

'My business will move back there as well.' Mae kept smiling. 'I am sure you will be pleased that it is doing very well. And since the house has so long been in the family Chung, I was wondering if Old Mr Chung and my brother-in-law Mr Chung Siao would not like to occupy it with me.' Mae smiled. 'So. You see, I have not come to trouble you. I really wish to speak to the Chung family.'

'And not your own family,' growled Ju-mei.

'My own family does not invite me into their house, even when it is snowing. From that, I conclude I am not welcome. I do not wish to intrude.'

Ju-mei was very angry with her. 'Very well,' he said – and closed the door in Mae's face.

Mae heard a singsong wailing from behind the wooden door. That, she realized, would be Mama. She had time to wonder if Ju-mei had actually wished to spare Mae a scene with Mama. Mama presented her life as a continuing tragic opera.

Then the door was flung open, and Mae's mother, wearing her Quivering Flower face, stood trembling in the doorway. She held her head back with defiant pride.

'How dare you! How dare you show your face at my doorway!'

'Mother, you're being silly,' said Mae.

'You talk to me! You judge me! When you have behaved as no woman should behave. When you brought shame to me – yes, me. What do you think people are saying about me: "There she goes, the woman who cannot control her wild daughter, who brings down re-spectable life in the village." I cannot believe you would do that to me!'

'I didn't do it to you, Mother, I did it to myself.'

'Everything you do, you do to me. When your father was killed . . .'

Here we go, sighed Mae.

You can tell the truth so often that it becomes a lie.

Mae had not spent a day in her mother's presence without Mama telling yet again the full story of how their brave father was shot by the Communists, and how she was left alone in the world with three young babies. Then followed the sacrifice, the work, and the endless worry, only to be repaid with desertion and coldness. Then – and this was best of all – how she had never complained, was always silent, had left the past behind her, but now . . . now, because of Mae's behaviour, was forced to speak of what had been left behind.

'You! You! You have made me cry, you have made me remember, you have broken my triumph over these terrible memories!'

'I need to speak to Mr Chung,' repeated Mae.

Her mother by now was wracked with sobs, and Ju-mei was holding her, patting her and glowering at Mae.

'You see-*hee-hee*!' her mother sobbed. 'She cannot admit she was wrong!'

'I was wrong,' said Mae.

'You see! She has no remorse!'

'It was a disruptive thing I did.'

'She has no feeling. She has not been to see me once! She was staying next door, and she would not deign to see me! She does not care that I am old and sick and alone!'

Suddenly, Siao in his T-shirt had inserted himself sideways past the Wangs, and his steady face was wrinkled in an embarrassed smile. There was no accusation in the face at all. Mae saw at once: He had absolutely had his fill of the Wangs. She also saw his Karz blue-grey eyes, and his fine dark beard, and his slim workman's arms. She found herself thinking: He has grown up.

'Come home?' Mae asked him.

Siao nodded yes, very slightly. 'It would be pleasant to be in my old house,' he said.

'I am sorry for what happened,' Mae said.

Siao stayed smiling and calm, while his shoulders equivocated. 'It was a terrible thing you did.'

Mae nodded. *Yes.*

Siao turned back to the doorway. 'Mr Wang . . .' he began. 'I must speak to my father.'

'You cannot go back with that woman after what she has done!' roared Mr Ju-mei.

Siao rocked slightly in place. 'I am so grateful for what you have done for us, but I am aware that we cannot stay as guests for ever. It is a burden for you. Please, I am very cold, we all are, can we not simply ask Mae to come inside?'

'Never!' wailed her mother.

Ju-mei stood up straight. 'You heard what my mother said.'

His wife chipped in: 'The baby is freezing.'

Siao nodded once, politely, and smiling, stepped inside. 'Just a moment, Mae, I will not be long,' he said, bowing slightly. He closed the door.

When he opened it again, he had Old Mr Chung with him. The old man looked confused now. He had on a filthy quilted jacket, with his box of tools. 'Is it a job?' he asked, looking eager.

Still in his T-shirt, Siao stepped outside with his father into the snow and closed the door after him.

'Your family has been very generous to us,' he said to Mae. Mae saw his bare arms and took off her coat and put it around Siao's shoulders.

They were all cold. Mae spoke quickly: 'The house is restored to you as long as I can pay rent. The business is now in the barn. How are you, Old Mr Chung-sir?'

'Ready. Ready,' the old man said, stepping in place as if held back by a harness. 'They are driving me crazy.'

'Father, that is rude.'

Old Mr Chung looked at Mae. 'I know they are your family . . .'

Mae heard herself say, 'You are my family. Whatever was between me and Joe, I always loved his family.'

The old man blinked. 'We loved you.'

The door blurted open like an awkward remark. Ju-mei stood glowering at the door. 'You keep a poor old man outside!' he accused Mae.

'Then perhaps you can let us inside,' said Mae.

Mae won. Reluctantly Ju-mei admitted her. Her mother sat enthroned and avoiding her gaze. Young Mrs Wang had taken the baby elsewhere. The inside of the house, as always, was as empty and as clean as an iceberg. The tiny brazier did nothing to warm it. On the wall was the framed photograph of all of them as children, and another photograph of her father, so familiar that it looked nothing like him.

Mae's mother cowered in black trousers and jacket and a long flowered scarf. She looked tiny and frail and unhappy. There is nothing in her to be frightened of, Mae thought. Then she thought: *Frightened?*

Siao said, bowing, 'We have decided to take Mae's kind offer.' Something in the way he said it made Mae realize: Siao is head of the family now. Joe's going has been good for him.

Ju-mei glowered. 'I cannot believe you will accept any help from that woman.'

'We have taken much already from her family who owed us nothing and were so kind to make space for us in their home,' said Siao. 'We are impoverished and through our own efforts have lost everything we inherited. At least this way, there may be some small illusion that we live in our own home.'

Ju-mei glowered at Mae. 'Your sentiments are noble, Siao, and I can only add that I am deeply ashamed that my own sister has left you in such a terrible situation. You have been an ideal guest . . .'

Ah, thought Mae, they've all been driving each other crazy.

'. . . and I feel that as a mark of my respect and affection for you, that I will assist in carrying your cases and goods.'

He wants to see what is going on, thought Mae.

And he did. Ju-mei went into the barn and saw the giant weaver with its lights and display, and its speaking voice. His eyes boggled.

'You make money from this?'

Mae used her little formula: five hundred collars at ten dollars each.

Ju-mei looked so forlorn that part of Mae wanted to hug him. He looked like such a disappointed little boy: he pouted and looked sad and yearning, and hung his head. Ju-mei had always thought that if someone had something, they had got it by stealing it from him.

'*Tuh*. Who will work for a woman like you?'

'About half the village,' chuckled Siao, 'since it makes them so much money. Your sister has appeared in the *New York Times*.' He even gave his sister-in-law a little hug about the shoulders.

'Hmm. And you think you can run a business of this size by yourself?'

'Oh, I do not *think* that,' said Mae, ringing her little bell voice. 'I know I can. So I will not be needing your help.'

Mae moved into the attic.
She wanted it that way, to keep her new TV out of the way of thieves, she said. She did not mention the Flood to Siao.

'That will be fine,' said Siao. 'I was tired of that attic. But, hoi, Mae!

Let me tell you – that attic is cold! Are you sure you want to be up there?'

'Siao. I am a fallen women. People will be more comfortable coming to your kitchen to offer you work if I am not there.'

His eyes looked briefly pained and then he nodded yes.

As if to make it up to her, Siao made a pulley. It had a strong net to carry things and strong wooden wheels and it could hoist her TV up and down from the attic. 'In case you want to take it outside in summer to teach,' he said.

Siao was plainly overjoyed to be back. He scampered, bringing in charcoal for the braziers, making a new bedspace for his father beside the fire, and screwing hooks into the roofbeam. He ducked and climbed and dangled, as lithe as any monkey.

Mae warmed whisky, and around their old wooden table, they all toasted the Chung family and its house. 'The new house,' they called it, as if it had been rebuilt.

And then, alone and wearing every single piece of clothing she possessed to keep warm, Mae sat alone in her attic, in front of a television of her own.

'Please say hello,' it asked her, to start the process of getting to know her.

'Hello,' replied Mae. It was like meeting a female cousin for the first time and knowing you were going to become friends.

She entered a new e-mail address – the one she had told Kwan's machine to forward e-mail to – and at last began to work on her own. She sipped yet more warmed whisky, and went to work.

---

audio file from: Mr Hikmet Tunch

17 December

I have been looking at a particular site in America about history and have found it very interesting. Perhaps friends of yours would like to know it is available. Strange indeed are the uses to which we all are put. I myself come from a long line of peasant soldiers of the Karz. Throughout history, we have laid down our rakes and picked up our axes to march off to bash the Happy Province into submission. But it is like a walnut that does not break open, but is only driven into the mud, so that it sprouts again. I seem to have been used to help plant it afresh. Once there was a dictator. He drove millions to various kinds of deaths, by war, in prison, or simply in harsh deserts farming their lives away. He destroyed temples, burned books, and ruined the art of calligraphy. He wrote terrible poetry and forced everyone to learn it, so destroying the literary taste of one quarter of humanity. He remained a warrior even as Chairman. He was at his best as a warrior, because as a warrior, he was fighting for his people, dreaming for them. After that, he only ground them down. But I forgive him for saying one beautiful thing:

'Women hold up half the sky.'
—Chairman Mao Tse Tung

19

audio file from: Mrs Chung Mae
26 December
Mr Oz

Kwan has an e-mail saying that Teacher Shen has lost his job and is to be replaced. How? The snows have come. You can't get even a tractor up our road now. So is Teacher Shen supposed to go on teaching unpaid? How will it help our children if there is no school? Look, okay, Teacher Shen gave me a big blow and did the Party of Progress great harm. But this will do no good. Please listen to his wife, our friend Shen Suloi.

Mr Oz-sir, I am Mrs Shen Suloi, the wife of Teacher Shen. Gracious friend, you have been all kindness to us and we need your help again. My husband is wrong about the TV and Air, he sees these things as a great flood that will sweep everything away, but he is a good man and he wants the best for the children of our village. Gracious friend, it is a very bad thing that the message he lost his job came through the TV, and came after your visit. This makes many men here think of the TV as an enemy. They think it spies for the government. They think it takes away a man's whole life. Many say they will not let their children go to school if it is taught by a government replacement woman. My husband goes on teaching now for no money, but he is brokenhearted. We are poor people, Mr Oz, okay? That is hard for us to admit – easier perhaps for the women. We have four children ourselves, and no farm. My husband goes to the school with his shoulders hunched. He does not comb his hair. He sits at night by the single candle and weeps. All his life he trained to be Teacher. It was a great accomplishment for a boy from Kizuldah, and now that has gone, and his wife makes more money than he does. So can you talk to the people who did this and explain we have no Teacher? Can you get them to give my husband back his job?

This is Mrs Chung. Tell them this mail comes from me, whom he harmed.

Winter is when our children traditionally do their lessons. It does no good to have no Teacher here now.

_____

audio file from: Mr Oz Oz
27 December
Mae, I am angry, too. They didn't even tell me. It is like that – you make a report, and they go off and do something and don't even consult with the person who was there. It is typical of the Central Office to work in that way. I don't know why I stay with them. They never listen. They have no management skills. I feel terribly embarrassed but it is not my fault. What can I do?

_____

audio file from: Mrs Chung Mae
27 December
I don't care about all of that – what are you going to DO NOW?

_____

e-mail from: Mrs Wing Kwan
29 December
Dear Secretary Goongoormush,
I am a partner with Madam Chung Mae. Our business was recently featured in the *New York Times*. The attached files of access statistics and business turnover shows our venture to be one of the most successful under the Taking Wing Initiative. My husband is manager of Swallow Communications, also funded by the Initiative.

I say this only to show that I, along with Chung Mae and others, represent what we here call the Party of Progress. Your representative Mr Oz Oz accurately reported that our efforts have been hampered by the local schoolteacher, Mr Shen Yoh.

However, removing Teacher Shen from his post at this time will slow progress. His replacement will not be able to get up our road in winter. This could leave our children without schooling during this crucial year of Taking Wing.

Teacher Shen has not seen the benefits of Info. But he is a good man, and we of the Party of Progress request his reinstatement.
Yours,
Mrs Wing Kwan

---

audio file from: Mr Oz Oz
30 December

Mae, are you crazy? A letter from Kwan? She is not the best-regarded person in Kizuldah. I have raised the issue, but my boss tells me it is all down to the Office of Discipline and Education, and their own 2020 Vision campaign. So, you see how I am prevented at every turn from helping.

---

audio file from: Mrs Chung Mae
30 December

I do indeed see what stops you helping us.

It was dawn, and in her loft, Mae could hear the weaving machine at work.

It made a neat whirring sound that reminded Mae of hummingbirds. She could hear it through her walls as she worked. She could imagine it extending a tongue of beautiful new knitware.

Her new TV was strung in a hammock and held up by Siao's pulley. It was early morning and Mae was building a new site. It was not going well. Well, at least one screen worked.

OLD CARS NEVER DIE,
they just go to Mr Pin-sir's
DYNAMIC CAR SURGERY.
Also their cousins tractors, trailers and vans.
All vehicles are charmed by the Car Surgeon's bedside manner and kind, skilled hands.

Mae had written letters telling everyone about her new Net services. Her first customer, Mr Pin, had shown up two days ago.

Mr Pin did not want to speak to Madam Owl. He sat with Siao, ignoring Mae and twisting the letter in his hand. He had no more idea of what to do with the Net than use it to make himself seem more modern. That meant, more modern than his great and murderous rival, Mr Enver Atakoloo.

Siao kept trying to defer to Mae, to direct Mr Pin's questions to her.

Finally, to relieve everyone's embarrassment, Mae had gone back upstairs into the loft.

She listened from upstairs, and was surprised at how useful Siao was. Mr Pin was a difficult man to help. He did not understand what the TV was for, and was frightened that the government would see anything about him.

Siao kept explaining. It took hours and a bottle of warmed rice wine. Siao's idea was to put a list on the machine called, 'Mr Pin's Helpful Service that Answers Your Questions.'

It would give people advice on how to check the car was working or to make simple repairs themselves. Mr Pin did not understand the principles of Info mat-unrolling – giving something away for free. Siao evidently did. He explained that free Info made friends with the customers and showed you were expert. More importantly, it got rid of the less profitable parts of your business by giving away all the little pieces of advice that made no money.

Pin, drunk by now, finally got it. 'Ah, Mr Siao-sir, what a brain you have! You should be running a bank, sir!'

Siao coaxed out of Mr Pin everything that could go wrong with a car and whether most people could fix it themselves, and if not, how much it would cost.

Siao then clambered up the ladder with a written list. His manner had no pride in it. Businesslike, he had read it out to Mae and into the machine.

Mae was using that information to make her first intelligent voice-form. It was supposed to ask questions and leave time for the innocent to reply into the microphone.

'*Nature of the problem?*'

'The car won't start when . . .'

'*Huh? Please repeat the nature of the problem.*'

'Won't start . . .'

'*Huh? If you are having difficulty, please make an appointment with Mr Pin. Can you bring the car in? Answer yes or no.*'

'No!'

'*Can you bring the car in? Answer yes or no.*'

'Yes!'

The voiceform did a kind of flip and started to repeat over and over. '*Answer . . . Answer . . . Answer . . .*'

'Shitcakes,' said Mae, and thumped the TV. 'Stop. Save.' Mae arched herself backwards to bend her spine in the opposite direction. 'Create e-mail to sloop@karzphone.co.kz. Attach program file Pinform Three.'

Mae sent the form to the Sloop, the telephone engineer in Yeshibozkent who had first tried to explain TV to her. He helped her with difficult encoding. For a fee. How was she supposed to make money from this?

Mae sighed and thought about breakfast.

She went downstairs and was surprised to see Siao and Old Mr Chung were up this early and at breakfast. Then she saw the time. It was eight-thirty A.M. Siao had his head in his hands.

Siao held out a paper towards Mae. 'Your brother,' he said, shaking his head.

'What has he done now?' Mae was prepared to be breezy about her brother. He was inconvenient, like burnt porridge and a pan that needed to be scrubbed.

Siao's face curled inward on itself, lips disappearing. 'You will not believe it. He is claiming your business.'

'What! How can he do that?' Mae made the face she got when she shooed midges from her eyes, a squinting and a shaking of the head.

Siao read the letter to Mae. It was a from a city lawyer.

Under section 99.54 of the Worldly Property Act, it is evident that Madam Chung Mae, having deserted her husband, has no claims on the family property. The residence Down Court 2 on Lower Street having been sold, this leaves only the family's business interests. Since Mr Chung Joe has residence in Balshang, plainly the family business in fashion, Net design, and clothes production has been taken over by his deserting wife, who has no legal entitlement to it.

Mrs Chung has shown continual lack of judgement and bizarre behaviour since an unfortunate incident resulting from the Air Test. This has been fully documented; see affidavits from Dr Bauschu, who attests to an induced schizophrenia following the Test.

Mrs Chung's bizarre behaviour has included attacking a village elder with cleavers, desertion of her husband, an illicit love affair, and a complete rejection of her own maiden family, causing her elderly mother great distress.

As male head of her family, I therefore claim immediate control of all these business interests in order to preserve and protect them and to put them under rightful management . . .

Hatred came to Mae – pure and whole and all-consuming. She sat down with a bump. Ju-mei was very lucky that he was not in the room, for she would surely have picked up her cleavers again.

'I cannot believe this. He can do that?'

'It is an old law. It is to avoid women taking over things. But the law exists.'

'I will kill him!'

'That will just leave you in prison.'

Siao lit a cigarette and looked Mae in the eyes. 'How much do you trust me?' he asked.

Mae blinked at the unexpected question. 'I don't know. I have never had to trust you, Siao.'

He nodded, and his eyes turned momentarily inward towards himself. He had not made himself present before. 'We could say that this is a Chung family business. And that therefore Mr Wang can keep his nose out of it.'

Mae could see why he had asked. 'We could indeed.' And she did indeed feel mistrust. She did not want Joe or Siao taking it over, either.

'I could say it is Chung family business, and that Ju-mei may be a head of family, but it is the wrong family. We could say that whether you are suitable or not, is not for him or his lawyer to say.'

Old Mr Chung shook his head. 'They take everything away.'

'Not if we don't let them, Papa,' said Siao.

'We will need a lawyer,' said Mae. 'Lawyers know people, they know how the government works. *Inshallah!*' She put her own head in her hands. 'Oh, I do not need this! I tell you, all of this will drive me mad!'

'I should not say things like that for a while,' said Siao.

Mae went to her machine and voicemailed Kwan. Kwan gave her the name of a lawyer, and suggested that it might be better if she, Kwan, wrote the letter.

'Mae, when you get angry you sometimes say things.'

'I never want to see any of my family ever again.'

'That is exactly what I mean.'

Kwan produced a draft in her own name, writing as a member of the Circle. It was the complete expression of a reasonable, ladylike person, setting out a situation in which she herself had rights. The business apparently belonged to everyone in the Circle, including Kwan.

I hope, Mae thought, I am not about to have trouble with her too.

Siao looked pensive. 'That is another line to take, and perhaps even better than saying it is a Chung family business. But consider. It could be that Ju-mei does not do this because he thinks he can get the business. Maybe he just wants a cut.'

'He wants a cut, all right, I'll give him a cut. He knows nothing about Info, nothing about Air, nothing about anything, he is just jealous and always has been.'

'He is those things. You have to accept that. You can't change who your brother is.' Siao knew something about accepting difficult brothers.

Mae said nothing. Siao said, 'Mae, I don't think it's money he wants. I think he wants respect. That is why he is always in city overcoat and city hat. It is why he is an insurance agent up here in the hills, even though none of us can afford insurance.'

Mae was furious. 'I will never talk to him ever again. For me he ceases to live. A toad has more of my notice than that city suit of pretension and jealousy.'

'You and your sister ran the family,' said Siao. 'All he sees is his power-grabbing sister who is always, always, ahead of him, and he yearns, just once, to win. I would say that what he wants is for you to need him.'

'*Tuh!* Him? You are too nice, Siao. Ju-mei wants success and loot.'

'What a man wants more than anything else, Mae, is to be needed.' Siao's voice was very quiet. 'If a man is not needed he does one of two things. He gives up and becomes quiet and angry. Or he rages and becomes loud and angry. Both are the same.' Siao's eyes said, *I know.*

And Mae thought: He means himself.

She said, 'Ju-mei has his wife and child to need him.'

Siao shrugged. 'That will not be enough if you are a cloud over his head.'

'So. What do you suggest we do?'

'I suggest you spend no money on lawyers. That is what he wants you to do so that he can go to court and humiliate you.' Siao was thinking. 'You can apologize.'

'What!'

Siao could not help but smile. 'A-ha, you see, you like being right, too. You are both from the same family.'

'Apologize for what?'

'Lying to him.'

'I never lied to him.'

'Did you tell him about your plans for the business?'

'What? No! Of course not!'

'Ah, so you did not tell your own brother the truth. And what is not telling the truth, Mae?'

Mae was flabbergasted. 'But, but, it it it it . . .'

Siao was starting to chuckle. 'You hid the truth. Hiding the truth is a lie.'

'But it is not like I told him I was *not* doing any business! What business is it of his?'

'He is your brother. What he is doing is trying to make the law enforce that. Yes, he wants to do it in a way that hurts you, but that's because you have hurt him, and he thinks you must have done it deliberately. I know! You didn't do anything to hurt him deliberately. But you hurt him. What is he looking for here? To be head of family, and to be your brother. He knows in his heart that you married, and are no longer a Wang.'

'*Tuh*. He knows in his heart he wants money.'

'I know in his heart he wants much more than that. I tell you. Let me write the letter.' Siao could not resist a little joke. 'Women are so insensitive. They cannot understand a man's finer feelings.'

'Nonsense!' said Mae.

Siao touched the tip of the pencil to his tongue to begin writing. Siao enjoyed writing. Mae had never noticed that before.

> *My dearest brother,*
>
> *I am sorry to have concealed all my business dealings from you. It was not honest to do so. I have lost much because of this. I have lost your aid and your counsel. Instead you have become my enemy at a time when I most need friends.*
>
> *I have a wonderful idea, but I do not know how to progress it because I am so ignorant of the insurance business. And here at hand I have a brother who knows all about it! I think you and I together could come up with very intelligent ways to use the TV to get our local village people to see how important it is to have insurance.*

I need your help. Please can we meet so that we can talk all through this.

Your sister,
Mae

Mae was scornful. 'It says nothing about the case. It does not even ask him to give the case up!'

'Ah. You noticed.'

'You are asking me to lie down and be screwed by my own brother.'

'I am asking you to give something up so that he sees it is in his self-interest to give something up, too. So that he will be on your side, as a brother should be. I am willing to bet, Mae, that he would give anything to be by your side as a brother should be.'

Mae snarled. '*Hmph*. Okay, we send your letter, eh? And just see the reply we get from my charming younger brother!'

Mae,

Your idea for television insurance is interesting. Of course, it would have to be linked with Yeshibozkent Home Guardian, whose interests I represent. But I am sure they would have no objections to screens that carried their brand and sold their products in a way that suits our locale. I will need to discuss this idea with them first.

I do have doubts whether we can work together. Your behaviour in the past leads to grave concerns about your state of mind. However, families must show solidarity in the face of adversity. If you are willing to allow my greater knowledge of the field to direct policy, then perhaps we can consider this further.

Your brother,
Mr Wang Ju-mei
Happy Province Sales Conqueror, Yeshibozkent Home Guardian

Mae was furious. 'My behaviour! My state of mind! What about his, suing his own sister! Trying to take away all that she has done!'

Siao sipped his tea. 'Shall we look at what he really said? First, he has grave doubts about the two of you working together. Is that not something you can agree with?'

Mae puffed out air. 'Poh, yes, that at least.'

'So. Shall we regard that as a simple statement of fact?'

Mae shrugged her shoulders. 'He sued me, I did not sue him.'

'He hasn't sued you. He has stated his intention to. In fact, he gave you fair warning. Isn't that so? Mae? It is so.'

'You are a man and you are on his side.'

'You are perfectly right to call him jealous and scheming. Let's just look at what he says in the letter. Now, he then mentions your behaviour and your state of mind. Have you not chased a man with cleavers? Did you not have a careless affair with the neighbour? Did you not threaten to kill Ju-mei?'

Mae did not like this. She wanted to fight, but there was nothing to fight.

Siao whispered, 'He is frightened of you, Mae. He is terrified of you. You are his big, brave older sister, and he knows you take on the *New York Times* and that you chased big strong Mr Haseem out of your house, and he is scared!'

There was something in what Siao was saying that made Mae laugh.

'I'm frightened of you, Mae! The whole village is terrified of you! So, okay, Madam Owl, who is violent and aggressive, hates him. People know when you hate them, Mae. They also know when you love them.'

Mae was still smiling.

'So he is saying he will talk to his company, he is saying families must stick together. Mae! You've won! So now you must act like you have won.'

Mae started to puff out.

Siao said, 'You must go and visit your family. And make amends.'

Mae was left to wait alone in the icy diwan.

Her family burned tiny amounts of coal. Two grey chunks of it smouldered on the brazier. Mae sat on the cushions and tried to warm her feet and still her butterfly hands, her butterfly stomach. Mae, Mae, why are you so scared?

She heard them whispering outside the room. Why were they so scared? Why was the whole family Wang frightened of itself?

It's like this for Ju-mei, she thought. He shows up in people's houses, they don't want to be discourteous, so they show him in into the diwan and have a quiet fight hissing behind curtains, trying to make each other be polite to him. He sits alone and pretends not to hear.

But the least you can do is let people wait in warmth. If coal is such a luxury, then burn shitcakes. Except that the family Wang can't be seen to burn shit, only peasants burn shit.

We used to wrap birthday presents in the red paper napkins that came with the tea at the teahouse. We would wrap up something precious like an orange. And we would carefully pick off the tape so we could use the napkins again. Every little present came wrapped in the same red napkins.

Poor Mama. All we ever had to eat was soup, one bowl of soup a day. And I remember one day we had to eat grass stew, just to fill our bellies. The next day, Mama went to every house in the village and begged. Someone gave her hen's-feet. Someone gave her an onion. And she made us soup, out of almost nothing. And then one of us little monkeys spilled kerosene from the lamp into it. And she fell on the floor weeping. She did not even punish us. She just lay there crying.

Mae looked at the photographs on the walls. There they were, all children lined up in white shirts, white dresses in the Golden Age, as Mama called the time when Papa was alive. Even then, she would have beaten those clothes white on the rocks under the bridge.

There was Papa with a photographic face like burnished bronze in a city suit, with a moustache and a pipe. Mae remembered the day it was taken. They had all ridden down from Kurulmushkoy in a cart, and he had sat up straight and proud in his best clothes. He was the local candidate for the Party of National Unity, and that was why his picture was to be taken. That was why he was killed.

It was okay for Missy and me, we were girls, we could go on being girls. It was Ju-mei who had no one to show him how to be. And that's why Papa's picture now hangs in the middle of the wall.

Mae remembered: Ju-mei didn't talk for six months after Papa was killed. He just sat in silence, looking at his little scuffed shoes.

Mae remembered. It was Ju-mei who had found him dying in the diwan. We had to keep using the cushions, with Papa's blood on them.

Suddenly the diwan curtains snapped back as if Ju-mei wanted to tear them down. His chin was thrust up, he was in full city regalia, and he had on his glasses.

Suddenly she remembered her father's dead face and the answer came.

He is frightened of the past. He is doing everything he can to escape it. And the more he fights, the more he's trapped in it. And so am I.

Something in Mae seemed to snap and unwind. She uncoiled and relaxed.

Poor Ju-mei, you can never give up fighting, not even for a moment.

Mae stood up and gave her brother a respectful bow. Even she was amazed. She did not feel a tremor of resentment.

'Brother,' she murmured.

'Sister,' he growled curtly, and jerked his head up and down. It was more like he was hitting her with his head than bowing in respect.

He didn't know what to say. They both stood staring for a moment.

'May I sit down?' Mae asked.

'I am amazed that you have to ask,' he growled back. He thought she was trying to show him up for bad manners. Which meant, of course, that he knew he had been bad-mannered at leaving her alone for so long.

Mae sat down and looked at the walls and thought the Karz equivalent of, *To hell with it.* She gave up trying to do anything at all.

'Your photographs reminded me strongly of the old days, when we lived here with our auntie.'

'*Tuh!* I am too busy to think about the past.'

'Me too, mostly. But you know, it was not all bad. It is good to remember how dedicated Mama was to keeping us clean and fed. How we all worked.'

'It is pleasant to hear you acknowledge Mama for something.'

Mae couldn't be bothered with fighting. 'She will always be Mama. It was very difficult for her; she relied on Papa for everything. In those days, it was possible to believe that if you were a woman you would never have to grow up. You could just go on doing what you were told. And suddenly . . . *poof* . . . no one there to tell you.'

'She has never recovered from Father's death.'

'None of us has. We are so far gone we would not know what recovery looks like. Who we might have been if Papa had lived is so far away we cannot even imagine it. Only, I think we keep thinking we will one day grow up to be that family.'

Ju-mei suddenly stood up. 'What do you want?' he asked roughly. Mae couldn't figure out if he was angry or threatened or impatient or bored or sad.

She might as well answer his question for real. She sat and thought for a moment and the answer came as a surprise. 'A little peace and quiet,' she said.

'*Tuh*, there is little chance of that for anyone else when you are around.'

And there probably was some truth in that. 'Maybe that's why I need some myself.'

Ju-mei stood up straighter. 'We are here to talk about a proposition.'

Mae's eyes felt heavy. She had a choice. She could let them have the argument Ju-mei wanted, or she could choose to hold on to what Siao had shown her: something new.

Mae found she was doing this for Siao.

' "Insurance" is too big a word for people who make their own candles,' she said. 'They have to see it. They have to see themselves. So. Your company will have something called *day tah*. It is Info the company uses to calculate answers to insurance questions. Maybe the company has videos, maybe about real people the company has helped.'

It was like a fire kindled in herself. Mae suddenly sat up.

'So what we do is, pull all this stuff together into a show. And we have Number One Expert. That's you. Maybe we put the show on in Mrs Wing's courtyard. We make it social. Maybe in spring. Food, flowers, everything is abundant. Ah! And you come, and you explain. You show some films, but also, you invite people to talk to the TV and it gets answers especially for them.'

She'd done something wrong. Ju-mei's face was closing down. 'I've been selling insurance to this village for many years, Mae. I don't need you to tell me how to do it.'

I have made a mistake. Here I am, the big older sister, telling him what to do.

'I . . . I have let my enthusiasm carry me away,' she said. 'Plainly, this scheme would rely entirely upon you.'

'You have never bought any insurance yourself,' he said.

What, I should spend all that money with you, because you are my brother? Mae had to quell the rising-up of anger. After all, Mae, his wife bought your dresses. Families buy from each other. Solidarity.

'That was my husband's decision,' said Mae.

'Joe? Joe never made any decisions.'

Ju-mei is being more honest in this encounter than you are, Mae.

'I never thought we needed it,' said Mae.

Until now. They needed it now, and for a reason. 'I don't expect you to believe me, Ju-mei, but I have only just realized what I want out of this.'

'Money,' he said flatly, dourly, without hope.

'I want you to get our village insured. Against flooding.' She thought for a moment. 'And I want my family back.' She felt a little sting of tears around the base of her eyes.

Mae thought it was to no avail. It ended like a business meeting, with Ju-mei promising to consider her proposal. Before she turned and left, she looked about the house. There were small thin rugs on the floor, and a picture cut from a magazine in a frame. The shelves were empty except for an encyclopedia Ju-mei had bought second hand for his children's education. The room was clean and tidy – so much work and so cold. Her mother did not show her face.

Mae got home and decided to buy some Flood insurance. She made tea, climbed up the steps to Madam Owl's attic. There was an e-mail for her.

> *Sister,*
>
> *I have talked with the family and we have decided to accept your proposition. We think it would be better if we had the show here, in our own home. Mama is talking about about decorations and food. Would you or Mrs Wing be able to loan us the television?*
>
> *There is something I did not understand. I did not understand before how much of what you do is done for the village. I thought you did it to make money. You dressed down and looked bad and I thought you had given yourself a different kind of air and grace, that you had set yourself up as something. It simply did not occur to me how much of what you were doing you were doing without thought of yourself.*
>
> *And so I find that I am more than happy to join with you in your project.*
>
> *Together we will get Kizuldah insured.*
>
> *Your brother,*
>
> *Ju-mei*

'Siao! Siao!' Mae called, overjoyed. 'Siao! Come see!'

Mae and Sloop the engineer from Yeshibozkent put the demonstration together.

Siao and Ju-mei wrestled her television into the Wang family house. There were indeed flowers, but winter flowers, made of paper, and tables full of food. Someone from every household in the village came. The grates were piled high with coals, and there was rice wine.

Ju-mei stood in front of them all, and showed people how much money they could make, and how they could pay, so little each week. The faces of other farmers explained: They were buying protection. These were not videos; Yeshibozkent Home Guardian set up live links. Lined, weathered faces like their own answered the villagers' questions. 'Oh, yes, we lost all our sheep to foot and mouth, but the company paid back our losses.'

The director of Home Guardian also came on a live link. He told Ju-mei that his show was a model of how to bring the insurance crusade to the people.

Siao was there and bought insurance on behalf of the family Chung. He made a handsome gesture of paying for the insurance of Mae's weaving machine.

Throughout, Mae sat quietly in the corner, wearing her best white dress.

After the shaking of hands, and good-nights, and seeing her brother's overjoyed smile, Mae climbed up the ladder to her loft and went to bed alone. Her arms held nothing, except the memory of the party. She cradled it all night alongside the swelling shape of her unborn child.

But she found herself thinking of Siao's smooth arms.

20

Teacher Shen came to call.

Mae opened her door and saw him against the glowing white-grey sky, and her heart thumped. 'Teacher,' she said, greeting him in the formal fashion, with a bow of respect.

Shen looked awful. Disordered wisps of hair were on his chin. They were grey, like an old woman's whiskers. His eyes were encircled with concentric pouches of flesh.

He stared at her.

'It is cold for you; please come in, Teacher,' she said.

He looked poor, he smelled poor. His coat was old, black, held shut. Something had been spilt on it. He had beautiful Eloi mittens, knitted by his wife.

Mae kept talking. 'Oh, such weather to come visit, let me make you tea.'

'It's not cold,' he said. 'It is unseasonably warm.'

'Please – please sit at the table.'

Mae cleared away Siao's breakfast things. 'I know what you mean about warmth. All that snow on the hills, in this warm weather. I fear there will be a Flood.'

Shen's lip curled.

Mae kept smiling, rattling out cups. 'There was one, you know, in 1959, and all the village of Aynalar was washed away. We need to be prepared in case it happens again.'

Stop it, she told herself, you say that to everyone now. You chatter. He is not here for that.

Mae bustled the kettle onto the brazier and rattled out cups for them both. She smelled his breath. Old sour wine. Chinese men could not drink well; the condition was called *kizul*, 'red' for the flushed cheeks, and the anger. It should also be called 'white,' for afterwards they were pale and shivery, like easily broken ice.

He sighed and dug his fingers into his thick black hair.

You were always so handsome, she thought. Friendship flowed down old familiar channels.

'I didn't sleep last night,' he said.

'I don't wonder at it. You have been removed from a most honoured position, most unjustly.'

'*Tub*,' he said, looking at her as if she were the TV. His look said: *You did it*.

'I did nothing, you know,' Mae said, sitting away from him. She found she was calculating how far he could swing if he went to hit her.

Teacher Shen, I would ride in your cart upholstered with hops for the beer factory. That was always my favourite way to go to the city. You, me, and Suloi up early, all the four A.M. birds singing all around us. The dawn would come up on your friendly faces and we would eat buns and you would tell all your old village stories.

Shen said, 'My wife tells me you have been writing letters. You are trying to get me my job back.'

Shen's face shivered, the ice broke, and he was weeping.

'They won't give me my job!' He sounded exactly like a little boy, his face wrung like an old washing-rag. He stared at the table, drawing breath, trying to swallow. 'I am not a farmer, I have very little land. What I am to do for money?'

He patted his pockets. Looking for a cigarette. Then remembering he had none, could not afford them.

Mae leaned forward. 'You studied so hard to be a Teacher. It was not right of them to fire you.'

'Fire me they did,' he said.

'Kwan is trying to make a collection. Trying to get enough money from the village to pay you . . .'

He shook his head over and over. Who had the money for that in winter? Who became a Teacher to end up living on village charity?

Mae tried to explain. 'I would help collect it but . . .'

Shen sighed and nodded. 'But no one will talk to you. Hard to lose a job, isn't it?' He looked up at her. 'It is what I did to you.'

She shrugged. 'I was able to do something else. As we all will have to, Teacher. The world will not let any of us stay the same.'

Shen sniffed; he sat up straighter. 'I have been thinking,' he said, 'that there is something I can do to help myself.' He sighed, sniffed, and repaired the damage to his manhood by wiping his cheeks. 'I can learn how to use the monster.'

He pulled in a breath as if smoking self-respect cigarettes. 'If I use it, they will say, "Oh, he is no longer stopping progress." '

Mae paused. Her response must be gentle. 'You are wise, Teacher Shen,' she replied.

'How do I do it?' he said with a snap.

She replied cautiously. 'It will take time, Teacher Shen, and the village needs you to be Teacher now.' Mae considered how to unroll Shen's mat. 'The effect we need to create is that you already know much about Info. And that you are willing to teach it.'

Shen swayed in his chair. He looked trapped. He turned away and looked as if he desperately wanted a lungful of cigarette smoke to blow out.

'Okay,' he said.

'I can tell you what to say to the machine to set up an e-mail address. If you do it vocally, the machine will record that the commands came from you personally and that will be better, yes? The Office of Discipline and Education sees it comes from you. Then, we will send them a videomail. So they see that you don't just know e-mail, you are full Net TV person. So we must spruce you up a bit.'

He almost laughed. 'Fashion expert.'

'No longer,' she replied. 'But I am good at selling things. And make no mistake, Teacher. We are now selling you. Ah? I'm sorry, but we must be clear on what we are trying to do.'

He was dismayed, he was helpless, and his picture of the world no longer worked. He nodded tamely.

'I still have some things of Joe's,' she said, and stood up. 'Oh! The tea!' She quickly poured water into the pot and left him with it. He sat nursing the cup. He wanted to be comforted and to wash away the booze.

By the sink were Joe's things, male things: razor, comb. When Joe left, he had hurled everything about the house. He and Tsang had flung everything about. They must have been drunk. Or very happy.

'Here. You must shave. You must wash your hair.'

Shen seemed frozen. Of course, he would have to take off his shirt. Imagine the scandal if one of the ladies of the Circle came to find him with Madam Owl and his shirt off.

'I will check the machine and be back,' Mae said. She was growing very adept at zipping up and down that ladder.

She unhooked the TV from the beam. It did not take much strength to wheel the machine around and crank it down onto the kitchen floor. 'Tell me when you are ready, Teacher Shen!' she called.

Mae looked out from her skylight. The whole house clicked like knitting needles as water trickled continually down the eaves. The water butts were overflowing. It was cool, her breath was vapour, but only because the air was so wet it could not contain any more moisture; it was the vapour of fog, not of deep chill.

Too warm, too warm, too warm.

Mae broke off the thought. She talked Mrs Tung down. We will go on TV and get Teacher Shen back his job. The weaving machine is making all kinds of things, new things that never existed before. California ladies order bags, women in Japan order embroidered caps. Isn't Info great? Isn't business fun?

'I'm ready,' Mr Shen called.

Mae clambered down the ladder. Her heart went out to Shen. He stood up straight, head back, as if to brave the buffeting waves of examination. His hair was black again, from being damp. There were shaving suds around his ears and Joe's old razor had left a rash. But he looked shiny and he sat up straight.

'Oh, you look so professional,' said Mae.

She talked him through setting up an account on her machine. He spoke the words slowly, hesitantly, through a stone face in which even the lips hardly moved.

But the screen did a fan dance of pages, confirming, informing.

I love this stuff, thought Mae. At no other time was her mind as clear. At no other time was Old Mrs Tung farther from her, less in step, more powerless inside her. So joy reinforced joy. Her beautiful TV was like a fount from which she drew something sparkling, wholesome, and clear.

Shen was a double name. If he was Karzistani, and there was a lot of doubt about that, then the name meant 'Happiness.' If it was the Chinese name Shen, then it was too ancient to mean anything. It could even be an Eloi name, if you pushed – Shueng. What nation was he?

Someone called Shen came from a people with too much history. They could be killed for the history embedded in their names. That made them permanently afraid, buffeted by fate. They were a peasant people only wanting to be left alone, and to not have to worry about which continent they belonged to or which tribe. That was all Shen wanted – to be left alone unnoticed.

'Okay. Now you must look like you are going to your daughter's graduation.' She pulled the old coat from him and was grateful that he had worn a black shirt. It was rumpled and of variable colour, but on TV its darkness would be pristine. She wiped the soap from his ears.

'Excuse me, you have a rash,' she said. 'Can I put some makeup on you?'

Finally he smiled. 'I am a Talent,' he said, shuffling his feet even as he sat.

Mae dabbed his chin with her own colourings.

'I will be talking to the Secretary?' he said, something like terror overcoming him.

'No,' she said hurriedly. 'No, no, of course not. What you will do is talk into the TV but the video will be sent like a letter they can open later. They will see that you are a good man, a serious man, and that you are at home with Info. They will see that they are wrong about you. Okay?'

She looked into his eyes. The village hated the government, mistrusted it. He could bolt at any moment.

'I'll tell you what, use the big screen like a mirror. That will show you how you look, and that can help you.'

Shen seemed to wilt. 'I should not do it now. I should write out a speech first. What if I make a mistake?'

'If it is a bad one, we make the movie again, okay? But listen, Shen, don't read a speech. You are a Teacher, you are used to talking all day in front of people. You are a smart man, I promise, you will do this well. Okay? Okay?'

You poor good man.

Mae turned on the camera and went onto RECORD, and swapped the screen so it would show what the camera saw. Shen was suddenly struck by seeing his own face on TV. He opened his mouth and stared. Sweat from the heat trickled down his face, as if he were melting snow.

'I don't know what to say,' he said. His face was slippery with panic.

'Stop. Cancel,' she told the machine.

Mae mopped his face and told him, firmly, 'You know what you need to say. The Secretary knows he is powerful, so don't waste his time grovelling. He knows you are asking for something. Just ask quickly. But make sure also that you say what you need to say.'

He began again, and the Teacher in him emerged.

'Secretary Goongoormush,' he said, and swallowed. 'I am Teacher Shen Yoh of the village of Kizuldah in Yeshibozkent Vilayet. I have recently been removed from my post of Teacher.' He cleared his throat. 'I understand why this has been done. It is my job to teach Info. And it is true that I did stop Madam Chung from teaching this subject. However, the village has no Teacher at all now. In winter, this means that the children receive no schooling. I request that I be reinstated. As you see, I have begun to learn Info from Madam Chung herself.'

He paused and then said, 'We have always been the best of friends, and I am sure she will help me to become a good Teacher. Thank you for your time.' His breath rattled, and then he said: 'Queue message.'

When had he learned that?

'That's it!' she said, to encourage him. 'You've done it!'

'Yes,' he said. 'Thank you.' His eyes were heavy, his whole bearing was weighted. As if lifting rocks, he stood up to go.

It was time for them to be honest. Mae stood up, too. 'What you did to me was a very bad thing,' she said to him.

'Yes,' he said. Still he did not, could not, apologize. He moved towards the door.

'I am only trying to help us, help us all,' she said, finding herself trailing after him. 'We all must learn, to be part of the future!' What did she want from him? Something in return?

He was being pursued, and speeded his progress towards the door. He picked up his stained coat and wrapped his scarf around his throat. His back was towards her. He was at the door, through the door, gone. Nothing else was said.

Not even a thank-you? She went to the window. Shen's shoulders were hunched. He took a hand and mussed his tidy hair. His hands shook as they fought to open the ancient latch of the courtyard gate. Then, as if in a rage Shen flung the doors back so they shuddered against the cobbles and only slowly swung back to close after him. Before they did, Mae saw Shen hide his face in his hands.

Then she looked to the other side of the courtyard. She saw Mr Ken, glaring after Shen, ready for a fight. She saw Kuei turn towards her window, and she darted back, into the shadows.

PARTY OF PROGRESS
Today's Events

SUNNI-MA'AM's *review of good dress high fashion. See how Info makes it possible to select the very dress in your special fabric and colour. Sunni-ma'am's house. Come and have tea at 9:30 after the morning's tasks are done.*

EYE OF THE BEHOLDER CIRCLE

begins work every day at 8:00 A.M. See our happy ladies at work as the intelligent machine weaves special clothes for each one of our customers. The ladies make even more special handmade items. These are sold for big bucks to our friends in America. If you come at 10:30, Madam Chung will be pleased to show you the Info she has designed and created for your neighbours' businesses. She will tell you

HOW TO MAKE BIG BUCKS FROM INFO.

HAPPY FAMILIES

Both of Kizuldah's TV Houses are open to all every evening. Come in for friendly hello-cakes, tea, and village chat with Sunni-ma'am, or Wing-sir and Kwan in their own homes, at their own machines.

This is a very good thing that has happened to us: the government says so, and the New York Times says so.

6:00 P.M.–9:30 P.M. every night except when snow is too deep.

INSURANCE PARTY

Ten households in our Happy village are even happier, safe in the knowledge that if misfortune falls, they are protected. Mr Wang Ju-mei, our village insurer, will be holding another midwinter Jamboree. Come and be warm with wine, Old Mrs Wang's home-cooking, and a free TV show with a difference. You will be the star . . . a TV show about you.

7:30 P.M. Friday night. Modern music by our modern girl, Sezen!

---

audio file from: Mrs Chung Mae
10 January

Dear Miss Soo. I have taken to heart your kind advice of some months ago. I have given this all the thought of which I am capable, and I see so clearly how wise you are. If Balshang is imitating my native costumes, they will take my business because Americans will not see or care that we are real and Balshang is not. So I think: Our own people see America on TV, and will want to look like America. Your house must be planning to sell good cheap clothes for households. The ladies of my Circle are good and cheap. We will give you great deal on duplicate American houseclothes. Maybe your house or maybe even you yourself would be interested?

Your friend,

Chung Mae

e-mail from: Office of Meteorological Investigation
14 January

Dear Madam Chung,

We were pleased to receive your unusual offer to take readings for us in the Kizuldah sector of the Yeshibozkent Villayet. It is true that we have no regular records of weather from your locale. However, the standards we apply to data collection are very rigorous. This data must then be interpreted via use of n-constant equations before our own database can make use of the information.

Many thanks for your offer, but we see little point in accepting it, either from your point of view or ours.

Bedri Eyoobogloo

e-mail from: the Office of Agricultural Development
18 January

Dear Mrs Chung,

We are pleased to be able to offer our local weather prediction system. Combined with our partner Office of Land Surveying modelling package, it offers an all-in-one solution for those seeking to predict weather and its impacts on particular geographies. The licence fee is 100 riels a year. This includes an annual update, full online support and Smart Helper installation. As you are a Taking Wing Initiative Centre of Progress, we are also able to offer ten per cent discount.

We await your answer.

Goksel Kartal

audio file from: Mr Goksel Kartal, Office of Agricultural Development
20 January

It is true that the system does not offer n-constant interpretation. But it is very unusual for normal agricultural use to require such a sophisticated weather prediction system. Why would the Happy Province need to mesh data from Balshang and Beijing?

---

audio file from: Mr Bedri Eyoobogloo, Office of Land Use
22 January

Madam Chung, you are quite correct; the process you describe would meet our rigorous standards for data collection, but are you sure you want to do it? You are talking two hours' work a day, I think. Please understand, I think maybe you have this wrong; the government cannot pay you to do this work. Nor can we give you n-constant software. You only pay the licence fee once, but it is one thousand riels! Why are you doing this?

---

audio file from: Mrs Chung Mae
22 January

Dear Mr Eyoobogloo, I want to know about the weather. We depend on land here, and water and sun and all those things. N-constant means Chaos theory, right? That means that if I know patterns in Balshang, I know how they affect us, right? This is important because this winter we have high snowfall and warm temperatures. In 1959, this meant a terrible flash flood. It happened with the Erjdha Nefsi, Dragon's Breath, hot wind from the Northern Desert, from Balshang. You see?

---

audio file from: Miss Soo Ling
24 January

Your message came at good time, as I am considering setting up my own business. I am replying in haste, and will reply again at leisure. Your friend, Ling.

---

audio file from: Mrs Chung Mae
24 January

Mr Tunch, my constant watcher, I finally had the TV read out to me your article. Just to be clear, I cannot read. Which is one great advantage I have over many people. I move by my gut, not my head. But Info has taught me that I have a very good head attached to a very good gut. It gives me such secret pleasure to know that none of you understand Air. Not you, not your Sistemlar, not the UN, not the Gates Format, not all you scientists and Talents and politicians. I know something you do not, something I suspected but hid from you. So I got the better of our deal. So I make another deal with you, Mr Tunch. I will tell you this great thing I know, if you get me the best, most powerful, most accurate software for weather forecasting, with n-constant interpretation. When you have done that for me, I will tell you what Air is and it will blow your world away.

Yours with deepest affection, Chung Mae.

---

audio file from: Mr Hikmet Tunch
25 January

Mae, Mae, my darling girl, I think you have spent too much time in the hills. You go crazy like an old trapper. I know what you have to tell me. In Air, gravity and thought are the same thing. You know that, because you seized hold of gravity-as-thought and used it to tear my metal fence to shreds when you decided to go home. And you want to tell me that this can be an amazing weapon, that we can use thought-as-gravity to tear whole cities apart. I can tell you that we are already working on that. You are a bright, bright girl. Sorry about the deal, but no deal. Your wise contender, Hikmet.

---

audio file from: Mrs Chung Mae
25 January

Ha-ha tee-hee. That is the words of my laughter. I am laughing at you. You are Foolish Gangster. In so many ways. The universe is a diamond of love, and whenever it decides to shine its light on us, you Foolish Gangsters always always try to turn the light that illumines into the light that burns. You take diamonds and turn them into knives to cut. But you have failed, haven't you, Arrogant Child? It has not worked, has it, this great new weapon that works only by thought? I know it will fail, it will go on failing. And since I am Wise Mother, comforting Arrogant Child, I will give away something for free. After all, I am selling Info. There is a thing called Kwan Tom, no? You see, I have other sources of information than you. I knew about eleven dimensions before I met you. Kwan Tom says that the world around us and the things in it are only probable. Atoms go in two directions at once and then suddenly make up their minds. Many realities exist as probabilities, only very, very small. Well, tearing fences is not a probability. It is a miracle. There have always been miracles, Mr Tunch. And they have always been small because they are not at all probable. You try to make your terrible miracles big, and probability will close over you, as if your thoughts were stones thrown into a pond. Your thought will create ripples. Something almost happens. And then the surface of what is probable closes over. Your weapon will never work. I have no words or education. I don't need them. I turn that into freedom, so I fly higher and deeper than you do into reality. I can blow your Foolish Gangster world away and replace it with a better one. Give me n-constant software, or I will keep laughing at you. Ha hee hee ha hee hee hee ha ha hee hee ha ha hee hee . . .

---

audio file from: Hikmet Tunch
26 January
Okay, laugh. The cost of the best n-constant and weather software is nothing to me. I know you only want it to predict the weather, my Weather Talent. You will find the code for it attached to this file with a full licence to use and a Help manual. So come on, then, blow my world away.

Your sceptical, very rich friend, Hikmet.

Agricultural Development Weather Predictor
Audio reading, 26 January: 17:57
    Location: School Ridge Drop
    Wind velocity: 3.7 kph
    Direction: north-northeast
    Air temperature: 7°C, 7.03, maybe
Okay, plug in direct. Oh, this is cold on the feet!
    Air temperature: 7.0298°C
    Air temperature with chill factor: 5.25°C
    Temperature of snow on surface: 2.7°C
    Temperature of snow at base: −1.8°C
    Temperature of runoff: 2.9°C
The village is all blue, like a memory. Every morning, I hear voices when I wake up, the children wailing, their mothers crying. It is the Flood. If I am not careful I fall into Air and I am there with it. So it is good to come out here, Weather Talent on my night patrol. The cold roots me in the Now. The Flood will come, this year or next, whatever. Ah!

This is the worst bit, right down into the muck. Maybe I find an onion left behind. Something for the pot.
    Soil Temperature: −1.7°C
I can really feel these stones, these terraces. They want to roll, they want to roll down and flatten us. At least all this is solid. Info keeps me sane.

There has always been a flood washing us all away.

Indeed, Mrs Tung, my dear, indeed.

THE FLOOD

Look across the valley. On the Mirror hill, you will see what is left of the village of Aynalar (Mirrors). It is a mirror for you.

In 1959, the whole hillside was wiped away in one night by a flash flood when all the snow melted too fast. Once, the terraces of Aynalar were rich and fertile. It was on the sunny slope of the valley and Kizuldah was the poor cousin, in shade. Now Aynalar is a heap of rocks. This happened during a winter of high snowfall and hot temperatures. This winter is another mirror, a mirror of that winter.

You have seen me. Every morning and every evening I go and measure snow. Three times a day I measure many things, temperature and wind and strength of sunlight through cloud. I am in touch with many government offices to calculate Info.

So far we are okay. It will need to be hotter than even 1959 for the flood to come here.

You will know the flood is coming if the Dragon's Breath happens in winter.

See these pictures? They show our village if the water melts. It shows how deep the water will get, and where you should go.

Don't go to the school. Big rocks will roll down from the terraces there and it could get buried. Everyone should get to Mr Wing's house. It is highest on an outcrop of stone. Those in the valley, like you, Mr Han, move your seed grain now; there won't be time when the Flood comes.

Move things into your lofts. If all else fails, if the Flood comes, get onto your roofs.

I will tell you the situation every day.

Madam Chung Mae

---

audio file from: Mrs Chung Mae

28 January

Whooooooooooooooo, Mr Tunch! That is the sound of my breath, blowing you away. Everything in Air is eternal, no? So I ask myself, How can we make the imprints? How can we change something that is eternal? Nothing new can happen there. So I think if we are in Air at all, we have always been there. These imprints you make of us have always been there. And then I think: So how do I get back to Mrs Tung's life? When I saw the Flood that destroyed the village of Aynalar, I was really there. The water was icy, I swallowed mud, I felt my child – I mean, Mrs Tung's – snatched away from me by the water. I was in Mrs Tung's life. Sometimes I look up over Kizuldah and I see great floating balloons, or hotels that do not exist, and I am not crazy. I am simply seeing the future through my Airself. I nip in and out of time like a mite living in a sponge. I just go through the holes.

Ah, but then, guess what else I have found, with my nipping? Everything lives in Air, Mr Tunch. Everything is in our balloon world and in Air at once. That means stones, flowers, and birds. And floods and funerals. That means everything is eternal, Mr Tunch. That means we have always had Airselves. If we live in Air at all, then we have always lived there, from the beginning. We have always been able to sometimes see the future or the past. We have always been able to make tiny miracles. Any child knows that. Many women do. It seem that only great big gangsters do not. Everything has always been and has always happened all at once. Which means nothing causes anything else. Which means stories only happen in this poor balloon-world of ours. Stories have no meaning. Nothing can be interpreted. Everything just is, without meaning, without needing your philosophy and your science or all our miseries and myths and tales and explanations. It is all just one big smiling Now. Whoooooooooooooooooooo. That is the sound of Air, blowing.

21

Mae came back from her morning weather Talent patrol and found Kwan and Sunni sitting at her kitchen table.
The house was chilly, the brazier burnt-out. Siao was out selling Info services.

'Good morning, ladies,' said Mae, pleased to see her friends.

'Good morning, Mae,' said Kwan, her hands steepled on the table. Sunni nodded, eyes averted.

Kwan asked, 'How long have you been out?'

'Oh. For two hours now.'

'When did you go to bed?' Kwan asked.

'Oh, I had a lot of mail. You see, we tell all customers to be patient with us, for we are snowbound and cannot ship until after March. Some of them find that interesting and write, and I try to answer.'

Kwan held up yesterday's leaflet. 'Did you run out the weather reports, then, too?'

Mae was unwinding her scarf. 'Oh! No. I do that now, in the mornings before the Circle. I would offer you tea, but I have drunk all my winter stock.'

They didn't want tea. Mae sat down with them and began to wonder why they were there.

'Did you really tell Mrs Pin that you know there will be a Flood because you have been to the future?'

Kwan's face looked burnished like wood: hard.

'Not in those words. But yes.'

Kwan and Sunni looked at each other. Sunni asked, 'Do you really believe that?'

Mae found herself adopting a fortified position, feet braced on the earthen floor. 'When you have been in Air for a while, you will see it is true. Air is forever, in both directions. Forward and back.'

Kwan drew in a breath, and said, 'You are saying that you have actually been into the future and stood in the coming Flood here in Kizuldah.'

'I have been in my future life. I suddenly find myself in my future life. Sometimes it is in the Flood. There will be a flood and that is why I warn people.'

Kwan uncrumpled the leaflet in her hand and read it again. 'Mae. We want you to stop worrying people.'

Sunni picked up the thread. 'It is foolish, people are bored with it. They say: "If this is what working with Info does, then let Mae drive herself crazy with it. We will leave it alone." '

Kwan finished: 'It hurts progress, Mae.'

Sunni sighed. 'As your friends, we are going to ask you to stop.'

No, no, no. These were her friends; this was a simple misunderstanding. Mae began to explain. The Flood. 1959. Temperature and snow. She stood up, got out her printouts, all elevation lines, and water flow. It was hard, practical stuff.

Kwan chuckled in exasperation. 'Honestly, Mae, if you do this one more time to me, I will scream! I have heard what you have to say about the Flood. Can I tell you what it sounds like, Mae? That you are afraid – not of the Flood, but of the future. All this talk of wiping everything away. That is what Air will do, not the Flood. Everyone sees you as a woman who is scared but cannot admit it.'

'And is driving herself and everyone else crazy,' added Sunni.

Kwan sighed. 'It reminds everyone that you have Mrs Tung inside you. It reminds them of the first disaster, that Test. It just makes them think all progress is madness.'

And I am the crazy adulteress woman and I am an embarrassment to you. I didn't think I was, but I am.

The two women looked at each other. Something was clinched.

'Mae,' said Kwan. 'We want you to stop working.'

'Take time out to sleep, eat, relax.'

'Leave the Circle to us, leave the new screens for the site to someone else.'

'Stop going out all over the hills pretending to be a weatherman.'

'Also,' said Kwan, 'there is a lady from Yeshiboz Sistemlar, called Fatimah, who has told us about the pregnancy . . .'

Sunni leaned forward with concern. 'For heaven's sake, Mae, get rid of it. You know what I am talking about.'

'Fatimah says it will kill you!'

The whole room started to buzz. It was as if the walls were full of hornets. Mae felt herself go dim and old, and she was frightened and alone.

Left upstairs all day, too weak to walk far, wanting to talk, wanting to be heard, always told you are too old, Gran, don't tax yourself. Stay still, stay quiet. You will be dead soon, and even quieter.

'Don't do this,' said Mae, in a very quiet, distracted voice, half hers, half Mrs Tung's. 'Don't leave me alone.'

Kwan leaned forward and took her hand. 'That's exactly what we will not do, Mae. We are your friends, and we will always stand by you.'

Sunni took her hand as well. 'Yes, Mae. We have had disagreements in the past, but we have overcome them. Listen to your friends; we do this out of concern for you.'

Kwan's eyes were firm. 'We think it is best if you just leave the TV alone.'

'For a while,' said Sunni. 'Until you are well and rested again.'

'Mae! You should see yourself! You look like a ghost. Your face is thin, your eyes stare, your hair is like a witch's.'

'You – who were the most elegant woman in the village,' said Sunni.

'You need help,' said Kwan, with finality.

'And,' chuckled Sunni, 'you need to leave that thing alone.'

'You need a rest from the TV,' said Kwan again, determined.

'Don't do this to me,' Mae repeated.

Her friends – her friends who had stood by her, who had not deserted her – why were they doing this now?

'Let Siao do the screens for Mr Pin and the others.'

'Maybe you could go to Balshang, stay with your son. Have tea with your new friend, Miss Soo. Have you ever seen the capital?'

'No,' said Mae, arms folded.

'There you go!' Sunni lifted up her arms as if everything were evident, settled. 'Maybe we could all go together. I would love to see the big city!'

'My work is here,' said Mae. 'The road is closed. What business is any of this of yours?'

'Come and live with me again for a while, Mae. Please!' said Kwan.

'No,' said Mae. 'I am happy living here with my family.'

Kwan leaned forward, her voice flat. 'Mae,' she demanded. 'Come with us.'

'I am happy as I am,' said Mae.

They tried for a further fifteen minutes, cajoling, tugging on her arm, offering her tea, saying she had worked harder than anyone and that she had won, she had succeeded, all the village was learning. Was the village not a Centre of Progress? Everyone knew that it was because of her.

'But even strong branches break when the load is too great,' said Sunni.

Everything they said availed nothing. They had stopped talking about making her stop work or taking away her baby, but that was what they intended.

Finally, sour, made angry and defeated, Kwan and Sunni left.

Mae sat still until she was sure they were gone.

Then she locked and barred her door. She thought about what Kwan might do next if she were determined enough.

Mae conferenced Mr Oz. 'Yes, yes, hello, it's always a pleasure. Look, I need a wireless account of my own for my TV.'

Mr Oz sounded relaxed and cheerful, away from the road. 'That should be easy enough. Just call the telephone company.'

'It's urgent. I need it done today.'

'Today? I don't know. You used to have a mobile phone, didn't you? You could try calling them. Why? Is there a problem with Swallow Communications?'

'Let's just say I just have a suspicion that Kwan might develop account problems.' She might cut Mae off.

Mr Oz groaned. Why was he upset? He was not the one with the problem. 'You've got extendable credit with the bank. Make sure they know that. Have the bank references ready, make sure you have your phone account number, and everything about your TV. It's a Hitachi 7700 PDTV. Okay? And Mae? What's wrong?'

Mae thought for a moment about future and past, and then said, 'I am too far ahead of them.'

Then she conferenced Sloop at his desk at the telephone company.

His round face glistened and he chuckled. 'There is no problem. We like new business.'

'I need it done today,' she said.

Sloop blinked. 'Today?'

It was complicated. Mae would have to download her new ID from their servers. Sloop would have to talk her through the process of reconfiguration.

She was at work on that when Kwan and Sunni came back. They hammered on the door. 'Mae! Don't be ridiculous! Open this door!'

'Mae, why are you leaving Swallow Communications?!' Mae looked out from her attic skylight. She looked down on them shuffling in front of her bolted door. They had Mr Wing with them.

Sunni's voice was shrill. 'Mae! We are your friends! We are trying to help!'

Mr Wing chortled, 'Mae, if we wanted to cut you off, it would be just as easy to cut the power!'

Kwan's voice was like a knife, shushing him in anger.

Mae unlatched her window. 'I have my own account, I have my own food, I have my own family. I will carry on my business, and I will continue to tell people about the Flood.'

Kwan puffed out air. 'You will end up damaging the thing you want to save.'

Sunni stepped forward. 'Mae! At least go to see doctors about that baby!'

'Thank you for shouting my business all over the valley,' said Mae. She latched the skylight shut, and went back to work.

'Mae! No one wants to hurt you!' Sunni called.

Mae heard Kwan murmur, 'I think we're just making things worse.'

Mae turned again to her beautiful screens and the messengers like birds.

There was another knocking at the door.

'Mrs Chung-ma'am,' someone called. It was Sezen.

And Mae's response was: What now? She went to the trapdoor. Suddenly it looked a long way down to the kitchen floor. Mae didn't want to move. She wanted to stay in her loft, above the floodwaters, with her machine.

'Please let me in,' Sezen called.

A thought of Mrs Tung's seemed to breathe through Mae.

We all end up alone, with no one understanding.

Mae went back to the TV. She watched as her morning weather data uploaded to Balshang.

There were footsteps on the roof. Mae heard boots skidding on stone tiles.

'Mae, this is Sezen,' said a voice from above.

'Get away, you silly girl, you will fall and kill yourself,' said Mae.

'I'm not one of them, Mae. I wouldn't do that to you. What did they say?' The voice through the stone tiles was as clear as if Sezen were in the room.

'They want me to stop working. They want to take everything away from me and they say they want to help me.'

'*Tuh*. Typical. You are a wild woman and don't wait for them to approve what you do. You go too far too fast.'

'They want to kill my baby,' said Mae, her voice thickening with rage. 'That bloody woman in the City has been trying to kill my baby all along, and she has been writing to Kwan.'

'Don't you worry, Mae, Sezen will never let you down. Ah? We are wild women together. What do you need me to do?'

'Get down off that roof before you kill yourself.'

Sezen laughed. 'The view is lovely up here. Okay. I am holding on to the crest of the roof so I cannot fall. So, what do you need me to do?'

Mae considered. She considered being accosted alone in the fields, surrounded by so-called friends. She considered all the hours she worked. She considered the baby in her belly made of fire. She considered the undoubted truth that she was doing too much. Above all else, she considered the village.

'I need you to help collect Info,' Mae said. 'Info about snow.'

'Mae!' someone shouted. 'What is going on?'

Sezen giggled. 'You have shut out Siao.'

'Siao, hold on, is there anyone with you?' For just a moment, Mae imagined that they might be with Siao; for just a moment, that Siao might even have joined them.

'I want lunch!' he shouted back.

Mae went down and let him in. Sezen joined them, grinning as Mae raged, pacing her own kitchen in fury. Siao and Sezen caught each other's eyes and mimed ducking.

'So I got a new wireless account, my machine is up in the loft! I don't need them!'

'Good,' said Siao, with a mild smile. 'You have needed to be independent of Kwan for a while. Don't worry, eh? If they cut off the electricity, I know how to get it going again. I'll put printout through doors, whatever.'

Mae hugged him in gratitude, and he kissed the top of her head. They hung together for a just a moment as if in outer space. Then they remembered Sezen was there. She made a mysterious and somehow knowing gesture, holding up both hands, palms out.

In the evening, an e-mail arrived from Mr Ken.
He had keyed it in, not spoken it, so he must not have wanted to be overheard. It came from Sunni's machine.

> If you are in trouble, I will help. You know that. Please call on me to help. But please, also tell me: What is this about a baby?

By all the stars, she hadn't told him. She had not told Kuei about his child. The room seemed suddenly colder, her cheeks burned. She could hear Siao below in the kitchen, cooking dinner for her. The metal spoon tinged against the wok; Siao was humming a song.

Mae! What are you doing?

22

It was Chinese New Year and Mae was alone.
Kwan was having a party. After everything that had happened, Mae
would not attend. Why should she – to be argued at, cajoled, and
entreated?

Something was up with Siao. He had come back from the Teahouse
looking distracted. He tore off the top of his thumbnail with his teeth,
kissed Mae on the cheek, and told her not to worry. Then he was gone
in young Mr Pin's car. Old Mr Chung shuffled and shrugged and then
left early, perhaps embarrassed, for a gathering of old village reprobates
like himself.

Mae had hoped at least to share some warm rice wine at New Year's
with her family, with Siao. Whenever she talked to Siao she always got
good sense, she always felt secure.

She didn't own him; if he wanted to go off and have fun, okay. He
wasn't married, he must need a woman, and perhaps he hoped to find
one.

And, ah, Mae, that is it. That is why your hands tumble over
themselves, round and round. That is why you cannot sit still. You see
another woman coming into the house, and that disturbs you, but
more than that, you see another woman with Siao.

Mae? What has happened here? Sit down, Mae, and look at your
hands. What do they tell you?

They tell you want to look into his calm, honest blue-grey eyes. You
want to see his smooth lean arms, with the silky skin that mixes
Karzistan with China. You want to hear his deep, measured voice. You
wish he were here. You wish you were with him.

Mae put her head into her hands. Oh, Mae Mae, Mae, Mae, what is
this?

Mae stood up from the kitchen table. I want him to work with me.
We work well together. He understands the things I understand. He is

even better than me at selling, he is better than me at understanding what all this new stuff is for . . .

Yes, Mae, and what else?

I want to hold him, I want to give him a home, I want to show him the respect his stupid brother never gave him. I want him to know that someone sees how smart he is, how kind, how patient. How wise.

Oh, Mae. You are in love with your husband's brother.

Well, it is traditional. The husband dies, the brother can take over. But when the husband just goes off? When the husband goes off because the wife went with his next-door neighbour?

And when she is about to have the next-door neighbour's child?

Oh, Mae, the knots you tie. If you were scandalous before, what will you be after this? And poor Siao, suppose he feels nothing for you but kindness? What will he feel if you declare yourself? You will be trapped together in the house, you see each other half-naked nearly every day, he has to think of his brother, he has to be neighbours with Mr Ken . . . Oh, Mae, nobody needs this!

Mae, if you go after your husband's brother, you really will lose everything. Maybe you really have gone mad.

But once given its proper name, the feeling would not go away.

I love his little beard, I love the way it makes his teeth shine out when he smiles, I love the slow way he moves, I love the way he turns everything around, stands it on its head, and it makes more sense that way. My God, I love his body, I love his mind.

When did it change? When did I notice as if in passing that he was also handsome? When did he wake up and start to speak? Or rather, when did I begin listening to him?

Mae, leave this. You don't like being alone, that's all. Being alone at New Year's is making me jealous. I do not like being the crazy lady of the village. I do not like being where I am. I am not Madam Owl, I am not Mrs Disruption, and I wish all this would stop. I want peace, I want quiet.

Mae went up to the loft to work. The moment she woke up the TV, it was invaded. The screen was cleared, and there was Kwan.

'Mae,' Kwan said, her living room ghostly behind her. Mae reached forward to restart. 'Please don't go. We must talk real-time. Open other channel.'

The picture was torn in half, and there, on her machine, uninvited and full of concern, was Fatimah, of Yeshiboz Sistemlar. 'Hello, Mae,' she said.

Mae felt herself go cold. 'Fatimah, I told you once before that you would find it impossible to do good,' said Mae. 'It is nothing to do with who you are. It is your job.'

'Mae, please listen,' said Kwan. 'This woman is a doctor.'

'Nurse. She kept me prisoner.'

Fatimah looked so sweet, made-up, groomed. Oh, she's wearing white, that gives her the right to kill people's children. 'Mrs Chung. There is no chance of it coming to term. It could kill you.'

'Oh, so it is by no means certain I will die?'

Fatimah sighed. 'Not if we could get you into a hospital.'

Kwan's arms were folded. It was the posture she adopted whenever she struggled against other people's stupidity. 'She is trying to help save both of you, Mae.'

'Mae,' said Fatimah, sounding conciliatory, 'Come to us, in a hospital, stay with us.'

'Okay. Maybe I will go and stay in a hospital in May. Maybe the whole month. Is that good enough for you? Goodbye.'

Mae unplugged the machine and detached the battery. The screen image collapsed as if punctured. All communication would be broken, and the invasive code disabled. She pushed the battery back in, and a fresh clear screen came up. She downloaded her written mail.

Her machine was invaded again. The image interlaced in stages.

'This is rude, crashing in on me like this,' said Mae.

'You are still distributing paper,' said Kwan, fixing her eye on her. 'You are still telling people, "No Flood just yet, but more snow and it will come." I had Old Mrs Nan in here yesterday, asking if I could keep her goats in my loft.'

'It's the safest place for them,' said Mae. 'Since no one is taking any steps to save people, maybe the goats will at least survive the flood.'

'Why are you having the child?' Kwan demanded.

'Why did you have yours?'

'Do you think it's some kind of magic sign?' Kwan demanded, still beautiful, little aging pouches of loose flesh under the determined mouth.

Mae thrust out her jaw. 'Yes,' she said. Since you phrase it that way.

Kwan's eyes widened momentarily.

'Look, Kwan. I am doing this weather work. The weather is all tied up together. But not like we think. We think that everything that happens has a cause. That I strike with a knife and that causes a cut. But sometimes a cut happens somewhere else, too, without a cause. Sometimes things happen because the world is held together by patterns. Things that are alike. So there are signs and portents.'

Kwan chose her words. 'You believe your child is a sign.'

'So is the Flood,' said Mae.

Kwan looked momentarily defeated. She wilted a little and ran her hand over her forehead. 'You really have been working too hard.'

'My baby is lodged in my stomach, it will be born out of my mouth. You know why Mr Tunch wants my baby dead? Because he thinks my child is a portent, too.'

'Mae,' said Kwan in despair. 'Listen to yourself. Please. You sound like some superstitious old woman from one hundred years ago.'

'I am one,' said Mae.

Kwan shook her head.

'Everything is changing and my baby is part of everything. You know what Fatimah does? She helps makes intelligent talking dogs. One of them helped me escape. His name was Ling. How is that for Karz people, ah? – they always give their dogs Chinese names. A talking intelligent dog, and it asked, *asked* to be put back as a dog.'

Kwan's face was shaking slightly from side to side. 'You really have gone, Mae,' she sighed.

'Who has gone? You threaten me, you break into my machine. Are you going to break down my door? Are you going to drag me off into the night?'

Kwan did not answer. Her face said: *Whatever is necessary to help you.* Her words said something else. 'Mae. You can believe any nonsense that you like. But you must shut up, because your nonsense is stopping the very thing you believe in most. Progress. Mae, I cannot tell people this is a good thing when you are being driven crazy.'

'Ah, so you are not concerned about me, really.'

Kwan scratched her hair, delicately. 'I am concerned about many things, including you.'

'So. How are you going to stop me talking? Shen couldn't. You are so concerned about progress. Is it progress to start bossing people around, like the government? The government thinks you are nonsense, Kwan. Who saved you then?'

'You.'

'Then leave me alone.'

Kwan looked very determined. 'I am going to return the favour, Mae. I am not one to give up on a friend.'

It was Kwan who cut off communication this time.

Mae was left quaking with rage. Who was Kwan to tell her what to do? To tell her what to say, to tell her to get rid of her baby? Kwan, you have been important in the village too long, you have come to think of yourself as Head Woman.

She read her mail.

---

e-mail from: Mr Ken Kuei
20 February
Dear Mae,

Happy New Year. E-mail gets easier all the time. It reminds me of when I learned to ride a bicycle. Suddenly for no reason you can do it. I wish, though, that I had learned from you.

Since these messages can go round the world, I thought I would send one an even greater distance. Across our courtyard.

---

audio file from: Lieutenant Chung Lung
20 February
Tsang has left Dad. I knew trouble was coming when she started to lose weight and wear black, and took even more trouble with her grooming. She got a job with some crook of an estate developer. She would talk in front of Dad about all the opportunities he was offering her. Dinner with clients. She thought she had become a Balshang Beauty. She was always a very stupid woman. She used to be falsely fond of Dad, but at least she would praise him in front of the officers. Suddenly all that stopped. She started to say things to make Dad look like a fool, and he would sit with that hazy grin of his, looking really foolish. This drove my sister Ying crazy. She said she would not be in the same room with Tsang.

Tsang was very bitter about me, too: 'Oh, but then Asian women are not good enough for you, so you want to leave Kizuldah so far behind.' 'Like you?' I said back. 'Is this boss of yours married?' So finally she has gone off with her gangster and Dad is alone. He wants to come and live here with me. I can't have him, Mama. I have to entertain officers here, it really is not possible. He came here two nights ago when the colonel was visiting with us. Dad was drunk and he was weeping and cursing Tsang, and cursing you and cursing life, and looked like a real peasant. I tried to keep him under control. I said he could stay the night if he wanted to. Sarah tried to take him into the kitchen and he threw off her hands and started calling her 'a Western whore.' And he started telling me that I thought I was a big man now, but I wouldn't when my Western wife found out I had a small cock. All this in front of my colonel. Truly awful. I know he was upset, but really, he cannot behave in this way. Neither I nor Ying has heard anything from him for two days. I will try to visit him after work today. I will let you know what happens.

---

e-mail from: Mr Bedri Eyoobogloo
20 February
Mae,
Thanks for data. The attached file shows what happens when we run it against what's happening here. You are getting more snow *because* it is warmer. There is more evaporation, which then falls on the higher slopes.

We get Dragon's Breath when an inversion over the desert is suddenly pushed south by a cold front coming down from the north. Usually this happens in summer, when the air has baked. It is usually in massive, single movements.

We have an inversion now – it is 32 degrees Celsius in Balshang! We are getting little Dragons. Mustafa here calls them 'Dragon Sneezes' – whirls of cold coming down in spiral patterns, making very hot blasts, very localized. The front itself is not moving nor the inversion. However, this is the foundation situation.

Your data is going patchy, and that disappoints us. Your assistant Sezen is no substitute for you.

Mae opened the attached file and entered it into her own database. She stood up and looked through her skylight. It was snowing heavily. It was so warm the flakes seemed to have cohered into lumps, almost as if someone were throwing snowballs or marshmallows.

She told her machine, 'Calculate the chances of a flood.'

50–50 Chance of Flood

This is the last warning I can print. I have run out of paper. Please take precautions. The map shows a map of Kizuldah, and where water and avalanches are most likely.

If it gets hot, day or night, if you feel the Dragon's Breath on your back, leave the west of the village. Go east and up. It is best around Kwan's house. Now is the time to get your seed grain up in lofts; don't wait for the flood to begin. Mrs Tung says, when it comes, it sounds merry. The water laughs, the rocks applaud.

If you hear that sound, get yourselves away, get yourselves away, for the love of God.

Your friendly madwoman,
Chung Mae

Mae ran with her leaflets to Mr Ken's house and knocked on his door.

His mother opened it. Old Mrs Ken glared at Mae. She was a plump, overworked woman in her sixties, sweaty, with hair astray.

Mae did not give her a chance to speak. 'The government says there is a chance of the Flood, there is cold in Russia; if it decides to move, all the pieces will fall into place, the Dragon will wake up, the snow will melt. Okay. So. If it gets hot, go up to Kwan's. It is bad for us at this end of the village. See?'

Mr Ken's mother stared at her like a stone. She took the paper Mae offered her and held it out away from her as Mae pointed to the map.

Saying nothing, Mrs Ken tore up the paper, calmly, neatly.

'I will put this where it belongs,' she said.

'I am carrying your grandchild,' said Mae, and left, having no more time to waste.

Mae was wrestling with the courtyard gate, and heard footsteps.

'Don't mind Mother, she is still upset,' said Mr Ken. His face was phosphorescent-blue from snowlight, and outlined in gold.

'I'm used to it,' said Mae. It seemed as if Ken Kuei had stepped out of her life from many years before.

'Can I help?' he asked.

Mae paused. 'Yes,' she said, and divided her papers in half and passed them to him. 'Take these along Lower Street, that will be a big help. I will cover Upper, and I will ask Sezen to cover the Marsh. If the Flood comes, get your mother up to Kwan's.'

'Where will you be?'

'I will go to the mosque, so I can use the Muerain's speaker. Okay, thanks for helping. You go that way, I head up there.'

Ken stood his ground. 'Is the baby mine?'

Mae thought: This is what I get for not clearing this up; I am being held up at just the wrong time. 'Of course. Who else's?'

'Will you marry me? After the Air comes?'

The snow fell, like fainting in reverse. White flakes, not darkness, closed from the side of her vision. Blue-and-gold light reflected on the cheeks of this beautiful faithful man.

'Yes,' she said, and then hedged. 'Probably.'

'Probably,' he said, disappointed.

'Move, please. Please?' Her eyes and her voice were pleading. Of course I need help with this – please help.

Mr Ken nodded, serious, solemn, not entirely bright, but good. He stepped out of the gate and turned up Lower Street. Mae found herself gazing at his broad, silent back. Oh God, she thought, I love him too.

She turned and walked northeast.

She climbed up the hill to Sezen's house. She pounded on the door. 'Sezi! Sezi! It's me, Mae.' Hatijah opened the door, looking nervous but pleased to see her patron at New Year's. The courtyard goat began to bleat at the disturbance.

'Hello, Hatijah. Fifty-fifty chance of a Flood, so this is the last of my paper.'

Sezen hopped in, pulling on a boot. 'Mrs Chung-ma'am. Are you going to Kwan's party?'

'No, and neither are you, just yet. You are taking these to Lower Marsh Street, okay? The Macks, the Chus, the Hans.'

Sezen's lip curled. 'Couldn't we let An drown?'

'No time for jokes. I want to be back at my machine before Wing finds out I'm not there.'

'Oh, Mae. Just one drowned traitor. Please?' Sezen pretended to wheedle like a child. Her no-good boyfriend emerged sleepily. He wore no shirt and his plump, hairless belly wobbled.

'Tell your boyfriend he is enough to put people off their food, and to dress himself.'

Sezen giggled. 'We've just been fucking.'

'This is not a joke, Sezen!' Mae's voice was raised in warning. 'Look, the whole point of being wild is to have more style, not less.'

Sezen swallowed her grin, embarrassed. Yes, Mae was right. 'What can you expect, with my home background?'

'Better,' replied Mae. 'Move!'

Already the warm snow had filled in her footprints. Mae struggled farther up the hill to the school, where Teacher Shen lived. She pounded on the door. Why, *why* did no one ever answer? She pounded again. 'Yes?' inquired Suloi's voice.

'Suloi, please open up, just for a moment. I am so sorry to intrude.'

The little room beside the schoolhouse was full of candlelight and smelled of wine. Suloi was all smiles, but a screen had been pulled across the entrance and behind it her husband snored.

'Hello, Mae! Happy New Year. Are you going to the party tonight?' She wished everything was normal, she wished everyone could be friends. Mae passed her the paper in silence.

'Oh,' said Suloi, disappointed. She looked trapped, ashamed.

'I'm not saying necessarily, only fifty-fifty.'

Suloi looked sad. 'Are you going to everyone in the village with this?'

'Of course,' said Mae. 'What do you think, that I would leave anyone out?'

'I know you mean well, Mae.' Suloi sighed. 'Mae, you know what people used to do to eldritch women?'

'Cast them out,' said Mae.

'Into the snow,' said Suloi.

'Unless they told the truth,' said Mae. 'I must go.'

'Happy New Year,' Suloi said quietly, and went back to her snoring husband.

Mae marched down the hill to the first house on Upper Street.

The Okans were an old couple, all their children and grandchildren had moved to town. They were delighted to receive company. 'Happy New Year,' they chorused, and hobbled forward with the warm wine they were not sharing with anyone.

'This is so kind,' Madam Okan said toothlessly, under her best coloured headscarf.

Mae did not have the heart to make them feel deserted at the New Year, so she sat with them and sipped the warm wine and itched to be away throughout, sitting up straight on the diwan.

'She sits so prettily,' said Mrs Okan.

'Relax, sit back, drink with us!' said Mr Okan. 'Allah forgives on this day, and besides, it is not made from grape, eh?' He winked, his skin like old stained leather shrunk onto bones.

They began to talk about children, grandchildren, even great-grandchildren. Photographs, a tumble of babies, and babies who now sat babies of their own on their laps.

'If . . .' began Mae, 'if you hear a funny noise tonight—'

'Oh! New Year's. We don't mind the noise.'

'There could be a Flood,' Mae said. 'If there is a Flood, you need to get to Kwan's.'

Their smiles faded, they grew confused. Mae tried to explain. Mrs Okan's heart plainly sank. Mae had not come to be social; she had come because there was some kind of trouble. It was good when someone came because there was trouble, but even nicer when someone came to have fun. They nodded, and tried to smile. But their little glasses were lowered. Mae felt awful for them.

'How are we to get to Mr Wing's?' said Mr Okan, smiling with a shrug. 'I can only shuffle.' He moved his slippered feet back and forth and his wife of fifty years chuckled and put a hand on his arm.

How, indeed?

'I have to go,' said Mae.

At the door, the Okans chorused, 'How nice to see you, Happy New Year!' On impulse, Mae leaned forward and kissed them both.

'Oh-ho,' Mr Okan joked. 'I have a new girlfriend!'

Next door was Mr and Mrs Ali.

Mrs Ali opened the door, looking sour.

'You know why I have come,' said Mae, and passed one of her papers.

'I fear I do,' said Mrs Ali, Sunni's old ally. 'Is that all you have to say to me?'

'Happy New Year,' said Mae. 'Say hello to Sunni for me.'

Ali will be off to the others like lightning. I know that, but it would be wrong to leave anyone out.

Next door, the Dohs were having a party.

'Ah! Madam Owl!' called out Mrs Doh, red-faced and friendly. 'Hello!' She took Mae's hand and pulled her inside. Her house was full of people – her large family, the Lings, the Soongs, and the Pings.

'Our favourite madwoman!' said Mrs Doh, and crumpled a paper hat onto Mae's head. 'Oh, look, another piece of paper from our Mae!'

'You just stop work and get drunk like us,' said Young Mr Doh, and thrust some rice wine into her hand.

The radiocassette was on, and the younger people were dancing. Young Miss Doh wiggled up, took all of Mae's papers from her, and made her join the dancing circle.

Mae danced, and calculated. This party had saved her having to visit three other houses. She warned Young Miss Doh, who was pressed next to her in the circle. 'The main danger on Upper Street will be rocks falling from the terraces. Houses like yours will take the full force of them. You must leave everything.'

'Stop!' said Young Miss Doh. 'Have fun! Life is short!'

Mae allowed herself one dance. Then she cut everything off with a nod of her head, got her papers back, and left.

Mae climbed up and over the steep arch of their bridge. The next house belonged to Hasan Muhammed. Mae swallowed hard and knocked on his door.

It was answered promptly. Tsang's deserted husband stood, clean, pressed, and proud. He carried his young son in his arms.

'Yes?' he asked, his head held back, away, as if from a bad odour.

'Mr Muhammed-sir, I am sorry to intrude. Just in case.' Mae held out a paper towards him.

He didn't take it. He pondered her for a moment, and then shifted his child to the other arm. 'I already have everything in the loft,' he said, entirely serious. 'When it comes, we shall all go directly to the house of Mr Wing, me and my children.'

Someone believed her.

'You are well prepared,' said Mae. She took hold of the little boy's foot and held it.

'Bad things happen,' said Mr Muhammed. 'As both of us know too well.'

'Keep an ear listening. Happy New Year!'

He merely nodded, and closed the door.

'Thank you, Mr Muhammed!' she added, facing the blank door.

She turned and began to walk up towards the Atakoloos'. As she came around the corner of her brother's house, she came upon a group of people struggling up Lower Street.

'There she is,' said Kwan.

A flashlight darted over Mae's face, making her squint. The Wings, Sunni, and Mr Haseem strode towards her.

'Mae,' said Mr Wing. 'This has got to stop.' They all wore waterproofs. Kwan – neat, slim, and in black – was in front of them, all with papers in hand.

'We mean it, Mae.'

'Are those my papers?' Mae demanded. Kwan was nearly up to her. 'Are those *my* papers?'

'You are not going to make a fool of yourself on New Year's. Now, give me the rest.'

Mae felt fury. '*You* give me that paper. Who said you could have that paper?'

'We took it from Sezen, if you must know. She spat at us, but I expect no better from her. Give us the paper, Mae.'

'It is not your paper, it is my paper.'

Kwan nodded over her shoulder. 'I am sorry, Mae, you can't go around spoiling everyone's New Year with these fantasies.'

Sunni, hiding behind Kwan, said over her shoulder, 'Mae: You are a traitor to yourself with this foolishness.'

Wing and Haseem came towards her.

'You keep your hands off me,' Mae warned.

Kwan shook her head. 'I am sorry it has come to this, Mae, but the madness must stop.'

'We are friends no longer,' warned Mae again.

'That is your choice.'

Mae was hugging her leaflets, the last of her papers, to her breast. Wing already had grasped them. 'Come on, Mae, don't make it worse,' said Wing.

'Your friendly madwoman,' chuckled Mr Haseem.

'Please, Mae,' Sunni wheedled.

'I have no friends,' said Mae in a small voice; jerking away from Mr Wing.

Mr Haseem took her arms. Mae doubled over, to clench the papers to herself. Fire burned in her belly. Wing reached around her.

'This really is getting us nowhere,' Mr Wing said, still neat, still smiling.

Mae began to yell. 'They are stealing from me! They are robbing me! Thieves! Help!'

The paper was shiny so that messages could be burned cheaply onto it. It was slippery, and it began to slide now.

'Sezen! Ju-mei! Siao! Help! Ju-mei!'

Fire shot out of her, fire like Dragon's Breath, and she turned and let them have it. Fiery juices shot out of her burning stomach and over Mr Haseem's face.

'Ah!' he yelped, and backed way. 'God! She spat at me.'

'Mae,' said Kwan, rolling her eyes, shaking her head. She looked at Sunni. 'She just gets worse.'

'Her and Sezen,' Sunni shrugged.

'It burns. It really burns!' yelped Sunni's husband. The acids gnawed at his skin.

And Mae froze, for she was indeed beginning to believe in sympathetic magic.

Dragon's Breath.

Oh God, what if I've helped it happen?

Suddenly Wing was shaking her. 'Mae! Enough!' He got the papers.

'There is a fifty-fifty chance,' said Mae, in a weak voice. 'I'm not saying it must happen. I'm saying it could. I'm saying we must be prepared.'

Kwan looked at her with something like sympathy. 'I'm sorry, Mae. If you feel like coming to the party later, you will be very welcome.'

'She must be like a nuclear furnace inside!' said Mr Haseem, wiping his face with a handkerchief.

'I'm trying to digest my baby,' said Mae, a little stupid from everything that had happened.

They left her.

She listened to the falling snow.

The front door of the Wangs' house opened. In the warm light stood her brother Ju-mei. 'Mae, what is going on?' he asked.

'Oh, Ju-mei! They have taken the last of my papers! And there is a good chance of a Flood.'

'Come in – come and get warm,' he said. He gave her rice wine. He had a new little clock of which he was very proud. Mae relented, and toasted the New Year as her brother's prosperous little clock chimed.

She ignored the sounds of a party at Kwan's, and very slightly tipsy went back down Lower Street. Maybe it won't happen. There's a good chance it won't happen, she thought.

She got home. Siao was still not there. She pulled herself up into her loft and dragged a heavy trunk over the trapdoor. She opened up the connection.

More mail.

---

audio file from: Lieutenant Chung Lung

21 February

So what has happened now is even worse. I think Dad has gone back to you. I went to his room, and he was not there. Mum, Balshang is a mess, the place has roads and pipes for a million people, and no one knows how many have come here, between nine and sixteen million. I had not seen his place before. Mum, there was a lagoon of sewage behind it. All his things were gone. There was no sign of breakfast, just one very old dirty plate with hard food on it. That may mean he has been gone some days. He has no money, so must be hitching. He may think he will be able to get back to you through the snow. He is beside himself with despair. I don't think he even cares about getting through the snow. I think right now he probably wants to die. I thought I should warn you. If he turns up here with me or my sister, I will let you know. Try under the circumstances to have a good New Year.

What else? thought Mae.

Her spirits and her body sagged. What else can possibly happen? She turned off her machine. She pulled out the mattress and laid it on the plywood sheet that rested between the slats of her floor. The roof was the thinnest part of the house.

If the Flood came, she would hear it, and if it did not – thank God. She turned out the light.

23

Sweat woke Mae up.

She sat up in the dark, suddenly wide-awake and gasping for breath. She had been dreaming of the Flood; she had heard it, the spreading crash of water and stone.

She listened. Everything was silent and still, but she was soaked with sweat.

The air! It was hot, hot as summer, as hot as those nights when you have to sleep outside. She heard a rustling in the eaves, like something breathing.

Erjdha Nefsi.

Mae threw off the covers and stood up, listening. Very faint under the sound of moving air, was a sound as if the hills were being tickled.

She switched on the light, and looked at the TV.

Forty-five degrees Centigrade.

'Wake up,' Mae told the TV. She threw on old jeans, rubber boots, and a light coat. She strapped on a rucksack filled with blankets and tins of food. She jerked the trapdoor out of its socket and dropped the bag down to the kitchen floor below.

'Siao!' she called. 'Siao, are you there?'

There was no answer. If Siao had gone down the hill, and was in a house or a cafe, he might be all right. If he was on the road when it hit . . . Mae did not have time for imaginings. She spun back around and sent an audio file.

'Bedri. It's forty-five Celsius, the Erjdha is breathing, and I can hear the meltdown. I don't know if it's Flood or not, but please tell people: if it is at the worst, we will need help. It's four-thirty a.m. now, and I need to store battery power, so I'm sending this off, and leaving. Don't bother replying, I won't be here. If it's bad, I'll be at Kwan's.'

Mae pushed the machine off, and lowered herself through the trapdoor, badly scraping her forearm. She could hear her breath rattling like gambler's dice. She dropped to the floor, and hauled back the curtains to Siao's alcove.

Old Mr Chung slept, quietly smiling. He smelled of rice wine. Mae called him, and shook him. 'Mr Chung-sir! Mr Chung!'

She dragged him blinking out of sleep.

'It's here, Mr Chung, it's here, the Flood – get up!'

He had fallen onto the bed fully clothed. Mae knelt and jammed his feet into string shoes. 'Come, Mr Chung, come!'

She rattled him out of the house, into the courtyard under the stars. The hot wind had blasted the sky clean; everything was hot and clear. She explained to Mr Chung that Siao was still down the hill, he must get to Mr Wing's Big House.

Then Mae pounded on the door of the Kens.

'Kuei! Kuei! Old Mrs Ken. Get up! Get up! Erjdha Nefsi!'

The window overhead was thrown open, wood clunked against the wall. Silhouetted against the whitewash was Mr Ken's mother, hissing.

'Go away, you madwoman. My son is asleep. Take your fancies and go.'

'Feel the wind! Feel the air! It's hot; it's nearly fire. It . . . is . . . here!' Mae thought: I don't have time for this, or for you. 'Mr Ken. Ken Kuei! Wake up!'

It's come, said a voice. *This is what it was like.*

Mae began to feel a kind of panic. 'Ken Kuei! You said you would help!'

The air is like fire and the water moves the earth.

Mr Chung suddenly said, 'I'll be back.' The old man trotted away bowlegged towards the barn.

'Mr Chung, we have to go!'

Mr Chung's voice had an unexpected edge. 'I can't leave my tools!'

Oh, no! Mae held her head. She shouted to them all: 'We all have to leave here now! Our court is in a very bad position. Both rocks and water will wash here, nobody must stay here!'

And suddenly, Old Mrs Tung spoke, calling Mrs Ken by her childhood name: 'Ting! Do as you are told! No more nonsense! Even as a little girl, all you ever wanted to do was stay inside the house. I've told you and told you what happened last time. The Flood is here. Darling daughter, you . . . will . . . have to leave this house!'

At the window, Old Mrs Ken's face fell. Hot wind buffeted the shutters.

Someone touched Mae's arm, bringing her back. 'I'm here,' said Mr Ken.

Mae gasped, recalled to herself. 'She's with me. She's using my voice!'

Mr Ken put an arm around her and kissed the top of her head. 'I will get your father-in-law to safety,' he promised.

'And your mother and the Okans.' Mae swung her bag higher up her shoulder.

Mr Ken smiled, amused. 'Is there anything else?' They started to walk towards the gate.

'Yes. Start yelling.'

' "Happy New Year"?'

Mae saw him smiling, moonlight making him look young and merry. Okay, she admitted. I love him.

Old Mr Chung returned with his bag of tools. He bowed and greeted Mr Ken sweetly. 'Happy New Year.'

Ken swung open the courtyard gate for her. His smile cracked wider and he started to bellow, as if in a child's game: 'Happy New Year! The Flood is here!'

Mae joined in. 'This is no joke! The snows are melting!'

He looked up into her face. 'You *know* don't you?'

That he loved her.

'Yes,' she said. 'Yes, yes I do. Now, let's go!'

Mae turned left down Lower Street. 'Get everyone up to Mr Wing's!' she shouted again to them both, and began to run.

The air pulsed as if there was something, huge and hot and alive, breathing down the back of her neck. Mae shouted as she ran: 'Dragon's breath! Wake up. Wake up!'

Already, down the cobbled slope of Lower Street, water ran in a current. Her feet made plashing sounds and her thick boots clunked on the uneven stones. She tripped and knocked her wrist against the side of Mr Kemal's house.

Her plan was to get to the mosque, to use the PA to warn everyone. She turned up the slope towards Sezen's.

'*Inshallah!*' gasped Mae.

In hot starlight she saw: Already the snow from this lower slope was gone.

Mae ran up the hill, slipping on a glossy surface of mud and moss. The ground creaked with water as if it were an overfull barrel. Where her feet did not shoot backwards out from under her, they sank into mud.

Mae shuffled sideways to one of the usual runoffs. As she had hoped, it was gravelled, swept clean. It was also ankle-deep in racing water. Mae struggled up the slope against the current.

'Sezen!' she shouted. 'Sezen. Flood!'

Ahead of her on the hillside, a light went on. The wet slope reflected electric light like a field of broken mirrors.

The door opened. 'Madam Chung?' said a hesitant voice. Hatijah leaned out of the doorway, her husband looming behind her.

Mae stopped and windmilled her arms for balance against the current.

Hatijah called, 'Sezen has already left. She goes to wake the people of the Marsh.'

'Oh! She is a *good* girl,' said Mae.

'She has become one,' said Hatijah.

'You! What are you doing? Get to Kwan's! Get moving, now! Those terraces will be full of water, the walls will break!'

'We wanted to wait for Sezen.'

Mae felt a familiar stab of exasperation. She struggled up and out of the ditch. 'Hatijah! Sezen is not your mother, for heaven's sake; you have other children, get them out of here, now, now, now! Sezen has packed your bags, I know, just take them and leave!'

Hatijah was weeping. 'We can't leave our goat,' she said.

Inshallah. Mae relented 'Of course you can't, it is all your family's wealth. But Edrem, please tell her, life is more important than money. Let the goat go, perhaps it can save itself.'

Edrem's silhouette, tall, skinny and slow, murmured to his wife: 'We must go.'

Mae started to struggle higher up the hill, to the Shens. She shouted as she walked: 'Edrem, I rely on you! You take the children, Hatijah the bags, okay? Okay? And leave your lights on. We will all need light!'

Mae struggled up the hill, leaning on her hands. The hillside was sheathed in water, a solid rippling sheet that was seasoned with tiny cutting flints. The stones sizzled against her fingers like fat on a stove. My God, the whole hillside is moving!

All around her, suspended in the air, was a sound like sighing, a rushing sound of water, in a hundred thousand streams. It was a terrible sound, huge and gentle at the same time, vast as a world. As if Mae had heard the world for the first time.

That's it, that's the sound.

Unexpectedly, the ground flattened and Mae stumbled forward. She was at the schoolhouse. Already the dusty playground was a polished lake, reflecting the children's swings. Water poured out from one corner of the school as if from the spout of a pitcher.

Mae waded to the door and pounded. 'Teacher Shen! Teacher Shen!'

The door seemed to bounce open.

Mae felt another hot breath, but not the Dragon's. Moist, weepy, there was Suloi, her face sticky with tears. 'He won't come, Mae,' she said, and shook herself into sobs.

Mae hugged her sister from the Circle. 'What do you mean?'

A voice out of the darkness, like the darkness, growled, 'There will be no Flood. It is foolishness.'

'Oh, Shen, don't believe me, but believe the water, look at the ground! Shen, please come!'

Something wavered in the darkness, as if it were coiled, legless.

'There will be no Flood.'

Suloi backed away. 'He will not leave.'

Mae pleaded: 'Shen! Come outside! You can hear it. The snows are melting!'

'And the snows will run off, as they have for two thousand years. Do you think those machines of yours can change the world?'

'Do you think you can hold back a Flood? How? By teaching it arithmetic?!' Mae's voice broke with fury.

The darkness, the despair finally uncoiled and stood up. It cocked a rifle. The gun clicked in the darkness.

'I will not have scandalous filth such as you telling my family what to do,' said Despair, who once had been called Happiness.

'Go, Mae,' whispered Suloi, and gave Mae an invisible, loving push.

Shen growled, 'We stay here where we belong.'

Mae pulled Suloi to her, hugged her, whispered in her ear, 'Run in the dark.' Then she pulled back and ran and called over her shoulder, 'Live!'

The hills were laughing.

There was a giggling sound, thousands of chuckles as the water shook itself over rocks, down gullies. It slapped its way across the rock faces of the terraces.

Mae skittered down the slope to the square box of the mosque that had the public-address system mounted on its gable. She came to the door. She rattled it. The sound beyond was hollow. It was locked.

Who locks a mosque? It's never been locked! Mae had calculated, she knew it would take three hours to rouse each house in turn. Mae was near tears. She had planned and planned, but she had never planned that the mosque would be locked.

She would have to run to Mr Shenyalar, the Muerain. He would have the keys.

At least it was downhill. She turned and let the water and gravity carry her.

Mae staggered and slid down the hill. She skittered through the space between the Alis' and the Dohs'. She got tangled in old rusting bedding that someone had discarded. The springs made a merry *sproing* sound as she pulled her feet free. She half fell onto the cobbles of Upper Street, and spun herself into the concave frontage of the house of the Doh family.

Mae shouted up at the shuttered windows, 'Old Mrs Doh, all Dohs, wake up, wake up, there is a Flood, there is a Flood!' She had danced with them only hours before. 'Please wake up!' New Year, and everyone will be asleep, drunk, exhausted, happy.

Mae spun away onto the bridge. The little river roared, enveloping the arch in mist that stroked Mae's face and danced happily into her lungs. Over the stone balustrade, moonlit rapids shot white and hot and fierce down the gully. Mae remembered the ducks, the geese. Already they were a memory, already washed away. Below, the village square looked like an ocean, all glinting waves.

On the other side of the bridge, there was a huge puddle. Even here on Upper Street, a pocket of the road was flooded. Mae plunged down from the bridge and water poured in over the tops of her boots. Even now, the village was still asleep, still dark.

'Flood! Flood!' she shouted. Suddenly a flashlight flared around the corner of the back of the Haj's house.

'Mae, this way,' said a voice. It was her brother. 'We've got Mother up at the Wings. I've just been down to Lower Street.'

'Ju-mei! I need to get to the Shenyalars'.'

'Good, this is the way, down here.'

Mae waded towards him, the water above her knees. Ju-mei reached forward and grabbed her arm. Together they threshed their way down the rocky gap between the house of the Haj and his neighbours. The alley was like a water garden, all ferns and waterfalls. Mae and Ju-mei fell into Lower Street as if plunging into a river.

The current nearly swept them away. It poured around the corner of Ju-mei's house, rucking up like bedding, white as sheets.

Across the street was the Muerain's tall stone house, with its bronze plaque. Clinging to each other, Ju-mei and Mae crossed the torrent. It made them trip downstream as if dancing. They crammed themselves into the porch of the al Gamas' house to brake. Holding on to the rough walls, they pulled themselves upstream, as if up a cliff.

Something crackled. Mae turned to see the Haj's straw outhouse spin out into the current and down into the square. The square was a lake. The village's one streetlight glowed golden on waves rocking against the front doors of the Kosals' and the Masuds'. The outhouse roof, like a straw hat, swirled away on the current. The surface of the water roiled as if full of serpents.

Ju-mei pulled Mae into the doorway of the Shenyalars'. He pounded; Mae howled.

'Muerain! Muerain Shenyalar! Oh please, *please* open. Please wake up! Oh, Muerain! Muerain!'

Why, *why* didn't they move? They were religious Karz, they did not drink, they did not celebrate the New Year, why didn't they hear?

'There is a Flood, Muerain, please wake up!'

From somewhere down in the valley came a terrible spreading crash, as if someone had dropped a dresser full of china. The sound of breakage rolled, settled and then shushed to a halt.

The small terraces below the village were falling, collapsing into the waters.

The houses of the Pins and the Chus. Where Sezen was?

Mae was spurred by terror. 'Shenyalar. Wake up! Oh please wake up!'

A shutter moved.

'Who is it?'

'Mrs Shenyalar, it is Chung Mae. Listen, did you hear that noise?'

'Yes, yes indeed.'

'The Flood is here! Mrs Shenyalar, can your husband come with me, can he come and open up the mosque, so we can use the public-address?'

'Wait there, Mrs Chung,' said the wife.

Ju-mei began to shout at the other houses. 'Mr al Gama! The Haj-sir! Mrs Nan!'

A light went on at Mrs Nan's.

'Mrs Nan! Get up, get your things – go!' Mae shouted at the light.

The door of the Shenyalars' opened.

'Oh, Muerain!' Mae cried in relief.

'*Inshallah*,' breathed out the Muerain. He had taken time, the foolish man, to dress in his religious robes. He saw the river and its surging current, and the new lake at the foot of the streetlight. He heard the roar. He turned and looked at Mae, and his fine, thin features said mutely: *You were right.*

'We have to tell everyone,' she said.

Unhurried, the Muerain strode back into his house. 'Wife! Get the children, get food, and go at once to Madame Kwan's.'

His wife called, 'Surely it is too soon to worry?'

'It is too late to worry. I order you, wife: Out of this house and up to the house of the Wings'!'

'What are you doing?' his wife asked.

There was a flurry of footsteps on stairs. 'My duty!'

At that moment, the entire village was plunged into darkness. The power went.

'*Inshallah!*'

'Husband!'

'Get to the Wings'. I go!' shouted Mr Shenyalar.

Mae wrestled with her backpack, and felt the rubberized surface of a waterproof flashlight.

'I have two,' she said, and passed him one. The light flashed on the wet walls like fairies in a play, dancing ahead of them.

Mae turned to her brother. She kissed his cheek. 'Thank you,' she said. 'Don't go down. Lower Street is lost. Go up to the Soongs', the Pings', and Mr Atakoloo. Yes?'

'My place is with you,' said Ju-mei.

'It has always been with me, brother. But it is also with your wife and neighbours. Please go?'

Ju-mei paused, and then, very deliberately, gave his sister a long, low bow of respect.

Then he turned, shouting, 'Go to Wing's, don't go on Lower Street!'

Mae shouted, for a Muerain could not lose dignity to that extent. 'Everyone up! The Flood is here! Everyone up!'

Mae and the Muerain fought the current back up the gap between the Haj and the Nan households. Overhead, the stars glinted with merriment, the hills roared, everything was comic. The little people were finally seeing who their master was.

The current on Upper Street had gained strength. It sounded now like a waterfall; the little lake had reached up into the house of Mr Ping, and its surface rippled as it sluiced its way out between houses.

The Muerain hoisted up his skirts to show long hairless legs. He reached back for Mae, and ran, holding up his skirts like a dancing showgirl. The stars laughed. Around their feet stones swirled like the shards of broken pots.

The Muerain ran up the cobbles of the bridge. Below, through the pursed lips of the bridge's arch, the river made a noise like a child blowing through its own spit. Mr Shenyalar and Mae cleared the top of the arch.

More like a stallion now, all in white, the Muerain plunged down into the cascades that swept around both sides of the Dohs' ancient house. His sandals were snatched away from him. The Muerain nipped and minced and hopped across the stones on tender feet. *Ouch ooch eek ouch.*

The stars clutched their sides, their tiny eyes narrowed, wet with tears of laughter.

Ahead of them was movement. Mae shone her torch.

Mr Ken was giving a piggyback ride as if at a party, Mrs Okan's arms around his neck. Mr Okan shuffled beside them, clinging to the edge of his wife's dress and murmuring to her.

Behind them came Sezen's two sisters; Edrem, carrying his youngest child; and Hatijah, who was carrying the goat. Its eyes were round and pink with terror.

The Muerain said, 'Hurry up to Kwan's. The bridge will not hold.'

'The current is terrible,' said Mr Ken. 'Mae, come with us.'

'Not yet.'

'Mae, do not be so foolish. Please!'

Mae said instead, 'Loan the Muerain your shoes.'

A moment's pause, the sense of it was seen, and Mr Ken kicked off his galoshes.

'Is your mother out?'

Kuei shook his head. 'My mother is packing!' The Muerain hopped on one leg, pulling on the shoe.

'Packing! Does she think it's a picnic?'

'I know!' Mr Ken began to run to gain momentum to get him and Mrs Okan up the steep slope of the bridge. 'I'll have to go back for her!' he shouted.

The goat blinked and kicked in Hatijah's arms. Mae and the Muerain ran.

They ran straight into the rusting bedding now washed into the roadway. Blindly they bobbed and bounded their way over the springs. On the moonlit hill, Sunni's house was dark.

Out onto the bare slope, all trails gone. The stars glistened on the sheen of water. Ahead of them the white walls of the mosque glowed.

They reached the door of the mosque. Mae waited, panting. The Muerain suddenly slapped his own forehead.

'I've left the key behind,' he said.

'You *what?*' Mae felt like the water – torn, broken, swept away.

The Muerain stood back, raised a leg, and kicked at the lock. He was tall, strong, a herdsman. With a splintering sound and a shuddering of wood, the door chuckled its way backwards.

The floor was flooded. He grasped the wooden railing of the prayer stall, splashed across the floor to a staircase, and ran up the steps to the tower. Mae ran after him. The flashlight licked hungrily over the back of the speaker down to the batteries. Mr Shenyalar bent and kissed the batteries, tasting them to see if they still worked. He flicked a switch; there was amplified crackling. He began, low and dark, to sing.

Mae grabbed his arm.

'Muerain. Please!'

The flashlight glared angrily at her.

'I'm sorry, Muerain-sir. But most people sleep through a call to prayer.'

Pause.

'They turn over in their beds.'

Pause.

And his voice, rich and deep, said, 'The Flood has come. For our sins, our godlessness, the Flood is upon us.' It was strange. Mae could hear his voice, which was so close to her, roll and fall away all across the valley.

Then he said, 'Follow the advice of Mrs Chung. Take food, take blankets, and go to Mr Wing's. Do not go on Lower Street. Already you will not get past. Go on Upper Street. Now. The Flood is here.'

He turned.

'You go,' the Muerain said.

She paused. Somehow she had pictured herself calling the faithful.

'You must go and wake people. I can stay here.'

'Not too long,' Mae warned him.

'I have a duty,' Mr Shenyalar said. 'Go.' He passed her back the second flashlight. She turned and the Muerain's voice ballooned out over the sound of the water. 'The Flood has come.'

Mae staggered down the steps and then had to lean over. Acids shot like venom up from her stomach and out of her mouth. The fumes were acrid; she had difficulty breathing. Her throat was raw and sore. She knelt down and scooped up some of the water and drank.

Where could she do the most good? Sezen would have roused the plain, the houses in the low south. It was Sunni who had farthest to go; she was high, but next to the river. She would need to go down to the bridge to cross. Mae looked across and saw Sunni's house, high and alone. She blinked, and thought she saw it move on its foundations.

So Mae ran to save Sunni.

The hill between the high mosque and the high house was no longer flowing with water. It was pouring mud; the mud stirred around her like porridge, but porridge with teeth, for it was also full of stone. I will have to give up soon, Mae thought, I will have to save myself.

Already.

Another voice spoke, unbidden:

The hillsides dissolve like sugar in tea. That undermines the terraces and they fall. The houses fill with mud or are crushed by stone.

Ahead, the river leapt up, white and snarling. The river had become a kind of dragon, rearing up over its banks, leaping, challenging, and opening its maw.

Mae thought of Sunni, of their delicate chats in the ice cream parlour, of adjusting each other's hair. The stones nibbled her ankles, the mud tugged playfully. A boot was pulled free from her foot. Mae forged on, against what was becoming a tide of mud.

Sunni's high stone front step was already an island. Mae pounded on the door. She shouted. The river was louder.

The door was not locked. Mae ran into the darkened house. It looked so calm and normal and safe, with its rack of kitchen pots and new pool table in the living room.

'Sunni! Sunni! Mr Haseem! Wake up!'

Mae ran up the stairs – narrow, steep, unfamiliar. She had never been upstairs. She bashed her head on a beam. There were many doors. Which one? She pushed her way into a bedroom full of snores and reeking of booze. Starlight through the window fell over the bed, making chessboard squares.

'Wake up, wake up!' Mae cried.

Sunni jerked and sat up and then wailed and covered herself with the bedding, her face full of fear.

'What are you doing here? Get out!' Sunni wailed.

Her husband snored, fully clothed, still in his boots.

'Sunni, the Flood is here.'

'Get out of my bedroom!'

'Sunni, please, just listen. The snow has melted. Listen to the river.'

'Madwoman!'

Sunni was in a rage. She tried turning on a light. Nothing, no power. She got up and threw on a robe and stormed towards Mae and pushed her. 'Madwoman, get out of here!'

Mae pushed her back.

'Ow!' shouted Sunni, scandalized. 'Husband, wake up, she will kill us both!'

'Stupid cow, I don't know why I bother with a woman with cowshit instead of brains!' Mae raged, and seized Sunni by the wrist and pulled her out of the room.

'Husband! I am assaulted. Help!'

Mae's strength surged out of panic and anger, and Sunni was dragged to a corridor window.

'There,' said Mae.

Outside, the river was full and white. It filled the gully; it was pouring all around the bridge. It hauled itself over the top walls of Lower Street and down, a waterfall now. Under the steaming moon, they saw the entire valley. It glittered like a sea.

'My God,' whispered Sunni.

'See! See!' raged Mae. 'Who is the madwoman now!'

'It's terrible.'

'You are nearly dead! The hill outside this house is moving, whole and entire.'

There was a sharp breath; Sunni spun into the dark, wisps of white twirling after her, and went back to her husband. 'Wake up! Wake up!' Sunni shook Mr Haseem's bright-red face by the ears. She looked back at Mae.

'I know him when he is like this. He won't wake up,' she said.

'Leave him,' said Mae.

'Oh, you would say that – you hate him.'

Mae limped forward. 'I don't, Sunni, but it is too late for all but final things. Do you want to die with him?'

Sunni looked at her, blankly.

'It's come to that. If he doesn't wake up now, you either love him enough to die with him, or you go with me now. *Now!*'

'You hear her? You hear her?' Sunni shouted. She slapped Faysal hard on the face. He snorted.

'Wake up!' She slapped him again. He turned over. Sunni said to Mae, 'Okay, let's go.'

Mae turned and clattered down the steps.

'Don't hit your head on the beam,' Sunni said. Too late. Mae's eyes watered a second time.

Sunni grasped two tins of food as she soared through the kitchen. Out into moonlight.

'Okay, we're together,' Sunni said. 'If one of us goes, the other tries to pull them free, but only for so long. We promise each other, ah. We save ourselves, but we try to help the first.'

'Right,' said Mae. 'But I'm going to Lower Street.'

'Madwoman!' said Sunni, again.

'I have to see if Siao has come back, if Mr Chung got out, if Sezen is okay!'

'Okay, but I'm not coming with you,' said Sunni.

'At last you are talking sense.'

'It will make a change, I admit,' said Sunni. The moving earth was unstable. Both of them fell into the mud. They thrashed their way to their feet, and held each other up.

'The flashlight!' said Sunni.

'I've got it, it's covered in mud.' Mae wiped it on her coat, and the light shone dimly again.

She pointed the light ahead.

On one side of the Dohs' house, the river had risen up. On the other, mud was mounting the back of the house like an unwanted lover. Mae and Sunni would have to cut down through the gap between the Dohs' and the Alis'. There was no other way down. Mud and water carried them down into Upper Street.

At some point the calling of the Muerain had fallen silent.

'Zeynap,' panted Sunni, thinking of her friend Zeynap Ali. They tumbled together onto the street. Mae shone the light. The doorway of the Alis' house was open.

'They're out,' said Mae.

From inside the house of the Dohs came yells and shouts. Mae cried, 'Dohs! I have a flashlight.' She ran. Inside the kitchen Young Miss Doh was flinging food into bags amid unwashed glasses and crumbs.

'Go upstairs, get my parents *down*!' Miss Doh raged – as if Mae were stupid, standing still.

Mae turned and ran up the stairs. In the upper corridor, Old Mrs Doh spun into the flashlight beam, waving her arms as if fighting cobwebs.

'This way!' said Mae.

'Who's that?' wailed Old Mrs Doh.

'Chung Mae.'

'What are you doing here?'

'Trying to help. These are the steps. Come on.'

Mrs Doh felt like a loose bunch of sticks in strong wind. She shook. 'What,' she said. Not even a question. Mae passed her to Sunni at the foot of the stairs.

'Here we are, dear,' said Sunni, as if it were a party.

Mae turned and ran through each of the rooms. She heard the river's roar. She heard a creaking, in the walls, in the wooden beams, and she felt the weight of the mud leaning against the house.

'This house is going to go!' she shouted to anyone who could hear her. She went from bedroom to bedroom. The good fairy of the flashlight blessed the walls of each room.

In the last of them, Old Mr Doh stood, sobbing. He was trying to button his shirt and could not.

Mae imitated Sunni. 'Oh, good Mr Doh. This is Mrs Chung. It's time to go.'

He flung off her hand, impatient, sobbing, still fighting his way into his best shirt.

'No, no,' she cooed, and laughed. 'You look wonderfully elegant. Come down now.'

'My wife,' he said, dazed.

'She's waiting.'

The whole house groaned and listed forward.

'Mae!' screamed Sunni, from the street outside.

Mae simply seized him and pulled.

'Oh, oh,' he said, fighting the dark. She hauled him towards the stairs. The walls suddenly snapped forward, leaning, dust puffing out where the floorboards joined them. Everything was looser underfoot. She pulled him down the stairs, he lost his footing, and they skidded together in the dark, slammed vengefully by gleeful wooden steps, until they both tumbled into the kitchen.

'Leave me!' he said. He started to fight Mae, the light careering over the walls. Someone entered, seized him, and pulled. Out they all went, clattering against chairs, slipping on oil spilled from bottles, as if all the contents of the house had been upended. In the street, the Dohs waited.

'I told you he was not outside,' raged Miss Doh, to the others. 'It took Chung Mae, as always.' Miss Doh pushed the old man, turned in the darkness, seized Mae, and pushed her tongue into Mae's mouth.

'In case one of us dies,' Miss Doh said, and darted back.

All the world was careering like the light; the stars themselves seemed to threaten to fall.

Over the sound of water Mae heard a grinding rumble. She turned and saw headlights trailing up the road. Against the lights she saw water gushing up against tyres.

Siao, she thought. That could be Siao.

'You go on,' Mae said to Sunni.

'Where are you going, fool?'

'Back home.'

'Okay.' Sunni was suddenly in front of her. 'Mae. You were right,' she said. Mae began to move. Sunni gripped her. 'You heard me say that, didn't you? *You were right!*'

'Sunni! Yes. I heard. Go!'

'You go! And come back quickly!'

Nothing else was said.

Mae ran past the backs of the houses of the Hos, the Matbahsuluks and the Kemals. She held on to the corner of Mr Kemal's house to wrench herself around into Lower Street.

A sound like applause. If you hear it above you, you are dead.

This is it, Mae; one check on the house, and then you go yourself.

Her old house glowed white, like a cake under the stars. In front of it rested one of Mr Pin's old vans, empty and dark. The courtyard door was open. Mae ran in.

Her courtyard was knee-deep in mud.

'Siao? Siao?'

Mae shone the light. The door to the barn was shut firmly, mud already pushing against it. Across the surface of the mud, rivulets of water flowed. If there were no one here, she would run.

From inside Mr Ken's house someone wailed, 'I can't get out!' It was Old Mrs Ken.

Above them something hissed, like water on a skillet.

'The terraces are going!' Mae screeched. And she felt a *click*.

I have been here before, she thought.

Mrs Ken began to pound on the inside of the kitchen door, the weight of mud pushing it shut.

'The window. Break the window!' Mae called. She waded forward. Mud was a slow and heavy evil. It sucked at her feet, and held her back like glue. She could not advance. 'I can't get any closer.'

A chair was punched through the glass, which sparkled like snow, in the air on the liquid earth.

'Mae!' someone called, from by the courtyard gate. Mae turned and it was Kuei. He surged forward, pushing through the mud up to his waist. 'Mother! Mother!' He jerked, thrashed, tossed himself from side to side, rocking through the mud towards the broken window. Suddenly the mud heaved him forward and off his feet.

For the first time the thought came to Mae: We've left this too late. We could die.

A head, arms, then legs came through the kitchen window. 'Oh. Oh. Kuei! Help me out!'

The mud gripped Kuei and held him fast. His mother was out of reach.

'Kuei,' called another man. 'Walk on this board.'

Siao? Mae turned. Three men were carrying the lid from the coal-bunker.

There was Siao.

And there, helping him, was Joe. Joe! Where? How?

The three of them flung the broad plywood lid on top of the mud under the window.

'Jump down onto it. Maybe it will take your weight for long enough. Try to walk forward to us.'

'Mother,' Kuei said. 'Just fall forward. I'll catch you.'

Old Mrs Ken without another word pulled herself through the jagged window frame, and fell gently forward onto the raft. It listed down into the mud and she scuttled forward towards her son's hands. Kuei grabbed her and pulled her forward. Joe and Siao rocked forward and pulled as well. Kuei cradled his mother, who juddered out a single sob.

'Mae!' demanded Siao. 'What are you doing here!'

'Trying to find you!'

A current of mud pushed them back away from the gate, like some kind of living thing, a slug.

'How do we get out through this?' Joe despaired.

Mae remembered her washing line, strung across the courtyard. 'This way,' she said, flashing her good fairy light along the rope. Then she reached up and began to pull herself along it, through the mud.

Mr Ken said, 'Okay, Mama, pull, like Mae says.'

All of them seized the rope and pulled themselves forward. Mae turned at the gate, and shone the light on them.

There they were, her three men: her husband, her lover, and Siao. She looked at Siao's steady face. 'I got a message at the Teahouse,' he said. 'Joe had got to the Desiccated Village.'

Joe looked up at Mae, and then down, quickly, in shame.

Did Mae hear applause?

She turned to the open door, not daring to breathe, and looked behind.

There was a sound of delight – massed clapping from the eastern slope. The sound had a shape, a shape like a blade, sharp at one end, but widening behind. A wedge of the walls had fallen.

'That's it!' she keened, her voice box tight, wet.

Ssssh, said all the stones. They trickled like water, made a sound like water, were borne by it and their own weight down the hillside, one collapse knocking into the terrace below, catching it, knocking it free.

Mae fought her way to the street and, glinting in the moonlight, she saw it, a flow of rocks on the eastern side of the bowl.

A river of stone.

'Come on!' she screeched again.

She looked behind her wildly; Ken and Joe were up to their ankles, and pulling Mrs Ken free.

Mae fought forward and pulled.

Then the applause started on the hill directly above them.

It was so slow, the fall of stone. Above them on the hill, a terrace wall turned sideways, grumpily, forced to move by the weight of stone settling on top of it. All of it slumped forward towards the school, to Sezen's.

They would not be able to get back to Upper Street.

'We've got to go this way,' said Mae.

They all ran. Mae shone the light. Doors left open, doors closed, Mae found she no longer cared who had managed to escape. As if something were jamming needles into her ears, there was a terrible sensation, a shivering in the air, in the earth itself, that was not quite a noise. It was something inside her head.

There was another sigh, in front of them this time. The hills groaned with relief, as if finally able to let loose their bladders and bowels. Three houses only, and they would come to the square.

The beam of light teased them, showing them glimpses of the flood. The square had indeed gone. Most of the Kosals' house had collapsed. The western corner of it still stood, but the rest was spread as rubble across the new lake. A chair stood on the stone. Beyond the rubble, the river roared.

'We can't get across,' said Mr Ken.

'We could try climbing the rubble,' Joe said.

'Just beyond it would be the gully. We would just disappear into it.'

'Let's go back,' Old Mrs Ken pleaded.

'The house will be buried,' said Mae.

There was grinding, as if the sky itself were being milled, as if the hill were peppercorns – and in the light of the moon and stars they saw the bridge above them come away from its foundations.

The bridge heaved up and shrugged forward and skidded down the slope with a fall of earth and stone, down from Upper Street. There was an explosion of water, great white shooting jets of it. Wooden beams spun upwards into the air. A tangle of roots rose up, snagged itself, whiplashed down. The One Tree had fallen. The bridge moved down the hill. The bridge settled, still upright, leading nowhere.

Another crash spread out just above them. The Dohs' house would have finally gone.

One of her men jerked her. Which one? All of them moved into a veil of water. It pummelled their heads. It tried to drive them down onto the ruins of the Kosal house. They had to climb up a broken wall of stone. Someone reached down for her. She looked up into his face. It was Joe's face, looking worn, handsome, and sad. But not slow – fast, lean, and as awake as he had been when he was the leader of the young men. He hoisted her up.

First they climbed up the Tree. They walked along its ancient oaken trunk, all rough creases.

And then walked as if nothing were awry, across the old bridge. A waterfall thundered next to them, scented with earth and the mineral smell of freshly melted snow. A beautiful river huge and green washed under them and down onto a valley that was a sea. The Tuis' house stood above the water, its upper storeys only. Otherwise, the southern wing of the village was simply submerged. Kizuldah looked like a seaside town, as if it had always been that way, with a breakwater of stone.

Lower Street fell away below them to the west, and the hillside was flowing across it. Everything was moving: rocks, shrubs, earth, as if in migration. The earth looked like a herd of buffalo going to a lake to drink.

'Oh! Oh,' sobbed Mrs Ken. 'Everything's gone!'

They had to jump down from the bridge, twice the height of a man, into swiftly flowing water. The current slammed into Mae, taking her breath and her strength. One of her men caught her; she caught him; they both caught Mrs Ken and whoever was holding her. Together they pulled each other up onto the street that was gushing water, white rapids over the cobbles. Cobbles were solid underfoot.

They were going to live. They ran up the hill towards Kwan's.

24

Wing had his generator running.

The courtyard was full of light and people. The Haj, their pilgrim to Mecca, stood at the courtyard gate. He had crammed onto his head a funny hat with a teddy bear's face. Perhaps he wanted to cheer people up. He had a list.

'Chung Mae,' the Haj called out. People surged forward. 'Ho-ho! With all the Chungs – Old Mrs Ken and . . .' He paused, ballooning out his eyes. '. . . Mr Ken.' He coughed and then murmured, 'Quite a family group.'

Mrs Shenyalar threw a blanket around Mae's shoulders. 'Mrs Chung was first!' the Muerain's wife shouted to the villagers. 'She roused my husband!'

Sunni's mother, Old Mrs al Gama, took up Mae's hand. Sunni hugged Mae. 'Are you all right, darling?' Sunni asked.

Mae turned back around to the Haj. 'Mr Haj-sir. Where is Sezen? Miss Ozdemir – has she come in yet?'

The Haj kept smiling, but his eyes narrowed. He said nothing.

'Kwan has hot food for everyone.' Sunni was tugging at her shoulder.

'Haj? You have been keeping count? Who has come? Who has not?'

The Haj looked sweet, like a calf, and shrugged. He was blinking. 'So many have been saved,' he said, looking down at the list.

'Where is Sezen?'

The Haj sighed, and reached forward with his plump hands. 'She has not come here.'

'Who else?'

'The Shens, the Chus . . .'

Mae knew. 'The people in the south wash.'

The Haj shook his head. 'The Macks and Pins are all right.' He sighed. 'They believed you.'

Mae found she was weeping. 'Who else?'

Sunni stopped pulling, surrendered, and hugged her.

Mae asked, 'What about Han Kai-hui? Her daughter?'

The Haj simply shook his head and said, '*Inshallah.*'

'Almost everyone else is all right,' said Sunni. 'You did everything.'

Mae let herself be led through the throng. All the Soongs had survived and were huddled in one corner of the court. The cluster of grandchildren played with toys. Mr and Mrs Okan shuffled up to Mae and showered her with thanks.

Sezen was gone. She had died saving An, the traitor. Han An, the last person in the world you could have seen Sezen giving her life for. Mae thought of An and their clipboards. Mae remembered Kai-hui's face when they were little girls, both poor, catching turtles in the reeds.

From somewhere there came a sound like thunder or fireworks, a crackling and a boom. Someone's house had fallen. Involuntarily, the villagers groaned.

Some of the Dohs surged around Mae now, and took hold of her hand. They were thanking her. Was their house still standing?

'Have you seen Mr and Mrs Ozdemir?' Mae managed to ask. Mrs Doh stared back at her, as if she was far too important to know or care about sharecroppers.

'Wild girl,' said Mae, and suddenly her legs left her.

Mae slumped down onto the ground. Siao, Joe, and Ken Kuei were ranged all around her and that was too much as well. Her brain buzzed.

Someone else was using her mouth.

We all go, we are all washed away, down into the dark, and no one will find us ever again.

Sunni was making Mae sit up. 'Sezen is probably cut off some-where, Mae. You know Sezen: She'll come roaring up here tomorrow on her boyfriend's motorcycle.'

Indeed, it would be just like Sezen. Mae tried to smile. Joe and Ken between them helped her to her feet. Her shins were numb.

Somehow she was on the stone staircase, being led down into Kwan's kitchen. All around them, the noise of the flood was gently falling asleep. Sssh, the waters seemed to say, sssh, the worst is over. The wound is lanced, the pus is draining. Sssh little ones, sleep.

In the kitchen, everything was feverish: the single orange light, the heat of the stoves, the bustling women.

Something bony and hard flung itself around Mae's neck. Mae

burped vile juices into her mouth and felt only elbows. Kwan, desperate, clung to her. Kwan leaned back, looked at Mae, and her lower face crumpled.

Mae felt nothing. Who was this person?

Kwan took her hand and led her to a table. Mrs Pin leapt up, and with a kind of whirligig speed, spun bowls and village bread onto the table in front of Mae.

Wing and Mr Atakoloo looked up from their food. Both bowed deeply and in silence. Mrs Pin ladled soup into Mae's bowl. Mae picked up the spoon, and found it was too heavy to lift.

She collapsed into tears and lowered the spoon and sat helplessly. Kwan crowded in next to her and Mae gave her an angry shove.

'I tried to tell you!' Mae shouted at Kwan. 'No one believed me. No one did anything!'

The kitchen fell into an embarrassed silence. From outside came the rushing sound of water.

Kwan, Wing, Sunni, Young Mrs Doh – all stared at her with those same round, helpless eyes. What were they waiting for? For her to say: I forgive you?

'That's all I have to say,' she told them abruptly. She tore at a newly moistened piece of village bread.

Mae found that the only person she cared about right now was Sezen. Not Joe, not Ken, not Ju-mei, not Kwan, none of them. It was a strange thing to discover. If she told the story of any of them, it would not move her. Only Sezen's life had a meaning. Sezen, who loved Air.

'Where is Mrs Ozdemir?' said Mae, very carefully, very angrily. 'That is what I have asked people. Sezen's mother. Or is she not important enough to be allowed into the kitchen?'

Kwan looked up, questioningly. 'In the courtyard somewhere?'

Without saying anything else, Mae stood up and walked.

'Mae?' someone called after her.

She broke into a run, fleeing from them. Leave me alone! She heard her feet on wet stone again, as if the Flood was still behind her.

The flood never goes away, it pushes – pushes, and washes all away.

Bunched up like a fist, Mae pushed her way unseen through people too concerned with their own loss. The sky was going silver. The rooster crowed on Kwan's barn roof.

Mae found Hatijah huddled in a corner of a barn in the dark. Her head was covered and she sat rocking slightly. She was singing in a wan, private voice.

'Mrs Ozdemir-ma'am? Hatijah?' Mae rubbed the woman's shoulder. The family goat was loose, rooting in hay. Edrem sat with his back towards everyone.

'Hatijah? Don't give up hope. Suppose she rescued all those people and got them up to high hills. What a heroine she will be, ah? Think how joyous we will all be when she comes back to us? Hatijah?'

The woman kept singing – a thin, wheedling, wordless lament. Hatijah stared unblinking and dry-eyed, ignoring the baby on her lap. Mae hugged the red shawl and thought of fleas and the stricken household and how Sezen had fought – fought everything. And she won. Sezen had won.

'Hatijah? Do you want to talk?'

Hatijah kept singing tunelessly, and rocking back and forth. The older daughter sat plucking her own shawl, scowling, ignored. The useless back of her useless husband was turned towards them.

'*Can* you talk?'

Nothing.

Edrem answered instead. 'We saved the *goat*.' He snarled the last word. His hands were over his eyes and he creaked like an old leather chair.

Born in poverty, die in poverty. Born in shit, die in shit, die without hope. Oh, but live in hope, oh yes, only to have those hopes broken, ground down. And for what? To want to slit the throat of a poor animal because it is alive and your daughter is not?

To break your back, weep into the earth, be beaten by the sun, and for what? For the sometime song of the nightingale? The once-a-year feast? The sometimes-full belly that is mostly empty? Love? When love is what makes it hurt when someone is destroyed?

Edrem began to sob – great, heaving, heartbroken, helpless, useless sobs. His skinny, bent body, his wide, flat shoulders swelled and shuddered. Mae hugged him too and smelled sweat, old hides, smoke, bread and yogurt. Like his wife, he was beyond being hugged.

Mae was useless too.

So Mae stood up and stepped back out into the last of the starlight, looking up at the stars, so perfect, so white, so cold. The Dragon's Breath was still blasting and hot. People still stood in silent circles, kicking the ground. The Haj was still at his post, trying to tell Dawn and her friends a story, but looking – looking as the sun rose, for anyone coming up the road.

The rooster cried, saying, *Work. Work should begin.*

Mae climbed up her friend's stone steps. The steps belonged to others as well, to a thousand years' worth of families. Mae's legs were made of bags of wet earth. Fire burned in her belly. Kwan sat exhausted on a chair in the diwan, hand buried in her hair. Kwan did not see her.

Mae climbed up farther.

Footsteps followed.

Mae turned and on the landing of the staircase, three men looked up at her. She pieced together who they were. Joe and Mr Ken were lined up side by side, as if for a firing squad. Behind was Siao. Siao's eyes were full, and full on Mae.

Beautiful men, so much alike really. Useless. Useless, their beautiful brown eyes, their fat male hands, their lean legs.

'Mae,' said one of them, 'Joe and I have been talking.'

'About the weather?' Mae asked with a crooked smile. 'Everyone talks about the weather.'

'We have decided not to fight,' said Joe. 'Mae. You are expecting a child?'

'It is expecting me,' she replied. She had to sit on the stairs.

Joe walked forward. Joe, she thought, you are beautiful again. Maybe you become beautiful when you are really needed. Maybe somewhere, you are always beautiful. Maybe if you had been born rich . . .

'I was the one who left,' said Joe. 'I will leave again.'

He leaned forward and kissed her. He took her face in his hands. 'My little Mae.'

His shoulders said: *You don't need an idiot like me. I have ruined everything. I lost my father's farm. I want to wander the earth in shame.*

'Don't feel useless, Joe,' Mae pleaded. 'We're all useless. We just do things and hope.'

'Lung thinks I'm a fool,' he murmured. 'I am a ghost here.'

The teenage boy had suddenly found cracks in his face. Who needs a teenage village hero in his fifties? What could he do? Nothing. Except to be someone's sharecropper.

'I could buy you some land,' Mae said.

Joe paused. 'I hate farming,' he said, smiling. 'I think I want to drive a truck.'

'So did I,' said Mr Ken, in recognition.

But you grew up, thought Mae.

So, I still love my husband. And I am going to let him go. She stood up.

Everything was very suddenly clear, as if washed clean by flood-water. She looked at her old husband, who was going away; and at faithful simple Mr Ken who had fathered her last-chance child; and at Siao, who was wise.

'I am going to live with Siao,' Mae announced. 'I'm sorry.'

Without a glance at Mr Ken, Mae climbed again. She remembered her first day at school, and seeing the older boys playing football. The captain of one of the teams stopped the game and began to fight. 'That is not fair,' he bellowed.

A little boy Mae's own age came up and stood beside her. He was the first child in the school to talk to her. 'That's my brother,' little Siao said proudly, quietly. 'Are you going to live here?' he asked.

'Until I'm grown up,' little Mae had answered.

Mae went into her old, high room, and there was the machine in front of the high window and she looked out over the courtyard. The sky over the broken roof and the bowl of the mountains was already blue-grey against silver. Somewhere farther down the valley, in the future, the sun was bright, but Kizuldah was still in shadow. The rooster was crowing over and over, having sensed at last that some-thing was wrong.

And there was her old friend, Kwan's TV.

'Chung Mae. Wake. Full audio and video, no queuing, sent in real time and saved to Bugs at Nouvelles. Also to Bedri at Metoff.'

A flick and buzz. The little seeing, detachable eye. Mae held it up in the palm of her hand.

'Hello, Bedri, hello, Bugsy, this is Chung Mae. There has been a flash flood. This is our village now at seven-fifteen A.M.'

The bowl of the shadowed mountain was no longer in orderly lines. White rocks were spread in wedge-shaped lines down the hillside. They rested at crazy angles like eggs in the mud. The treasured and nurtured earth had escaped, wasted itself in bursting down the hillside.

'It may not look too different to you,' said Mae. 'But yesterday it was covered in snow. There was snow on the high hills, and today, looking at the hills across the valley, there is no snow. That is the first time I have seen that.'

She swallowed. She traced the two parallel streets of Kizuldah with her eyes.

'It will not look different to you, but our stone bridge was washed away from Upper Street into Lower Street. I can remember . . .'

Mae had to break off, and swallow – she felt her eyes swell and heat up. But this was real time; she could not afford mistakes.

'I can remember when the Chinese engineers visited, to volunteer to make the bridge. They came with trowels and concrete because Kizuldah had none. We were too poor.'

Her voice, like a carpet, was worn thin. It straggled away like torn thread. Mae swallowed and continued.

'We loved the Chinese because they were told not to be snobbish, to mix in, and they did, and they worked hard, and they left that bridge behind. And those of us here who are Chinese, thought of them every time we walked across it. The big handsome men, the happy women, who lived in our homes and praised the food. How we all admired them and their bridge. And see the house next to it? Oh!'

Mae had to stop again. She hauled back in moisture and sadness, for she had to keep talking.

'That was Mr and Mrs Kosal's house, but it was the house on the square, and on its benches we spent our lives sitting. Old men played dominoes, our Haj would talk about his travels, and Old Mrs Kosal, now gone, would come out and give the children bonbons. In the square we had the harvest. We would pile up the hessian sacks full of rice, and build bonfires for barbecues. Year on year we would lay out rugs and hire a band, and all of us – the old women, the boys, the little girls – danced and ate our fill of roast and yams and new rice. We sat under the tree. We called it the One Tree. It had been planted there so long ago and was big and huge; it was like a friend, it was like all our fathers taken root. And it's been washed away. It had a swing on it, and all the children – the children of the 1950s, and the 1960s and '70s, '80s, '90s – all of us swung on that swing. So high, so hard, I think some of us must have tossed our spirits into the air. And they are still in the air. The spirits of the children, playing.'

Mae had to wring the moisture out of her eyes.

'The gully is where we kept our ducks and geese. Maybe some of those lived. And the house that has fallen across Upper Street, that was my friends' house, the Dohs' house, and they have lived there for one thousand years. The Dohs were Chinese warriors who stayed, and the house is older than the One Tree. And just above it, that was our new mosque. Every morning our Muerain would sing, and he sang so considerately in the early morning – soft and low and sad, as if he was sorry to wake us, wanted to let us sleep, sorry that we would have to wake up to empty bellies, or cold, or scorching sun. We all built the mosque. We all paid for it, even those of us who were not Muslim, and all the children ran to help with hammers, and the dogs barked, like when the trucks come to take the harvest.'

Mae broke down. She couldn't speak. Her face was not her own. It was like the laundry she saw in Old Mrs Tung's hands, wrung clean.

She wiped her face and her mouth, and swallowed and kept on.

'That's the roof of the mosque in what is left of Mr and Mrs Ali's house. They are a fine old couple, of our Party of Progress. And there is the Okan house; they are as old as the hills. And I am so happy, because their house is whole, it isn't touched, and all the circular rugs that Mrs Okan weaves herself, with old hands, over candles at night, they will have survived. We can wash them. We can wash them and put them on her floors and it will all be as it was. And next . . . next to them.'

Mae drew a breath and grew grim. 'Next to that is the house of my dear friend Mrs Ozdemir. You cannot see it. But I can. I can see it as if it had never left, was still there, as if a girl called Sezen still drew at a table, and still fumed at her mother, for being sad and frightened, as if it were still full of corncobs that the family used as furniture because they were too poor to have anything else, with beautiful naked babes and words from the Koran written in crayon on the walls. I can still see it, but that girl died, and they have lost their home. But Mrs Ozdemir's heart is broken and so is her head, and she just sits and rocks and weeps.

'And there is my house, too.

'My house in many ways, because it was my husband's house, and in that house I gave birth to three children. One whole side of it is gone. I can see inside it; it's so familiar, even flooded with sunlight, my bed, and my kitchen. I think I see my own TV in part of the loft, sunning itself. But the barn is full of mud, so I think my beautiful weaving machine will be gone.

'But look at the beautiful new sea. Look at it sparkle. Look how full of hope it seems; look, it has seagulls, who could hate such a beautiful sea? Even if it covers houses – houses where you played as children –

even if dear friends are trapped inside, their mouths full of mud. Even landscapes die, and give birth to new ones.

'And here comes the sun.

'See it? It is creeping over the hills, and the terraces, and the terraces are gone. Every spring after harvest, up we all would go, men and women and children with levers and stakes and hammers and pulleys, and all of us, even the ones who hated each other, would stand together and pull up the rocks and hammer in the stakes, to repair the terraces, to hold the earth.

'And that earth, what it did not contain? Our blood and sweat, our shit, our stillborn babies, anything to make it rich and keep it rich. What you see spilled is not mud. It is our blood, our blood of two thousand years – that is why it is so red, and that is why it seems to me that the earth screams. For it is lost now, like a beautiful child that bursts free into danger. It will be washed away, washed away down into the valley, and so much of what we are, will go with it.'

The corner of the room was dark, and Mae was swaying, and the constant fire in her belly gnawed at her. She saw the school high on the hill swamped with mud.

She saw its open door.

Farther down the hill, stumbling over the ruin of Mrs Doh's house, she saw people walking.

'It's Shen!' Mae shouted. 'Oh, the people you see walking – see, that is our Schoolteacher, Mr Shen! We thought he was dead, surely – look at the wreck of our school – but look, he is there. Oh, tell the Haj, tell our pilgrim, that one more of us has lived, and lovely Suloi, she lives, too – beautiful Suloi and her daughters!'

Shen shambled as he walked, everything shaking: legs, arms. But his head was held erect, stupidly high, dumbly proud, as if he had been proved right, as if he had defeated history.

The littlest child – too young to understand, except to wonder – her mouth was open. In the beautiful sunlight, she held out her arms and began to spin.

'She dances,' whispered Mae. 'The daughter dances.'

Mae turned to tell someone that Shen lived. She turned and saw that crowded and silent in the doorway were Kwan and Wing and Sunni and Kuei and Joe and Mr Pin and Mr Ali and others looking over their shoulders.

The room was going darker. Mae heard the sound of children

playing in a courtyard. She heard the Muerain, year on year, and the harvest festival and the winter party, and the spring replanting with its songs, and the late-night barking of the drowned dogs.

That's when it came into the room. Mae had seen it before: something dark and whole, something like a dog, loyal in a sense, patient, waiting. Except that it meant the end of everything she had known and loved. The black dog settled in the corner and licked its chops.

Mae sat back onto the bed. She dropped the camera. Kwan walked forward and picked it up.

'The road has been completely washed away,' Kwan said, to the machine. 'We are cut off and have only limited supplies of food.'

'Wait. Look,' said a handsome man Mae once had known.

There was a sound like sheets in the wind, clean sheets being shaken.

'It's a helicopter.' The handsome man spun in joy. 'They have already sent a helicopter!'

'Mae, did you send a message last night?'

'*Blurpble ah*,' said Mae. She was not well.

Mr Ali came forward with his hat, and Mr Atakoloo and even Mr Masud.

'So,' said Mr Ali. 'You will have to teach us all now, Mae – all how to use it.'

'We will need it,' said Mr Atakoloo. He tried to smile.

But everything was slipping into darkness, closing down. Someone else was dancing.

Old Mrs Tung won.

25

Progress passed into the hands of the habitual leaders of the village: the Wings, the Muerain, and Mr Atakoloo.
They set about rebuilding Kizuldah. As a blacksmith, Mr Atakoloo was disposed to building shelters of prefabricated metal. Mr Wing knew stone was best. Stone would hold warmth.

'It takes too long to build!' Mr Atakoloo protested, gesturing, puffing out his handsome white moustache.

'If you only have two or three people building. We have one hundred men, with nothing to do.'

'*Tuh*. Most of them unskilled,' said Mr Atakoloo, brushing flakes of village bread into his cupped palm.

In the end, they had to build with both metal and stone. The cold came back. Ruined houses like the Dohs' or Mae's had small shelters built against whatever walls were still sound. For this, the stones of the ruined terraces and houses served better than tidy sheets of aluminum. The men and the women carried rocks, in wheelbarrows or in gloved hands. The aluminum sheets formed the roofs. Concrete was poured on top of that to stop them radiating out all the warmth of the fires.

Fifteen families had bought Mr Wang's insurance. Ju-mei, his city clothes gone in the Flood, made a point of giving them their cash himself. He passed them wads of bills to replace their houses, folds, and flocks. They gaped at him in wonder.

So it was that Mae's computer was seen even to provide money. The village people were related to each other and showed solidarity. They shared their payouts, and so the village had money to restore itself.

The TV brought other things. News, for example, that the Office of Discipline and Education had reinstated Shen in his job. The e-mail wished him a productive partnership with Mrs Chung. The Office seemed unaware that there had been a flood.

People temporarily shared their houses. The Kemals and the Ozdemirs found shelter in Ju-mei's house. Mr Wing put up the whole tribe of Pins. The Alis stayed with the Haseems in what was left of their house.

Faysal Haseem had awakened late on the day after New Year, to find much of his house missing. It looked, he said, rather like his own skull felt, broken open and washed away. His garage, his white van, all his tools were gone! He thought there had been thieves. He thought that Chung Mae had finally gone crazy and driven a tractor into his house. It had its funny side, waking up hungover, having slept through disaster. He had to laugh. He told the story over and over. He did not look at his wife as he laughed. Sunni looked down at her hands.

Food was dropped from the air: bags of flour or rice, paid for partly by money donated by the Nouvelles magpie. On cold, clear days, the village could hear the rumble of machinery, up from the valley. The road to their village was being repaired.

Kwan thanked Bugsy, thanked the world. She still had requests by voicemail for Mae's last narrowcast. Kwan always referred to the Nouvelles address. She could not bear to listen to it herself.

At times Kwan stood looking out of that same window, to see how the village was healing, and to think of Mae.

The wind had a different sound now. Kwan was sure she was not making that up. Some of the wind spirits had left them: The invader wind had frightened them away. Some of the spirits would never come back; the air itself would sound forever different.

That, at least, is what her mother would have said. Her mother, Mrs Kowoloia, would have said many things.

Kwan's mother would have said, There are four principal spirits, called Earth, Air, Water, and Fire. In times of change they become unbalanced. The Eloi despised the Chinese with their paltry system of opposition: yin and yang. The Eloi had layers of struggle and synthesis.

Earth was female and solid, and nourishing and dark and fertile as the womb. It was the lowest layer.

Water was the force of time that carried everything forward. It flowed, making the earth turn, the air spin. Water was the engine of the world. Water was change.

Air was the spirit, high in heaven. Between Earth and Air was Fire.

Fire was people. Fire was their desires, the things that made them move. Fire and Water were change; Air and Earth were what continued.

Oh, Mrs Kowoloia would have had no trouble telling them what had happened. Air had usurped the place of time and desire. The world of the spirits had come to earth, like ghosts, and the fire-demon Erjdha had blown across the hills.

Old Mrs Kowoloia would have had no difficulty knowing what Chung Mae was, either.

Some people bore the weight of the world. It was not their fault. They could not be blamed. Air and Fire and Earth and Water churned within them exactly as they churned without. They did extraordinary things and were to be avoided, for they were maelstroms; and they were to be watched, for whatever happened to them, happened to the world.

Such people became oracles to be read like yarrow stalks.

So Kwan would sit and ponder the meaning of the oracle.

What the oracle told her was simple and final, and all that Mae had been saying since the beginning.

Their old and beloved world had died. It was right to mourn it. But they could not resist the movement, either. Water, spurred by Air, had changed its course. Water was time. Time had moved, very swiftly, and so must they.

And Old Mrs Kowoloia, long since burned by funeral fire to join the world of the spirits, would also say: Do not fear for your friend. The Water in Mae has responded to the usurping Air. The Water has swept her away.

Mae lives in the future.

Thinking this, looking out over their darkened village, Kwan let hot water fall from her eyes. And her mother would have said to Kwan: Cry, daughter. Tears are good for people who grieve. Tears are time. The tears help bear you away beyond the time of grief.

Why does it work, Mother? This old stuff. Why does it work? When you tell me it is dead. Why does it help me understand?

Kwan had wanted her son to be modern and scientific. The Eloi had to be, to live in this world, and to fight the Karz if the time ever came again. But her son knew none of his people's wisdom. And he would go away, like Mae's son did, and come back a stranger.

Look to oracles, they live out the future.

Kwan wiped her eyes and went down to the diwan, still crowded with people. Her son's name was Luk. He was big, quiet, kind, and part of a group, not its leader. Was now the time? She saw his face. It was a university face; he might not become a soldier. He could become something even worse than a soldier.

See the water? See the tears? See the candle burning in our little boat of wishes? He is going away, daughter. This is his last winter in Kizuldah.

So Kwan made herself smile, and collected the stone mugs and murmured to friends, not wanting to disturb their viewing.

They were watching a programme about Mat Unrolling.

Kwan was glad to see Suloi there. Suloi would understand. Two Eloi sets of eyes caught each other's glances.

Kwan said, 'Remember Mae? She talked about her Mat all the time.'

Very solemnly, Suloi nodded downward, once – yes. *Mae was our oracle.*

Kwan came to Luk. 'Son? When this is through, could you and I go for a walk?'

He glanced at his friends, two of the Pin brothers, all bucktoothed and sweet. Kwan was glad he had such good friends.

It was unusual for her to ask. He looked at his friends and said, 'I can go now if you like.' Mat Unrolling bored him, maybe.

Kwan was careful not to tell him how to dress; he did not want to hear his mother telling him to bundle up. And she promised herself as she slipped on boots that she would not let her worries run away with the night. She would not worrit him about studying, about not spending, about writing her. Nothing he could do would fill the gap that would be left behind when he went. Nothing she could do would make his life better if he failed to fly by himself.

We must meet as equals, she thought.

So they trudged out together, and her son had bundled himself up in sheepskin coat, scarf, and gloves, almost too carefully.

And this made Kwan think: Where is the swagger in him? Is Luk a bit too quiet, even a bit dull?

Don't worrit, Kwan.

They walked out into the courtyard.

Kwan asked her son, 'What do you make of Chung Mae?'

That surprised him. If he had been dreading a motherly discussion, that would have reassured him.

'I don't really know,' Luk said, finally. 'She is your good friend. I'm sorry she is not well.'

'That's what I think, too, of course. But what do you think she is?'

Luk looked back at her askance. Was this a trick question? Adults asked questions when they knew the answers.

Kwan did not want to play a guessing game. 'The Eloi in me thinks she is something very mysterious.' Kwan found herself smiling and wiggling her eyebrows, almost making fun of it. They both stood in the courtyard light.

Luk grinned. He understood. 'She is a bit spooky,' he said.

'Your grandmother would have said she was *oiya*,' said Kwan. 'That means "disturbed," which means the elements are out of balance.'

'Many people would have called her disturbed,' said Luk. 'Only, she turned out to be right.'

Kwan stepped out of the courtyard, and began to walk out of the village, up the hill. It was so cold that the stars seemed to be made of frost – as if her own wreathing, white breath blew up into heaven to freeze there. Stars and breath, it's too big, she thought. You can't cram all of the Eloi world into someone all at once.

'The Elois said that stars are solid places in the air, for spirits to rest,' she said. 'They are like frozen air.'

'Well, they're fire instead,' said Luk.

'Do you ever think about the Elois?' she asked him.

She could hear his sheepskin shrug. 'Only that I am part Eloi. My first name is Eloi – I think. It doesn't seem to make any difference in the way people treat me.'

'You don't have any sudden urges to stand up and herd sheep on the high hills?'

She heard the rustle of a smile. 'No. No urge to tattoo my legs, either.'

'You should try it, it looks beautiful.'

'Ah, but my legs are just a bit too hairy for it.' He was joking, but it was also the truth. His legs were Chinese.

'And they don't allow tattoos in the military.'

He sighed. 'Well. That might be a good reason to get one, then.' Then he said, 'Okay. Tell me about the Eloi.'

The air was still.

'You really want to know?'

'Not as much as you want to tell me. But I don't know it.'

Good, said the stars.

'Okay. I'll talk. But if a nightjar churrs, we have to go back inside, because birds can talk to the air. If a nightjar calls, it is warning you.'

'About what?'

'That you are betraying the secrets of the spirits. Or that the spirit inside the body you are talking to is not ready yet. Things like that.'

'Mom. You don't really believe this, do you?'

Kwan had to consider. 'Not really. Not with the top part of my head. But, this old stuff – it produces the right words. You just say what the old people would have said, and something is explained. Somehow it's all easier to bear.'

Even now, down the hillside, water trickled.

Luk spoke next: 'There's something about Earth resting underneath, and being the foundation. And Air on top, with Fire and Water as the filling in the sandwich.'

'Yes, but I think those are the wrong words.'

'Ah. I am a modern fellow,' he said.

Kwan said. 'There are two kinds of time. There is time in motion, measured by clocks, and there is "the Time." The Time is the situation you live in. You make it, the world makes it, most of the time it is like a punch you roll with. You make your choices, and do not resent them, and wait for the season to pass. And the season is made of the four elements, all of which have characteristics, powers. They all kind of swirl together.'

Those are the wrong words, too, Kwan.

O, Mother Kowoloia, O spirits of the Air, the Water, the Earth, speak for me.

The nightjar also churrs when you are not ready to speak. It sleeps in the road, dazzled by headlights, only because the asphalt is still warm.

'In Mae, all these forces are gathered together. So Mae is the Time. Do you understand? Mae is like a picture of the Time. Your grandmother would say that Mae has solidified the Time, like water solidifies into ice. And ice breaks – when the season begins to move. You see?'

Not yet. Luk waited.

Kwan continued: 'So Mae is the Earth, like women are – she derives her power from women, from the Circle, from Bugsy. You see how it works? The old words? So, you have Mae, who is in her character most like the Earth, she is an Earth person: rooted, least-moving of all people. But her head – her head has been filled with Air; this is the Age of Air. And so she is disturbed. Spirit mixing with Earth, swept away by the enraged waters, which are change, which drive change.'

Luk said, 'Mae is Earth moved by Air and moved by Water.'

'Yes!' Kwan was pleased. Luk understood.

'What is the fire?'

She still remembered him at five, all innocent toddling nakedness. She remembered him at sixteen, how soft and troubled he looked back when Tsang had been seducing him.

'Don't you know?' She prodded him. 'Think. You know. She is disturbance – so what was disturbed?'

Luk was embarrassed. 'Ah. Well. Her husband and things . . .'

'Fire is desire, and Fire flared up. Your grandmother would have said that was only to be expected, too. But Fire is not just sex, it is yearning, for everything, here, now, on Earth. It makes us have children, it makes us love them, love our friends. Water carries us, but Fire makes us swim.'

There were the stars of fire.

Rather clumsily, her huge son put a sheepskin-muffled arm around her shoulders. She felt how small and frail she must seem to him.

She pointed to the stars. 'You see? In the world of the Air, there is no time. Even Fire is still. Fire becomes permanent.'

Why was she crying? 'Fire becomes love. In Air.'

He stood beside her and she was not sure what he felt.

'You see? You see? You see?' Even to herself, Kwan sounded like a bird.

In March the road was finished, and in one of the first cars up, it carried Fatimah from Yeshiboz Sistemlar.

Fatimah asked where Mae was. Sunni and Kwan greeted her with firm smiles.

'Mae is gone away,' said Kwan.

Fatimah looked suspicious and disappointed. Kwan had been her ally.

'Where? May I see her?'

'Oh, I think not,' said Sunni.

'No,' said Kwan, shaking her head. 'No. She went up into the hills, to live with an old aunt. She takes care of her now.'

'Yes,' said Sunni. 'How lucky is the woman who has family. We did not even know the aunt existed.'

'Where is the village?' Fatimah nodded, vaguely uphill.

'There is no road,' said Kwan.

Fatimah stood just outside the interior of the car, the door open between her and the villagers. Above her, the ruin of terraces was a jumble of stones.

'I feel it is only polite to point out,' said Sunni, 'that for you, there will never be a road.'

Fatimah's face went pale, and worked in helplessness. She got back into the car.

The Circle's weaving machine was replaced by insurance money. There was a celebration when it arrived. The Nouvelles Chung Mae Fund had ordered over four thousand collars, enough to keep even the machine busy. Each Disaster Collar had IN HONOR OF CHUNG MAE woven into it. Inside the package, in English, was the recipe for a thank-you cake. The huge sums of money from the sale were distributed to those outside the Circle as well as those within.

The men repaired some of the terraces, only a few, enough to plant some rice, enough to feed the village and generate some more grain.

A hired bulldozer came and scooped up the last of the ruins of the Chu, Koi, and Han households. Rugs, cups, clothing, came to the surface, but not the missing bodies.

Finally, halfway down the plain, they found a body which must have been Han Kai-hui. Sezen, Kwan decided, had been carried by the Flood even farther into the future than Mae. She would never be found, except perhaps in a spaceship going to the moon.

High on the hill where their mosque had been, the villagers gathered for another funeral.

And Chung Mae was brought out for it.

Chung Siao came with her, holding her hand, keeping her quiet. And on her other side stood Mr Ken.

'Who is it? Who is it?' Mae demanded, too loudly.

'Han Kai-hui, Granny,' Mr Ken said to her. 'You remember her. She was Chung Mae's little childhood friend.'

Mae's face looked angry. 'She must have died very suddenly! Was it an accident?'

Pause. 'Yes, Granny,' said Ken.

Mr Ken struggled to keep the fighting hands still. His face looked worn but enduring. How can he stand it? Kwan wondered.

'Oh! People should be more careful!' Mae flung the news away with a toss of her head. Old Mrs Tung could not learn. She looked around the crowd, outraged, like an angry lizard. 'And children should show respect! Where is Han An, at her own mother's funeral? Where is Chung Mae, if it is her friend? Mae should be here!'

This was beginning to look like a mistake. Kwan moved through the village crowd. They stood in their anoraks or sheepskins, all heads bundled in scarves. The fire was mostly broken furniture and kerosene, with a rug wrapped around the body.

Maybe Kuei can bear it for the sake of his child inside her.

Maybe he can bear it because he shares it with Siao. It is strange, the two of them and her. Who can say how they make it work?

Except through love. Fire in Air.

Kwan nodded to them both, eyes catching. Then she looked deep inside the eyes of the woman beside them who was no longer Chung Mae.

Kwan denounced her. 'You horrible old woman. You are dead, too. You died, you horrible ghost. We loved you in life, but you should be a spirit now, in the air. You are a disease. At least let Mae mourn her friend.'

The eyes went confused and watery, the young mouth shook like an old one. For just a moment, Kwan thought she saw Mae.

'Mae. We're winning. Everyone uses the TV. We love it. Mae, we want you back.'

'Uh!' said the struggling Mrs Tung, and pushed Kwan away from her.

Kwan saw struggle in the helpless confusion of the face, the shuddering and the shaking.

'She's fighting, she's there,' said Kwan. She took hold of the hand and kept talking to her. 'Come on, Mae. You can come back. The old witch only has part of your soul. You have the rest. Come back, Mae!'

Kwan visited Mae most days.
Siao and Ken Kuei lived together with Mae in the ruin of their houses. The village had decided not to regard this as a scandal. Both men loved her; of course they would stay with her in misfortune.

Only the barn and the back corner of the house still stood. The wound had a scar of piled stones over it, bandaged with plastic.

Daylight peeked through, but the room was warm. There was room for the brazier and the table, and the alcove with the bed. Part of the loft remained, but was unused.

Kwan would duck through the low doorway and bow with respect to Old Mr Chung, who sat in the only standing corner of his old house. Kwan would lay food on the table – village bread, a few dried vegetables, and at times even a bottle of rice wine saved from the Flood.

Siao and Mr Ken would both then busy themselves with the cooking. Politely, they would pass each other the knife, the soy. Kwan had once asked Ken Kuei how it was, all three of them living together. 'Oh,' he said. 'There is no problem. I have lived next to Chung Siao all my life. We have always been friends.'

Kwan felt a quiet pride. Such behaviour is only possible, she thought, among a truly civilized people.

It was best for Mae to sleep in her own bed. It might help to bring her back. Certainly Old Mrs Tung did not like it. The old creature quailed, *Why are we in this place?* She was confronted with the fact that she did not belong.

The tiny bedroom alcove was kept as tidy as possible by Mr Ken. Old Mrs Tung would sit disgruntled next to the tiny window. She kept turning out the electric lights; she hated them. She lit candles. Mr Ken put them out. Candles in such a crowded space were dangerous.

'Hello, Siao,' said Kwan. 'Is she eating?'

He shook his head no: *No, she is not.* 'She says her tummy burns.'

Her stomach ballooned out just under the rib cage like a pigeon breast. You could tell just from looking at her shape that something was terribly wrong. Old Mrs Tung could learn nothing new, so she could not remember that she was pregnant or where the pregnancy was. She felt full so she never ate. Mae's starving face was becoming more and more delicate. Mae was beginning to look like Mrs Tung.

Kwan said, 'Mae's not fighting.'

Perhaps there is no more Mae left to fight.

'I found the onion in my old store. And Mrs Ozdemir, bless her, she still keeps giving me bits of her goat for Mae.'

It was smoked scrag-end. Siao went for the cleavers. 'The famous cleavers,' he said. He added the onion and curry powder to cover the taste of stale meat. They sat and talked of village things. The two men took turns to stir the fry up.

Kwan looked at Mae's beautiful old dresses hung in an orderly row. 'It's been a long year,' she said.

'Huh. More like a century,' said Kuei.

'Remember, last April? She was already beginning to talk to people about graduation dresses, showing them fabric, bustling about the place. She always wore high heels for that, remember?'

'Oh! Do I!' Kuei rolled his eyes, as if he had never seen anything as beautiful. 'With her hair always up. I would look out, and it was like a dream to see her, like someone from TV had dropped down by mistake into our village.'

Kwan smiled wryly. 'That was the effect she wanted.'

'She was a different Mae,' said Mr Ken.

Which Mae do you love? Kwan wondered.

Old Mrs Tung shifted with discomfort and frustration. 'Where is Mae?' she demanded. 'And, Kuei, why are we are we eating old goat? Can't you find anything better?'

Siao made a space near him for Mr Ken to moisten the bread. In the corner, Mae's TV still received voicemail. Kwan considered. It is probably Siao, who loves the Mae she became – Unrolling Mats and TV screens.

'I will have to get back soon to the girls,' Mr Ken warned Siao. His daughters lived with their cousins at the Teahouse. Siao nodded. The two men were a household.

And, Kwan considered, it is probably Siao who keeps it together.

As soon as the shreds of goat were cooked, they offered the food. Kwan leaned forward. 'Mae? Mae, eat something, please.'

'I am not hungry,' said Old Mrs Tung. 'Kuei! Take me home. We have been here long enough. It is evident that Mae and Joe will not be back.'

'For your baby. You must eat,' said Kwan.

'What . . . what . . . what . . .' Mrs Tung shook her head no – no, over and over. 'What are you talking about?' Old Mrs Tung demanded. 'I don't want your food, woman! I want to go home. Why can't we go home?'

'Sssh, Granny,' said Kuei, coming from the stove.

'We have been here for hours!' Old Mrs Tung started to weep from frustration.

'Sssh, Granny. The house is gone; it was washed away in a Flood.'

'What?' Old Mrs Tung looked up in horror and her eyes shivered with all the despair of fresh discovery.

Old Mrs Tung could only live in the past.

Mae lived, fascinated, in air.
Air was real life – all of life all at once, for it made all times one time. For Mae, time was a breakfast table, with everything in reach. She would stretch across eternity and feel herself expand, out of Air and into any moment of her life.

Mae would walk to school hand in hand with her brother Ju-mei. She threw acorns at him, and they ran, laughing, round and round the One Tree.

Joe took her on a date, down the hill to Kurulmushkoy. The Teahouse there catered to young people and had a radio.

Dazzled, at sixteen, Mae sits in a booth and listens to U2. It is only two years since the Communists have gone; there is all this new stuff. Joe seems to be king of it.

'U2 are from Ir Lang Do. They are not English, not American. They had a big event, all the big stars sang for poor people. It went round the world. Yah.' Joe looked into his tea. His hair is buzzed short, he wears a chrome necklace. Joe is the future. His eyes are sad. 'We missed it.'

Mae is entranced. She is moved. 'We will not miss it next time, Joe,' she says. She ventures forth, and puts her hand on top of his. This is simply because she finds she feels the same. 'Next time, we will be part of the future.'

'We can bet on that,' he says, and pushes his hand into his tight jeans and pulls out a quarter-riel. He slams it on the table.

'It is a wager!' Mae giggles, at sixteen, and covers her teeth with her hands because she thinks they are huge and make her look like a horse. But her eyes are fixed on Joe.

And then this time shrinks and folds down into itself. It is the room and the people and the smell of boiled water and cigarettes that collapses, not Mae herself. Mae is always there.

Mae can do frightening things. She balloons herself back into the womb before she was born. She can feel her mother's terror and misery seething around and inside her. She hears pumping and muffled voices. She sees gentle light. It is like dying, a gentle dying that is not fearful because you know that this is the beginning.

The unborn infant knows that too, connected in Air to its own future.

We live and we die in eternity. Our physical bodies occupy the balloon world. The balloon world has space, and we are trapped in one part of it. The balloon expands and we are trapped with that expansion. And that is time.

But, oh, in Air!

Air has no time.

Air is everything that has been and will be, waiting its turn to puff out of its tiny dot into our brief world.

And Mae's life is hinged with that of another.

It is the first day of autumn school and Mrs Kowoloia comes with her little daughter Kwan.

Mrs Tung thinks: My, but the child is solemn. And Mrs Kowoloia, oh, she is so beautiful, ethereal. She floats – and all that embroidery!

'Mrs Kowoloia, you are as beautiful as the butterfly!' hoots Mrs Tung, seizing her client's hands with gratitude, for this is the first arrival of the school year. The courtyard will soon be full of children.

Mrs Kowoloia says, 'Mrs Tung, may I say what a benefit this is to all of us. To run a school for us year in and year out. And we all know of your education.'

'Ah! But all my books were lost,' hoots Mrs Tung, holding up her hands and laughing for the dead.

The little girl looks seriously ready for work and disgruntled that there is none to do.

'Kwan, dear, I have some paper and paints.'

Kwan wrinkles her nose. 'It's all right,' says Kwan. 'I'll read my book.'

Every time the boys play football together in the white dust of my courtyard, I say, 'Ahmet would have played with them.' When all the little girls sing or skip rope, I close my eyes and imagine I hear Lily chanting with them. My Lily, who I let fall and drown.

Two little girls slip through the gate all by themselves. One is tall and skinny, and angry. The other is tiny, so small that her chin hits her chest as she scowls.

I know who this is, thinks Mrs Tung, and she walks forward, bending at the middle.

'Are you the little girls who lost their daddy?' Mrs Tung asks.

The oldest looks at her with frightening directness. 'He was shot by Communists.'

'And what is your name?' Mrs Tung half hopes it will be Lily.

'I like to be called Missy,' says the elder. 'So that's what everybody calls me.' She looks down at her sister with a mother's pride. 'This is my sister, Mae,' she says, in a way that makes Mrs Tung want to weep, it is so full of love and care.

The little one is shy. She holds up an autumn leaf. 'It's red,' she says. 'I found it on the ground.'

'Leaves fall. That's because autumn is coming. I'm Mrs Tung.'

'It's beautiful. It looks like a cushion. All red.'

'Where is your mother?' Mrs Tung asks.

'Nowhere,' Missy says coolly.

Missy coughs, and from deep within her lungs comes the authentic crackle of TB. She coughs again, and passes Mae to Mrs Tung. 'Mae's clever,' says Missy. She ushers Mae forward, arm around her shoulder. Her solemn eyes meet Mrs Tung's. Mrs Tung feels a prickle up her spine, as if Missy is passing Mae to her, to care for.

Missy coughs again, Mrs Tung is sure.

Mrs Tung could taste Air.

'Come, Mae. We have another clever little girl for you to meet. Her name is Kwan.' Mrs Tung moves them forward together. The older one is lean and already grey as a ghost.

Mrs Tung gazes at the round face of the little girl and to her it is like an egg that will hatch. She can half see who this Mae will be – oh, clever, yes, but not in any way that school can capture. She will turn herself into Missy, to honour her and love her and remember her.

The children run around her, swirling like dust, and Mrs Tung can see them all hatching, into Shen, into Joe, into Kan-hui. It is her job to warm them, love them into life.

Mrs Tung sits in her big kitchen, darning wet socks.

You darn them wet so that they will dry and heal shut. Her smelly, kindly old husband is in the fields. Her young man is off in the hills. Mrs Tung feels heavy and weighted, as if going up a fast escalator. She is pregnant, and she knows the child is not Mr Tung's. She becomes aware that she is hearing gunfire. Has the war moved back here?

Suddenly, the guns batter so loudly that it is as if the guns are in the kitchen. Mrs Tung jumps. She hears a cry, from nowhere.

Then everything is still again, just dust turning in rays of light. Suddenly Mrs Tung is certain.

Kalaf is dead.

Something that was in the air is there no longer. Like music that is suddenly turned off. Like the sudden smell of burning food. He is dead, she thinks, and I will be getting a telegram.

She puts the sock down on the table, and ponders. It will not do for her husband to see any telegram about any man. She ponders a moment, and wonders why she is not crying when there is no doubt.

Mrs Tung goes up Lower Street to the Teahouse, and she slips sideways into the room with all the men and cigarette smoke. The men in cloth caps look up and glower. She is a woman, even if her head is covered. Only whores sit in cafes with men. Mrs Tung sits at a table and starts to darn socks. She focuses on the yarn and the thread. The morning passes. She nods yes to a glass of tea, but does not drink it.

Her cousin Mr Tui comes up and suggests she should leave. Mrs Tung just shakes her head, for she finds she does not trust herself to speak. She keeps her eyes on the socks.

Then the machine in the corner of the room chatters. Mrs Tung sees the shadow of Mr Tui turn away. Mrs Tung puts her hands in her lap and waits.

The shadow comes back. 'This is for you,' he says, leaning down, so that she has to see his walrus face looking sad.

'You should have said you were waiting,' says Mr Tui. Mrs Tung knows that if she speaks, she will start to weep. Cousin Tui stands up. 'She was waiting for this!' He shakes the telegram at the men at the bar.

He folds it flat and puts it in her limp and waiting hands.

Dear friend, beloved cousin Kalaf is dead.

'He was kind to me when I was young,' says Mrs Tung, and scrunches up the telegram as if it were her face. Her face becomes a rag to be wrung; she can feel water seeping. She stands up, and holds up, and swiftly strides out of the Teahouse. She keeps her head high, walks back home through the narrow corridor of houses, and cannot tell anyone that the father of her child is dead. She finally closes the door of the kitchen, and hides her face in her husband's wet socks.

Mrs Tung knew before she could have known.

Mrs Tung had been a traveller in Air. Before there was Air.

So Mae went to find her.

Mae went back to the day of the test.

Mae burgeoned back into her old life.

The cauldron is boiling; Joe has eaten his rice. Old Mrs Tung is led in, chuckling at herself. Kuei helps her, blind to his own future, as blind as this time-bound, work-bound Mae.

TO *Chung Mae Wang*

CERTIFICATE OF APPRECIATION FROM THE GRADUATING CLASS OF 2019

FOR FASHION STUDIES

And all around them are the magnetic fields, the arcs emanating from the fire in the heart of the earth – unnoticed and of no importance to Kizuldah for two thousand years.

Until now.

There is the flash and the buzz and the inflation of the mind. Every neural pathway is jolted at once.

A kind of Question Map of the self. Every question answered, complete.

Buzzed and jolted and in that moment stamped for ever on eternity, in Air. A complete, unchanging, unloving, unnatural Map.

And, oh, murmuring, here comes the Format.

Mae has to chuckle. It was such a cheap and tinny thing, the Format, like a child's plastic space-helmet clamped on the head. A few lines of code, a bit of information added to the mix.

'Chocolate. I smell chocolate,' coos Old Mrs Tung.

Here it comes, thinks Mae-in-Air, *here it comes*.

The cauldron is knocked, and topples. It will fall forever. That white steaming sheet will like a shroud cling and scald the old thin flesh for an eternity.

Mae is moved by pity and jumps forward, her mind addled and stirred by the unfamiliar immanence of all-time one-time. She plucks away the scalding shroud.

Mrs Tung? another Mae demands, riding on the shoulders of her old life. *Where are you, Mrs Tung?*

Mae-in-Air seeks the eternal soul.

In time, Mrs Tung takes another Mae's hand. There are sticky trails across Mrs Tung's face, as if from snails. Her hands are lumpy and blue.

'I can see!' Mrs Tung whispers. Her eyes waver back and forth, skipping, leaping, but they move in unison.

Mrs Tung, it's me, Mae!

Air was saying, *'To send messages, go to the area called Airmail . . .'*

Mae watches her early self swoop clumsily across a virtual courtyard and overshoot the graphics. She embeds herself in the blue stone. Seen from enough distance, anything is funny.

Air says, *'For an emergency configuration, simply repeat your own name several times.'*

And Mae-in-Air hears her other self say over, and over, 'Mae, Mae, Mae . . .'

Mrs Tung cries out in unison, *Mae! Mae!*

Click.

That was it. That was it right there.

Such a simple thing, a mailbox address. You don't need to talk about souls, or wonder how your imprints got entangled. It's nothing to do with the Gates or the UN Format.

All you have to do is chant the same name together when they configure your mailboxes.

Mae starts to laugh. Their mailboxes had the same name! That was the problem. They would have the same name for eternity – all eternity, both past and future.

The imprint had the mailbox, but the imprint was connected always to the real self, the real person who controlled.

All I have to do, Mae realizes, is talk to the real Mrs Tung.

Water, says Granny Tung, as if in prophecy. The 1959 flood comes gurgling back, but Mae is gone.

Mae pierced and repierced air like a sewing needle, looking for the real soul of Mrs Tung.

Mae sat on her own shoulder, morning visit after morning visit to Mrs Tung's attic.

There Mrs Tung was in her chair at ninety, the wind blowing in her face as if fresh from a Cossack campfire, looking back at memories of the hills.

'Is that you, my dear Mae?' Mrs Tung would banter and then laugh again from heartbreak. 'Well, well, come and sit near me child, and tell me all your news. Hoo-hoo-hoo!'

Mae would collapse. 'Woh! Nothing Granny, just laundry.'

'Oh-ho-ho, I used to so love doing laundry. Watching it hang out in the sun all those colours. I used to love the smell of it you know.'

That's because you loved the people who wore the clothes, Granny.

And Mae-in-Air, on her own shoulder, would whisper: *Granny, Granny Tung, can you hear me?*

And it seemed sometimes, that the old catlike face would go still and listening, as if just catching a whisper.

Granny, Granny, I'm here.

'Hoo-hoo-hoo, strange how the mind plays tricks. I suddenly remembered – oh, I don't know why – something long before your time.'

And Mae-in-time, fresh from laundry and Joe's noodles, and the smell of Siao in the loft, would lean forward, hopeful for novelty, wanting beauty. 'Remembered what, Granny?'

'Oh!' Mrs Tung waved it away. 'I remembered . . . I don't know why – hoo-hoo-hoo – I remember one year, the rice fields were full of poppies. Just for no reason. And we all left them there, because so many of our young men had died. Poor souls.' Her old blind eyes still glittered with joy. As if they could see the eternity beyond.

And Mae would stand up to go, and Mae-in-Air would collapse herself back down.

Then she would huff and puff and blow herself back up to another day, another visit.

Mae followed herself, haunted herself, trying to find whenever Mae had been near Old Mrs Tung. She reasoned that there might be some closer link, the closer she got to their final relationship, their final state.

Then, finally, Mae went back to the day just before the Test.

Mae-in-time thumped her way up the stairs to Mrs Tung's room. It was a duty visit. Her head full of dresses and how she could deliver them all in time by leaving off lace collars. She was feeling impatient, a tickle of nerves making her jump as she collapsed onto the chair Mrs Tung kept for guests. They talked about wishboats and pumpkin seeds. Mae, outside time, could see now that Old Mrs Tung was in a mysterious mood.

'I remember the day you first came to me,' Mrs Tung said as if the time had come to talk of final things. As indeed it had. 'I thought: Is that the girl whose father has been killed? She is so pretty. I remember you looking at all my dresses hanging on the line.'

Yah, yah, yah, a sweet old lady's memories, thought Mae. She replied, half thinking, 'And you asked me which one I liked best.'

Another Mae thought: *Pay attention, Mae, this is precious. This is the last time this will happen.*

Mrs Tung giggled. 'Oh yes, and you said the butterflies.' She sat straight up in her chair as if surveying all of her life from a high cliff. The air from the open window blew her hair. 'We had tennis courts, you know. Here in Kizuldah.'

'Did we?' Mae pretended she had not heard that before.

'Oh yes, oh yes. When the Chinese were here, just before the Communists came. Part of the Chinese army was here, and they built them. We all played tennis, in our school uniforms. Oh! They were all so handsome; all the village girls were so in love.' Mrs Tung chuckled. 'I remember, I couldn't have been more than ten years old, and one of them adopted me, because he said I looked like his daughter. He sent me a teddy bear after the war.' She chuckled and shook her head. 'I was too old for teddy bears by then. But I told everyone it meant we were getting married. Oh! I wish I had married him.'

There were so many people Old Mrs Tung wished she had married – from her Cossacks to boys in other villages and of course her Kalaf. She even managed to love the ones she had married.

It's all so precious, thought Mae-in-Air, *it's all so beautiful, we have to ignore it, to get on with the laundry.*

And Mae felt a wind blow, a movement in Air.

Old Mrs Tung did a slight jerk, and turned her head and tried to chuckle. 'Ooh. Hoo-hoo-hoo. Someone just walked on my grave,' she said, in time.

And outside time, dim and confused something rippled, like a voice: *Mae?*

Dying people say their fathers return. The dead sit down beside them, to comfort them. They give them kisses in dreams. Missy lay dying in summer, in an attic room that was always hot and smelled of old sweat in clothes. Mama would not let Mae visit, for fear of making her ill as well. But Mae still crept in and marvelled in horror at the dark circles under her sister's eyes and the dew of sweat. Missy looked at her, said sweetly, 'Isn't it lovely that Papa lies so quiet next to me?'

Again: *Mae?*

It was just a whisper, unclear, unformatted, a swirl, an eddy in time from a place where nothing can move.

Mae-in-Air reached across for it, across the breakfast table of time.

And very suddenly, like the incomplete thing it was, the room, the space it contained and the bodies in it, collapsed like cards, fell back and down.

And there in infinite layers reflecting back, reflecting forward, babe, child, woman, Granny, was Mrs Tung.

Mrs Tung was a weaving blur around the landscapes of three villages lost in forgotten hills. Mrs Tung was a serpent-weaving pattern of someone's entire life, a sinuous wild shape through time, folded in on itself.

Folded in on Mae.

Mae didn't use one name to call it. She used all names: Young Miss Hu, Ai-ling, Mrs Yuksel, Mrs Tung, Granny. The names were a weaving serpent blur as well.

And the entirety seemed to rouse itself, in something like recognition. It rose up like a ghost.

There was no speaking to it. There was nothing clamped to its head to translate and set other people's messages in order. It rose up and then settled down, into the most probable shape. But it could be teased down the hill, edged towards the imprints.

'Help me,' whispered Mae.

And the entirety lifted up its aged, young, beautiful self and corralled its separate parts like hundreds of waving chiffon scarves, collected itself, trying to recognize and learn in a realm where time and learning were complete. Finished, meaning, accomplished.

Mae nipped in and out of that life like a mouse through floorboards. Mae called, and the entirety tried to lift its head as Mrs Tung slept.

Mae whispered to Mrs Tung in dreams.

A young wife tossed fitfully in her bed in a village called Mirrors. Mae tried to lead her back to the moment when the cauldron spilled, when the fire shot through the Air.

Little Miss Hu shivered on the grass as she slept by a campfire, trading horses. Mae called.

Granny shook her head, aching in a wooden chair, asleep in dreams, in Air.

Dreams are a way for the finished self in Air to live again, to have a before and an after in which to think. We learn through all eternity in our dreams.

And so did Mrs Tung. The dream had recurred all through her life.

It was a terrible dream, always the same. A friend, a daughter, even Lily perhaps, needed her. She, Mrs Tung, had done something. She didn't mean to do it, she had not known she had done it, but it was something she had done. Sometimes, at its most nightmarish, she had somehow stolen her friend's body.

And the answer was always the same.

Old Mrs Tung lifted all of herself up like a thousand ragged ghosts. And she was blown by love towards one particular time.

'Mae Mae Mae Mae Mae Mae . . .'

And she met a friend, and that friend seemed to pour her like slithery silk scarves to one particular thing.

That thing was a part of Mrs Tung's life. A moment of her life that had been taken and frozen and held. It was like a burn victim, so scarred that it could not move, embittered and incomplete. Incomplete and angry, after the beautiful pattern should have been finished. Mrs Tung settled on it with her whole self, and enveloped it and welcomed it and hugged it and stilled it. She was reunited with a tiny, hardened, mean little part of her life. She wove it back into the beautiful carpet.

And then said, very clearly, quoting the poet through all her life:

'Listen to the reed, how it tells a tale, complaining of separations.'

Somewhere in time, Mae's eyes fluttered and opened again.

She was in her kitchen, back in herself.

'I'm back,' she managed to whisper. There was a sound of scraping chairs as two men jumped up from the table.

But somewhere else, two spirits sat together as if in an attic exchanging memories, joined forever, remembering the poets.

'Body is not veiled from soul, nor soul from body, yet none is permitted to see the soul.'

In the future, everyone will be able to talk with their dead.

26

Mae, Siao, Mr Ken and his children all strolled together towards the celebration.

They were a new kind of family. Mr Ken walked on ahead, cajoling and calming his two daughters who were beside themselves with impatience to get to the square to join their friends.

Mr Ken's arms were full of little paper boats. Each one had a birthday-cake candle balanced in it. The girls kept jumping up and trying to snatch them, as if they were full of bonbons.

'Careful, careful!' said Mr Ken. 'The candles are only held by a little wax, and these are for Auntie Mae and Siao as well.'

'Let me have mine,' said the eldest, trying to look more mature. She delicately peeled a boat from her father's grasp. She looked at it with experienced eyes. 'What happens if the candle falls over and the boat catches fire?'

'Oh, that is very good luck: That means your wish gets to Heaven even faster.'

Mae thought, I think Kuei has just made that up.

But, oh, he was handsome, his hair combed, his broad shoulders in a nice new shirt, his round legs in beautiful new slacks.

Mae and Siao strolled slightly behind them, holding hands.

Siao had caught her glance and grinned. 'I have found you out,' he said, teasing. 'I know you have a lover. But I am not sure who it could be.'

'Ah, now I am undone,' said Mae. She played along, but she could still be taken aback by Siao's unexpected habit of turning the most painful things into jokes.

'People even say that once you had a crush on my brother Joe,' said Siao.

'Joe? Don't be silly. Maybe when he was younger and more fashionable. I only like fashionable men.'

'Ah,' said Siao, who even on this big night wore his stonemason's grey sweatsuit. '*That* is what you see in me.'

He grinned at her with his beautiful catlike face. That was the village face when it was beautiful, like Mrs Tung's, I love both of my men, thought Mae.

She walked, ponderous with contentment and pregnancy. I feel like a ewe on the pastures at lambing time.

'Mrs Chung-ma'am!' someone called. Mrs Hoiyoo, Kwan's sister, was waving from a high window. 'Your special dress is so beautiful!'

It was airy and embroidered. 'Shen Suloi made it for me!' Mae called back.

'The girls look excited.'

'They are beside themselves. See you there!'

The village square was already full of people. Mr Ken's daughters saw friends, squealed and ran off, clutching their boats of wishes.

The village square was newly paved with honey-coloured stone. Their once wayward little river was now firmly disciplined in a decorative zigzag channel. The bridge which had conveniently dropped down from Upper to Lower Street was now firmly mortared in place, and hung with lights.

Once, the lights would have hung from the One Tree, and the children would have been in the swings soaring higher and higher over the heads of the festival. The children did not even miss the tree now.

'Dad! We'll need more duct tape!'

Genghiz Atakoloo shouted down from scaffolding at the edge of the drop. It would hold all the village TVs, for everyone to see. His father, Enver Atakoloo, bristled his white moustache. Mae remembered that her first real crush had been for Mr Atakoloo, who in those days had been strong and bull-like with his black eyes and black stubble. On the terrible day that he killed Mr Pin and was carried off to prison, Mae had wept. Joe came up behind her and said that she must get used to that, because one day, he, Joe, was going to kill someone and go to prison, too.

'I miss Joe,' Mae said to Siao.

'I know,' said Siao, and gave her hand a shake.

Mae coughed up bile, and moved her handkerchief over her mouth.

Dawn came bouncing up, pulling her mother, Mrs Ling.

'My mother says you are no longer pretty,' giggled Dawn.

'Oh!' exclaimed her mother.

'She says that you are an Imam instead.' Dawn dissolved into giggles. 'Where is your white turban?' She kept chuckling.

'Mae,' said Ling, in apology.

'It is nice to be called an Imam,' Mae said with a shrug.

And suddenly Kwan was there with Sunni, and the women gave each other a quick hug. And Ken and Siao and the girls were all hugged in turn.

'Well!' sighed Kwan. 'We're all here.'

'Not all of us,' said Mae.

She thought of Sezen, Kai-hui, Mrs Tung, Old Mrs Kowoloia. Someone's car radio was pumping out Balshang Lectro.

'Ah,' Kwan said. 'Indeed.' The song faded away and a Talent raved over and over the Air was coming, it was Airday, and the air was 27 Air degrees.

Food came up on legs – the Pin children brought Mae plates of food. People straightened her collar for her.

Young Miss Doh approached, still yearning for love. 'This is your day,' she said to Mae.

'We are all so lucky!' said Mae.

'Lucky? Kizuldah?' said Young Miss Doh.

'We are high up, so we have rain and do not live in a desert. Our people had to fight to stay here, you know. This was the most valuable place.' Mae looked up at the ruined hills. 'We were cut off from all the madness until the very end.'

Mae looked at Miss Doh and saw that she did not feel lucky, cut off high in the hills, but it was important that she acknowledge. 'We are the last, you see,' said Mae. 'The last human beings. After tonight, everywhere, we will be different.'

The Teahouse had a new awning, and tables and chairs laid out on the new pavements. The men played cards or dominoes; some of the women knitted. Mae felt a constant churning like illness in her belly. Suddenly she felt sick and sagged slightly.

'Let's sit, shall we?' Sunni suggested.

Mr Ali stood up and offered a chair. Mae settled, still holding Siao's hand. Kwan seemed to flicker like a knife being sharpened. She shot a glance at Sunni, and Sunni stood up to fetch something or someone.

'I wonder . . .' Mae began. There was too much to wonder about: Where Joe was now and what he was doing; what Sezen would have done with Air if she had lived; what would happen to Mae's village after Air.

Suloi pulled up a chair, then Mrs Pin, and Mrs Doh. With a sound of scraping chairs, the Circle was suddenly gathered. Out came the clay pipes and tobacco. Siao leaned back and shared his cigarettes with Kuei.

The chat was light and distant, about Soong Chang, who was to wed one of the Pin boys. Mrs Pin must be excited. Had plans proceeded? Siao stood up and craned his neck, trying to catch someone's eye.

'I shouldn't have had anything to eat,' said Mae. She put down her plate.

The food was simply fire, raw on her ulcerated stomach.

'Ooh. All this excitement,' she said.

Sunni came back with Mrs Kosal. 'The new toilet in my house is now working, Mae, if you should need to use it.'

As if on a signal, Siao, Kuei, and Kwan were on their feet.

'Come on, Mae darling, you should see how Mrs Kosal has been able to restore the house.'

Mae chuckled. 'I just need to use the toilet.'

Mrs Hoiyoo was also there, suddenly. Kwan's sister had become a much better friend since the night of the Flood. For some reason she had a towel.

'We all want to see the new house,' said Sunni. 'Better than sitting around waiting for eleven o clock.'

On the radios all around them, Yulduz was singing about Fate, and the fate of the nation being like the fate of a person.

So they dutifully admired the paint on Mrs Kosal's wall, and agreed that there was no trace of damage now, and Kwan drew Mae off into the loo.

'It's 10:40,' warned Mrs Kosal. Her smile shook.

'Don't be frightened,' Mae said to her.

Kwan and Sunni gasped in mock approval at the modern toilet. 'Oh, they have done so well – look at this!'

'So convenient and hygienic,' said Kwan.

'Hot water,' said Sunni, in approval.

'I'm going to be sick,' Mae said shyly. She wanted them to leave.

'Poor darling,' said Kwan, and would not leave her. She patted Mae's back. She looked at Sunni, and Sunni suddenly darted away.

'I'm all right,' Mae said.

'Is it moving?' asked Mrs Kosal.

Mae flung herself forward and Mrs Pin's delicious fish salad shot whole and glossy out of her mouth.

'There,' said Mae. 'That's it.'

Sunni, smiling, stuck her head around the doorway. 'Can we come in?' she asked brightly. She prised the women apart, and Ken Kuei blundered his way forward and then settled, relieved. Siao stood respectfully behind him.

'*Ach*,' said Mae, 'all of you. Mrs Kosal's new toilet is not more fascinating than the Air. Come on, all of us, or we will miss the show.' She looked at Kwan. 'I feel better, really.'

This time her two men took hold of her, one on each arm.

Mae asked, 'Kuei, what about the girls?'

'They are fine; they are with their cousins. You just think about yourself for once.'

Outside the house was a crowd of people. They stood in silence, turned away from the screens, the car headlights, the radios and the food. They faced the Kosals' house, waiting for Mae.

'She's fine,' Kwan said to them all, in a singsong voice.

'And Mrs Kosal's toilet is very modern,' said Mae, which brought a bit of a chuckle.

Hatijah came forward with a paper boat. She had started to wear black trousers, like her daughter. 'Mrs Chung-ma'am,' she said. 'Have you made a wish?'

'Oh, no! I've forgotten,' said Mae, and took Mrs Ozdemir's arm in gratitude.

'Hurry up,' said Kwan. It seemed that the entire crowd bustled Mae forward, to their little stream.

Since the Flood, the gully was steeper. Their little stream was walled, channelled to the edge of the square, where it dropped away as a waterfall. Mae was supported as she knelt down beside it. The fire in her belly moved again.

'I want another boat!' Mae exclaimed. 'One for my baby!' She looked back and there they all were, all the villagers. Shen had joined his wife, and all the Pin babes crowded round.

'Have mine,' said Ling Dawn.

Two boats of paper with birthday candles.

'Light the candles first, or the boats will float away first,' said Dawn.

Kwan pushed a cigarette lighter into her hand. Mae lit the first candle and set the boat adrift. The boat was made in the old way. It seemed not to soak up the water. It was stable, and it spun away, bearing fire. Mae lit the second, beginning to feel self-conscious, with all those people watching – and her second boat of wishes was borne away, separate from the first.

'That's it, show is over,' she said, standing up. She turned and saw both little boats drop suddenly over the edge.

Then it moved.

Her whole stomach rose up, crammed like a hard pillow. It caught in her gizzard, and something tore. There was another wave; she could feel her gullet clench, relax, push like a serpent. The thing caught, and her gut began to thrash.

'It's coming,' she managed to gasp.

On the scaffolding, Mr Kwan's TV was lit with the face of the tiger Talent. *'It is almost here, everyone,'* the Talent boomed. *'In just two minutes' time, there will be the second coming of the Air. Are you all counting?'*

Her sharp, high little voice began to count.

'One minute and fifty-seven seconds.'

The screen shifted to the crowds outside the National Assembly in Balshang. The President was counting.

Mae vomited and vomited, but nothing moved. Her chest heaved.

In Singapore a dancing dragon moved through the crowd.

Push!

Old Mrs Tung was fighting with her.

The dragon inside her moved. The lump reared up and stuck and Mae could not breathe.

Her whole body heaved and fought. Kwan shouted something. Mae felt hands, hands on her wrists, everything about her was slimy with sweat; no one could hold her, she was hot and wringing wet.

'One minute, thirty-five seconds.'

In New York, people were holding hands and singing: *'I heard the news today, oh boy . . ."'*

In Kizuldah, Mr Wing's fireworks erupted, crackling above the ancient fields. Blue and white fire danced in the air, smoky, trailing down like snow made of light. The light also danced on the water. The irrigated fields were full of little boats made of fire, tracing the pattern of the ancient canals.

Mae heaved to suck in air. It came with a thin popping sound, slithering up and over the thing in her throat. She roared again with the sound of vomit, and bent over.

'Forty-nine seconds.'

In Japan, there was a new building made all of wood to celebrate, and balloons were bobbing, ready to be released.

Fire burned the inside of her nostrils. Everything strained, pushing – her new empty hungry belly, the lacerated gullet – it all shifted, and something stuck just behind her mouth, like everything Mae had ever wanted to say:

> *I love you, Kuei. I love you, Siao.*
> *Kwan, you are a true friend.*
> *Sunni, I am sorry, but we are friends now, yes?*
> *Sezen, I am your mother.*
> *Joe, you will always be my husband.*

And like a bubble something burst.

'Ten seconds to go.'

Mae's knees gave way; out it moved, something encased. She felt it move – move of its own accord – and the envelope tore and something sugary and sweet suddenly poured forth.

Kwan was shouting over all the noise, and stroking Mae's throat. 'It's coming. She's giving birth through her mouth.'

And then the Flood came.

A flash and a falling backwards, and then a waterfall of sound/ taste/images sense, rising up out of the earth, catching fire. A flood of Air roaring into her head with a sound like bells, washing away the breakage of the previous Format.

Mae thought, this time it will be right, this time it will be safe.

The people were imprinted again.

Because of Mae it was still the UN Format. It was not the UN Format that had made her ill, but the mailbox program. There was no need for a different Format. She had wrote and told Bugsy that. Bugsy had written a second, powerful article: 'Do We Want a Company to Own Our Souls?'

There were voices in the air like birds, and they shouted in all languages, *Hello! hello! hello!*

Mae understood them, understood all the languages; she tasted the tang of New York, the restraint and pride of Japan, the waves of salt from her own people.

And Bay Toh Van.

'Come sing a song of joy!'

Air bloomed as gently as knowledge itself; thing after thing was learned, as ignorance was healed like a suppurated wound. Cars, telephones, the Kings of England, the Japanese yen, the euro, the space shuttle, the iron molecules on old computer disks.

And the joyful ghosts. They came running even as Mae choked and clenched for one last time.

'bugsy@nouvelles: Babe! Honey, did you make it?'

'My baby! I've just had my baby!'

Bay Toh Van boomed, Bugsy did a virtual dance in the air, and Mae looked down, under crackling light.

'tunch@kn: Well, Mae, you won. You beat even me. We all won.'

'chungl@arm: Hiya, Mom, show us Kizuldah. We can see with your eyes, Mom!'

And Mae looked down at the thing that hung out of her mouth. Sunni held one hand, Kwan the other, and Kuei's arm was around her back.

The newborn was tiny, the size of a hand. How could it shrink so small? And it was burned black – black by acids. Its tiny fingers seemed melted together, and its tiny genitals were a blur of ruined flesh and its eyes had been seared shut.

And the child beamed – smiling, joyful, dazed.

The babe had been Formatted.

It was full of Beethoven, the history of Karzistan, the hysterical voices of joy live from Beijing, a new wall of Collab music rolling across the landscape from New York, and a sudden, huge warm hand of love reaching into it. Mae spoke to it through Air.

'My little future. You are blind, but you will not need to see, for we can all see for you, and sights and sounds will pass through to you from us. You have no hands, but you will not need hands, for your mind will control the machines, and they will be as hands. Your ears also burned away, but you will hear more in one hour than we heard in all of our lifetimes.

'I am called your mother.'

And then Mae looked up.

'You're alive,' said Kwan.

'We all are,' said Mae, and she caught up the dangling child and its father reached out for it, held it and cradled it. 'He burns!' Kuei chuckled. 'The child burns.' But he cradled him to his breast.

The light flicked and crackled for one last time; the fireworks of Kizuldah fell away to nothing. Kwan gave her a tug. Mae and Kwan, Sunni, Siao, Kuei and his new son, Old Mrs Tung, all of them, turned and walked together into the future.